I0847243

Wistful in Wyoming

Antelope Rock Book 2

J.B. HAVENS & SAMANTHA COLE

Prologue

August

"I apologize in advance if this is none of my business, but why are you single? You're handsome as all get out and a great guy. Any woman would be lucky to have you. No one around that strikes your fancy?"

Willow Crawford's question wasn't surprising, but his habitual answer didn't spill forth. Lying about himself was second nature to him at this point—sometimes, the lie felt like the truth. Until those moments when he stretched out in his big empty bed at night, and his heart ached for a pair of arms to surround him. Arms that were strong, muscled, covered in coarse, dark hair, and gripped him tightly. Arms that belonged to the faceless, nameless man of his dreams. In that quiet dark of the night, truths are easier to see, even those that we don't want to.

"I don't like any of the women around here. Actually, I don't like women at all. I'm—I'm gay." That was the first time Jeremiah Urban had ever uttered those words aloud. He still wasn't sure what had prompted him to confess his darkest secret to the woman who was quickly becoming the best friend he'd ever had, but it was too late to take it back now. He was just tired of hiding behind a shroud of guilt and fear since figuring out his sexual orientation at fifteen.

Growing up in the Midwest town of Antelope Rock, Wyoming, with a population under a thousand and full of disparaging rednecks and Bible-thumpers, hadn't been easy. Slurs, threats, and harassment often befell those who were deemed "different" by some people's standards. As far as he knew, he was the only gay man living in the Rock, which would make him a target if he ever came out publicly, and he didn't think he was strong enough to risk it.

But Willow Crawford wasn't from the Rock—she'd only arrived there from Philadelphia a few months ago after Jason Hillcrest, the father she'd never known, had passed away and left her his cattle ranch. Jeremiah had only been about six or seven when twenty-three-year-old Jason had come to work at his uncle's Skyview Ranch, eventually inheriting it when the old man died. As far as Jeremiah knew, no one had ever been aware the man had a daughter until Jason's lawyer had arranged for Willow to claim her inheritance.

Antelope Rock had not been prepared for the pink-haired, tattooed tornado that had blown into town, and most of the residents hadn't expected her to stay. However, with nothing left for her in Philadelphia, after a divorce and the death of her mother, Willow had decided to build a life in the Rock. Jeremiah couldn't be happier about that since he felt as if he was developing a kinship with the woman. They were complete opposites in so many ways, but she was nonjudgmental, and little seemed to faze her. She was dealing with the disapproving glares and whispers from some people in town with grace and her head held high. Maybe that was why Jeremiah had let down his guard and blurted out the one secret he'd never told anyone in his life.

Their friendship had blossomed over the past few months as he'd given her advice and helped out in any way he could while she'd cleaned out her father's home and made it her own. Jason had been an unhappy man who'd isolated himself more and more as the years passed. Most people living in the Rock hadn't had a kind word to say about him, but there had been times when Jeremiah had seen glimpses of longing and regret replace anger and resentment in the man's eyes. Jeremiah just hoped Jason had found peace in the afterlife.

"So, does this mean we can check out hot cowboy

asses together? There's just something about a tight pair of Wranglers . . ."

Jeremiah threw his head back and laughed so hard tears welled up in his eyes. "Oh, woman, you never cease to amaze me. Thank you for that. Coming out is never easy for anyone, and you're the only person I've ever told, not even my family or anyone in this backwater town. I'm sure my parents suspect at this point, but we don't talk about it. They're retired and live in Arizona, but we see each other about twice a year and chat on the phone every few days. And to answer your question, yes, ma'am, a nice, tight ass in Wranglers is a sight to behold."

Coming out is never easy—who am I kiddin'?

He didn't know dick about it. He was out to exactly one person in his everyday life.

Willow.

Fear had kept Jeremiah's mouth shut about his sexuality his entire life. Even if he wanted to come out, he had no idea how to go about it. The only other people on earth who knew his sexual orientation were the random, nameless hookups he'd been with after driving two-and-a-half hours to a gay bar in Cheyenne. Every few weeks, he'd make the trip whenever he needed the human connection he couldn't get with just his hand, and he'd always been terrified someone he knew would spot him going into the club. Once inside, it was dark and anonymous enough to relax and get what he needed—a warm, willing body with no attachments.

That night, Willow had invited him to dinner to thank him for teaching her how to shoot earlier in the day. Almost every Wyomingite had at least one weapon in their house, and many carried one on their person. Willow had never picked up a gun in her life, but her father's shotgun had come with the house. There were critters and snakes aplenty in Wyoming, and she needed to know all about firearms and how to shoot them in case a situation ever arose when the shotgun would become necessary. She'd been a fast learner and an excellent student. By the time they'd run out of ammo, she'd hit the target with every shot. Besides her shotgun, he'd introduced her to several of the rifles and handguns he owned. While she might not purchase any other guns, at least she knew how to handle them if needed.

During their meal, after he'd bared his soul, he'd asked her if she was interested in any of the men in town. He hadn't expected her to tell him about a deployed military man she'd been writing to through an organization called Any Soldier. Nathan sounded like a nice guy, and Willow seemed quite smitten with him. Jeremiah hoped it worked out between them because not only was Willow becoming his best friend, but he couldn't help but feel she was another kid sister to him. He didn't get to see his only sibling much anymore—it'd been over a year since they'd gotten together—although they did talk on the phone at least once a week. Six years his junior, Jenna was a big-shot corporate lawyer in Denver, a long way from the small, Podunk town she'd grown up in.

As for Willow, he wanted her to be happy, and if Nathan was the man to do that, then Jeremiah was all for it. Especially after her ex-husband had called her after dinner and made a nuisance of himself. Apparently, the bastard had cheated on Willow and with her best friend, of all people. If he ever showed up in Antelope Rock, Jeremiah would greatly enjoy rearranging the guy's face. He'd been glad to see Willow block the man's number on her phone.

"Willow-girl, that meal was delicious, but I'm stuffed. I'm half-tempted to leave my truck here and walk home to burn off those extra calories." It wouldn't be a hardship since their ranches were adjacent to each other, but his house was far enough away from hers, between her 1200 acres and his 7900, that it couldn't be seen from her porch.

After bidding her goodnight, he drove home to his ranch. His employees were done with their work for the day and hanging out near the bunkhouse, sitting around a fire pit, and having a few beers. Sometimes, Jeremiah would join them, but tonight, he felt lonesome in a way that couldn't be fixed with a friendly conversation with his employees. It was too late to drive to Cheyenne, so instead, he found a pint of butter pecan ice cream in the freezer, despite his full stomach, and plopped down on the living room couch. One of his guilty pleasures in life was the Hallmark Channel. If he couldn't have a happily-ever-after with a man, at least he could watch some women get theirs in a few sappy movies.

Toeing off his boots, he got comfortable and turned on the TV.

Chapter One

September

Jeremiah had taken care of his horse and removed his chaps following his calf roping event at the rodeo in Butterfield. *I'm not as young as I used to be*, he thought, rubbing his shoulder as he headed behind the chutes to watch the next contestant in the charity event. His gaze snagged on a gray hat, and he did a double-take. In a sea of cowboys wearing similar hats, he didn't know what had grabbed his attention about this particular one.

What the hell—who are you tryin' to fool? You know damn well why he's on your radar.

Dale Harris was the owner of that hat—Jeremiah had spotted him earlier, much to his combined annoyance and interest. As Jeremiah watched, the soon-to-be foreman at Willow's ranch took off the Stetson and slapped it against his leather-clad thigh, setting free a cloud of dust. Jeremiah's mind immediately began to imagine what the man's tree-trunk legs would look like in the chaps he was wearing without the benefit of the Wranglers beneath. The black leather framed his tight, round ass in the back and his crotch in the front. The arrogant bastard was sculpted to perfection, every hard inch of him.

It pissed Jeremiah off that, out of all the men in the world he could be physically attracted to, it was a man he'd despised since knowing him all of three minutes after they'd met last week. While the man was freaking gorgeous, his smug attitude toward Jeremiah that day had rubbed him the wrong way. Jeremiah had accompanied Willow and her now-boyfriend, Nathan Casey, to an alpaca ranch in Redworth, where Dale was the foreman. The ranch's owner had passed away, and the family wanted to sell the herd and equipment. It also meant Dale would soon be unemployed.

Willow had done a bang-up job negotiating with the deceased man's nephew for a good deal that included not only the odd-looking, fluffy animals and the equipment but three horses, two goats, and two herding dogs. When all was said and done, Dale had also agreed to come work for her. He'd be living on her property in an RV in just a few weeks—close enough to be a maddening temptation for Jeremiah. Shit, the guy was probably as straight as they come too.

Shaking loose his wayward thoughts, knowing it

wasn't the time or place, he turned his attention back to the arena, where a rider he didn't know had just beaten his roping time.

"Dammit." Second place was going to have to do. It was for a good cause in any case. A local soldier had suffered a traumatic brain injury in Afghanistan, and the money being raised would be used for several things to make his life easier, including renovating his family's home to accommodate his wheelchair. Hopefully, there would also be enough to buy a van he could be easily transported in. As with past charity rodeos Jeremiah had participated in, the winners of each event would most likely donate their cash prizes to the family, keeping just their buckles and ribbons. He'd already decided to do that if he came in first or second.

"You'd think a lifetime of being a closet case would teach you to keep your eyes to yourself, boy."

Jeremiah's head whipped around, his heart hammering as his fear rose so fast he thought he'd faint on the spot. Instead, he did his best to mask his near panic with anger. "The fuck?"

"You keep checking me out." When Jeremiah opened his mouth to protest, his words were cut off when Dale glared at him. "Don't try to lie to me. I won't blacken your eye since I like the attention, but there are plenty of guys here who would. Or worse."

The man leaned his elbows on the fence. He'd managed to sneak up on Jeremiah while his mind had been elsewhere. The devastatingly handsome man's voice was low enough that only Jeremiah could hear him—thank God. Unfortunately, that deep, raspy tone was sexy as all hell, too, and doing all sorts of things to Jeremiah's body that he fought to thwart. "Most don't see it. But I do. Be careful, sweetheart."

"I don't know what the fuck you're talking about, but you keep it up, and I'll show you that even Wyoming ranchers can kick Marine ass."

Willow had learned her new foreman was a retired Marine when she'd spoken to him a few days after agreeing to buy the alpaca operation and hiring him. She mentioned it to Jeremiah, and since then, he'd been imagining what Dale looked like in dress blues— without a doubt, he had to be freaking gorgeous in them. Had he been an officer? Did he have a saber to go with his dress blues? Jeremiah couldn't help but want to see Dale play with his . . . sword. God, that was so miserably corny.

Chuckling, Dale eyed him for a moment before leaning his head closer—close enough to kiss. His chiseled face was cloaked in the deep shadow of his gray Stetson. "You're hot as hell, neighbor." He stressed that last word like he was reminding Jeremiah exactly what they would be in about two weeks. "There's no denying that. I love the ginger thing you got going on, but I don't fuck in the closet. When you decide you're not afraid anymore, you come find me. It'll be more than eight seconds and a hell of a lot more fun." Grinning, he licked his lips, his amber gaze burning holes through Jeremiah's clothes as he raked his eyes over Jeremiah's body from head to toe. "Might still hurt a bit, though."

With a wink and a tip of his hat, Dale walked away. Despite the man's warnings and the surprise and irritation coursing through him, Jeremiah's eyes were glued to Dale's ass, framed in those damn black leather chaps, with the silver fringe slapping rhythmically against his thick thighs.

Harris is gay? Jeremiah was so shocked you could have knocked him over with a feather. *And how the hell did he know I was in the closet?*

Regardless of whether the man was gay or not, Jeremiah wouldn't touch him with a ten-foot pole—not after Dale's declaration. He wouldn't be forced to come out for a hot piece of ass. Not now, not ever. His ranch, livelihood, and family legacy rested on his shoulders. He was fine with his twice-monthly trips to the city— he got what he needed there without complications. So, the guys in the club seemed to be getting younger as he got older. It shouldn't bother him that he always awoke with a sour taste of regret in his mouth the next day. It was a sacrifice he'd made his entire adult life and would continue to do so. No matter how much he craved the dark-haired Marine, who both pissed him off and fascinated him simultaneously.

Chapter Two

May

Jeremiah straightened his bolero tie for what felt like the third time in as many minutes. He couldn't wait to get his damn tuxedo off. It was the first time in his entire life he'd worn one, and if he had his way, it would be the last. But Willow had asked him to give her away today, and he'd do anything for that girl—including wearing a monkey suit. At least she'd forgone the traditional bow ties and cummerbunds in favor of vests and boleros. And as soon as the ceremony and pictures were done, he was getting rid of the jacket and rolling up his shirt sleeves.

Pacing at the back of the small Methodist church, he waited for the bride to arrive. Thankfully, the happy couple hadn't chosen the Baptist church up the street because Jeremiah would've never stepped foot in there.

Pastor Whitehouse was not only a religious fanatic, but from what Jeremiah had heard over the years, the man was also a hypocrite.

Jeremiah checked his watch—Willow should be there at any moment. The last he'd seen of Nathan, he was sweating bullets at the altar with the preacher and his best man, Zach Ramsey. You'd think the guy was being led to the gallows instead of into wedded bliss with his self-proclaimed soul mate.

Despite Nathan's nerves, Jeremiah knew he was madly in love with Willow and would do anything for her. Jeremiah was so happy they'd found each other since both had lost their families years before. Nathan's parents and sister had been killed in a car accident about ten years ago while he'd been deployed. Willow's mother had passed away a couple of years ago, and the father she'd never known, just last year. She'd been an only child.

Now, the couple was on their way to starting their own family together. Willow was carrying their first child, and in addition to giving her away today, Jeremiah would be the baby's godfather. He was tickled pink over that honor since he wasn't sure his own sister would be giving him a niece or nephew anytime soon. Jenna was married to her work—hell, as far as he knew, she hadn't dated anyone seriously in well over a year or two.

The sound of the door opening had him turning and lifting his gaze. Willow stepped into the antechamber, the sun shining in behind her and her friend, Maddie Carmichael, following. The bride was a vision in her white gown. She wore no veil, and her hair was down, falling in waves over her shoulders. Her colorful tattoos were front and center with the strapless dress, covering her entire right arm and shoulder and extending across her chest. The skirt mostly concealed her small baby bump, and as she stepped closer, he caught a flash of pink from under the hem.

He kissed her on the cheek, careful not to disturb the subtle makeup she was wearing. "Willow-girl, I've never seen a prettier bride, but I gotta know—are you wearing your Converse sneakers under that fancy dress?"

She grasped the skirt with one hand and lifted the hem, showing off her odd choice of footwear for the occasion. Of course, it shouldn't surprise anyone who knew her well. "Bet your ass I am! This is my wedding day, and I'm not going to spend it with my toes smashed into high heels that are going to kill my feet. I'm here to get married and party, and there's no reason why I can't do it in comfort."

"I tried to talk her out of it, but she wasn't having it," Maddie interjected from where she stood beside her friend. "And I thought *I* was stubborn. Personally, I think it's the baby hormones making her go looney-toons."

Dressed in a blush-colored, calf-length, maid-of-honor dress, Maddie was as gorgeous as ever. Her long, blond hair was arranged in a simple bun on the crown of her head.

Laughing, Jeremiah pulled Willow into a tight embrace. "I'm so damn happy for you. You ready for this?"

"I've been ready since I got his first letter." Placing her hand on the swell of her stomach, she blinked rapidly. "And now that this little one is on the way?" A tear escaped, and she brushed it away. "I'm not waiting a minute longer to start the next chapter of our lives. I don't want this baby to ever doubt for a single second that her mommy and daddy don't love her and each other. This is a new beginning. So, come on, let's get this show on the road."

When he held out his left elbow, Willow looped her right hand through his arm while clutching her bouquet of wildflowers with her left. Maddie kissed her cheek and winked before stepping between them and the set of double doors leading into the church. Jeremiah nodded to the two ushers who opened the doors. The music swelled, and he glanced at his best friend, seeing her lift her chin and beam. The joy shining from her eyes was enough to almost make him tear up, and they hadn't even walked down the aisle yet.

When Maddie reached the altar and took her place beside the preacher, the organist began the wedding march, and the people filling the pews stood to face the bride. As Jeremiah escorted her forward, matching their steps to the classical music, Nathan's love-filled gaze didn't stray from Willow as she drew closer. Jeremiah couldn't help but feel lucky to be there for the happy couple. He was so grateful to be a part of their big day, the moment when two of the nicest people he'd ever known exchanged their wedding vows.

As he handed Willow over to her future husband and what he knew would be a lifetime of happiness, Jeremiah swallowed a bittersweet lump in his throat. Joy always seemed to go hand in hand with heartbreak for him. He'd long since given up the idea of a wedding for himself, but as he took his seat, his gaze landed on Dale, who was sitting across the aisle in the third row.

Damn that man. Just the sight of the dark-haired retired Marine confused him. He couldn't decide if he wanted to knock out some of Dale's ridiculously-perfect teeth or kiss him until neither of them could breathe.

Weddings always messed with him, but thankfully, Willow and Nathan had opted for a short ceremony, and before he knew it, they were at the reception at the American Legion Hall, and he had a welcomed ice-cold beer in his hand. He stood with his back to the wall, watching the newly married couple hold each other close and sway on the dance floor. Neither of them could dance worth a lick, but they were so lost in one another that he didn't think they even heard the music.

Quite a few other couples were out there,

including Maddie and Zach. Nathan's best man had arrived two days ago and had been charming the woman ever since. Nathan and Willow had suspected the two would hit it off, but since Zach was still in the Army and stationed in Kansas for a few more months, Jeremiah wasn't sure if anything lasting would develop between them.

Jeremiah took a sip of his beer and let his gaze roam around the room. As if being pinged by radar, it settled on Dale—dammit. He was across the room with Beth Loach, a deputy with the sheriff's department, who was flirting and practically drooling over Dale. The curvaceous woman was a knockout in uniform—out of it, she was devastating, even from a gay man's point of view. Moreover, Dale was definitely flirting back—which was odd, to say the least.

When they'd first met, Jeremiah had figured the guy was straight, but then at the rodeo, Dale had implied he was gay. Now, Jeremiah wondered if the foreman was bisexual—not that it should matter because he didn't want to be attracted to him at all. Speaking of which, the asshole looked so damn delicious, it was difficult for Jeremiah not to drool too. The guests had been invited to dress casually despite the dressy bridal party, and Dale wore black jeans, which molded to his long, muscular legs, Tony Lama snakeskin boots, a light-gray western shirt, and a black Stetson. Yummy with a capital Y.

As if sensing Jeremiah's gaze, Dale winked at him. Fucking winked! Argh, what an arrogant bastard!

* * *

Dale knew he was pushing Urban's buttons but couldn't help himself. The guy was hot, and Dale was drawn to him like a moth to a flame. Urban was also off-limits in so many respects, mostly because he was Dale's employer's best friend and neighbor and in the proverbial closet. But that didn't stop him from wanting the guy . . . and pushing those buttons to rile him.

He'd first noticed the man when Jeremiah had accompanied Willow to check out the alpaca operation Dale had been in charge of. And now that Willow had hired Dale to continue tending the herd he knew so well, he got to see a lot of the sexy owner of the adjacent ranch. He'd never been attracted to a ginger before, but Jeremiah's flaming red hair, green eyes, and freckled peaches and cream skin, which probably required tons of sunscreen to prevent burning, had Dale's engine revving. At five feet eleven, Jeremiah was five inches shorter than Dale and a little stockier. Dale guessed the guy was around his age—forty-three— maybe a year or two younger.

Dale had known since his teens he was pansexual and had been in the military when "don't ask, don't tell" had still been in effect and for a few more years after its repeal. By the time he'd left the Marines seven years ago, he'd been out and proud, refusing to ever crawl back into that stuffy closet he'd hated with a passion. He didn't care if someone was male, female, transgender, or undefined—he was attracted to the person, not their sexual orientation. As long as they caught his interest, their gender didn't matter to him. He'd had relationships with several men and women over the years, but never simultaneously. Monogamy was just as important to him as the person he was with being true to who they were.

Yeah, he'd caught some shit from other Marines when they'd found out he was into men as much as women, but most of his teammates had stayed by his side, ready to defend him just like they had in combat. A few had distanced themselves and talked smack about him when he wasn't around, but that had been the worst of their disapproval.

Frowning, Jeremiah thumped his beer bottle onto an unoccupied table with a little more force than necessary and stormed toward a hallway leading to the restrooms. Unable to help himself, Dale decided to follow the man—for what reason, he wasn't sure yet. Smiling at Beth and gesturing toward the hallway, he said, "Will you excuse me for a moment?"

She glanced over her shoulder at the sign for the restrooms. "Oh, sure. No problem. Just save me a dance later, okay?"

Beth was a nice, attractive woman and, from what

he'd been told, a damn fine deputy. Not that there was a heck of a lot of crime in Rockland County, but she'd reportedly held her own in several high-risk situations over the years. While many of the larger towns in the county were covered by police departments, the smaller ones, like Antelope Rock, were under the sheriff's department's jurisdiction. Dale had heard of one domestic violence incident where she'd single-handedly arrested a man who'd been beating his wife bloody. The injured woman hadn't been the only one in need of an emergency room physician by the time Beth had been done with the man, and she'd done it without firing a shot or deploying a Taser.

Dale winked at her. "Sure thing."

Striding across the room, he silently reminded himself that pursuing Jeremiah was a bad idea and would end in disaster, but even knowing that didn't stop him from going after the man right then.

He pushed the door to the men's room open and frowned. No one was at the urinals, and the two stalls were open and empty.

Where the hell is he?

Stepping back into the hallway, he glanced to his left and noticed an exit door. It was slightly ajar, and he headed for it. Before fully opening the door, he peered through the gap and spotted Jeremiah pacing back and forth on a small patio, mumbling to himself and running his hands through his red hair. His hat rested on the retaining wall that bordered the patio. There was no one else out there.

The corners of Dale's mouth ticked upward when he heard the words "arrogant bastard," with a few choice curse words filtered in. If he had to guess, he'd say his earlier wink at the sexy cowboy had made an impression.

He opened the door just wide enough to slip out into the night. Surprisingly, the hinges didn't make a sound. The muted festive music floating out from the party muffled his footsteps. The patio was lit up by a yellow bulb in a lantern hanging above the door. Flaming citronella torches were spaced out evenly along the perimeter of the patio that'd been created with gray stone pavers. Two picnic tables and about a dozen or so plastic chairs provided seating, and in the center of it all was a large fire pit. While it wasn't ablaze, someone had set up several logs and kindling, probably anticipating the wedding guests coming out here later. The temperature hovered around fifty degrees—pretty normal for the region in mid-May after the sun went down. A half-crescent moon hung low, surrounded by countless twinkling stars. Dale would never tire of the Wyoming night sky. In all his travels, both in the United States and abroad, he'd never seen a more magnificent and humbling display of the universe.

Leaning against the brick wall of the building, he eyed the object of his lust, who still hadn't noticed he was no longer alone amid his muttered grumblings. An amused grin spread across Dale's face. "You know, it'd be a shame for you to pull all that fiery hair out of your head. I might be forced to shed a tear at the loss."

Jeremiah spun around, gaping at the unexpected intrusion of his bitch-fest. He quickly tried to shutter his face but failed. There was a mixture of anger and lust in his beautiful green eyes, and Dale would give anything to be staring down into them as his naked body covered the other man's.

As strong as his desire was, though, he wasn't about to play games with a closeted gay. He'd been burned once before and refused to open up to that kind of heartbreak again. The only thing worse than falling for a man who wasn't out was developing feelings for a straight guy. He had no idea why he couldn't just walk away from Jeremiah and leave the poor guy alone.

"Fuck off." Turning away from Dale, Jeremiah tipped his head back, staring at the night sky. "I came out here to get away from you."

"Did you really want to get away from me? Or were you secretly hoping I'd follow you out here?"

He scowled and snorted at Dale. "You think highly of yourself, don't you?"

Dale smirked. "Not really. I just know when someone is attracted to me."

Unexpectedly, the man didn't deny that statement, although the desire in his eyes flared just as much as his fury did. The combination had Dale closing the distance between them. Whether Jeremiah would try and deck him was a crap shoot Dale was willing to risk —for some insane reason. He didn't stop until his chest brushed against Jeremiah's, his gaze never leaving the other man's.

After several heartbeats, Dale lowered his mouth to Jeremiah's ear, inhaling the rich scent of his skin. He made his voice rumble, low and seductive. "Admit it, sweetheart. If we were anywhere else, where there was no chance we'd be interrupted or found out, you'd be on your knees right now, blowing me halfway to heaven before begging me to fuck that hot ass of yours."

Jeremiah swallowed hard, hunger and passion swirling in his eyes. He wanted this. Craved it. That much was obvious to Dale. However, actually giving in to his basic carnal lust was a different story altogether. Jeremiah would never make the first move, not without some encouragement.

Dale slowly licked his lips, drawing an almost imperceptible moan from the other man's throat. His jeans got tighter in the crotch as his cock swelled with need. Leaning into Jeremiah just a little bit more, Dale commanded more than dared, "Kiss me."

As his eyes rounded, Jeremiah's breathing became nearly frantic. The pulse in his neck raced as a shiver rippled throughout his body. He was as terrified as a rabbit trying to outrun a predator. But the man didn't run. Didn't move. All he had to do was lift his chin and let their mouths meet. Dale would take over from there.

Jeremiah shifted, bringing him closer to Dale instead of farther away. His head tilted back a scant inch or two. Dale lowered his mouth, reveling in the soft puffs of Jeremiah's gasping breaths against his own lips, giving the other man every opportunity to take what he so obviously wanted.

Laughter reached his ears a split-second before the door burst open behind him, and several wedding guests filed out onto the patio, chatting away. Jeremiah jumped away from Dale as if he'd been burned and spun around, facing away from everyone, most of whom had no idea what he'd been about to do. Dale was the only one aware of how close Jeremiah had come to kissing him. If only they'd had a few more minutes alone.

Damn it.

Jeremiah strode over to the retaining wall and snatched up his hat, slamming it down on his head. Someone bumped into Dale, diverting his attention and causing him to reach out and steady the other person.

"Whoops! Sorry, Dale," Ginger Moore said with an alcohol-induced giggle.

He smiled at the young hairdresser. "No problem, darlin'."

Another titter erupted before she turned back toward her date—a man in his twenties whom Dale didn't recognize as being from the Rock. It didn't mean the guy didn't live there, but with a population under a thousand, Dale figured he'd met or at least seen most of the townspeople during the past seven months he'd been there.

As the group gathered around the fire pit, where Shane Rivers, the ranch hand Willow had hired a while back, started to light the kindling, Dale glanced around to find Jeremiah gone. The man had finally rabbited, and Dale wasn't sure if he was relieved or disappointed. Either way, he had to keep reminding himself that Jeremiah was firmly in the closet and would undoubtedly never emerge, so he would remain off-limits.

Easier said than done, asshole.

Chapter Three

September

Jeremiah strode down the path that ran along the fence lines of both his ranch and Willow and Nathan Casey's smaller one. Over the past year, the dirt had gotten well-packed from everyone using it to either walk on or ride the horses or ATVs. They'd long since added a gate in the fence between their properties. Ease of access had quickly become necessary for both him and the couple. They often ate dinner together, laughing long into the night.

He'd enjoyed every moment of watching Willow's pregnancy progress, not to mention the endless ribbing he gave Nathan over being so overprotective. Not that he had much room to talk. Jeremiah loved their little girl already, and she wasn't even here yet. Willow's due date of September 25 grew ever closer, just under two weeks away.

He tucked his hands into the pockets of his jacket. Autumn had arrived, along with colder temperatures. His mind was a riot of thoughts, scrambling over each other and making his nights sleepless and his days long. He felt as if he stood on a precipice, a decision hanging heavy in his mind, one that could change everything. He hoped to talk it out with Willow and Nathan, the two people who truly knew him—with whom he didn't have to hide parts of himself.

He was tired to the depths of his soul, but the fresh air on his face, the endless sky, and wide open vistas of the land made him feel a little less alone for some reason. After the rodeo and argument with Dale last fall, followed by their almost kiss at Nathan and Willow's wedding, then watching Willow and Nathan fall in love and begin their family, Jeremiah was out of sorts.

Hiding his true self was just something he did. He'd never considered coming out, not ever. He'd heard too many homophobic comments and seen the damage even rumors could do to other gay men in the ranching community that he'd resigned himself to making do with one-night stands in Cheyenne. He was forty-two years old, and he'd spent at least thirty of those years living in fear of being outed. He didn't know any way to live other than behind closed doors.

Nearing the house, he saw the couple curled

together on the porch swing, a blanket covering them, their heads touching. They leaned against each other, speaking quietly, the hushed words broken only by the occasional giggle from Willow. Jeremiah's chest clenched in envy, and he spun on his heel. He might be a lonely asshole, but he wouldn't break up such an intimate moment because he was feeling maudlin.

The sound of a door opening drew his attention. Glancing to his left, he saw a strip of light appear between Skyview's two barns. From where he'd stopped in his tracks, he had a perfect view of Dale's trailer. The gruff man had stepped out onto a small slab of concrete that served as his patio. A flame flared, briefly illuminating the man's handsome face, before extinguishing and leaving behind a red glow at the end of a cigarette.

Jeremiah's feet moved of their own accord. Hell, if he knew if it was the looming specter of his empty house behind him that had him closing the distance between himself and the man he couldn't stop dreaming about. It'd been a year since Dale had confronted him at the rodeo, and Jeremiah had thought of little else since. In the past, he would've headed into Cheyenne to blow off some steam and put whatever was bothering him behind him, leaving it at the feet of some random hookup. But since meeting Dale, Cheyenne no longer held an allure for Jeremiah. He'd avoided the man as much as possible over the past several months since the wedding, but it'd done nothing to quell the desire he felt whenever he caught a glimpse of Dale or when someone simply mentioned his name.

"Come on, Cowboy, I can hear your footsteps," Dale said in a low, husky voice as Jeremiah drew closer. It sent delicious shivers down Jeremiah's spine. "Don't worry, though—the lovebirds just went inside and never saw you."

Ignoring the evident dig at him, Jeremiah murmured, "Evening."

Seriously? That's all you got? Who says blah shit like that? Me, apparently.

Chuckling, Dale finished his cigarette, stabbing the butt out in a small metal bucket filled with sand. "Want a beer?"

Trying to act nonchalant, he shrugged. "I'm not a man that ever says no to a beer."

One step . . . two . . . three . . . he kept moving. His palms became sweaty, and a thick lump formed in his throat. He was close enough now to see Dale's face. Wreathed in shadows from his hat, he was more handsome than ever. He looked mysterious and dangerous, a deadly combination that woke Jeremiah's libido with a jolt of electricity, shooting straight to his cock, making him half-hard. Willing the response away, he closed the distance between them.

Dale smiled wryly. "You might say no to this one. It's my new batch of homebrew. It could be good, or it could taste like an old man's nut sack—no way to know until you try it."

"You've tasted an old man's nut sack?" Jeremiah laughed, feeling lighter at that moment than he had in months.

Reaching behind him, Dale pulled the trailer door open and waved him forward. "Come in, I'll tell you all about it."

Jeremiah climbed the steps, feeling as if he was entering a wolf's den and he was the prey.

Heaven help me.

He remembered the argument at the rodeo last fall just as much as he recalled their near-kiss at Willow and Nathan's wedding. Both incidents should've had him running home with his tail between his legs, but he was helplessly drawn to Dale like a magnet. He wasn't sure what he was getting himself into, but he also knew he didn't want to be alone tonight. He was lonely—painfully so.

He supposed he saw in Dale an opportunity to really be himself, for once in his life, and for longer than a quick fuck in a bathroom stall in some gay bar two hours away from home. It wasn't even fully about sex, though the desire was there, the evidence of which pushed against his fly. It was about being around someone who knew what it was like to be different with absolute understanding. To be afraid of being jumped and scorned for no other reason than who he loved or was attracted to.

"You going to stand in the doorway, letting my heat out, or come inside?"

"Shit, sorry." Stepping inside, Jeremiah glanced around as Dale came in behind him and pulled the door closed. The inside of the RV was clean and functional, basic to the extreme, but somehow it suited Dale. Being a retired Marine, orderliness was probably a deep-seated trait he couldn't shake, even if he wanted to.

After wiping his sweaty palms on his jeans, Jeremiah doffed his hat.

"You don't have to look so nervous. Seriously—sit down and chill." Dale waved him over to the small dinette table.

Taking a seat, he set his hat on the bench next to his hip. "I'm not nervous." He tasted the lie even as he said it—his anxiety level was nearly through the roof.

Dale crossed his arms and glared at Jeremiah. "What? You think I'm going to jump you? Consent is sexy, dickhead, and mandatory when I take someone to my bed. Nothing will happen without you first saying you want it—and with actual words, not just your bedroom eyes. I can be attracted to someone without pushing them into something they don't want or aren't ready for."

Jeremiah gaped at the other man, unsure what to say or do in response to his little speech. *Consent is sexy? Bedroom eyes? Attracted?* His mind was a whirlwind of possibilities, and his body reacted to each one.

Again, Dale was an enigma—a contradiction of terms. Jeremiah didn't really know if he was gay or bisexual. Plain straight seemed to have been taken off the table at some point. It was clear the man was interested in Jeremiah in a way that wasn't just neighborly or friendly.

With a single nod, Dale turned away and opened one of the kitchen cabinets to retrieve two pilsners and bottles from the fridge. After pouring beer into the glasses, Dale passed one over to Jeremiah before sitting across from him. Their knees brushed against each other's in the narrow space under the table, and Jeremiah fought the urge to hook their legs together and run his foot up the back of the other man's calf. Playing a childish game of footsie shouldn't be a turn-on, but damn him if the thought didn't make his dick twitch anyway.

"Try it." Dale saluted him with his glass, then took a long swallow of the cold beer. Jeremiah tried not to stare at the other man's throat but couldn't drag his gaze away. His Adam's apple bobbed as he downed the liquid, and Jeremiah couldn't help but fantasize about what it would be like to see him swallowing something else.

Pointedly ignoring Dale's earlier comments, he raised the glass to his mouth and took a drink, licking the foam from his upper lip. "It—it's good." He cleared his throat. "I've never had homemade beer before. I like it."

"Thanks. It's a new recipe. I usually get a kit, but this is a Harris original."

Staring at the dark amber liquid, Jeremiah swirled the glass around in his hand, the cold condensation on the sides slicking his palm and fingers. He hesitated a moment before finding the balls to ask, "Are we really going to talk about beer?"

One of Dale's eyebrows arched. "Why not? Unless you're going to tell me why you're really here. Why you're walking around in the dark like a stalker or something."

Barking out a laugh, Jeremiah took another long drink, enjoying the bitter, hoppy flavor. "Why I'm here?" Shrugging, he set the glass on the table. "I don't know. My house is big and empty."

"So? You came to my *small*, empty trailer?"

"You're here, so it's not exactly empty now, is it?" Dale didn't respond but just gazed intently at Jeremiah, who hesitated before adding, "Not going to make this easy on me, are you?"

"Nothing in life is easy, Urban, as you well know."

"Are you gay?" he blurted, immediately wanting to smack himself as soon as the words passed his lips.

Dale's chuckle was low and sexy. The corners of his sensual mouth curved upward in mild amusement. "I don't like labels, and I don't see their point. I've been with men, women, and people who don't identify as either. If I like a person, I like them—it doesn't matter to me what's in their pants."

Mulling over the unexpected answer, Jeremiah took another sip of his beer. Dale continued to puzzle him. "That's surprising, I guess. What's that like?"

"What is what like? I won't sit here and play twenty obscure questions with you, Cowboy. If you want to talk, talk. If not, finish your beer and be on your way."

It was confusing why this man's abrasive personality turned him on so much. If it'd been anyone else, Jeremiah would've already stormed out of there and never looked back. He must be a glutton for punishment because, instead of leaving, he opened his mouth and let words come out. "Being free. I mean, what's it like being free to be who you really are?"

"Freedom is relative. Have I had slurs shouted at me? Absolutely. Have I been in fights because someone called me a fag and wanted to beat the queer out of me? Yup. I'm not more or less free than anyone else. I just don't give a shit what people think most of the time. That being said, some things I won't let slide, but I firmly believe that whatever two, or sometimes more, consenting adults do behind closed doors is their own damn business. If someone doesn't like it, they can fuck right off."

"God, you make it sound so damn easy, but it's not! Coming out is . . . " Scrubbing both hands down his face, he groaned. "It's not like I haven't thought about it a million times. Of course, I have! I'm so fucking tired of hiding, but I don't know any way out. I'll be crucified in the community, and my family legacy will go down in flames."

He had no clue why he was baring his soul to this man. It wasn't like they were friends, more like acquaintances. They were friends of friends. Neighbors. Neighbors who'd butted heads since the moment they met. But all that hadn't stopped Jeremiah from dreaming about Dale being in his bed. Nor did it stop the verbal diarrhea spilling from his mouth whenever they spoke to each other without anyone in earshot. Dale's pull on his psyche was almost as strong as the physical draw he felt when finding himself close to the man. He wanted to hand himself over into Dale's safekeeping and just forget the world for a while . . . or forever.

"I never said you *had* to come out—that's your decision. And a big one at that. I've never come out in the traditional sense either—I didn't send out engraved announcements or shout it from the rooftops, but I haven't hidden my sexual orientation from anyone in a very long time. As a result, I'm not going to be with someone who's gonna to try and hide me away. I refuse to be treated like someone's dirty little secret. Been there, done that, threw away the T-shirt.

"I'm not ashamed of who I am, and you shouldn't be either. If we start a relationship that includes any kind of intimacy, at no point am I going to ask you to wave a rainbow flag and march down Main Street in sequined hot pants. But I will ask you to kiss me in public, hold my hand, and act like a couple. If you can't do that, there's the door."

"What if I don't want to date? What if I feel like we're better as friends?" Ugh. This conversation was damn heavy for two people who didn't really know each other that well.

"Then I'd say you're deluding yourself. You want me, and I sure as hell want you. If you don't want to date, fine. But then you don't get to fuck me, and I won't be fucking you either." Sighing, Dale stood, taking his now empty beer glass with him. "Here's the truth of it, Cowboy. I'm too damn old for fucking around. Clubs and one-night stands don't do it for me —they haven't for a long time. I want to meet someone I can date and do all that other couple shit with. But I won't compromise my happiness waiting for you or anyone else to accept me and what we are together. What you see is what you get. I won't hide or pretend to be something I'm not. If you can accept that, I'd love to take you to dinner. If not," he shrugged, "well, I guess I'll see you when I see you."

Taking Jeremiah's half-full glass from him, he put it in the sink and walked to the door, opening it wide. "Go on. Go home and think. The offer stands. But I won't wait forever. If I meet someone else in the meantime, I won't say no on the off-chance you'll decide you're ready for something real for once in your life."

"You're a harsh bastard, you know that?" Rising, he slapped his hat back onto his head angrily before walking through the door and descending the two steps. "Throwing ultimatums around like fucking candy. One day that'll bite you in the ass."

"Maybe, maybe not. See you around, sweetheart." Dale unceremoniously slammed the door in his face, forcing him to jerk back so he didn't get his nose smashed.

"Fucker."

Chapter Four

December 24

It'd been a little over three months since Dale had delivered his ultimatum. Since then, the two men were back to being "friendly neighbors." It was frustrating as hell for Jeremiah, especially since he was having wet dreams—something he hadn't had in years—about the other man. Being forty-two and waking up in a puddle of his own cum in his boxers was something he thought he'd left behind with his teenage years. It was embarrassing as hell, even though no one else on Earth knew about it.

A few weeks after Dale had slammed the trailer door in Jeremiah's face, Willow and Nathan had welcomed their daughter Shannon Cherry Casey into the world. As Jeremiah stood at his stove, waiting to take out the homemade bread he'd made for Christmas dinner at the couple's place, his mind recalled the day Willow had gone into labor.

It was an unseasonably warm Sunday for that late in September, but according to the forecast, the cooler temperatures would be coming in full force by the end of the week. Jeremiah was sitting on the side-porch swing with Nathan, shooting the shit and talking about the upcoming calving season and the pregnancy checks they'd perform at the JP Ranch in a few weeks. He'd brought over a surprise for the happy couple—a beautiful wooden cradle he'd made from scratch. It was one of the few times he'd ever given away one of his creations. His workshop was filled with crafts he'd constructed from pieces of wood, but he never showed them to anyone, aside from the ones he used to decorate and furnish his home and a few he'd made for specific people. His workshop was his sanctuary— where he could just be himself, not a rancher, not a boss, and not a gay man impersonating a straight one.

He'd made an ornate puzzle box for Nathan to give to Willow, that matched the one he'd made many years ago for her father. After that, his best friend had tried to convince him to sell some of his pieces at the Rockland County farmer's market that took place every Saturday from late spring until the middle of October, weather permitting. In addition to local produce and edibles like homemade jams and bread, there were many vendors with non-food items, such as crafts, antiques, and flea market finds. Jeremiah still couldn't bring himself to show others his talent, although he honestly didn't know why. Like being gay, he just found it hard to share personal things about himself with anyone.

A gray bundle of fur sashayed from around the back of the house and then flopped down in front of them. Willow's cat, Ethel, was now fully grown and the queen of the castle—in her own opinion, of course. Chuckling at the feline's antics, Jeremiah was just about to ask Nathan a question when a loud crash from inside the house caused both men to jump to their feet and rush to find the source.

They found Willow standing in the kitchen, broken glass and a puddle of lemonade all around her. She'd dropped the pitcher she'd been bringing out to them and was hunched over, breathing heavily.

"Willow, stay there. I'll lift you out of the glass," Nathan ordered while striding closer to his wife, who was still wide-eyed and silent amid the mess. "Jeremiah, get the mop and broom, will ya?"

"Nathan . . . that's not all lemonade," Willow gasped between breaths as she stood in place. She pointed to the wet spot on the lower half of her loose-fitting maternity dress—an ugly muumuu she'd called it in disgust on more than one occasion. Still, she ran out of clothes that fit her comfortably, and she'd refused to buy more that late in her pregnancy.

"My water broke, and I'm having a contraction—damn, that fucking hurts!" She moaned, grasping her belly and bending forward.

Nathan immediately paled, and Jeremiah could swear the man swayed, about to faint, before gathering himself together and rushing forward to sweep Willow off her feet, away from the broken pitcher.

"Jeremiah! Get the car!" he yelled, not putting Willow down but carrying her right out of the kitchen to the front door.

"Nathan, honey, we need the hospital bag." Her voice sounded calmer after the worst of the contraction had passed.

"Take her out to the truck," Jeremiah ordered. "I'll get the bag for you." A few weeks ago, Willow had told him it was next to her dresser in their bedroom, just in case, God forbid, Nathan was out on an errand or something when she went into labor. Clasping his friend on the shoulder, Jeremiah kissed Willow's forehead. "Hang in there, Willow-girl, you're about to be a mama."

"About damn time. Oh, call Dale for me and let him know we're on our way to the hospital, please. He's in Butterfield picking up some stuff."

"Got it." *Wonderful.*

He strode down the hall to retrieve the bag, chuckling at Willow, who insisted to her husband she could walk. Of course, the father-to-be wasn't listening to her. Once she'd settled in Nathan's truck, Jeremiah followed them to the hospital in his own vehicle, commanding the Bluetooth feature to dial a phone number as he drove.

A gruff voice filled the cab. "Yeah?"

Dale.

Just hearing the man's voice sent a lance of pain and desire through Jeremiah, but he managed to push it aside and keep his voice steady and unaffected. "Willow's water broke. We're on our way to the hospital—looks like you'll be handling the chores on your own for a bit."

"Fuckin' awesome." The words were said with genuine joy. Dale had grown fond of his new employers and vice versa. "Nathan freaking out?"

Laughing softly, he replied, "Yeah, the man is usually cool under pressure, but I thought I'd be driving them in—he went white as a sheet before recovering. I think his combat training kicked in."

"That'll do it. Keep me updated if you don't mind."

"No problem."

A click told Jeremiah the call had been disconnected before he could say anything more. Apparently, Dale had been done talking to him. Bastard. That phone call was probably the most they'd spoken to each other since Dale had kicked Jeremiah in the gut with his ultimatum.

Forcing the man and their issues from his mind, he called his own foreman, Anthony Garner, to let him know he was heading to the hospital and didn't know when he'd be back. The man whooped loudly over the phone when he heard the baby was coming. Many of the JP ranch hands loved Willow as if she were their own sister. They'd all been counting the days until she went into labor. Of course, a money pool was going for the weight and length of the baby—$500 was riding on the results.

Butterfield General Hospital was small compared to the medical center on the other side of the county, and Jeremiah knew the head nurse working in the labor and delivery ward. Since it'd been a slow night there, she hadn't banished him to the waiting room. After six hours of pacing outside her room, with a few short breaks here and there, the angry squall of an infant broke the silence of the hallway Jeremiah had traversed while anticipating his goddaughter's arrival. Falling back against the wall, he sighed, glad it was finally over. If he was that relieved over it, he couldn't imagine how Nathan and Willow felt.

Smiling, he scrubbed a hand down his face and settled in to wait some more. Hopefully, she had ten fingers and ten toes, all her mama's gumption, and maybe a bit of her daddy's sweetness.

A short time later, his vigil was interrupted when Nathan poked his head out of the room and waved him inside. "Come on, Willow wants to see you and show off our baby girl." Nathan's grin was bigger and brighter than Jeremiah had ever seen.

He stepped nervously into the delivery room,

taking off his hat and running the brim through his fingers. A team of nurses and a doctor were throwing things into bins with red plastic bio-hazard bags—it was controlled chaos, which he ignored. His gaze landed on an exhausted-looking Willow, covered with a clean, white blanket and propped up on pillows with a tiny bundle cradled in her arms.

He tiptoed closer, not sure why he was walking so carefully.

"Come here, Uncle Jeremiah—it's okay," Willow said, not taking her eyes off her brand-new baby girl. "She's so beautiful."

He leaned over the duo and gently pulled the blanket off the baby's fuzz-covered head. Her eyes were closed, and her mouth was open slightly as she slept in her mother's arms. Her skin was a little red but smooth and flawless. She had her daddy's dark hair and her mother's nose.

"She's the most beautiful thing I've ever seen." His voice was hushed, his eyes filled with joyous tears, and he felt his heart crack open for this perfect little girl. "Congratulations, you two."

"Do you want to hold her?" Willow finally dragged her eyes from her daughter and met his gaze. She had heavy, dark rings under her eyes, and sweat had stuck her brown hair to the side of her head, but she was as gorgeous as he'd ever seen her, glowing with motherhood.

"No. Not yet. You guys need time together. I'm

going to head out now that she's here and you're both doing fine. Between Dale and my guys, we'll keep Skyview running. You take all the time you need to be a family." He kissed her forehead before softly stroking his finger down the baby's soft-as-silk apple cheek. "I'm so damn happy for you guys I could bust."

Straightening, he'd exchanged handshakes and back slaps with the new daddy, then turned to leave. He hadn't even left the room before Nathan rushed back to Willow's side. The little family had been oblivious to everything but each other.

The shrill beeping of the timer on his cell phone jerked him back to the present. Grabbing a pair of mitts, he bent at the waist and removed the bread from the oven. Setting it aside to cool, he headed upstairs to change for the party. Willow and Nathan were hosting a Christmas Eve gathering, and he was incredibly nervous. He hoped Shannon was fussy, so he could disappear with his goddaughter and avoid Dale. Cowardice soured his gut, but he wasn't sure what he could do about it. His life had become the very definition of being stuck between a rock and a hard place. Just not the hard place he wanted to be stuck up against.

Will you ever have the balls to go for what and who you want?

He'd managed to avoid Dale as much as possible,

but the taste of regret was thick in his mouth every time he saw the dark-haired retired Marine. When they inevitably ran into each other at Skyview Ranch or in town, they exchanged the bare minimum that good manners demanded but didn't say much to each other beyond "Hello," "Goodbye," or "Crazy weather we're having, isn't it?"

After showering, he dressed quickly, opting for a pair of pressed dark gray dress pants instead of his usual jeans and a deep green button-down shirt that Willow had often said made his eyes look gorgeous. After tucking the shirt's tail into the waistband, he smoothed the material over his stomach, noticing for the millionth time he needed to add more crunches and sit-ups to his daily exercise. His age was showing with a softening of his midsection and some noticeable wrinkles on his face. Lately, he'd also been finding some white hairs mixed in with the red on the top of his head. He wasn't overly vain, but he liked to look good.

Some men aged well, like friggin' Dale, while others didn't. Willow's father had only been fifty-six when he'd passed away twenty months ago, but the man had looked fifteen years older than he'd actually been over the last two decades of his life. Loneliness and a near lifetime of regret could do that to a person. Jeremiah was so sick of being lonely, and he didn't want to have any regrets when he finally passed from this life. But wanting to achieve something and actually following through with it were completely different stories.

He slid the championship rodeo buckle that he only wore on special occasions onto his leather belt and snapped it into place before sitting on the bed and pulling on his best black boots. Adding a spritz of his favorite Ralph Lauren cologne, he headed downstairs, where he grabbed his black dress hat and a winter coat from hooks by the front door. He'd taken the gifts out to his truck earlier, knowing he'd be nervous about spending the next few hours in the same room with Dale and worried he'd forget them. Back in the kitchen, he transferred the bread into a basket, wrapping it carefully in a clean tea towel to keep it warm, before snagging his keys and heading outside.

"Here goes nothing. Maybe Dale will choke on a bite of my bread. Maybe the floor will open up and swallow me whole. Maybe the sky will fall, and angels will descend. Maybe Dale will tell me he doesn't care about me being out, and he'll bring me home and fuck me through my mattress. Yeah, dream on, Cowboy." Sighing at his own ridiculousness, he shook his head. "Now you're like Willow, talking to yourself, friggin' asshole."

Starting his truck, he girded his proverbial loins in preparation for the night ahead. "If things get weird with Dale, I'll just play with Shannon and ignore everyone else."

Chapter Five

Dale stood in the kitchen, nursing a bottle of beer, with one hip propped against the counter. Coolers loaded with ice, beer, and soda were on the back porch. Platters of appetizers covered the counter behind him and the dinette table across from him. The kitchen's island was home to at least seven different kinds of dessert, including colorful Christmas cookies, éclairs, and what looked like two different pies. There was enough food to feed a small army.

Nathan and Willow had gone all out on the decorations, too—well, actually, Willow had. A grand seven-foot, brightly lit Christmas tree, with dozens of cute ornaments on it and a star on top, stood in a corner of the living room, and garland framed all the doorways. There were Santa figures mingled in with elves, snow-men, and angels on every available flat surface. A roaring blaze crackled in the living room fireplace while a pine wreath with a humongous bow hung above it. Six stockings dangled from hooks on the mantel, one each for Willow, Nathan, baby Shannon, Jeremiah, Dale, and Shane Rivers. It'd been very sweet of her to include the three men in what she called her new family tradition.

However, the woman hadn't stopped there with the decorations. Hell, she'd also gotten stockings for Ethel, her gray cat; Fred and Little Rickie, two prairie dogs that made a daily mecca to her back porch for the seeds and vegetables she left out for them; Lucy and Desi, her two goats; and Johnny and June, the ranch's herding dogs. Those were all hanging from the top frame of the bay window Willow and Nathan had hired someone to install in the living room over the summer—Willow had always wanted one. It faced the front yard, which had about a dozen giant, blow-up holiday characters scattered about since the weekend after Thanksgiving.

There were also strings of Christmas lights wrapped around every porch post and spindle and hung along the eaves. Dale couldn't imagine what their next month's electric bill would look like. Willow knew she'd gone a little . . . well, *a lot* crazy with the decorations, but she'd told everyone she'd wanted to make their first Christmas as an extended family special. Nathan had apparently put his foot down, though, when she'd also wanted to order stockings for their three horses, ten chickens, and the twenty-four alpacas on the ranch—five of which had been recently weaned from their mothers and were being sold in the new year. However, Nathan had given in when his wife asked for a compromise of green garland and red bows hanging in the barns.

The entire house smelled like sugar, pine, burning oak, and food. Scents Dale had always associated with the holidays. Willow and Nathan didn't know it, but this was the first holiday season of his adult life that he'd spent at home with a group of people. During his time in the Marines, he'd often been halfway around the world, and then afterward, he'd either worked or spent Christmas alone. Carl Faulkner had always gone to Cheyenne to spend it with his family, leaving Dale to run the ranch for a few days—not that he'd minded. It'd been a long time since his folks had passed away, a year apart, and without siblings or close family, the holidays had lost their appeal to him. That changed after he'd come to work for Willow and Nathan.

Dale had forgotten how much he loved this time of year. The lights, the parties, and the smiles on children's faces as they waited for Santa to come. It was magical.

He nodded a greeting to Anthony, Jeremiah's foreman for the past two years or so. Most of the staff from the JP Ranch were there, Nathan and Willow having adopted the group of mostly bachelors. In his time there at Skyview, Dale had come to learn that neither of his bosses had immediate family left and were more than happy to grow their chosen family at every opportunity. They loved having people at the house and throwing small get-togethers. Now that Shannon was a little older, the baby never wanted for a pair of arms to hold her or a knee to bounce on. The child would grow up with the biggest passel of uncles in three counties. Poor thing wouldn't be allowed to date, *ever*, by the looks of the group filling the house. It was kind of amazing to see a bunch of rough and tough cowboys going ga-ga over the little girl who hadn't even said her first word yet and wouldn't for a while.

Taking another sip of his beer, Dale left his post by the counter and headed into the living room just as the front door opened, sending a gust of cold wind blowing through the house.

Shouts of "Shut the door!" were called out to the person coming in. Dale didn't even need to see who'd entered to know it was Jeremiah. Whenever he was in the room with the gorgeous redhead, a shiver raced down his spine and his heart fluttered. It was unexplainable and frustrated him to no end. He hated that Jeremiah had even this small measure of power over him without any effort, either.

"Merry Christmas!" Willow called, shuffling over to her friend, with Shannon propped on her hip. Earlier in the day, she'd dressed the baby in a fluffy, bright-red dress with white tights and shiny black shoes. The shoes had apparently gone missing while

Dale had been in the kitchen, and if he was seeing things right, the tights were also now gone.

Chuckling, he stood back, observing Jeremiah as he greeted his friends. He'd handed a basket of something off to Nathan and dropped a large, red, Santa-like sack, bulging with gifts, onto the floor, before hugging him and slapping his back. He then took Shannon from Willow, blowing raspberries on the little girl's neck, making her giggle. Once the baby was tucked against his chest, her head resting on his shoulder, he gave Willow a one-armed hug, kissing her on the top of her head.

Dale tried not to notice how good Jeremiah looked in his dress clothes, the green of his shirt bringing out the sharp emerald of his eyes and setting off his gorgeous, thick red hair. Dale kept getting a flash of auburn chest hair and pale skin at the open collar of his shirt. He was helpless not to imagine how all that ivory and freckled skin would look spread out on his sheets. He wanted to suck hickeys on the insides of the other man's thighs and leave finger-shaped bruises on his hips.

"Fuck," he muttered, trying to will away his growing erection, knowing it was useless.

Why did I give him that ultimatum again? Oh, yeah, I'm a dumbass, that's why.

Jeremiah's sparkling eyes and laughter brightened the whole room until his gaze strayed to Dale. When he saw Dale staring back at him, Jeremiah's smile slipped, and his cheeks flushed. Dale couldn't help himself—he winked, knowing it would get a rise out of the other man.

What the hell? Are you a schoolyard bully? Picking on the person you like instead of talking to him?

He drained the last of his beer and then left the empty bottle on an end table before snagging his coat from the back of a kitchen chair and heading outside. He needed a fuckin' cigarette.

Jeremiah forced his gaze away from Dale as the foreman left the room, refusing to give in to the desire to chase the guy down.

Beside him, his best friend gave him a hip check. "You know," she said softly, "whatever's going on with you and Dale is kinda hot to watch. The sexual tension is so high in here, I feel like I'm going to get pregnant again just being in the same room with you two."

"Willow!" he scolded, his face flaming with embarrassment as his gaze darted around the room. Over a dozen people were there already, milling about, but no one was paying attention to him and their hostess. He lowered his voice. "You can't . . . Jesus Christ, what if someone heard you?" he hissed, leaning closer to her. "Shut. Up."

Rolling her eyes, she gestured around them at the house full of their friends, hired hands, and chosen family. None of them except Willow, Nathan, and now Dale had any clue he was gay. "What? You think any one of these people will care? Newsflash, they won't. They love you and just want you to be happy, whatever that means to you."

Patting his cheek none-too gently, she kissed her daughter's head full of black curls and left him standing there with his mouth hanging open.

She was crazy. In a small town like Antelope Rock, filled with rednecks, there would be a load of judgment slammed down on him by at least half the population, if not more. However, as he looked around the room at the men who worked for him and others he considered his friends, he wondered if maybe she could be right.

When Willow had moved to the Rock, many of the townspeople hadn't held her ancestry or her unusual appearance against her except for a few uppity religious types and some others who'd hated the father she'd never known. She'd expected far worse, coming from Philadelphia to a town with less than 1000 people in it, with her sleeve of tattoos, her nose stud, and her short spiky hair dyed pink at the time. Maybe if the town could welcome an out-of-the-norm woman like Willow, they could accept an openly gay man, or a gay couple even, in their midst.

The thought wouldn't leave him for hours as he ate, changed Shannon into her jammies, fed her a bottle, and drank some beer with his hosts and their guests. Dale had come in from the porch, filled a plate, then gone back outside. Jeremiah knew that because he'd been watching the back door.

"Here, baby girl, go see Daddy." Giggling and kicking her feet, Shannon seemed more than happy to be handed over to her adoring father. Nathan grinned and opened his arms wide to take her before cuddling his daughter close to his chest and kissing her. Jeremiah's heart clenched, knowing he'd probably never have a child of his own. "I need some air."

Jeremiah didn't say anything more. He just slipped on his coat and went out the back door, shutting it behind him. Realizing he'd left his hat inside and his gloves in his truck, he cursed under his breath and tucked his hands into his pockets. The man who'd become an obsession was nowhere in sight, but a whiff of rich tobacco tickled his nose. Recognizing the distinctive aroma of Dale's cigarettes, he followed the scent down the long porch and around the side of the house. Leaning over the porch rail, he found the man standing ankle-deep in the snow, hidden in the shadows of the wraparound porch with his back against one of the posts. Just out of reach of the lanterns on the side and back of the house, it made a perfect hiding spot. The tip of his cigarette glowed brighter when he took a drag, then pale white smoke was blown outward, curling around itself as it disappeared into the night. The man had to know Jeremiah was there—or at least someone was, between the door opening and closing and the footsteps—but he didn't acknowledge the fact.

Walking back the way he came, Jeremiah passed Willow's swing and stepped off the porch. He crunched through the snow and ice, cursing Dale in his mind. His dress boots were *not* meant for this. When he reached the other man, Jeremiah muttered, "Cold night."

God, you are so fucking lame! You can easily have a conversation with every other person on the fucking planet, but with this guy, you sound like a twelve-year-old kid trying to talk to his first crush and failing miserably.

"Yeah, it's winter. In Wyoming. It gets cold." Dale was gruff, even more so than normal, refusing to look at him as he took another long drag on his cigarette.

Jeremiah scowled at him. "You know, I never understood people who smoked needing a cigarette bad enough to stand outside freezing their asses off for a hit of nicotine that tastes like ass."

"It's a nasty habit. I'm trying to quit—have been for years, actually."

The man's simple confession surprised him, and he felt like a jerk calling him out like that. Addiction came in many forms. Cigarettes. Drugs. Booze. Hiding in a closet.

It was true. If Jeremiah really thought about it, he had his own addiction. He couldn't stop feeling like he had to pretend to be someone he wasn't. Overcoming that fear was probably just as difficult as someone else trying to conquer their own vices.

"Sorry—I didn't mean to sound judgmental. What I wanted to say was . . ." He was uncertain how to put his thoughts into words.

Dale put his cigarette out on the bottom of his boot, tucking the butt into his pants pocket to presumably dispose of it later. "What? You wanted to say what, Cowboy?"

"I don't fucking know!" he snarled as anger and frustration flowed through him. He stalked closer to the taller man, stopping only when he was toe-to-toe with him. This time, when he spoke, he kept his tone low and in check in case anyone else came outside for a breather. "I know I want you. I know I'm dying to know what you taste like, how you kiss, and how your hands feel on me. What the skin over your hipbones feels like between my teeth. What sound you make when you come. I know I want all of that, but I don't fucking know how to go about getting it. I want to know you, not just your body, but your mind. I want to know what you did in the Marines and if you have any family. *Everything!*"

"Fuck," Dale said softly, almost to himself, as his eyes blazed with both rage and hunger, the combination potent and heart-stopping.

Jeremiah's breath left him in a rush as his cock hardened in his pants, and he bit back a moan. He'd just opened his mouth to say something else, anything else, when Dale reached out, palmed the back of Jeremiah's head, and crashed their mouths together. Jeremiah gasped, his arms going around the other man's waist, pulling him tightly against his own aching body. In a move that was almost choreographed, Dale spun him around, slamming his back against the post. Snow showered down on top of them from the eaves, both too wrapped in each other to notice the cold flakes.

The kiss went on seemingly forever, with much biting and licking. Dale's tongue swept into Jeremiah's mouth, causing him to moan again. The man tasted like smoke, beer, and something spicy-sweet that seemed to be unique to him. Jeremiah normally hated the taste of cigarettes, but with Dale's lips against his, he found his need to consume him quickly overrode any negative feelings about it.

Lifting his arms from Dale's waist, he knocked the man's hat to the ground, filling his hands with the thick strands of his dark hair. *So soft.*

Dale grabbed Jeremiah's ass, rubbing their groins together, sliding their hard cocks against each other's. Dale thrust his hips forward, over and over.

"Please," Jeremiah begged, unsure what he was begging for, as Dale's mouth left his and trailed kisses down Jeremiah's neck, laving and sucking on his skin. Shivers racked Jeremiah, and he shot his hips forward, desperate for more. More friction. More kisses. More skin. Just more everything.

"Please, what? Fuck you in the snow?" Dale

released Jeremiah's ass and gripped his jaw, twisting his head to the side, granting himself more access to the exposed skin of his neck. "God dammit, you taste amazing, I knew you would."

"Yes, just . . . fuck." Jerking his head free from the man's grasp, Jeremiah kissed Dale again, sucking his bottom lip into his mouth before sweeping deep inside. Groaning at the sensations bombarding him, Jeremiah tried to pull the other man even closer, though they were already as close as they could be with their clothes still on. He couldn't get enough of him—he wanted every inch of Dale's naked flesh pressed against his own.

"You want to be on your knees in the snow? You want me to choke you with my cock?"

"Yeess!" Grinding harder against Dale's hard-on, he was breathless, so close to coming in his pants it was ridiculous.

All at once, Dale released him and stepped back. Jeremiah stumbled, his legs weak and wobbly as a newborn foal.

"No." Bending, Dale picked up his hat and brushed the snow off it before settling it back onto his head. A firestorm raged in his eyes. "I want you, Cowboy, there's no denying that. On your knees, on your back, up against the wall, bent over that railing. However, I can get you. But I also want to take you on a date, open doors for you, and put my hand possessively on the small of your back. No matter how tempting you are, I won't be hidden. Never again."

Without another word, Dale stormed away toward the barns and his trailer.

"Fuck!" Jeremiah shouted, spinning around. He smashed his fist against the porch post, busting his knuckles open. His chest heaved in a combination of frustration, anger, and lust. Bracing his hands against the railing's spindles, he stared down at his boots, cursing himself for being a stupid, stubborn fool. He could've gone his entire life not knowing what it was like to kiss the arrogant bastard, but now that he'd tasted the man, Jeremiah didn't think he could last an entire minute without needing to do it again.

Chapter Six

April

Jeremiah drank the last of his coffee before slamming the empty travel mug into the cup holder as he drove over to Willow's. His bad mood had started on Christmas and showed no signs of abating, even after four months.

Willow's fussy-ass alpacas wouldn't eat the last shipment of hay she'd ordered, so he'd offered to swap hers for some of his. Cows don't give two shits what cutting the hay was from, but apparently, the alpacas did. They would turn their fuzzy noses up at the hay, piss on it, and walk away. Willow had been beside herself with worry, but he'd talked her down and told her he'd be over today to exchange the bales. The nursing mamas wouldn't have to go without their preferred forage. Later this year, the Skyview Ranch would be reaping a field of its own hay for the first time, but it would only be enough for half a year's feeding of the alpaca herd. Still, it would be a money-saver.

The only problem Jeremiah was having with making the delivery was Willow and Nathan had the baby at a well-child check at the clinic in town. He and Dale would have to work together. Honestly, Jeremiah could do it himself, but it would take him all fuckin' day, and he had his own shit to deal with at the JP.

"Fuck me." He picked up the coffee mug again before remembering too late that he'd already finished it. "Dammit." He hadn't been sleeping well, and his normal one-pot-a-day coffee habit had increased to nearly two. "Get it done, get home, and forget about the man."

Yeah, right. Like it was possible for him to forget anything about the hotter-than-Hades retired Marine.

Every night, he fell asleep recalling the feel of Dale's lips, his hands gripping him tightly, the taste of him thick in Jeremiah's mouth like a candy that never fully dissolved. The sexy foreman lingered in his mind, no matter how many times he wished it otherwise. No matter how many times he jerked off, the ghost of Dale hovered nearby, taunting him. Jeremiah was fairly certain he was cracking up, his mind breaking under the strain of his deepest desires being so close yet impossibly out of reach. He hadn't been to Cheyenne for an anonymous hookup in almost a year. Every time he'd decided to make the trip to blow off steam, visions of Dale had prevented him from even stepping out the front door.

He turned onto Skyview's long driveway, bouncing over ruts and keeping an eye on the trailer behind him. It would just be the icing on the cake of his day if any of the hay fell off into the mud. The last of the snow from a moderate storm over the past weekend was mostly melted, and the ground was soggy. It made for long, dirty days, but he'd rather deal with mud than snow any day. The cold sapped his energy worse now than it did when he was younger. Spring had always been his favorite time of the year—everything fresh and new as the sun warmed the earth enough that sweaters, jackets, and gloves could be shed. Unfortunately, it was still early in the day, and the sun was behind a sky full of clouds. A cold front had swept down from Canada late last night, and the cooler temperature had required Jeremiah to grab a lightweight jacket on the way out the door that morning.

Making a wide U-turn behind the house, he pulled the trailer loaded with hay around before backing it as close to the alpaca barn as he could manage. No reason to haul the bales any farther than they had to. Glancing in his rearview mirror a final time, he saw Dale standing outside the barn, a black hat shading his face and his thick arms crossed over his broad chest. The man looked pissed off and sexier than he had any right to be. The herding dogs, Johnny and June, were nowhere to be seen. Dale had probably closed them off with the alpacas in their pasture while they worked—Jeremiah had seen the foreman do it a few other times. Apparently, the dogs liked to try to "help" with certain chores when, in reality, they just got in the way.

Jeremiah climbed from the cab, stepping directly into a deep puddle he hadn't realized was there. "Fucker," he said with a growl when the water covered the tops of his boots. His jeans and socks were now soaked. Sighing in aggravation, he tipped his head back and stared at the sky for a moment. Someone up there had it in for him today. "Thanks a lot."

Determined to get the job done as fast as possible so he didn't have to be around Dale longer than necessary, he strode forward, ignoring the other mud puddles and stomping through brown, slushy water everywhere. The mess suited his mood—chaotic and uncontrollable.

"Throwing tantrums now?" Dale smirked before stepping forward and releasing the first few tie-downs holding the hay on the trailer.

"Not doing it with you today, Marine. I've got plenty of shit to do without dealing with your smart-ass mouth."

Shoving the larger man aside, Jeremiah made quick work with the rest of the ties. "You going to open the damn barn or just stand there glaring at me?" His newly volatile temper was burning hot and high, it seemed.

"No need to be a dick," Dale jabbed back, anger tightening his stubble-shadowed jaw. Jeremiah ignored the desire to feel that coarse hair rub against his own, to see beard burn on his neck and cheeks. He didn't need anything from Dale. Not now. Not ever. Being sexually attracted to a guy and actually liking him were two totally different things.

"Where's Shane?"

"In town, picking up some stuff at Ducky's."

Turning his head so the other man couldn't see him, Jeremiah rolled his eyes. Of course, the ranch hand had run the errand to the local feed and supply store instead of the foreman, who was pissing Jeremiah off more and more with every second that passed.

Donning his gloves, he hooked his fingers through the baling twine and hauled the first bale up and off the trailer. "You just gonna fuckin' stand there, or are you gonna help? If you want to gawk at me, at least do it while moving some of this shit."

"Damn, you're sore today, huh?" Dale snapped, leading the way to the barn and throwing open the double doors. Jeremiah pushed past him, dropping the hay where Dale pointed. "What's stuck up your ass?"

Certainly not you.

Clamping down on the retort before it could burst from his mouth, Jeremiah worked in silence. Back and forth, they carried the heavy bales, then returned for more, avoiding each other as much as possible. It wasn't long before the trailer was empty, and they began to load the hay the alpacas wouldn't eat onto it. Once he got home, he'd have to haul all the hay again. Even with his men's help, it would be more back-breaking work. He was sweating through his shirt in response to the physical labor he'd gotten used to decades before.

Pausing before grabbing the next load, he stripped off his jacket and flung it over the side of the trailer. Under it, he wore only an old, faded, blue long-sleeved T-shirt. The material stuck to him around his neck, under his arms, and down his back where he'd sweated through it. He stank, too, but he didn't really give a fuck right then.

"I'd ask what's got you so pissed off, but I'm sure I know."

Gritting his teeth, he did his best to ignore Dale and the way his words fired an arrow of rage and want into his heart. He also didn't allow himself to notice the way Dale's gray T-shirt rode up in the back when he bent over, revealing a strip of tawny skin above the black waistband of his briefs peeking out the top of his worn jeans.

"Just like you know everything, huh? About every-one? Without even needing to be told. You should take your mind-reading skills on the road—you'd make a mint." Jeremiah had let his frustration get the best of him again, the words pouring out before he was aware he would say them.

"Jeremiah, we should talk about this." Dale stopped in front of him, blocking his path to the barn, propping his glove-covered hands on his denim-clad hips.

"Oh? Now you want to talk, huh?" Stripping his gloves off, he shoved them into his back pocket. "Now you're talking to me instead of *at* me? Not throwing demands in my face? Not telling me how it has to be without giving any fuckin' consideration of what I might want and need?" He'd passed anger about two months ago and was fixed solidly on rage and torment.

Dale sighed heavily. "Yes. I realize now that at Christmas and before then, I might have been a little . . . well, harsh." He maintained eye contact with Jeremiah, letting him see the truth in his gaze. "I thought maybe I could explain."

He stepped closer, standing within touching distance. Jeremiah could smell the salty musk of his sweat and the underlying spice that was all Dale. "Explain? You kiss me and rub your hard cock against mine, you tease and push and . . . and . . . demand shit from me! What makes you think for one fuckin' moment I would listen to anything you have to say after all that? I was worth a grope in the dark but not a conversation then, but now I am? Fuck you!"

Jabbing his finger into Dale's sternum, he let loose with every ounce of fiery hurt and shame he had buried in his soul. "I'll say it again, fuck you, Dale! It's not easy for me. You think I want to risk everything—my business, my legacy, and my family—on a night in the sack with you? No! No fucking way! I won't do it.

Yeah, you make my dick hard, and I want you more than I've wanted anyone in a long time, if ever, but if you can't show me the common fuckin' courtesy of giving me a chance to explain where I'm coming from, then you can go pound sand! I'm worth more than that!"

He didn't realize until he paused for a breath that tears streamed down his cheeks. His chest heaved with the force of his emotions, and his hands shook. He wanted to punch the handsome bastard in the mouth and then kiss him until they both passed out.

"Jeremiah, I'm . . . I'm sorry." Taking off his hat, Dale ran his fingers through his hair before jamming it back on his head. He lifted his hands as if he was going to touch Jeremiah's face but then seemed to change his mind, tucking his thumbs into his jean pockets at his hips. Sheer regret filled his eyes. "I've been thinking a lot since Christmas. I was wrong. You have to under-stand—before . . . " He swallowed hard before continu-ing. "Years ago, I was hurt—badly. I waited and waited for him to come out. We were out of the Marines, and there was no more danger of going public, but he kept putting me off. Every time he said he would come out, he didn't, giving me a shit-poor reason each time. But I was in love, and he said he loved me, so I waited some more. Until one day, I came across pictures he'd been tagged in on social media. He was with someone else— a woman—kissing her and showing off her engagement and wedding rings."

Jeremiah felt the blood drain from his face, and sorrow filled his heart for the man standing before him.

Dale shrugged. "He'd always said he wasn't like me —into both men and woman—he only liked men. Well, that was either a lie or confused thinking. He liked women just enough or convinced himself he did to actually marry one behind my back. She was some girl he met right before our discharge who wanted a meal ticket and a Marine on her arm. He went for it, knowing he'd never be happy but unable to fight for who he really loved—me. He painted on a heterosexual face and refused to say he was anything but absolutely straight as an arrow."

He glanced away momentarily before returning his gaze to Jeremiah's face. "After that, I swore I would never again allow myself to be hidden away. If I were ever with someone again, no matter how new the relationship was, it would be out in the open for everyone to see. But you, goddammit, Jeremiah, *you* make me want to break my own rule."

Wiping his sweaty face on his arm, Jeremiah met Dale's gaze full-on. As bad as he felt for what the other man had been through, he still held onto his own hurt and anger. His tone was nearly a shout when he retorted, "I never, not once, told you no. I said that I didn't know how to come out, that I was unsure and afraid, but I never said no. Maybe you could try some patience and compassion. Until then, I'm out of here.

I'll send someone by later for the rest of the hay. I can't look at you right now."

Without another word, Jeremiah stomped back to his truck, splashing mud farther up his pants and not giving a single shit. Absorbed in his own thoughts, he didn't notice Nathan's truck now parked in its normal spot near the house, nor did he see Willow scowling at him as he drove away.

Chapter Seven

Dale stared at the tailgate of Jeremiah's truck as it flew down the dirt drive to the road, the half-full trailer bouncing over the ruts and splashing in the mud.

Damn it. I picked the wrong fuckin' day to quit smokin', didn't I?

He'd fucked up. All this time, he'd been playing with Jeremiah like a cat with a mouse. But instead of a plaything, the other man was turning into something more . . . someone Dale was craving to a greater extent with each interaction. He'd told Jeremiah the truth—he refused to hide who he really was—but somewhere along the line, he'd forgotten what it was like to take those first few baby steps out of the closet. It could be scary as hell. The least he could do was give the guy a chance to take those same steps one at a time.

He got where Jeremiah was coming from—the

Rock was much smaller than Redworth, where Dale had lived before coming to work for Willow, which had a population of approximately 15,000 people. The city of Laramie, Wyoming, where Dale had grown up, was a little more than twice that size and less than an hour away from Cheyenne, which had over four times the number of residents than Redworth. He'd been able to explore his sexual orientation without sticking out like a sore thumb, but Jeremiah had been born and raised in a town that was barely a blip on a map. If you were driving through the Rock and blinked, you'd be halfway to the next town before you realized it. And if you sneezed, your neighbor two miles away would bless you and then get on the rumor mill to tell everyone you were on your deathbed.

Footsteps approached on the dirt and gravel, and he turned around to face Willow. Yeah, he'd seen Nathan's truck pull up a little while ago and wasn't surprised she'd witnessed his confrontation with Jeremiah. His boss's frown increased the guilt he felt. Stopping in front of him, she crossed her arms. "I told you before that I didn't want any pissing contests between you and my best friend. He's a good man—one of the best I've ever known—he doesn't deserve to be toyed with. If you want to play tit-for-tat with a guy, then find someone else. Jeremiah's emotions are raw as hell. Everyone has their secrets, and it's not up to anyone else to say if and when the time is right to expose them.

"This is a small town—everyone knows everyone.

There are still some people who disapprove of me simply because I'm not from here, I have a sleeve of tattoos and a nose stud, and I used to have pink hair. They also didn't like my father, so I have that cross to bear too. But I don't give a crap. I didn't know these people all my life, and the ones who won't accept me, well, that's their problem. I don't give two shits about them.

"But Jeremiah grew up here. He's seen what happens to people who're different around here. He knows what'll happen if and when he comes out. When I tell him no one will care if he's gay, I know that's not entirely true. The people who really care about him will stay by his side, defend him even. But he'll still face ridicule and disgust from others. Would you be willing to risk everything you've ever known for someone who's done nothing but tease you and demand you come out? Someone you have no idea if you can trust? Someone you really like but are afraid to take that first step for, worrying if you'll be tossed aside when the thrill of the chase is gone and the damage has been done?"

God, the woman really knew how to thrust a knife into someone and twist it when they'd fucked up and she was in mama-bear mode. Sighing, he dropped his gaze to the ground, where he toed a pebble before meeting her eyes again. "You're absolutely right. I screwed up."

Her eyebrows nearly hit her hairline. After a

moment, she nodded. "Okay, then. What are you going to do to fix it?"

And wasn't that the million-dollar question?

* * *

Jeremiah had just popped the top on a fresh beer, his third since finishing up his chores, when Willow came barreling into his kitchen. He looked up in surprise and alarm. She usually knocked before walking right in, so his mind immediately went to something being wrong. However, her blazing eyes and tense frown told him she was furious, and he hoped that rage wasn't directed at him.

She stood before him, wearing heather-gray leggings, her neon-pink muck boots, and an oversized baby-pink hoodie. Her hair was flat on one side and tangled on the other, not to mention what looked suspiciously like a spit-up stain on her shoulder.

She slammed her car keys down on the counter and crossed her arms. "You should be happy I waited until I had a nap with Shannon before coming over here. She just had shots, so she's cranky as hell, and I got my period for the first time since I had her. To say that I'm in a *mood* is an understatement."

"Okay." Totally confused, he stood back, well out of reach, and racked his brain, trying to figure out what he'd done to make her so angry. He may not have much experience with menstruating women, but he knew enough that caution was probably the best approach.

Or with chocolate? Is there any chocolate in the house? Ice cream? Shit!

He'd finished off his last pint the evening before while binging on Hallmark movies again.

Willow stomped her foot. "What I saw today makes me want to smack you into next week. I'm your best friend, so I'm allowed to say this—what the fuck is your problem?"

"What? Willow! What are you talking about?" He raised his hands to his sides, stepping closer to her. "Sweetheart, I can see you've had a hard day, and I want to help, but you're gonna have to fill in the blanks for me."

Snarling, she propped her hands on her hips and glared at him. If looks could kill, he'd be a pile of ash. "I saw you! I heard you! The way you talked to him today is *not* the Jeremiah I know!"

Fuck, she'd been home and heard him yelling at Dale. Shame heated his face, and he hung his head.

"Don't you give me that hang-dog, aw-shucks crap either—I don't want to hear or see it. I've tried to ease you gently into this, but since you're a stubborn asshole, we're just going to rip the Band-Aid off. No. One. Cares. You're. Gay." She poked him in the chest with each word, and he fought the urge to rub the spot.

Damn, that hurt.

"I love you, Jeremiah. Your family loves you, and

so do your friends. No one who cares about you gives a single fuck who you love or who you have sex with. All anyone wants is for you to be happy. I'm not saying you need to make an announcement in the paper and paint your house in the colors of the rainbow but going on a date with Dale is a great place to start."

"W-what?" he sputtered, his eyes round and large as saucers. "How do you know no one cares?"

"Because, *dumbass*, dollars to donuts, everyone who knows you well enough to love you has always known! My gaydar doesn't operate too well most days, but even I could tell almost right away! I was more surprised you came out to me than anything else.

"You like to play hide the sausage with dudes. So fucking what? You're an amazing person and a cornerstone of this community. That's all that matters!"

"Are you done?" He didn't know what to think or feel right now. Hope was trying to blossom, and he was too afraid to examine his feelings closely.

"No! I'm not fucking done! You have it so good and don't even know it! Gay guys are the best! You don't have to worry about periods from hell or . . . or . . . getting pregnant or any of that crap! It's not fucking fair!" She buried her face in her hands and burst into tears.

"Oh, hell," he muttered before gathering her close. He held her as she cried, soaking his shirt. He was honestly at a complete loss for words right now. Baby hormones had fried her brain or something. "Um, should I call Nathan?"

"Yes! No! I don't know! I'm angry and happy and sad and stressed all at the same time!" she wailed, crying harder, her shoulder shaking. Keeping one arm around her, he pulled his cell from his back pocket and fumbled a text to Nathan.

> Your wife is sobbing on my shirt.
> Please help.

Thankfully, he didn't need to wait long for a reply.

NATHAN

> On my way.

After setting his phone on the counter, he rubbed his hands up and down her back. As he waited for Nathan to arrive, an idea formed in his mind. He mulled it over while consoling his best friend—over what, he still wasn't sure.

Willow was winding down to sniffles when Nathan rushed in, looking harried and worried, with Shannon on his hip. Jeremiah released Willow and immediately drew the baby into his arms so Nathan could take over, comforting his wife.

Cuddling Shannon against his shoulder, he left the couple alone, ducking into his living room and plopping onto the couch, his beer and foul mood forgotten. He rested his feet on the coffee table and propped

Shannon on his bent knees. "What do you think, Sunshine? Think you would want to hang with me for a bit and give your mama and daddy a break?" Staring at her blue eyes, framed by those gorgeous dark curls, he nodded to himself. "You're right, we got this."

Nathan led Willow into the room with an arm wrapped possessively around her shoulders. Not giving the man a chance to speak, Jeremiah said, "You two go pack a bag. Sunshine and me are gonna hang out and watch some movies. Don't worry, I'll cover her eyes if there's any kissing involved." Yes, they were aware of his Hallmark Channel addiction. "Bring me whatever stuff she needs, and I'll take her for the night and all day tomorrow. Go rent a room somewhere and relax. Dale and Shane can handle the chores just fine. Plus, I'm only a phone call away if they need help."

It wasn't as if he'd never babysat his goddaughter for an hour here and there before. *A few more can't be that bad, right?*

Willow opened her mouth to protest, but Jeremiah raised his hand, silencing her. "You're right, everything you said—I just need some time to think it over, and what better way than with this gorgeous angel to hash things over with? Go do whatever—Sunshine and me here have some plans to make."

Chapter Eight

Four hours later, Jeremiah knelt on the floor with Shannon—his sunshine, his goddaughter, and the destroyer of the multiple diapers laid out on and around the changing pad Willow had said to use.

"It's easy to clean," she'd said. Never, ever, in a million years had he anticipated that being something he would need to take into consideration. Little Miss Blowout had nasty-looking yellow liquid leaking out of the sides of her diaper, down her legs, and somehow, also up her back.

"Girl! How did this happen?" He had a pack of wipes beside his knee, with half of them already pulled out, along with clean clothes, a fresh diaper, and two plastic bags. One for the diaper currently leaking nuclear waste and the other for her dirty clothes that he would have to *rinse out* before he could wash them.

She babbled in response, waving her hands at him and kicking her feet.

Unsnapping her onesie at the crotch, he carefully rolled it up, trying his best to contain the mess within the garment. "Jesus Christ on a cracker, girly, I thought cow shit was horrible." Gagging, he tucked his face into his shirt.

What seemed like fifteen wipes later, he realized he should've just plopped her into the clean kitchen sink to rinse her off and bathe her, not pissed around with the wipes, but he was already committed and almost done.

A few moments later, he declared, "All right, young lady, now you're naked and clean. So, let's get you into a new diaper and fresh clothes."

Before he could get started, though, Shannon's sweet giggles changed in tone, and her cheeks turned red as she screwed up her face and let out a scream. Tears dripped from the corners of her scrunched-up eyes. She straightened her legs out, arching her back, keeping them tense and flat as boards, refusing to bend her knees, so he could lift her and put the new diaper under her little butt. Huffing in frustration, he tried again, unsuccessfully, to put the diaper on her. Her wails hurt his ears, and he was seconds away from bawling along with her.

"How is someone so small this strong? You're like the baby Hulk!" Sweat dotted his brow as his stress level rose. Willow always made this look so easy—two minutes, wham, bam, diapered baby! Nathan had the process down pat too. Jeremiah had even changed the baby a few times with Willow by his side. But this time, on his first solo run, his little Sunshine had turned into a tiny monster who didn't want to be naked but also didn't want a diaper on.

Maybe a toy would help distract her. Searching the baby-themed detritus that now covered his living room floor, he didn't see a single toy within reach.

What the hell? Nathan brought over an entire bag of them—where did they go?

Glancing around once more, inspiration struck, and he grabbed a nearby bottle that'd fallen out when he dumped half the diaper bag on the floor. "Talc-free organic tapioca starch? What the heck is that?"

Shannon's only reply was another screech to the high heavens. Honestly, it didn't freakin' matter what the stuff was. Kids didn't care as long as they had something to hold and look at. That's what he was going with anyway.

Once he gave her the bottle, she held it with both hands, inspecting it, and her crying and writhing slowed. He didn't hesitate, slipping the new diaper under her bottom and fastening the sides with all the speed he used when wrangling a bawling calf.

Lifting both hands in the air like a champion, he shouted, "Done!"

Later, he would swear he saw a devious glint in Shannon's eye as she pointed the canister at his face and gave it a good shake, releasing a large cloud of white. Jeremiah coughed and choked as the powder filled his nose and mouth. He hacked and gagged, waving his hands in front of his face, trying to clear away the billowy mass from the air. Meanwhile, Shannon was crying again, no doubt upset because he desperately tried to draw fresh oxygen into his lungs again so he wouldn't pass out.

Blinking cleared his vision—somehow, the spray had mostly hit his mouth and chest, missing his eyes. Glancing down, he saw they were both covered in a fine blanket of white, along with the floor all around them. She still had a good grip on the bottle, and the more she shook it, the more white powder exploded from the top of it. The cloying scent hung heavy around them, mixed with the smell coming from her dirty diaper, souring his stomach further.

"Well, fuck. I mean, shoot. You didn't hear me say that bad word. Don't worry, I'll put money in the swear jar later." Shaking his head, he took the bottle from her, which increased her upset from simply crying to scream-the-rafters-down level. "At least I didn't get your clothes on yet."

A change of clothes for both and two more hours had passed, and Shannon was *still* crying.

He paced with her, bouncing and rocking, singing in his off-key voice. He begged and bargained, promised her a pony, a sports car, and custom cowgirl boots, but none of it worked.

He thought about calling her parents, but an image of Willow's stressed and tear-stained face flashed in his mind. He couldn't do that to them. One name popped into his head—a person he was supposed to be thinking about anyway. He promised Willow he'd figure it out.

Dale.

He picked up his phone again. This was not how he wanted to start a conversation with the man, begging for help with Shannon, but he was desperate. His behavior earlier shamed him, even knowing his feelings were justified, but in order to get help, he was going to suck it up.

He dialed before he had a second to talk himself out of it. Putting the phone to his ear, he struggled to hear it ringing over his goddaughter's ear-splitting caterwauling.

"What the fuck is that noise?" Dale barked in Jeremiah's ear. Clearly, he'd heard the crying before he could even say hello. "Is that Shannon? What did you do to her, Jay?"

"I don't know! She won't stop, and I don't know what to do!" He was freaking out now as Dale's snappish tone broke the calm he'd been holding onto by a thread.

"Fuck," came the muttered response. "I'll be right there."

* * *

Dale threw his truck into Park and hustled into Jeremiah's large log cabin-style house, not bothering to knock or announce himself in any way. He'd never been inside the man's home before—only in the ranch's barns—but he could hear Shannon from outside and was terrified something was seriously wrong with her. He'd never heard her cry that way before. She was generally a happy baby and wasn't prone to long bouts of screaming.

"Jeremiah!" He found them in the living room—the path Jeremiah was pacing with the baby was the only clear spot on the floor. Toys, clothes, and what appeared to be dry, white snow were everywhere. Sniffing, he confirmed it was probably baby powder, the overwhelming fresh scent hanging in the air like a cloud, yet not enough to overpower the stomach-churning smell of shit.

Dale gasped, gagged, and coughed a few times before asking, "What the hell is going on?"

The other man was wide-eyed and harried, looking like he was about to burst into tears himself. "I don't know! She won't stop. Her diaper is fresh, and she won't eat. I tried burping her, but that didn't work either. There's tapioca starch everywhere! I don't want to call Nathan and Willow, but I don't know what to do here."

Shannon lifted her face from Jeremiah's chest, thrusting her whole body backward in a bow, arching her spine. Her face was bright red and streaked with tears and snot.

What the fuck is tapioca starch? Isn't that pudding?

Dale glanced around the room at the mess, unsure how to help. He knew Nathan and Willow had gone to dinner and a drive-in movie—their first night out since the baby had been born—and he didn't want to disturb them any more than Jeremiah did. "Come on, let's go outside. Maybe the fresh air will help." It reeked in there. The combination of powder and baby shit was horrid and would probably be stuck in his nose for days.

Grabbing a blanket off the couch, he shook it out, sending a new cloud of powder into the air. He waved it away from the baby's face, then laid the blanket over her shoulders and back. Jeremiah nodded as he tucked the material around Shannon's torso, his expression more stressed than Dale had ever seen it. Worry had carved deep furrows into his brow, and sweat dotted his forehead. His red hair stood straight up as if he'd been running his hands through it. Smiling to himself, Dale secretly thought it was adorable.

Quickly banishing that train of thought, he focused on the problem at hand. He held the front door open for Jeremiah to walk through, a screaming Shannon still thrashing in his arms.

"Hand her over, take a minute, and then tell me what happened." Dale opened his arms, settling the baby against his chest, trying to console her.

He kissed Shannon's forehead. She was warm, almost too warm, but it was hard to tell if it was from all the crying or if she was running a fever. He loosened the blanket but kept it around her. It was warm enough for him and Jeremiah to be outside without jackets but still too cool for a tiny baby.

In the meantime, Jeremiah paced the length of the porch. "I don't know what happened. She pooped all over, out of her clothes, and . . . and *everywhere*! I cleaned her up and changed her. Then she hit me with that powder and started crying. I got us both cleaned up *again*, but she just wouldn't stop. I tried feeding her, but she wouldn't take the bottle. Her diaper is dry. She won't sleep. I tried walking her, sitting with her, rocking her, everything I could think of. Is she okay?" His voice was thick with worry.

Dale pressed his cheek to hers. "She feels warm. Do you have a thermometer?"

"Maybe in her diaper bag? Let me go look." Jeremiah jogged back into the house—his fear that something was seriously wrong with Shannon was palpable. He loved her—that much was obvious. He was such a good man, Dale thought, as he rocked Shannon side-to-side, softly shushing her. Thank God some of his teammates in the Marines had little kids back then. Reluctantly, he'd learned a lot about infants and toddlers whenever they'd been stateside and over at each other's houses almost every weekend. Surprisingly, many of those lessons still came back to him at times like this.

Jeremiah hurried back out, the screen door slamming behind him. "Here, I found it." He brandished a bright pink thermometer in his fist. "How do you do it? We don't have to take it . . . um, *rectally* . . . do we?" Jeremiah's already white face paled further. "I don't think I can do that!"

Laughing, he said, "Here, you take her, I'll do it. And no, under the arm is just fine. You just have to add a degree to the temp."

"Oh, thank God." Lifting her under her armpits, Jeremiah took Shannon and settled her with her back against his chest. She threw her head back and forth, still crying, though it seemed a bit better now. The tone of her screams was softer.

Taking the device from the plastic protector, Dale pushed the on button and then pulled the sleeve of her onesie aside. He tucked the soft, rubbery end in her armpit and gently held her arm down. "There, there, baby girl. Uncle Jeremiah has you. It's going to be okay, sweetheart."

He tried to soothe her while they waited, kissing her forehead. He frowned—she really was warm. Shannon stuffed her fist into her mouth, drooling and chewing on her hand even as she kept whining.

The thermometer beeped a minute or so later, and Dale pulled it free. *100.5.*

"A fever but a low-grade one. Maybe she's teething." He gestured to where she was doing her best to fit her whole hand into her mouth. "Let's get her something cold to chew on and see if Willow packed her some baby Tylenol or something."

"How do you know all this stuff?"

"The wives of my Marine buddies made sure all their single teammates learned it so we could babysit when markers were called in or bets were lost."

Jeremiah nodded mutely and waited while Dale held the door open for them.

"Where's her bag?" he asked Jeremiah, glancing around the living room. Everything from the diaper bag seemed to be all over the place, but he didn't see any bottles of pain reliever.

The other man settled on the couch with Shannon on his chest. She kept gnawing on her fingers and whimpering. "Over there, by the chair."

Dale spotted a large pink and purple bag on the floor beside the recliner. Picking it up, he set it on the chair and dug around inside. He was surprised to see there was even more stuff still inside—diapers, clothes, toys, bottles, and a can of formula. Then again, that made sense because he remembered Nathan saying Jeremiah had taken the baby for the entire night.

Rifling through everything, he searched for . . . ah, there, in a side pocket, was a brand-new box of infant Tylenol. Reading the directions, he figured out her dose and opened the box. Inside was a bottle and a plastic syringe-looking thingy. After the cap was twisted off, the end of the syringe would fit into a hole in the top of the bottle, allowing him to draw the liquid directly into it. He measured the proper dose, re-capped the bottle, and put it back in the bag.

Sitting beside Jeremiah on the couch, he encouraged Shannon to turn her head. As soon as she did, he popped the blunt plastic end of the syringe into her mouth, turning it so it faced her cheek and not down her throat, and slowly depressed the plunger. He watched her throat, noting that she was swallowing. "That's a good girl. This will make you feel better." She sucked on the end of the applicator, finishing the liquid without a fuss. "Good job, baby girl."

Pulling it free of her mouth, he kissed the top of her head before standing and taking the dropper into the kitchen to the sink, where he rinsed it off. After shutting off the water, he leaned against his hands, which clutched the counter's edge. Closing his eyes, he took several deep breaths. Being around Jeremiah for any reason was nerve-racking. A constant battle was fought in his mind whenever he was within fifty feet of the man. Part of him wanted to tackle Jeremiah and fuck him senseless—closet be damned. The other part wanted to run as far away as he could. Dale felt that no matter what he did, he would get hurt.

"Dale." Jeremiah's gruff voice caught his attention as he returned to the living room. He bent, picking up a stuffed bear and handing it to Jeremiah, who tucked it under Shannon's hand. Her cries had finally stopped. Sniffles and hiccups were all that remained. Worn out, she gripped her bear and snuggled her face into Jeremiah's chest.

"Yeah?" He stared at his boots, not wanting to meet the other man's eyes. He was still hurt from earlier and how Jeremiah had yelled at him. Maybe he'd deserved some of it, but not all of it. He'd do anything to help Shannon—that's why he'd come without a second thought—and now that she was calmed down, he wanted to get out of there. Being near Jeremiah was too raw and painful right now.

"Thank you." Sighing, Jeremiah ran a hand through his hair again. "For everything. It seems like you really know what you're doing with babies. I have no damn clue, obviously. So, just, thanks."

"You're welcome, but I didn't do it for you. I did it for her."

Shannon had one fist wrapped in her bear's fur, the other held tightly to Jeremiah's shirt. She was out like a light, snoring softly, with tears still wet on her plump cheeks. Her jaw, mouth, and cheeks twitched as if she was suckling.

"I get that. But still, I appreciate it." Jeremiah swallowed audibly. "Also, I . . . uh . . . I wanted to . . . um . . . ask you something." Closing his eyes, he rested his head on the back of the couch, taking a deep enough breath that Shannon's little body rose and fell with the force of it. Dale crossed his arms and waited the man out. Finally, Jeremiah looked at him again. "Would . . .

um . . . would you like to, uh . . . go out to dinner with me sometime?"

"W-what?" Dale was gobsmacked, his stomach feeling like it'd fallen into his boots. "What did you just say?"

He couldn't have heard right—there's no way.

In the blissful silence of the room, Jeremiah glanced at the sleeping baby. "While I was walking Shannon, talking to her, begging her to stop crying—I have to buy her a pony now, by the way—I told her all about you and . . . about me." Blushing hotly, Jeremiah raised his eyes, meeting Dale's gaze head-on.

He glared down at the man. "You need to spell this out for me, Jay, because I don't want a misunderstanding now to come back and bite me in the ass later."

"I was wrong." He absentmindedly rubbed Shannon's back. "I'm sorry. Most of what I said today is how I feel, but it honestly comes from fear. I'm so scared, Dale—all the time. I just want to be happy, to be myself, but I don't know how. I *do* know that I want you. Not just in bed, either. I want to get to know you better, and I'd love to go to dinner—if you'll still have me after my behavior today."

Reaching out, Dale brushed his forefinger under Jeremiah's chin. "Just to be ten levels of clear here. This would be a date. Not friends eating out or buddies going for drinks. If this is what you really want, you'll have to be okay with me picking you up, holding your hand, and paying."

He swallowed hard but then nodded. "Yes. A date. In public. All I ask is that you try and be patient with me. I've never been on an actual date before, even with a woman, except for my prom date, Amy-Jo Hanson, but we were just friends. I have no fucking idea what I'm supposed to do on a date. Navigating that while also being *out* . . ." Jeremiah paused, gathering his thoughts, it seemed. "It's going to be difficult for me. I need you to respect that. And . . . and, if it's at all possible, could we go somewhere else—not in town or Butterfield."

Dale's eyes narrowed, but Jeremiah scrambled to explain. "I mean, I'm already terrified to go on a date with you. I'd rather not have everyone we know staring at us. The date can still be in public, just," he shrugged, "somewhere I'll be a little less self-conscious so I can focus on you and nothing else."

A few moments passed as he considered the man's request. He admired its honesty as he remembered his first date with a man and how nervous he'd been—more so about what other people would think versus the actual date itself. He nodded. "I'll pick you up Friday night at six. There's a place in Redworth that serves a great meal."

The relieved expression on Jeremiah's face told Dale he'd said the right thing. Thrilled, he stepped closer to the lounging pair and gently kissed Shannon's forehead, noting that she already felt cooler. Meeting Jeremiah's eyes, he braved the same thing, carefully kissing the man's temple. Straightening, he gathered himself, trying to contain his excitement. "I'll see you then."

"Yeah, I'll . . . um . . . I'll see you . . . uh, later," Jeremiah stuttered, color flushing high along his cheekbones. Hopefully, one day, Dale would see how far down the man's chest that blush went.

Grinning wickedly, he winked and left the duo.

Chapter Nine

Friday night arrived faster than Jeremiah ever thought possible. He hadn't been able to eat all day—his stomach was tied in knots, and his hands shook like an addict needing a fix. He'd been useless around the ranch. Anthony had bitched at him and kicked him out of his own damn barn after he'd dropped the tack they'd just de-tangled, not once but twice.

He'd showered and shaved before getting dressed and then changing his clothes four times.

What are you supposed to wear on a first date?

He wanted to look nice, but not like he was trying too hard, either.

Tie or no tie? Which hat?

Dress boots for sure, but other than that, he was at a loss. He currently stood in front of his mirror in just his jeans and boots. Staring at his bare chest, he ran a hand down his stomach, frowning at the definition that wasn't as noticeable in his abs anymore.

I need to add more sit-ups to my morning routine, he thought for the millionth time.

Twisting, he tried to check out his ass in the mirror—at least it was still as tight as ever, thanks to the hours he spent in the saddle every week.

Picking up his cell phone, he checked the time and saw he only had about thirty minutes before Dale arrived. Panic welled up. Not allowing himself a second more to think, he scrolled through his contacts and hit the button for a video chat with Willow.

Her smiling face filled the screen seconds later. But then she frowned. "What the hell? Did you call me by accident? Why don't you have a shirt on?"

"Help! I don't have a shirt on because I can't decide which one to wear!"

Scowling, she replied, "Jeremiah, you're a big boy now—you know how to dress yourself. Why does it matter what shirt you wear? The cows don't give a shit. Well, they do, just not about your shirt."

"Dammit!" Running a palm down his face, he remembered she didn't know he had a date. Should he tell her it was with Dale? No sense in trying to hide it—she'd figure it out soon enough. "I have a date . . . with Dale. I'm freaking out."

A shiver ran down his spine, and his knees quaked. *God, I'm going to throw up!*

"What? That's awesome!" Glancing over her

shoulder, she shouted, "Nathan! Jeremiah has a date with Dale and doesn't know what to wear!"

"Goddammit, Willow!" Jeremiah's cheeks flamed. "What the hell? Why don't you announce it to the whole friggin' county while you're at it, huh?"

"Clothes are a good place to start. Though if he opens the door naked, I doubt they'll make it to dinner," Nathan added from off-screen.

"Nathan, not helping!" *Fuck!* Now, he was thinking about being naked with Dale. Thank God Willow could only see him from his chest up because he was getting hard just thinking about her sexy foreman.

"Willow. Please. Concentrate and help me." He chewed on his lower lip until he tasted blood. He was two seconds away from canceling with Dale, locking his doors, closing the curtains, and pretending he'd moved to Timbuktu.

"Okay, you have jeans on, I assume?"

No way was he going to angle the camera down to show her his lower half, even though his nerves had his semi-erection deflating again. "Yeah, a new pair of blue jeans."

"Where's he taking you? And can I just say, I told you so? I'm so fucking excited for you two! I need all the details tomorrow!" God, she was like a squirrel, darting all over the place.

"Willow! Focus! We can talk about all this later. He'll be here soon, and I'm not dressed!"

His voice kept rising along with his anxiety. *How do people do this on a regular basis?* His heart would never be able to survive if every date was going to be like this.

"You're overthinking it. Wear that blue button-up I got you for Christmas—it makes your eyes pop. And your black hat because I know you won't go without it even though your hair is gorgeous. You'll be casual but dressy. Perfect. Don't forget clean underwear—oh! Wear a jockstrap! Gay guys have a thing for those, right?"

Rolling his eyes, he prayed for patience. "Willow, I am not wearing a jock on a first date. Jesus, woman, don't believe everything you read in those romance novels."

"Ha! You called it a jock—that means you have one!" Giggling like mad, Willow nearly dropped the phone.

He refused to think about his small collection of brightly colored jock straps and what Dale would think of them. Sex was off the table tonight. He was too keyed up even to contemplate it. He wanted to date, get to know Dale, and do all the things couples did. Hold hands at the movies, go for ice cream, and take goofy selfies. He might never get a chance to experience this again, and he refused to complicate it by jumping into bed too fast. Even if the thought of having Dale in his bed made him hard as concrete. And even if it had been over a year since he'd had sex.

The last time had been a sloppy blow-job in a bath-room stall with a nameless man whose face he couldn't remember. Fuck, that was so pathetic.

"Thanks for the help. Sort of, I guess." Checking the time, he saw he was down to fifteen minutes. "Shit! I need to go." Not waiting for her to respond—she would understand—he ended the call and tossed his phone onto his bed, which was currently piled with shirt choices. He grabbed the blue long-sleeved button-up and slipped it over his shoulders. Normally, he'd wear an undershirt, but the material was thick enough that he didn't think he needed one. He slapped on more deodorant, now that he was starting to sweat bullets again, and lightly sprayed his favorite cologne on his neck and chest before buttoning the shirt and tucking it in. His championship buckle sat heavily between his hips, and he almost took it off.

"Fuck it. I'm a cowboy—he knows that—if he doesn't like it, too fuckin' bad." Sticking his phone into his back pocket, he grabbed his wallet, keys, and dress hat from a peg on the wall and headed downstairs. His booted foot stepped off the last stair just as there was a knock at the front door. He unsuccessfully attempted to swallow the lump forming in his throat, wiped his sweaty palms on his thighs, and moved toward the door on shaky legs.

He mumbled a pep talk to himself on the way. "Here goes nothing. There's no going back now. Just don't let the closet door hit you on the ass on the way out."

Dale stood on Jeremiah's welcome mat, apprehension tightening his muscles until they were as taut as a guitar string, threatening to snap at any second. Jeremiah was someone special—he felt it in his bones. He just hoped neither of them screwed things up before they had a chance to see if it could be something more. They'd already had a rough start—now it was time to try and smooth it out.

The door opened, and light spilled out and haloed the man standing before him. Jeremiah's face was pale and a little green around the gills, but he was absolutely breathtaking.

"H-hey," he stuttered, his obvious nerves making Dale smile.

"Hey, yourself. You look amazing." Trailing his eyes down Jeremiah's body, he noted the snug fit of his jeans and the belt buckle that showcased his riding skills and drew attention to the enticing bulge behind his fly. Dropping his gaze to the tips of Jeremiah's black dress boots, Dale took a long, leisurely trek back up the man's body, tracking the fit of his sky-blue shirt over his broad shoulders, thick arms, and wide chest. He licked his lips as lust flared deep in his gut. His gaze stopped at Jeremiah's eyes, the sharp green blazing with desire as he gave Dale the same once-over. Dale had made similar choices with his own clothes, but all in black—jeans, a dress shirt that fit him perfectly, and his best boots. The only color was from the shiny, pearl snap buttons on his shirt.

"The man in black, huh? Don't let Willow see you—she'll make you sing Cash songs with her." When their eyes met again, Jeremiah's cheeks flamed before he ducked his head, letting his hat hide his face. "You look really good too."

Laughing, Dale held out his hand. "Ready?"

The question had a double meaning—more than if Jeremiah was all set to go. Was he ready to take this monumental step?

Nodding, Jeremiah grasped his hand. His palm was a little sweaty, and there was a slight tremor, but it didn't stop the electric awareness from zinging up Dale's arm, just like it did every time they touched. Grinning, he paused long enough for Jeremiah to shut the front door, then tugged his date down the steps after him. "Come on, sexy cowboy. Let's go."

The drive to Redworth passed quickly, with Dale tapping his fingers on the wheel along with the music. He wanted to reach out and hold Jeremiah's hand or, even better, have the other man scoot over to the middle of the bench seat so he could drape an arm over his wide shoulders as he drove.

Jeremiah filled the silence with updates about the JP and the upcoming pregnancy checks they'd be doing. Dale did his best to listen, but he was nervous too. No, it wasn't his first date—far from it—but if tonight didn't go well or Jeremiah freaked out, it might be the end of them before they even got started.

Now that I've got my head screwed on straight, I can be patient with him, but what if he jerks away from me? What if we see someone we know, and Jeremiah panics and runs?

Dale could deal with hesitation and could understand it, but he didn't think he'd be able to survive an outright public rejection.

Pulling into the parking lot of the Wagon Wheel, they had another fifteen minutes before their reservation time.

"We're a little early—do you want to wait here or at the bar?" Dale asked, turning toward Jeremiah, who'd removed his hat and set it on his knee during the ride. The yellow glow from one of the lot's lamps added a brilliant glimmer to his red hair, making him look as if he were wreathed in flames. Dale's heart stuttered, then began to pound, and he didn't give the man a chance to answer him. "Goddamn, you're so beautiful."

Jeremiah's neck, face, and ears turned beet red, and he tilted his head down, his gaze dropping to his own lap. "No one's ever called me beautiful before."

Reaching out, Dale lifted Jeremiah's chin with his fingertip. Even that small touch was electrifying. In that pivotal moment, he knew that Jeremiah was going to change everything he thought he knew about himself.

Everything.

"I don't lie. Ever. So, know that when I say you're gorgeous and you make me desperate, I mean it."

Jeremiah's emerald eyes darkened with desire, and he licked his lips while staring at Dale's mouth. Groaning in response, Dale let his hand fall, releasing Jeremiah. "Don't look at me like that right now, or we'll never get into dinner, and I want to do this right. That means not boning in the truck before the date even starts."

Laughing, Jeremiah nodded. "Okay, I promise I'll try not to drool over you, but it goes both ways, Marine. You can't look like you want to eat me for dinner and then be surprised when I offer myself up as the main course."

Chuckling, Dale shook his head and climbed from the truck. He'd intended to open Jeremiah's door for him, but the man got out and met him at the front of the vehicle before Dale had a chance to walk around to the passenger side. "Next time, I'd like to open your door for you."

Arching a brow as they made their way across the lot, Jeremiah scoffed, "I don't think so. This isn't the fifties, and I'm not the little woman. Open the restaurant door for me, sure, but I'll get my own damn truck door."

"We'll see about that." Smirking at Jeremiah's look

of disbelief, he held the large wooden door of the steak-house open for him, boldly resting his hand on the small of Jeremiah's back as the man proceeded him inside. The heat of his skin through the cotton shirt was hot enough almost to burn Dale's palm, and his mind immediately went to what it would feel like to have the other man's naked flesh pressed against his own.

Biting back another groan and dropping his hand, Dale kept his eyes glued to Jeremiah's back as they strode to the hostess stand, not letting his gaze check out the man's ass cupped in those tight Wranglers. If that happened, Dale would pitch a tent in his jeans in the middle of the restaurant.

"Do you have a reservation?" a pretty, dark-haired woman asked from behind her wooden podium. Dale didn't recognize her, so she had to have been hired sometime after he'd moved to the Rock because he used to know everyone who worked there, and they'd known him.

"Yes, for two, under Harris," he replied, setting his hand firmly on Jeremiah's back again. He stroked his thumb back and forth and grinned when Jeremiah shivered visibly. His reaction had to be from a combi-nation of Dale's touch and his nerves about the inti-macy of it while in public. Jeremiah's tense gaze darted around the bar area and restaurant, but no one was paying them any mind. After all, the popular Wagon Wheel was owned by a married lesbian couple who were out and proud. It was one of the reasons he'd chosen to bring Jeremiah there. While there were people in Redworth who refused to patronize the business because of "that couple," there were plenty more who did, not caring that Lizzie and Janice Wheeler were in love with each other. The food was good and the prices fair, and you couldn't ask for more than that of a restaurant.

The brunette checked the reservation book, retrieved two menus, and smiled at the couple. "Excellent. I have you in the back, as requested. Please, follow me."

Jeremiah leaned closer to Dale, whispering in his ear. "As requested?"

"Yes. I wanted privacy for our first date. I know you're nervous, and I thought it might make it a little easier on you if we weren't smack in the middle of the room. Plus . . . " he paused, boldly taking Jeremiah's hand in his own. When Jeremiah stiffened a little but didn't pull away from him, relief and pride surged through Dale. It was clearly out of Jeremiah's comfort zone, but he did his best not to run out the door in terror. "Being on our first date—I don't want to be interrupted by other people."

The gratitude in Jeremiah's eyes said everything, even as he opened and closed his mouth several times, unable to voice his thanks. Dale didn't need to hear the words—they were loud and clear. He tugged on Jeremiah's hand. "Come on, Cowboy, I'm starved."

Chapter Ten

After they were seated at a romantic little table, a busboy filled their water glasses, and then a young waitress named Diana approached the table. Both workers wore the usual Wagon Wheel uniform—black pants, black shoes, a white button-down shirt, and a cute tie. The owners allowed the waitstaff and bartenders to wear any tie they wanted, as long as they were in good taste, and it was a hit with both their employees and patrons. You never knew what you were going to see because most of the staff collected a bunch of different ones, each person trying to outdo everyone else. While the busboy wore a bright, yellow, smiley-face tie, Diana was wearing a black one with little pink elephants all over it.

She did a double-take when she noticed Dale. "Good evening, Mr. Harris. It's nice to see you again.

Someone said you moved a while back—I was very sorry to hear that. We miss you around here."

He grinned at her. "I miss y'all too. But I only moved an hour away—close enough that I could come back to my favorite restaurant whenever I wanted. Diana, this is my date, Jeremiah." His gaze flickered to the man sitting across from him—the one with an adorable blush and wide eyes. Clearly, he hadn't expected Dale to introduce him to anyone as his date.

As expected, the waitress didn't even blink at the announcement—she simply smiled and said hello to Jeremiah before Dale continued the introductions. "Diana's been working here for about five years now, and if I remember correctly, she should be graduating from college this year."

A huge grin spread across her face, and her eyes glistened excitedly. "You are correct—next month. Finally. Now I just have to find a job in my field—physical therapy."

"I'm certain you'll do just fine, although I'm sure Janice and Lizzie will miss you working here." He'd have to remember to leave an extra special tip for her tonight in honor of her upcoming graduation.

"I'll miss them too. They've become like family to me. Now, what can I get you two to drink?"

A few moments later, with drinks on the way—a beer for Dale and a glass of whiskey for Jeremiah—Dale sat back and looked his fill. Jeremiah by candlelight was spectacular. The flicking flames highlighted and complemented the different shades of red in his hair and caught on the silver strands, making them shimmer and dance. It was all Dale could do not to lunge across the table and devour the man. Jeremiah's forearms rested on the edge of the table while his hands twisted the burgundy cloth napkin from his place setting, folding and unfolding it over and over. He must have realized what he was doing because he put the cloth aside but then began fiddling with the napkin ring, twirling it on end and letting it fall. His gaze was pinned on the round, hollow piece of wood.

"Jeremiah." Dale kept his tone low in volume but firm.

His eyes lifted. "Y-yeah?"

"Relax."

He scanned the restaurant's interior as if he expected an angry mob to jump them at any moment. "I can't."

"You need to. I promise it's going to be okay. The restaurant is owned by an out-and-proud lesbian couple, and their patrons don't care. In fact, I doubt we're the only same-sex couple here tonight."

Extending his left hand across the snow-white tablecloth, he held it there, palm up, and waited. Jeremiah hesitated, staring at the proffered hand. The pulse in the man's neck raced, and his chest heaved with every inhalation. His gaze shifted to the people around them, happily chatting among themselves before returning to Dale's invitation. Both apprehension and longing vibrated from Jeremiah's body—Dale could almost feel his quivering muscles from across the table. He was about to give up and pull back, but just before he did, Jeremiah timidly reached forward and clasped their hands together. Sweat dotted his brow, and his skin was a little pale, but he grinned. The look of relief on his face, when there were no public cries of outrage or disgust, was so sweet, Dale could feel it in his own gut. This wonderful man was so scared yet wanted to be who he really was without ridicule or repercussions that Dale, emotionally and nearly physically, ached for him. He desperately wanted Jeremiah to know what it was like to be free to love whomever he chose.

"There. See? The sky didn't fall, and a hole didn't open up under the table and swallow us." Linking his fingers into Jeremiah's, he kept them there, holding hands in full view of anyone who cared to look. It was a small step to most, but Dale knew how much this simple gesture meant to Jeremiah. He was making a statement, stepping out of the closet with one giant stride, yet praying the safety he found behind the closed door wouldn't disappear before he was ready.

"I'm proud to be here with you," Dale assured him. "To have you on my arm, your hand in mine. Don't forget that."

Jeremiah's smile was so wide that Dale swore he could see his molars. "I won't. And I'm happy to be here with you. Like this." Jeremiah jiggled their hands slightly. "I never thought I could have this. Thank you."

"Trust me—it's no hardship."

"So, um . . . " He cleared his throat. "You've . . . um . . . eaten here a lot . . . before . . . I mean—"

Dale smirked at the question Jeremiah couldn't spit out. "Have I brought dates here?" He shrugged and told him the truth. "One or two, but it's been so long, I don't remember who they were or when we were here. Most of the time, I came here to relax with friends in a place where judgment was a rarity. That being said, I'm really happy you're here with me too."

Diana returned with their drinks. Reluctantly releasing Jeremiah's hand since it was closest to his drink, Dale picked up his beer and gave Jeremiah a silent toast. Bringing the glass to his lips, he downed half of it, hoping the beer would cool the lava, formally known as his blood, rushing through his veins. His attraction for this man grew more intense with every interaction, every uncertain yet brave word out of Jeremiah's mouth, and every tempting blush that spread across those ivory cheeks.

Jeremiah reached for his whiskey while trying to avoid the waitress's gaze that had momentarily flickered to their joined hands. There was nothing to be embarrassed about, though—in fact, Jeremiah missed the encouraging wink Diana had sent Dale's way. Picking up the glass, Jeremiah's fluttering fingers slipped on the smooth surface, and the entire contents spilled onto the tablecloth. The white fabric turned a deep amber as the smoky scent of whiskey filled the air.

"Shit!" Jeremiah jumped, trying to right his glass and knocking over the water goblet in the process. "Dammit!" Completely flustered, he stood quickly, escaping the cascade of water that had been heading right for his crotch.

"Hey, it's okay," Dale said, trying to calm the other man who looked moments from tearing out of the steakhouse. He threw his and Jeremiah's napkins onto the puddle to help soak up most of the liquid. Unfortunately, some of it had already hit the bench seat.

"I'm so sorry," Jeremiah gushed to Diana, who'd grabbed two more napkins from a nearby empty table. The place settings and menus were a temporary loss, having been splattered with whiskey, water, or both.

The waitress shook her head. "It's okay, really—it happens all the time. I've got it. Let's take you two over to another table." She stepped aside to let the busboy clean up the mess. "Please, come with me."

Hanging his head, Jeremiah refused to meet Dale's eyes. The other patrons had all looked over, unable to ignore the noise and disturbance. Dale felt every eye on their backs as they followed the waitress to a new table, a booth, even further into the back of the restaurant.

"Is this table okay?" she asked Dale.

"It's fine, Diana. Thank you."

"No problem. Have a seat, and I'll get new drinks

and menus." She smiled at Jeremiah as if trying to reassure him everything was okay.

"I'm so sorry," he repeated.

"Honestly, it's not a complete night without someone spilling a glass, but usually, it's one of the wait staff knocking things over. So, don't worry about it, please. Enjoy your evening."

Before she hurried away to reorder their drinks, Dale could've kissed the young woman for her little white lie about the restaurant's employees usually being at fault. Although he should've expected it—Janice and Lizzie trained their staff well, including how to treat the customers when accidents like that happened.

"We should just go," Jeremiah muttered as they sat down across from each other again.

Dale frowned and then slid around the booth until he was right beside Jeremiah, pressing against him—their shoulders, arms, hips, thighs, and calves getting intimately acquainted. Jeremiah was pale and shivering. Dale took his hat off, setting it beside himself on the seat. "No, we *shouldn't* go."

He tried to catch Jeremiah's eye, but the stubborn man refused to even take a peek at him. Dale sighed. "Jay, please look at me."

After a moment's hesitation, Jeremiah's eyes met his, misery clear in the emerald depths. "Seriously, I ruined our date. Let's just leave, please."

His gaze shifted past Dale to the mirrored wall, no

doubt looking for opinionated glares from the people around them reflected there, but they were all in his mind. Everyone was back to minding their own business.

"Stop it. Look at me, dammit." Not giving a single shit what anyone else thought about it, Dale turned and grasped Jeremiah's face in his hands. His knee rested on top of Jeremiah's thigh. Jeremiah's hat was tilted back on his head, partially shielding them from the wait staff and other diners. "Stop worrying about everyone else. You're here with me, and I'm here with you. *Just* you. No one else matters. Keep your eyes on me and *only* me." Resting his forehead against Jeremiah's, he fought the need to kiss him—to claim him publicly. He knew his sexy cowboy wasn't ready for it, but it didn't stop him from craving a taste of him like he did his next breath.

Jeremiah breathed hard, his chest rising and falling forcefully. "Dale . . . " Closing his eyes and trembling, he gently touched his lips to Dale's.

Dale was so shocked that he didn't even kiss him back at first.

Jeremiah is kissing me in public!

His heart was hammering and screaming joyfully, and he finally got it together enough to return the kiss. He kept it quick but sweet. It was chaste, but that single kiss cracked his heart open, and Jeremiah crawled into the yawning, empty space, filling it. With the most perfect kiss Dale had ever received, Jeremiah had replaced the loneliness inside Dale in a way no one else ever had.

"Jay . . ." The nickname he'd used only a few times before just slipped out. His hands shook where he still held Jeremiah's cheeks as his mind scrambled for something to say, something that would let this man know how special he was. Happiness bubbling over and spilling out, he fucking giggled over a kiss in a booth like he was a teenager. Not a single fuck given either. "You kissed me."

Yeah, that's all he'd been able to come up with at that moment.

"Caught that, did you?" Still a little pale, Jeremiah smiled shyly, ducking his head again like a boy with his first crush.

"I'm so glad I'm here with you. Glad I got my head out of my ass and let this happen."

"Me too, Dale, me too." Pulling Dale's hands free from his face, Jeremiah kissed the center of one of Dale's palms and then met his eyes. Hope simmered there, and longing, along with more than a little desire.

Chapter Eleven

The rest of the evening went smoother than Jeremiah had expected, with no more accidents or faux pas on his part. Dale, of course, had been the perfect date. Nothing seemed to rattle the man, and Jeremiah was able to draw some strength and courage from him. Where Jeremiah had gotten the balls to kiss the man in the middle of a public restaurant was beyond him, but it felt so right, so wonderful, that everyone and everything else had disappeared from his mind. All that'd mattered was Dale's lips had been on his, radiating warmth throughout Jeremiah's body. Something had clicked into place within him at the first touch of his mouth against Dale's. It'd almost been like déjà vu, but instead of feeling like he'd been there before, he *knew* he was where he was supposed to be.

After he'd recovered from that kiss, the conversation flowed between them as the tension slowly drained from Jeremiah's body. Dale had been right—no one paid them any mind except for Diana and the busboy, but it was their job to do that.

A delicious meal of Caesar salads, followed by T-bone steaks with all the fixings and a glass of red wine for each of them, was crowned with coffee and a shared slice of cheesecake while playing twenty questions. It was Jeremiah's turn to ask Dale something when they heard a raspy voice say, "Well, look what the cat dragged in. It's about damn time you came back for a visit, boy."

Dale grinned, and his eyes lit up as a short, robust woman in her late fifties or early sixties, with spiked silver hair and harsh-looking features, stopped at their table. When she smiled, it didn't soften her countenance, but the pure joy and affection in her voice made up for it. "Get your butt out here, Dale Harris, and give me some sugar."

Before she finished the command, Dale was already sliding back around the U of the bench seat. Jeremiah realized just how short the woman really was when Dale got to his feet and hugged her. He was over a foot and a half taller than her, and it was almost comical how far he had to bend down to embrace her. "Hey there, sweetheart. Missed you. Where's your better half?"

Her smile dimmed as they took a step or two away from each other. She had to tilt her head back almost as far as it would go just to look Dale in the eye. "Over at the hospital with her momma. Elise had a stroke the other day, and it doesn't look good. I've been there for most of the day but took a break to swing by and make sure everything was good here before going back."

Wincing, Dale put a hand over his heart. "Damn, I'm so sorry to hear that. Elise was always a hoot. Please give her and Lizzie a hug from me. I'll be saying a few prayers for all of you."

"Aren't you sweet—you're a good man, Dale." Her gaze flittered to Jeremiah. "Who's this handsome devil? You datin' a ginger? Good for you." She reached over and lightly punched Dale's arm. "I told you to find one. Mine is damn near perfect."

While Jeremiah blushed, Dale chuckled. "Yes, ma'am, you did tell me that—more than once. Janice Wheeler, this is Jeremiah Urban, and yes, he's my date." He gestured from Jeremiah to the woman. "Janice and her wife, Lizzie, own the Wagon Wheel."

Janice held out a weathered but hardy hand. "Pleasure to meet you, Jerry—can I call you Jerry? Any friend of Dale's is a friend of mine." The woman was a fast talker, and it was almost hard to keep up with her. When Jeremiah stood, affirmed that yes, she could call him Jerry, and shook her hand, she winked and tipped her head to the side toward Dale. "This boy's a keeper if you can get him to settle down. He needs someone strong enough to rope him in but gentle enough to soothe his battered soul."

For the first time all evening, Dale was the one to blush while Jeremiah reveled in it. He grinned and nodded at Janice. "I'll keep that in mind, ma'am. And it's a pleasure to meet you too."

"Oh, God. Another one who insists on calling me ma'am. It's Janice—ma'am makes me sound like an old fart."

The woman was a character, and Jeremiah liked her immediately. "Janice it is. My sympathies for your wife and her mother."

"Thank you. Now, you two sit back down," she gestured toward the booth, "so I can get rid of this damn crick in my neck, and enjoy your evening. Was everything okay?"

As the two men sat again, Jeremiah was the one who answered her. "It was fantastic, except for when I spilled my whiskey and water all over the place, and we had to switch tables."

She narrowed her eyes at him. "The water I can forgive. The whiskey, well, that's just a goddamn sin, boy." She gave him a good-natured slap on his shoulder. "Let me guess—nervous? First date for you two?"

His cheeks burned scarlet again while Dale chuckled, his eyes twinkling as he responded to the woman while keeping his gaze on Jeremiah. "Yup. But don't worry, Janice, aside from that little accident, the rest of the date has been wonderful."

"Glad to hear it. Dale, you stop being a stranger— Antelope Rock is only an hour away. I expect to see you and your handsome man here more often, under-stood?" She didn't give him a chance to respond before adding, "Now, let me check on my other diners. You two have a good night."

They bid her goodbye, and she moved onto another occupied table. Jeremiah chuckled. "Wow. She's some-thing else."

Dale snorted. "You have no idea. And Lizzie is the complete opposite. She's a redhead, just under six feet tall, and a small-time model—for local catalogs, adver-tising companies, and stuff like that. She's also a lot quieter. If there was ever an example of opposites attracting, it's those two."

Diana appeared next to them. "Can I get you anything else? More coffee or a drink from the bar?"

Arching a questioning eyebrow, Dale looked at Jeremiah, who shook his head. When they'd given their dinner orders earlier, they asked Diana to give them some extra time to relax and talk between courses. However, they'd been there for over two hours now, and both men had chores to do early in the morning. On top of that, they still had an hour's drive home. It was one of several disadvantages to ranching that Jere-miah had learned since he was a kid. For him, typically, late nights were usually the result of an issue with the livestock, such as an animal being ill, injured, or giving birth. It was a welcome change to be out past his usual bedtime for a completely different reason.

"Just the check, please, Diana," Dale told her.

"Dinner was amazing as always. Thank Chef Alan for me."

She grinned. "Will do. I'll be back in a moment."

Despite the fact that Jeremiah had asked Dale to dinner, the retired Marine insisted on paying. With a wink, he told Jeremiah he could pay next time. A thrill that there would be another date coursed through him.

The ride home was much more relaxing, partly from the whiskey and wine Jeremiah had drunk earlier and partly because of the man sitting in the driver's seat. Dale had done everything he could to get Jeremiah to laugh, smile, and completely forget they were out in public as a couple. Even now, Dale was driving one-handed—the other held Jeremiah's hand, their fingers linked together.

As it always seemed when you were having a good time, the trip back to the JP Ranch seemed much faster than it had taken them to get to Redworth earlier. Of course, the traffic was a little lighter, but Jeremiah knew that time had flown because he floated on cloud nine. The first date of his life, with another man no less, had gone better than he'd ever imagined. He wasn't naive, though. Dale had taken him to an LGBTQ+-friendly place in a much larger municipality than his hometown. Jeremiah was certain the experience would've been different and uglier if they'd gone to Bella Mia in the Rock, which was owned by a religious zealot and her family. He could just imagine the look on Chasity Jenkins's face if he and Dale walked into the restaurant hand in hand. She'd probably break out the holy water and throw it at them while praying for their depraved souls. The thought made him snort.

Dale glanced over at him as he drove down the road leading to both the JP and Skyview ranches. "What?"

He shook his head and smiled. "Just thinking about how different this night would've been if we'd gone to Bella Mia."

A bark of laughter filled the cab. "Chasity would've tried to drown us in holy water!"

"My thoughts exactly!"

Dale turned the truck onto the dirt drive leading to the JP's main house, and just like that, Jeremiah's nerves were back.

Do I invite him in? Do I want to?

When he'd been getting ready for dinner earlier, he'd firmly been against the idea of sex on the first date, but now, he wasn't sure if he could resist Dale if the guy wanted to take things that far tonight. Jeremiah grew half hard at just the thought. He wondered what the reality of Dale in his bed would be like. Mentally groaning, Jeremiah side-eyed his date, hoping something would show on the man's face and give him some idea of what came next.

Unfortunately, Dale was looking straight ahead, and his expression was unreadable. Averting his gaze, Jeremiah stared out the passenger window and tried to chill out. He knew he was overthinking things. They'd had a wonderful date, but he didn't want the night to end just yet.

Maybe Dale would come in for a drink? That was something people did, right?

The last evening that'd come anywhere close to being a date for him was about three years ago. He'd met a hot pilot at a club and gone to the guy's hotel room to screw around—something Jeremiah hadn't done often. He usually kept his hookups restricted to the bathroom or dark back hallway of the club, but for some reason, that night, he'd agreed to something more comfortable and intimate. They'd eaten take-out Thai food while lounging on the disheveled bed before starting round two. That'd been someone Jeremiah could've gotten into, seen more than once, but the guy lived in Texas, and the trip to Cheyenne hadn't been routine for him. Now, Jeremiah was grateful that it had only been a one-night stand because that pilot paled in comparison to this sexy Marine.

Jeremiah feared he would fuck up again and end the date on a sour note. Despite his assurances, Dale wouldn't be willing to take things slow and let Jeremiah ease out of his comfort zone. Soon, he'd give up and never want to see Jeremiah again. The sexy Marine could find someone far better than a closeted rancher in his forties.

Clenching his fists, Jeremiah bit the inside of his cheek while trying to fight the wild horses he felt stampeding in his gut.

"Are you okay?" Dale's voice broke through his spiraling thoughts, drawing his attention.

"What? I'm sorry, what did you say?"

"I asked if you were okay." Dale glanced his way and shrugged. "You seem, I don't know, tense."

He hesitated, licking his lips, as the truck stopped in front of the house. The porch light was on. A quick inspection of the small parking area by the bunkhouses told him his employees were still out on the town. Andrew's cottage was on the far side of that and out of his and Dale's sight. No one was around to see them. "How honest do you want me to be?"

Shutting off the engine, Dale grimaced as if expecting the worst. "My answer will always be the same. Completely honest. I'd rather a painful truth than pretty lies."

Jeremiah unbuckled his seat belt and turned fully to face the other man. His mouth was dry, and he swallowed hard, certain that at any moment, Dale would politely tell him things wouldn't work out between them after all. Jeremiah prayed that wouldn't happen. He gathered his courage and confessed, "I want to ask you inside. For a drink. And I'm really nervous."

Dale let out a heavy sigh, which had Jeremiah's navel puckering. "Come on, Cowboy, let's talk about this on the porch." Not waiting for him to respond, Dale climbed out of the truck and strode toward the house.

"Well, okay then," he muttered to the empty cab

before following Dale, slamming the truck door behind him.

The gorgeous Marine leaned against the porch rail, his hands gripping the banister beside his slim hips. Jeremiah groaned inwardly, not allowing his gaze to linger on the snug fit of Dale's jeans over his tree-trunk thighs or the enticing bulge behind his zipper. The man was sin on two long legs. He could easily be the hero in a Wild West movie and have men and women swooning after him.

Dammit. Jeremiah forced the reminder that not only was he competing against all the men in the world for Dale's affections, but the women too. His rivalry pool was double than usual. Dale could have anyone he wanted, and Jeremiah couldn't figure out why he was in the company of a middle-aged man who'd been a coward for most of his life.

Dale cleared his throat. "There's nothing for you to be nervous about because I'm not coming inside with you."

Jeremiah felt like he'd been poleaxed. He fucking hated being right. Dropping his gaze to his boots, he nodded and tried not to let the other man know he'd just crushed both his heart and soul. "Um, okay. Thanks for dinner, then. I had a nice time."

Pivoting, he gave Dale his back and stepped toward the door, feeling his heart splinter inside his chest. When something seemed too good to be true, it usually was.

When will you learn that there won't ever be more for you?

He'd grow old with nothing but a barn full of woodworking projects and this ranch to show for it. He'd never have a partner or a family of his own.

"Stop." A hand on his arm jerked him to a halt. "That came out wrong."

Jeremiah froze but didn't look back at Dale. He was too raw right now, his emotions scattered all over the place. He swallowed past the sudden burn of tears, refusing to give Dale the satisfaction of seeing him so upset.

"Jay, please, let me explain," Dale pleaded.

A shiver went down Jeremiah's spine at the nickname Dale seemed to have given him. Other than the family, who sometimes called him Jer, most people never shortened his name, and if they did, they'd always used Jerry as Janice had done at the restaurant. That'd been the first time he hadn't corrected the other person, and only because he felt it would've been rude in the woman's place of business. But when Dale called him Jay, for some reason, it felt special, like a lover's pet name.

Helpless to resist the other man's contrite tone, Jeremiah blinked several times before glancing over his shoulder and meeting Dale's gaze. Those whiskey-colored eyes shimmered with desire and need, which went right to Jeremiah's cock, making him instantly hard with a suddenness that stole his breath.

How can Dale look at me like that yet walk away?

Dale spun him around, walking him backward until his ass and shoulders hit the front door. Hands cupped Jeremiah's jaw as thumbs traced his cheekbones. Fingers pressed into his nape. Dale lowered his voice into a raspy but sensual whisper while his gaze roamed Jeremiah's face. "I'm hanging on by a thread here. I want you—though want isn't a strong enough word for what I feel right now. I'm desperate to explore every inch of your gorgeous body. To lick, suck, and taste you. I want to bury my face in your crotch and inhale your scent. I want to map your body with my fingers and tongue. I want to be all you see, hear, smell, feel, and taste. I'm dying to drive my cock so deep inside your ass neither of us will be able to remember our names."

A whimper of need escaped Jeremiah, but Dale continued. "I don't care how we come together, just that we do. I want to spend hours finding out what makes you beg, what makes you shout my name. Would you do that, baby? Would you scream my name when I made you come?"

He was too stunned, too on edge, to answer with words, so he just nodded. Dale's gaze dusted over Jeremiah's cheeks. "God, these damn freckles . . ."

Growling, Dale leaned in and slammed his lips down on Jeremiah's. Within seconds, his tongue demanded entry, and Jeremiah surrendered without hesitation. All awareness of being out in the open on his front porch fled his mind. Fire exploded from his mouth outward, racing down his chest and settling heavy and hot in his groin. Their tongues dueled, fighting for supremacy. The taste of Dale, beer, and something spicy made Jeremiah groan and slide his tongue deeper into the man's mouth, chasing the flavor. The man's lips were hot, demanding, and so incredibly soft it was unbelievable. Jeremiah wanted to feel those pillowy lips all over his body. He needed to see them wrapped around the girth of his cock while Dale stared up at him with those smoky, whiskey-laced eyes. The mental image lanced him with another shot of pure lust and greed.

Fisting Dale's shirt in both hands, Jeremiah tried to pull him impossibly closer. Aligning them from hips to chest, rubbing and thrusting, he fought to meld their bodies together while kissing Dale harder, deeper. He wanted this man—needed everything he was offering and more.

He hooked his leg up and over Dale's hip, digging his boot heel into the man's ass, tugging him even closer. Dale wrapped his hand around Jeremiah's knee, holding him up and open to him.

His thoughts scattered, leaving only one left—*more, yes, more.*

Tearing his mouth free and burying his face in Dale's neck, he nearly purred as he drew Dale's scent deep into his lungs. He wasn't above begging. Jeremiah would fall to his knees, submit fully at even the hint of a command. He craved this man, and somehow, he'd have him. However, he could get him. "Dale, please."

He dropped Jeremiah's leg and wrapped his long fingers around the man's wrists before lifting and pressing them against the door above his head. Dale thrust his hard length against Jeremiah's, driving them both higher. Rocking back and forth against the other man, Jeremiah moved as best he could while pinned by Dale's hands, chest, and cock. It was blissful torture. The entire town could've paraded up the driveway at that moment, with the high school band, cheerleaders, and color guard leading the way, and Jeremiah wouldn't have noticed a thing. His mind, body, and soul were focused on Dale, who could mold him into the free man Jeremiah longed to be or completely destroy him.

"Please, what, Cowboy?" The husky voice in his ear made him shiver and buck harder. Dale licked his earlobe before sucking it into his mouth and biting down. Jeremiah arched his back, moaning, as goose-bumps rushed across his shoulders, back, and arms, and his muscles seized almost painfully.

"Please," he gasped. "Take me inside, take me here, I don't care. Just have me. Or let me take you—I'm good with that too. Whatever you want . . . anything . . . please. I need . . . " He was babbling. He knew it but couldn't seem to stop.

Dale snarled like a predatory animal. "I'll take your ass, and then you can have mine. I'll suck your cock until your knees buckle and you feel like you'll pass out. I'll bend you over and eat your ass, jerk you off, and make you scream my name. Is that what you want, Cowboy?"

Jeremiah nearly came as he cried, "Yes!"

Writhing under Dale's hands and mouth, he was incoherent with blazing need. Dale's words were going to send him over the edge. He'd never been subjected to such a deliciously filthy mouth, but apparently, it was something that turned him on. *Way* on.

"But not today."

Jeremiah barely heard the words and ignored them. He was too far gone, hooking a leg over Dale's hip again and thrusting against the hard ridge of the man's denim-clad cock. Again and again, harder and faster, he built a rhythm that made his balls draw up tight, and he felt his orgasm building in the base of his spine. Dale sucked on Jeremiah's neck as if trying to draw blood, and the sharp pain spiked straight to his throbbing dick. Without further warning, the dam holding back his pleasure burst, and Jeremiah came. Babbling and nearly bellowing, he kept rubbing against Dale, working himself through the orgasm.

"Goddammit . . . Jay." Tucking his face into Jeremiah's neck, Dale shuddered and moaned, rocking his cock against Jeremiah's as he grappled his way through his own climax.

Panting and sagging against the door, Jeremiah wiggled his fingers, silently asking Dale to release him, which he did. His arms fell, boneless, around Dale's neck. At that moment, nothing else existed in the universe but the man in his arms and the sense of peace that draped over them. It took a little bit for Jeremiah's brain to come back online while his lungs tried to replenish the oxygen that'd been drained from them. "Damn . . . if it's that good with our clothes on . . . I don't know if I'll survive you naked."

Chuckling, Dale kissed his cheek, then his mouth, before leaning back and meeting his eyes. Their hats were on the floor by their feet, forgotten and discarded in the heat of their . . . whatever that was. Dale's hands rested on Jeremiah's hips, where he dug his fingers in, squeezing and releasing. "I haven't come in my jeans since I was a teenager, making out under the bleachers with Andy Torez."

"Lucky Andy." Jeremiah's grin was so wide it hurt, but he couldn't dial it down. Nor did he want to. He wanted to savor everything he was feeling. He'd had so few mind-blowing moments in his life, and this one topped them all.

"As I was saying, I'm not coming inside with you."

Smirking, he couldn't resist teasing, "No, you're coming outside with me."

Dale rested his head on Jeremiah's shoulder and groaned. "That was so bad."

"No, it was so *good*."

"You keep sidetracking me, Cowboy, and there *will* be consequences."

"I don't think your consequences are all that scary anymore, Dale." Jeremiah wiggled his hips, emphasizing his point.

"You're a menace." Dale stepped back, putting some space between their bodies. "As I've been trying to say, I don't want us jumping into bed together just yet. I want to get to know you first, but one step at a time. I want to date you and romance you. And I want us both to get tested because when we do make love, I don't want to use condoms, but we need to be safe. I haven't been with anyone bare in a long time, and I've been tested since, but we need to do this right."

Wow. He'd never expected to hear something like that from another man. Hell, Dale was throwing every one of Jeremiah's expectations into a deep well, drowning them, and surprising him left and right.

"Okay," he agreed. Maybe it was the lingering bliss from his orgasm or the joking around, he didn't know, but his anxiety had disappeared. He ran a seductive finger down the buttons of Dale's shirt, letting his blunt fingernail catch on each one. "I get what you're saying. Romance away, Marine. I've never had the pleasure. As for the other . . . uh . . . thing, I've never been with anyone without a condom, ever—even for blowjobs— but I'll go to the clinic in Butterfield and get tested all the same."

"Good, so will I. As for never being romanced before? That, Jay, is a fuckin' cryin' shame." Dale leaned in and gave him a swift, gentle kiss. "You deserve to be wooed. You deserve someone to bring you flowers and learn every single thing about you. During dinner, you told me your favorite dessert and color, and how you take your coffee, but I want to know more. I want to know if you snore. Are you a shower-at-night or in-the-morning kind of guy? What's your favorite meal, and what TV shows do you like? What music do you like and hate? I want to know it all. *Every. Damn. Thing.*"

Jeremiah gave him a shy smile. "Well, I didn't snore as a kid—my sister did—but I don't know if that's still true because I've never had someone sleep in my bed. I shower in the morning *and* at night. I hate reality shows, and I'm a sucker for the Hallmark Channel. Don't judge me. And my favorite meal is either Willow's stir-fry or strawberry shortcake. Yes, strawberry shortcake can be both a meal and a dessert. Don't judge me for that, either. Music—I love country and classic rock—I don't listen to anything else. The rest," he shrugged, "you can learn later."

Grinning, Dale brushed their lips together again, and Jeremiah's cock gave a halfhearted twitch. He wasn't twenty anymore, that was for sure, but Dale made him almost feel like he was Superman. "All right. All of that was noted. Are you busy tomorrow?"

"After chores, no. Being the boss has its perks." Jeremiah buried his hands in Dale's hair, loving the silky texture of the locks. The color was similar to that of a raven's wing, and he couldn't help but wonder how it would feel tickling his bare thighs, ass, and stomach. Mentally smacking himself, he tried to derail the erotic thoughts, but it was useless. To touch Dale, smell his intoxicating scent, and feel his heat was to burn for him.

"I have plenty of work to do, too, but I can take the afternoon off. I'll pick you up around one?"

"Wild horses couldn't keep me away."

Laughing, Dale pecked him on the lips again before slowly backing away. "You're such a dork sometimes, but I think I really like that about you."

Chapter Twelve

Jeremiah sat in a rocking chair on his front porch, carving a piece of wood with the pocketknife his grandfather had given him on his thirteenth birthday. He loved that knife and always took special care of it, keeping it nice and sharp. Whittling was the only time he'd work on a creation with other people around, carving different objects or animal figurines out of a small chunk of two-by-four. He often sat by the fire pit by the bunkhouse with the ranch hands, chipping away until the shape in his mind took tangible form. The men were always amazed at what he came up with, and several had tried to learn from him, but they couldn't bring their visions to life as he could. He could teach them the technical skills but not the ability to see the image in the wood.

Whittling relaxed him, just like puttering around in his workshop did—it always had, from the time he was ten or eleven. His mother's father had been a talented woodworker, too, and helped Jeremiah hone his skills over the years. He missed the old man. While he'd loved all his grandparents, Grandpa Joe was the one he'd connected with the most. When Jeremiah had been little, he loved to sit at his grandfather's knee and listen to him tell stories—real-life ones and others he'd made up. When they'd gotten a little older, Jeremiah and his sister used to take bets on which ones had been fabricated.

As a younger man, Jeremiah had imagined retelling those stories to his own kids one day, but with each year that passed, his dream and the window of opportunity faded a little further. He couldn't even see it anymore, most days not letting himself even think about it. It made him too damn sad.

As he sat there, his emotions were in turmoil. There was a combination of them, each battling the others to be the king of the mountain inside him. He was joyful over how well the date with Dale had gone the night before. Fearful about his friends and family finding out he'd gone out with a man and come in his jeans as they'd rutted against each other on the front porch where anyone could've seen them. And most of all, he was wistful for the freedom to be who he really was and fall in love with whomever he wanted.

His ranch was small compared to many in the Midwest, but at 7900 acres, it was huge by Antelope Rock and even Rockland County standards. Three-hundred-fifty acres were dedicated to the alfalfa fields, and another 300 were for prairie hay, both of which would be harvested and stored for the winter and periods of drought. Jeremiah's house, which he'd renovated after his parents retired to Arizona, several barns, two bunkhouses, and Anthony's cottage were spread out over another seven acres. Grazing pastures occupied the rest of the property. It was a beautiful spread, but even with his employees around, it could still get very lonely.

He'd been thrilled when Willow had moved into her deceased father's home. She was a firecracker, and they probably made the oddest pair of best friends—a tattooed and occasionally pink-haired "chick" from Philly and a born-and-bred redneck with all but a toe still in the closet—for them, though, it worked. However, Willow had Nathan and Shannon now—a loving family—and Jeremiah longed for that for himself. He wondered if he could find that with Dale.

The date last night had given him a glimpse of what life could be like for him if he ever got the nerve to truly be himself. Holding Dale's hand, eating at the restaurant, making out on the porch, all of it coalesced into a possible future he was desperate for. It wasn't just being out with a man, though. It was being with *Dale*. The alluring foreman was everything he'd ever dreamed of in a partner. Besides his stunning good looks, Dale was a person Jeremiah enjoyed being around—the man made him laugh even as he made him burn with desire and need. Dale challenged him and pissed him off in equal measure, both things he never thought he'd appreciate as much as he did. Maybe he didn't know much about being in a relationship, but he knew having a connection beyond the physical was important. Willow and Nathan did—they were friends first and lovers second, and they were so happy it made him half-sick with envy sometimes. If sex were all that mattered in life, he would've been satisfied with one of his hookups in Cheyenne.

He kept circling back to what Willow had said— anyone who really loved him wouldn't give a flyin' fuck who he dated, just that he was happy. If she were right, he'd never live down the "I told you so" from her. *But . . . can you really come out? All the way? Can you be the man someone like Dale could fall in love with?*

Pausing for a moment, he stared in disbelief at the piece of basswood in his hand and cursed. While he'd been woolgathering, his subconscious had somehow carved a penis of all fucking things! God, he had it bad for Dale. It was messing with his mind, turning him into a sex-starved horndog, and he hadn't even seen the man naked yet! At least not outside of his own dreams.

He eyed the dick in his hand. It had a flared head with a notch on what would be the underside, and the texture, grain, and cuts in the wood seemed to give it veins and blood vessels. It was freaking huge, and he wondered how it compared to the real thing. And great, now he was getting hard thinking about it.

An engine caught his attention. Someone was coming up his long driveway. It was too early for Dale —Jeremiah wasn't expecting him for another twenty minutes or so. He squinted, and his stomach flipped when he saw a Suburban with an emergency light bar across the roof and cattle-guard bars in the front protecting the grill.

Sheriff Grady Minor was Jeremiah's cousin and eight years older than him. Their mothers were sisters, but you'd never know it over the past twenty-five years or so. They'd had a falling out over God knew what and had barely spoken since. Over the years, Jeremiah had asked a few times what the fight had been about, but the responses had always been vague before the subject was quickly changed. With Jeremiah's folks living in Arizona now, it was doubtful the sisters would be burying the hatchet any time soon. However, their children, who included Jenna and Grady's brother and sister, were still pretty close to one another. Grady usually swung by for a visit once or twice a week, sometimes during his shift, just to chat for a bit, so it wasn't a surprise the man was there.

As the vehicle approached and stopped in front of the house, Jeremiah's gaze dropped to the big, wooden phallus still in his hands.

Shit!

With a quick glance around, he realized there was only one place to hide it before Grady got out of his truck and saw it. Leaning to the side, Jeremiah stuffed the damn thing under the all-weather cushion on the loveseat swing beside him. He stood and folded the knife before returning it to his back pocket. Wood chips were on the porch at his feet, but that was nothing new. His love of whittling was well known.

Grady climbed from the vehicle, carrying a bottle of water, and strode toward the steps. "Hey, cuz. Taking the day off?"

"Uh, sort of. Half day. Finished the last of the vaccinations and ear tags this morning."

His cousin joined him on the porch and . . . . *Oh fuck!* Jeremiah hid his cringe as Grady sat on the loveseat—

Right! On! Top! Of the covered dildo he'd carved with Dale in mind!

Crap!

The way Grady was sitting, one of three things could happen—he'd feel the lump and investigate, he'd move a certain way, and the thing would shoot out from under the cushion onto the ground, or three, absolutely nothing. Jeremiah prayed as he'd never prayed before that the third option was the winner.

Taking off his brown hat, Grady set it on the seat next to him and got comfortable before cracking open the water bottle and taking a long drag. Jeremiah slowly lowered himself onto the rocking chair as he tried to control his panic. Between the goddamn dildo and the fact Dale would be arriving soon to take him on a date somewhere, he sweated bullets. What else could possibly go wrong? Didn't things happen in threes? Though even thinking about it felt like tempting fate, and he really didn't want to find out what else karma could pull out of her hat for him today.

He wiped his damp forehead. "So, uh . . . how's Rissa doing?" He considered Grady's fifteen-year-old daughter, Larissa, a niece, and she, in turn, called him Uncle Jeremiah, as did several of his other cousins' kids. Grady had been a single parent since his wife Leah passed away of ovarian cancer six years ago. Starting as a deputy with the sheriff's department at the age of twenty-one, he'd spent the next decade and a half rising through the ranks to captain. He'd then been elected to the top position, where he remained for the past sixteen years. He'd beaten out two other contenders that first time and had run uncontested for every election since. The citizens of the county loved the man, and he gave them his all.

Grady rolled his eyes. "I'm the worst dad *ever* because I won't let her date some eighteen-year-old asswipe."

"Who is the little shit? I don't need a badge—I'll just bring my shotgun and tell him about how Marty Olsen's pigs don't leave any body parts to be found as evidence."

The lawman snorted in what seemed like agreement. "Yeah, well, she's grounded for the next two weeks for sneaking out of the house the other night around midnight. Her friend, who's also fifteen and not old enough to even have a learner's permit yet, let alone her license, took her mother's car without permission and picked Rissa and two other girls up for a joyride. I was at a town council meeting over in Butterfield that'd gone way too long. One of my deputies pulled the car over and then called me when he recognized Rissa.

"Needless to say, her friend's parents, who'd been at a wedding, had a fit and grounded her for two months. They assured me she also wouldn't be getting her permit until she was at least seventeen now. Of course, Rissa blames the whole thing on me. According to her, I should've let her friend drive home and not said anything to her parents—as if I would ever allow that." He ran a hand through his hair. "God, parenting was so much easier when she was younger and thought I hung the moon. Teenagers are a whole different ball-game—one you can never fully prepare for."

Jeremiah kept one eye on the dirt lane, expecting Dale to pull up any minute and not knowing what he'd say to Grady about it. What *could* he say that wouldn't sound stupid? *Fuck. Grady's always been good to me. Should I just tell him the truth?*

"What's with you?" Grady's eyes narrowed, and his mouth dropped into a frown.

"W-what?" he sputtered as a brief shot of courage waned. "Nothing's with me—I'm fine."

Leaning toward Jeremiah, Grady opened his mouth to say something but then glanced down at the cushion he was sitting on. Jeremiah watched in horror as the other man shifted his hips back and forth on the seat.

"What the hell is under this thing?" His cousin stood, picked up his hat, and reached to lift the cushion.

Panic-stricken, Jeremiah jumped to his feet to stop him. "Wait! Don't!" But his desperate cry was too late. Grady flipped the fabric back and stared in shock at what he found.

"Jer?" He looked pointedly from the wooden dildo to the wood shavings on the porch floor, then back again. "Did you—" Coughing, Grady's face turned scarlet but not as bright as Jeremiah's.

While Grady's gaze flashed in every direction, Jeremiah's mouth flopped open and slammed shut several times as he struggled to devise a plausible explanation for the hand-carved cock.

"Ya know what?" With more composure than imaginable, Grady replaced the cushion, covering the phallic creation again. "I'm just going to pretend this didn't happen, and we'll never speak of it again. Okay?"

He paused. "Listen, if you're whittling dicks, well, that's your business. I'm no one to judge what a man does in the privacy of his own home. I mean, sure, in my youth, there was a time or two I sorta wondered what it would be like . . . "

His gaze fell to his boots as he cleared his throat.

"But I've long since discovered that's not my thing. I will tell you this, though—you're my cousin, and I love you. Full stop and no questions asked." Setting his hat on his head, Grady tipped it, then walked down the stairs to his vehicle. After a glance back at Jeremiah and a nod of his head, he climbed into his truck and drove away without another word.

Groaning, Jeremiah plopped back down in the rocking chair. He rested his elbows on his knees, put his head in his hands, and hoped that the ground would open up beneath him and swallow him whole.

Can a person literally die of embarrassment? Because that has to be less painful than this.

For the rest of his life, he'd never be able to see or talk to Grady again without reliving the humiliation he was feeling. This date would forever be known to him as the Day of the Dick.

He rested there for several long moments until he heard another vehicle coming up his drive. Lifting his head, he spotted Dale's truck, and his whole body flushed hot at the sight. Flashbacks from last night shot through his mind, and desire stirred within him. Glancing over at the lump under the loveseat cushion, he debated between leaving it there and running the risk of it being found again or trying to hurry inside with it before Dale arrived.

His indecision made the argument moot when Dale's truck pulled to a stop, parking where Grady's had been moments before. The driver's door opened, and Dale stepped out, dressed casually in jeans and a light gray T-shirt. His usual cowboy hat had been replaced with a baseball cap. As always, he looked delicious.

Dale's whole face lit up as he eyed Jeremiah. The man was sin incarnate, but when he smiled, he was so beautiful that Jeremiah was sure angels were weeping as they gazed upon him. Helpless to resist, Jeremiah grinned back, his nerves forgotten for the moment.

"Hey, Cowboy," Dale greeted him, taking the porch steps two at a time, stopping in front of where Jeremiah still sat. He was at eye level with the other man's belt and licked his lips, glancing up at Dale and letting the heat of his thoughts reflect in his eyes.

Dale sucked in a sharp breath before taking off Jeremiah's hat and tossing it on the loveseat. Threading his fingers through Jeremiah's hair, Dale scratched along the back of his skull and down to his nape. Jeremiah moaned, letting his head fall forward and resting it on Dale's firm stomach. His ranch hands were working on the fence in the far pasture, and Anthony had driven to Cheyenne on personal business, so no one was around to see them.

"That feels amazin'. Love your hands on me." Jeremiah raised his own hands, tucking them into Dale's back pockets and squeezing both ass cheeks, relishing Dale's answering sounds of pleasure. Dale's denim-covered cock swelled before Jeremiah's eyes, making his mouth water and his own dick harden.

Down, boy. We said we'd take this slow, so chill out.

They stayed like that for a minute or so before Jeremiah inhaled the fresh scent of Dale's laundry detergent through his nose and realized something was different. "Did you quit smoking?"

"Yup. Hopefully, for good. Willow said I couldn't hold Shannon if I continued to smell like an ashtray." After another moment of silence and contentment, Dale asked, "Are you ready?"

Not releasing his hold on the man's glorious ass, he tilted his head back and met the other man's gaze. "Yes. Because if we don't leave, I'm going to drag you to my bed and keep you there until tomorrow morning."

Chuckling, Dale stepped back, forcing Jeremiah to let him go. With a smirk, Dale adjusted himself. "As fuckin' awesome as that sounds, I have plans for us."

"Yeah?" He stood, rubbing as much of his chest against Dale's body as possible, before grabbing his hat and settling it back onto his head. "What plans would those be?"

"You'll see." Dale quickly surveyed their surroundings before wrapping his arms around Jeremiah's waist and jerking him flush against his body, conjuring up images of the night before when they'd both come in their jeans. Dale gave him a swift kiss on the mouth. "For now, babe, you'll just have to trust me."

Chapter Thirteen

They'd only been on the road for less than two minutes when Jeremiah's phone chimed with a text. He pulled it out of his back pocket and swiped the screen. "What the hell? God, your boss is nuts sometimes, you know that?"

Dale chuckled, assuming Jeremiah meant his best friend, Willow, and not her husband. "What's it say?"

"She wants me to build a . . . get this . . . a *chick*-nic table."

"A *what*?"

"A C-H-I-C-K-N-I-C table for her fucking chickens to eat from. She even sent me a photo. It's a miniature picnic table with a lip around it so she can fill it with feed for the damn chickens. Look." He enlarged the image and turned the phone so Dale could see the screen. "I'm telling you, she's goddamn nuts. Hell, the woman has the cast of *I Love Lucy* on her ranch. A prairie dog named Fred, another one named Little Ricky, a cat named Ethel, and the goats, Lucy and Desi."

Dale grinned. "Well, to be fair, the goats came with those names." His old boss had dubbed the pair after the famous couple a few years ago. When Carl Faulkner passed away last year, Willow had purchased the man's alpaca herd, three horses, two working dogs, the goats, two ATVs and some equipment. Dale had liked the woman almost immediately and had easily accepted when she'd offered him the foreman job. "So, she knows we went on a date last night, huh?"

His eyes widened. "She said something to you?"

He couldn't stop the smirk that spread across his face. "Not exactly. You know that goofy expression and tone most people get when they know a juicy secret, and they're trying to be nonchalant about the whole thing and not blurt it out?" When Jeremiah snorted, Dale continued. "Yeah, that was her this morning when she asked how my weekend was going."

Jeremiah sighed and confessed, "I was panicking last night, not knowing what to wear, so I called her for help."

Taking his eyes off the road momentarily, Dale let his gaze roam the other man's body in a sensual caress before putting his attention back where it belonged. "I'll have to thank her then because you looked hot as hell last night. Just like today."

His cheeks and ears were pinkening as Jeremiah

ducked his head, and Dale felt like he'd been punched in the chest. One day soon, he fully intended to see how far that blush extended down Jeremiah's pale, freckled skin. He wanted nothing more than to strip Jeremiah bare, trace those freckles with his tongue, and see if the rancher tasted as sweet as he looked.

Shifting his hips, he tried to unobtrusively adjust his half-hard dick, a perpetual state of being when he was around the other man.

"Where are we going?"

"It's a surprise." Grinning, Dale tried to keep his excitement contained. He hoped the date he'd planned went well. It was the perfect day for a picnic—a sky the color of forget-me-nots, with scattered dandelion-fluff clouds, a gentle breeze, and a comfortable temperature in the mid-seventies.

They drove west for another forty minutes or so, past seemingly endless fields of crops and rolling pastures with grazing cattle and horses before a copse of pine and spruce trees took their place on either side of the road. The conversation flowed freely between the two men, and Dale hadn't been able to squelch the urge to reach over, grab Jeremiah's hand, and thread their fingers together, resting them on the bench seat. Jeremiah's shy smile lit up his face, warming more than just Dale's heart.

When he spotted the left-hand turn he'd been looking for, Dale steered onto an unmarked dirt road. Wild grass, weeds, and flowers flanked them, and the sweet scent of honeysuckle wafted through the open windows. The truck bounced over ruts, pebbles, and grapefruit-sized rocks, the road probably not having been maintained since its creation. He lowered the speed to a little more than a crawl to avoid damaging the undercarriage of his truck. While the vehicle was made for heavy-duty work and travel, there was no point in risking getting stuck there.

"Where are we?" Jeremiah asked as they pulled to a stop in a small clearing. There was nothing to see but a half-hidden trail through the trees on the left. There were no other vehicles and no signs indicating where they were. Dale had really hoped Jeremiah wouldn't be familiar with the site, even though he was a Rock native. Dale had only found it a few weeks ago while driving one day to relax and explore the area. It was something he liked to do occasionally—find places that were off the beaten path. He'd come back to this exact spot several times since—always alone. However, he looked forward to sharing it with Jeremiah and seeing the man's reaction when they reached their final destination.

"Come on, Cowboy." Unable to hold back his grin, he hopped from the truck and walked around to the bed, where he retrieved a hiking backpack, a small cooler he'd loaded with their food and a few other things, and a large flannel blanket which he handed to Jeremiah when he joined him.

Jeremiah glanced from the items to the path in the

trees and then back to Dale's face. "I feel like I'm either going to love this or a machete-wielding lunatic is going to run out here, screaming at us, and we'll never be heard from again."

Laughing, Dale grasped Jeremiah's hand and gave it a tug. "If a murderer comes after us, I'll protect you, I promise. I'm a Marine, remember? I can take Jason, Freddy, or Michael," he assured him, rattling off the names of famous movie serial killers. "Not too sure about Bigfoot, though."

Giggling—*Oh my God, he's giggling! How adorable!*—Jeremiah laced their fingers together. "Thanks—I feel so much safer already."

They started for the trail, and the smile on Dale's face was so full it practically hurt, but he didn't care. "So, I take it you don't like horror movies?"

"Are you kiddin'? I *love* horror movies. I remember watching *Nightmare on Elm Street*, *Halloween*, and *Friday the Thirteenth* at least three times each in the theater and then over and over again when they came out on video. Of course, they don't hold up against the stuff that comes out now, the graphics and fake blood were just terrible, but I loved them."

As his laughter spewed forth, Dale jostled the cowboy's shoulder with his own. Images of holding a terrified Jeremiah close as they watched a scary movie were very appealing. "That surprises me—I thought you and Willow were addicted to Hallmark movies."

"I am, but I can love horror too. I get into the whole

thirty days of Halloween thing every October." Jeremiah squeezed his fingers, rubbing his thumb across the back of Dale's hand as the path ended, and they stepped out into a clearing right in front of a small sand and rock-strewn beach. Stretching out into the distance before them was a serene lake fed by a snow-capped mountain rising high above it on the far side. The sunlight sparkled off the crystal-blue water, reflecting the sky in a near-perfect mirror image. Small ripples appeared as freshwater fish rose to the top before descending again. A bald eagle screeched overhead and then took a nosedive to the lake's surface, its claws extended, snatching up a nice-size perch to take back to its nest. The beauty of the scenery stole his breath as it did every time he came there.

Glancing over to Jeremiah, Dale sharply inhaled. Sheer joy looked amazing on his rancher, who tipped his hat back in awe as he stared out over the water. The wind rustled the grass at their feet as songbirds and ravens called to each other from the trees. A pair of trumpeter swans and a flock of mallards skated across the glassy lake. The majesty of nature was all around them, in all her glory, but Dale couldn't peel his eyes from Jeremiah. The man was beautiful, and everything else Mother Nature could come up with paled in comparison.

"What is this place?" Jeremiah whispered reverently as if not wanting to disturb their surroundings.

"I found it by accident one day and did some

research. It's Lake Anokasan, which is Sioux for eagle. Most of the area surrounding it is private land, but this section is public."

"This is . . . wow . . . I've never been here before." Pivoting, he met Dale's gaze. His voice cracked as he added, "Thank you for bringing me here. It's beautiful."

Dale's heart skipped a beat, seeing Jeremiah's bright and glossy eyes. No force on Earth could have kept Dale from kissing him right then. He set the pack and cooler on the ground, then took the blanket from Jeremiah and laid it on top of them before drawing the cowboy into his arms. Wrapping one arm around the man's waist, Dale cradled Jeremiah's jaw with his other hand. His green eyes glistened like jewels in the sunlight.

"Breathtaking," Dale murmured before lowering his head and taking Jeremiah's mouth in a deep kiss. Jeremiah's lips were soft and firm beneath his own. He pressed closer, aligning their bodies as he swiped the man's bottom lip with his tongue, then moaning as he gained entry into his mouth. The taste of his rancher exploded on his tongue—cinnamon toothpaste and something unidentifiable that was all Jeremiah. Need settled in Dale's gut and cock. He wanted this man in a way he'd never wanted anyone else.

Tearing his mouth free, Jeremiah tucked his face into Dale's neck, both his hands pressing against the small of Dale's back, keeping them connected. "Dale,"

Jeremiah whispered. "You . . . God, I want you so much." Jeremiah trembled in his arms, vibrating with need.

"Me too, Jay, me too." Lifting his arms, he knocked Jeremiah's hat into the dirt and buried both hands into his hair. He watched, fascinated, as the sunlight made the strands sparkle and shift from darkest auburn to strawberry and amber. Dale could paint a sunset with the colors he discovered there. "I want my hands all over you. My mouth. Everything."

"No argument here." Jeremiah chuckled, and the vibrations pulsated against Dale's chest.

He wanted to feel the arch of Jeremiah's back, the press of his skin, and his muscles trembling with ecstasy. He wanted to swallow Jeremiah's moans and taste his pleasure. Dale's desire for this man was visceral—a living, breathing animal within him, clawing to the surface.

"But we agreed to take this slow, right?" With a bit of mischief in his eyes, Jeremiah took a step back. "So, show me what's in that backpack."

"Yes. Slow. You're right. Of course. Yes. Sure." Dale was babbling but unable to stop the vomit of halting words spilling from his mouth. He scratched his head and glanced around. "Go slow, yup. We did say that. Of course, it's the best idea. This isn't just sex. We're dating, like *really* dating, and that's important."

Grinning, Jeremiah broke into his rambling. "Dale."

"Yeah?"

"You're adorable when you're flustered, but I need you to take a deep breath and relax."

His face was impossibly hot as his heart pounded against his ribs. Unbelievable. He *never* blushed! Couldn't remember the last time he had—probably in high school. "Okay, I'm trying here, you just . . . you're so . . . *you*." Sighing, he ran his fingers through his hair before dragging them down his face, trying to regain control. "Okay. Slow. Got it."

Squatting down and wincing as his jeans tightened around his nearly full-fledged hard-on, he handed the blanket to Jeremiah, who left the grass for the mostly sandy beach. After a brief scan of the immediate area, he found a spot that was free of rocks to spread the blanket on. While Jeremiah did that, Dale brought over the backpack and cooler and started pulling out the contents.

"You realize I don't know what the hell that means, right?" Jeremiah asked, from where he was now sitting on the flannel blanket. Resting on his back, propped up on his elbows, with his hat partially shading his face, he looked like a centerfold come to life.

Mentally groaning, Dale shifted his hips while trying to remember what Jeremiah had just said and what his response should be. The man scrambled his damn brains. "What?"

"You said, 'You're so you.' I don't know what that means."

It only took Dale two seconds to give up on answering because he couldn't think straight at the moment. Instead, he handed containers to Jeremiah, explaining what each one was as he passed them over. "We have turkey and cheese or roast beef sandwiches—I wasn't sure which you would prefer. If you don't want to choose, we can split them in half. Macaroni salad—my mom's recipe, by the way, with no damn hard-boiled eggs in it. I hate when people do that."

He shoved his hand back into the backpack and pulled out a bag. "Chips. And in the cooler, a few bottles of my homemade beer, some soda, and straw-berry shortcake for dessert."

"You brought strawberry shortcake?" Jeremiah's voice was soft, like a child who couldn't believe he'd been given a gift he'd always wanted.

"Sure. You said it was your favorite, right? I didn't get that wrong, did I? I also have whipped cream—I wasn't sure how you liked it."

Jeremiah leaned forward, gently setting the cooler with the drinks in it aside, before pushing Dale onto his back, causing a surprised *oomph* to erupt. Jeremiah climbed on top of him, straddling his hips. Bracing himself on his palms above Dale, he leaned down and kissed him, going straight from zero to sixty in two-point-eight seconds, devouring his mouth and sucking the air from his lungs. Jeremiah ground his pelvis down, rubbing his ass against Dale's hardness, making him hiss in a breath.

Thrilled and a little scared, Dale thought his heart would beat out of his chest. Something had changed just now, and he really liked where this was going but was also afraid to read too much into it. Yeah, the physical attraction was there in spades—there was no denying that—but he was starting to feel more for Jeremiah. It was so much more than he'd ever felt for anyone in his life, including Chris, the fellow Marine Dale had thought he'd been in love with but who'd broken his heart instead.

"Jay . . . " He groaned as Jeremiah writhed and pushed, rocking them both to heights that shouldn't be possible with their clothes still on. Jeremiah licked his neck and nipped at his ears before sucking on the lobe. Dale shivered, thrusting his hips up, needing more friction. More pressure. More Jeremiah.

"Don't say stop, please, Dale." Jeremiah sat up, scooching back so his ass rested on Dale's thighs. Both his hands went to Dale's belt. "Fuck slow. Fuck . . . waiting. I want you in my mouth. Say yes."

"Yes. Jesus, *yes*." Any other answer would've been impossible.

Grinning like a kid in a candy store with an unlimited budget, Jeremiah scooted down farther, kneeling between Dale's spread legs and undoing his belt and jeans before shoving his shirt up faster than Dale could even blink. Strong, calloused palms and fingers settled on his abdomen before running up to his chest, pinching his nipples, and descending again, stopping at the waistband of his boxers. Dale almost whimpered and begged him to go lower, but he'd already handed over too much control to Jeremiah. To protect his heart, he had to use caution.

"I've wanted to get my hands on you for so long." Jeremiah stroked his way back up to Dale's chest. His fingers raked through the coarse, dark hair there, following it down to his belly and then back up to his pecs again. Over and over, he repeated the motions until Dale was ready to jump out of his skin and take control of the situation. But he had to give this to Jeremiah, the chance to be free to explore and be with someone who wasn't a one-night stand.

"I fucking love your hands on me." Dale's words ended with a long, loud, and filthy moan as he threw his head back when a wet tongue lashed at one of his nipples. Jeremiah had leaned forward to lave and suck on the taut peaks, switching back and forth, before trailing kisses down Dale's torso until he reached the band of his underwear. He nestled his face against the hardness tenting the material, breathing deep and inhaling Dale's scent. At Jeremiah's urging, Dale lifted his hips, and the boxer briefs and jeans were dragged down to his knees.

Freed from its confines, Dale's stiff cock slapped against his stomach. Unable to resist, he stared down his body at Jeremiah, who in turn gazed up at Dale, his eyes full of wonder and pure salacious want. Jeremiah licked his lips, flattened onto his stomach, and buried his face in Dale's groin. He gently nuzzled Dale's balls, licking the skin where his thigh met his groin and sucking hard enough to leave a mark of possession. Precum leaked from the tip of Dale's cock in a steady stream. He couldn't remember the last time he'd been this turned on. Maybe never.

"You smell amazin'."

"Jay," he gasped, almost as if he was being strangled. "You're killing me." He raised himself onto his elbows, needing to observe every erotic act Jeremiah performed on him.

"Oh, baby, I haven't even started." Jeremiah took Dale's cock in hand, sliding his palm gently up the hard length. His thumb rubbed over the slit, spreading the fluid there around and using it to slick his way back down to the base, where he squeezed firmly, forcing a moan from Dale's throat. Jeremiah winked before leaning forward and taking Dale deep into his mouth.

"Oh, God! Oh, Jesus! Fuck!" His arms collapsed, and he fell back, thrusting his hips upward and shoving his cock farther into Jeremiah's hot mouth—so wet and tight and perfect. The cowboy's head bobbed, taking all of Dale's cock into his throat with nearly every pass. Saliva ran down, coating his balls. The sounds coming from Jeremiah were obscene. Grunts, moans, slurps, and muffled words. They were almost as hot as the skillful tongue that laved every inch of Dale's dick. He forced his mind not to think about who Jeremiah had practiced on to be so good at giving head. The man might've been unsure about some things in their budding relationship, but blowjobs weren't one of them.

Jeremiah drew up, holding only the top two inches of Dale's shaft inside his mouth. Hollowing his cheeks, he sucked hard as their gazes met. Dale's breathing increased to an unimaginable rate, his heart nearly bursting. Jeremiah's tongue ran over the sensitive bundle of nerves under the head of his cock, over and over, pressing and shifting while he sucked in tandem with his hand squeezing the hard flesh. His thumb and fingers wrapped around the other man's cock and met his lips, working in sync to bring Dale higher and higher. Up and down, steadily and with complete confidence. His eyes, now the color of moss, blazed with heat and passion, never leaving Dale's.

"Jay . . . I'm almost . . . "

Nodding, Jeremiah increased his assault, seemingly determined to suck Dale's brains out through his cock. The pressure was immense, and Dale was almost afraid to come as his orgasm barreled closer to the surface. Jeremiah snaked his free hand between Dale's ass cheeks, pressing a single finger against his hole. That was all it took to send Dale flying over the edge. Roaring, he bolted upright, curving his torso over Jeremiah's head, holding him tightly by the shoulders as he thrust his cock deeper into the man's mouth. Dale's vision blurred, his mind going off-line to where all he could do was feel the intense pleasure ripping through him. He gasped, unable to get enough air. His cum shot down Jeremiah's throat in multiple, seemingly endless spurts. He felt like he came for hours, and when the spasms ebbed and finally stopped, he fell backward, arms splayed wide as he struggled to recall his own name. Somehow, his lungs remembered to work again, and he panted.

Jeremiah rested his head on Dale's stomach, his fingers playing with the fine hair there. Dale's mostly soft and slightly sticky cock rested against the base of the man's throat, which he didn't seem to mind a single bit. "You okay?"

"Not sure. I can't—you broke me. Words . . . hard right now. Can't think." After a moment, he reached down and tugged on Jeremiah's shoulders, urging him up to drape over him. "I want to return the favor. I want to taste you too."

A chuckle erupted from Jeremiah, along with a sheepish grin, as he slid off Dale and cuddled into his side. "No need. I came when you did. Though, if you have a pair of shorts or something in your truck, I'd be grateful."

Dale's eyes widened as his jaw dropped. "You came from blowing me?" He'd heard of that happening, orgasms without physical stimulation, but always to other people or in some of the gay romance/suspense novels he liked to read occasionally. He'd never actually experienced it himself or had it happen to anyone he'd ever been with.

"Yeah." His cheeks crimson, Jeremiah wouldn't meet Dale's gaze, instead watching his own fingers as they skimmed back and forth across Dale's bare chest. "It was so hot—blowing you and your reactions—I couldn't help it. Though, I need to be honest here—if you're going to keep making me come in my jeans, we need to plan ahead so I can have a change of clothes with me."

A bark of laughter escaped him. "I think that can be arranged. Or better yet, you let me be in charge next time." Lifting Jeremiah's chin with his finger, Dale leaned down and stole a kiss. He kept it light, savoring his lover. He tasted himself on Jeremiah's lips, and it was almost enough to make him hard again. Almost. Ten years ago, it would've worked, but his recovery time had gotten longer as he'd aged. "And I do have a spare pair of shorts in my truck—there's a duffle bag in the back seat."

Knowing Jeremiah would be wearing his clothes sent another bolt of desire through him. He'd just come harder than he can ever remember, and he already wanted Jeremiah again.

"Thanks. You know, that's never happened to me before—I just couldn't hold back anymore. You brought me on a romantic picnic and remembered my favorite foods. No one has ever done something like that for me."

"I'll bring you strawberry shortcake every damn day if it'll get my cock in that beautiful, talented mouth of yours." Dale chuckled, hugging Jeremiah tight against his side, trying to absorb his warmth and scent into the very center of his being. "Seriously though, I love being with you and talking to you. Even just sitting and relaxing, not saying a word. I wanted to try and make you as happy as you've made me lately."

Smiling shyly, Jeremiah snuggled his face into Dale's chest, kissing the center before sitting up. "Come on, Marine, put your gorgeous dick away, let me change, and then we'll eat."

"Sounds perfect. I'm starved. After all, I didn't get an appetizer like you did."

Winking and grinning at the other man's blush, Dale pulled paper plates and napkins from the pack while Jeremiah walked stiffly to the truck. A few minutes later, he returned in a pair of baggy, black basketball shorts that hung low on his waist. He stared down at his cowboy boots, then the shorts and his exposed knees, sighing heavily.

Dale bit his lip, trying to swallow an amused snicker. "Look at you. Love the fashion statement, babe." Jeremiah's legs were so pale they were nearly translucent. The contrast of the milky-white skin was even more startling against the black material of the shorts. "We need to get you some sun. The light reflecting off your polar bear legs hurts my eyes."

Jeremiah flopped down on the blanket and glared at him. "Well, aren't you the comedian? Laugh it up, asshole."

Chapter Fourteen

After their picnic, Dale drove them back to the JP. Neither wanted the day to end, but duty called. The animals weren't going to feed themselves. Jeremiah was doing the evening chores at his place, so his foreman and five ranch hands could have the night to do whatever they wanted. On most Saturdays and Sundays, two hands took care of the basic work that needed to be done each day, such as feeding the horses and checking on the cattle. They rotated on a schedule each week, so everyone had some time off. He didn't want his ranch to be their entire lives, not like it was for him.

"I had a great time today." Dale stopped the truck next to Jeremiah's, put it into Park, and turned off the engine. "I want nothing more than to keep this going, make you dinner, and maybe watch a movie."

A glance toward the empty dirt lot in between the bunkhouses told Jeremiah all the hands were gone. Most likely, Anthony was somewhere on the property but nowhere in sight. Jeremiah had hired the pleasant but generally quiet man two years ago after his long-time foreman had been diagnosed with cancer and moved to Montana to live with his daughter and her family.

Jeremiah's shoulders relaxed a bit, and the quivering in his gut eased. He hated that he was so nervous about being caught in a compromising position, but he wasn't ready for everyone to know about them yet. However, it was hard to remember that when Dale was within touching distance. Jeremiah was still coming to terms with actually dating a man. "Next time, we'll do that. You can cook?"

"Yeah, it's nothing fancy, but I can keep you fed, Cowboy."

Letting his gaze drop to Dale's crotch and linger, Jeremiah arched a brow and chuckled. "Oh, yes, you definitely can keep me fed."

"That was dirty, Jay. So damn dirty, and I love it." Dale reached across the console, dragged Jeremiah closer by the back of his neck, and kissed him thoroughly.

He sank into the kiss, chasing Dale's tongue, then catching it and sucking it into his mouth. Their combined moans went right to his dick, and there was no hiding his raging hard-on in the shorts he still wore.

Releasing him, Dale leaned back, breathing hard. "The things you do to me, Jay." Shaking his head, he took off his hat, running his hand through his hair before replacing it. "Come on, let me at least walk you to the door."

"You realize I'm a grown man, and I can get inside all by myself, right?" Jeremiah asked, grabbing the bundle of his soiled jeans and boxers from behind the seat before climbing out of the truck and meeting Dale by the front bumper.

"Of course, I know that. But this is a date, and this is what people do on dates. I told you I was going to romance you. So, since you won't let me open the truck door for you, I'm going to walk you to your front door and steal another kiss before saying goodnight." Winking, Dale held out his hand and waited.

Hoping his assessment of the ranch hands not being around was correct, Jeremiah took Dale's hand, entwined their fingers together, and pulled the man up the porch steps after him. Not wanting the day to end, he led him to the loveseat swing. Tossing the dirty clothes onto the floor, he took a seat and then gestured to the empty space next to him. "I know you have to go —I have my own work to see to—but five more minutes won't hurt, will it?"

Dale shook his head and sat beside him, setting the swing in a gentle motion. They touched from thigh to shoulder, pressed together as close as they could get, neither willing to break the connection they'd forged by the lake. Dale frowned, shifting slightly away from Jeremiah and then back against him.

"Um, are you okay?" Jeremiah asked, his tone uncertain.

"Yeah, hang on." Dale stood, and then it hit Jeremiah.

Oh shit!

"Dale, no, wait!"

It was too late, though, as Dale flipped over the cushion and revealed the wooden cock Jeremiah had carved earlier . . . and forgotten all about.

"Jay?" Dale cautiously picked up the wooden phallus with his thumb and forefinger and held it up. "Something you want to tell me, babe?"

His cheeks flamed hotter than the sun. Certain he was about to keel over from embarrassment, he hid his face in his hands and groaned. "No," he mumbled, daring to peek out from between his fingers.

Dale turned the dick over, examining it from every angle. "Is this, um, carved from life?"

"What?"

"Did you have a model for this? I mean, it could be yours since I haven't exactly seen you in all your glory yet. Is this one of those live model things?"

Jeremiah dropped his hands between his knees and lifted his chin, steeling his nerves to meet the other man's gaze. He didn't think it was possible, but his face heated further under Dale's unreadable expression. He

swallowed a thickening lump in his throat. "No. I just
. . . whittled it. I was . . . .um . . . thinking about you,
and the next thing I knew—"

"Me?" Dale let out a snort and held the carved dick
next to his crotch. "Well, the size is close." Chuckling
as amusement filled his eyes, he was like a teenage boy,
playing with the dick as if it were his own.

Jeremiah moaned and stood. "Excuse me—I'm just
going to go put my head in the oven. Nice knowing
you."

"Jay, wait!" Dale called out, trying to speak past his
laughter. "Hang on, babe."

Tossing the wooden cock onto the loveseat, Dale
snagged Jeremiah's arm, hauling him back against his
chest, which still shook with an overload of mirth. The
heat of Dale's body nearly burned Jeremiah's skin
through their shirts. Arms wrapped tightly around
Jeremiah's torso, and he couldn't help but sigh and lean
back into the embrace.

"I've seen Shannon's cradle, so I knew you worked
with wood—I just didn't know you made woodies too."
A snicker came from behind him, and Jeremiah's ears
felt like they were on fire. "I like it. I think . . ." Dale
began, before running his hand down the center of
Jeremiah's chest to where his shorts rode low on his
hipbones. ". . . you should finish it."

He groaned and shifted his hips. "Why? I should
just burn it."

"What? No! You can't burn my cock!"

Now it was Jeremiah's turn to snort with laughter. "Why would I finish it?"

"Why would you finish my wooden woodie? So, you can get yourself off with it. Sand it down so it's smooth as silk, seal it, and use it on yourself." Dale's voice had dropped an octave, sending shivers racing down Jeremiah's back and desperate want pooling in his groin. "Damn! That would be so freaking hot to watch."

Dale's hand went between Jeremiah's legs, gripping his length through the thin fabric of the shorts, forcing a gasp from his lips and making him forget his embarrassment. "You know I'm waiting for you to start saying 'how much wood could a woodchuck chuck if a woodchuck could chuck wood?' right?"

Dale barked in his ear, and Jeremiah shook his head to get that damn tongue twister out of it. "Ugh, never mind. So, let me get this straight— you want me to fuck myself with the wood cock I carved while thinking about you?"

"Hell, yeesss," Dale hissed before sucking on Jeremiah's earlobe. The spot never failed to light him up like a firework on the Fourth of July. Moaning, he tried to thrust deeper into Dale's hand and back against the answering hardness nestled between his ass cheeks. The nylon of the shorts was so thin that he swore he could feel every ridge of Dale's length against him.

"O-okay," he stuttered, any other words failing him now as Dale's hand pumped his cock. The silky fabric between them enhanced his pleasure until he was crawling out of his skin with need.

Suddenly, Dale released him and retreated several steps. Jeremiah spun around, his eyes wide and words of denial on his lips. "Why'd you stop?" He was panting for more than just oxygen. Glancing down, he noted the sight of himself was nearly pornographic, with the loose garment doing nothing to restrain his obvious desire. There was no hiding what this man did to him.

"Because." Unashamedly, Dale adjusted himself, pressing the heel of his hand against his erection. "We're waiting and going slow, right?"

"What? No!" He lowered his voice, mindful that sound traveled farther than one would expect on the ranch. "You want me to fuck myself with a dildo I made by accident? How is that slow?"

His shoulders lifted in a shrug. "Well, because it's a fake cock—not mine. If I spend one more second with you in my arms with those sweet sounds pouring from your lips, I'm going to take you inside and own every inch of you. You won't be able to walk by the time I'm done without everyone knowing my cock was up your ass. And trust me, I fully intend to make you walk funny for at least a day." Dale's intense words were only matched by the fierce look on his face.

A flush raced up Jeremiah's neck and face as his eyes blinked rapidly. He cupped his nape, kneading it. Biting his lip, he dropped his gaze and toed an invisible pebble. After a few moments, he nodded. "All right. You're right." He took a shuddering breath and then bent to snatch up his jeans and boxers. "I'll, um, wash your shorts and get them back to you."

"Keep them—I like seeing you in my things." Dale took one step closer, just out of reach. "I want to kiss you, give you a proper goodbye, but if I do that, all my resolve will disappear." When Jeremiah smiled, Dale continued. "I'll text you?"

"Yeah. Yes, text me. I'll . . . uh . . . I'll be around. Can we . . . when . . . " Clearing his throat, Jeremiah struggled to get a handle on himself. "When can we do this again?"

"Soon as we get a chance." Grinning, Dale tipped his hat, descended the stairs, then whirled around and walked backward, not taking his eyes off Jeremiah's. "Don't forget about what I told you. I expect to see my likeness finished soon."

Winking, he did an about-face and strode to his truck. Waving one last time, he climbed into the cab and backed up before turning around and driving off in a cloud of dust.

"What have I gotten myself into?" Jeremiah asked himself. Shaking his head, he didn't give himself a chance to rethink it and added the wooden dildo to his pile of clothes. "Looks like I'll have to figure out which lacquer is safe for anal sex. Oh, my fucking . . ."

After dinner the next evening, Jeremiah sat on the rocking chair on his porch and rested his feet on a stripped and sanded piece of cottonwood tree trunk he often used as an ottoman. The sun was setting, painting the sky in the most majestic colors ever created, something he'd never grow tired of seeing. With a cold beer in one hand and his phone in the other, he pulled up Dale's contact and tried to think of what to say. He'd been busy all day, catching up on the ranch's bookkeeping, bills, invoices, and cattle logs while trying to distract himself from the thoughts of a certain sexy foreman.

It felt like a lot had happened yesterday—for both of them. It was as scary as it was wonderful. Jeremiah was closer to being out than he'd ever been his entire life. It felt . . . amazing, and somehow, that was overriding the terror he'd held onto for so many years, worrying if someone would find out his secret.

Unlocking the phone's screen, he thumbed open his text app and the thread he had with Dale. Before now, their electronic interactions had consisted of things like, "On my way" or "Willow asked me to tell you . . ." but now, he wasn't sure what to say, only that he needed to connect with the other man.

Is it too soon to be missing him this much?

"Hey," he typed and then pressed send.

A response came a few moments later.

DALE

Hey yourself, Cowboy.

Taking a sip of his beer, he gave himself a second to think about what he wanted to say. Another text popped up before he had a chance to respond to the first one. The words lit him up, spreading warmth throughout his chest.

DALE

I missed you today.

Oh, yeah?

DALE

Yup. I keep thinking about that wooden dick ;)

Jeremiah rolled his eyes and groaned.

I did more research into lacquer than I ever thought I'd need to do.

DALE

Ha! Love it. Can't wait to see the finished product.

What are you doing right now?

Jeremiah snapped a picture of his booted feet up

on the stump, a beer in his left hand, balancing on his knee, and sent it.

> Relaxing. I played businessman all day—paperwork, bills, etc.

DALE

> Fun. The joys of ranching. Wish I was there.

> Me too.

The sound of a car engine had Jeremiah lifting his head. A sheriff's department-issued SUV was coming down the lane.

> Grady is pulling up.

DALE

> Ooh, the fuzz is coming!

> Please don't say coming in the same sentence as my cousin!

DALE

> True. If we're talking about coming, I'd rather talk about you coming in my mouth.

His face flamed—even his ears felt like they were singed. He uncrossed his ankles and then recrossed them in the opposite manner, trying to stave off an impending erection the dirty messages had evoked.

DALE

You're blushing so hard right now.

Damn the man and his sixth sense.

Maybe.

Grady pulled to a stop just as another ping sounded on Jeremiah's phone. He ignored it, too afraid further embarrassment would show on his face and his observant cousin would notice and question him. Jeremiah was taking baby steps into the out-and-proud world, and he wasn't ready to be caught texting his . . . *boyfriend? Is that what we are?* Lover sounded too much like an illicit affair. Partner was too committed, too permanent, which they weren't yet. He made a mental note to ask Dale just as his phone pinged twice more in rapid succession.

"Hey, how's it going, cuz?" Climbing the steps, Grady was dressed in civilian clothes—jeans, a brown and gold T-shirt from his alma mater, the University of Wyoming, and scuffed, chestnut-colored boots—the attire he wore on the weekends when he wasn't scheduled to work. However, as always, his duty weapon and badge were attached to his belt since he never knew when he'd have to respond to an emergency and not have time to change into a uniform.

"It's going. Pull up a seat, grab a beer." Jeremiah

gestured to a small ice bucket holding two more cold brews he'd brought outside. "What's up?"

"Nothing much. Rissa's still grounded and not speaking to me. Lorraine told me she'd keep an eye on her if I wanted to get out of the house for a while."

The sixty-five-year-old widow was a sweetheart and lived across the street from Grady. After Leah passed away, Grady hired Lorraine Culpepper as a housekeeper and nanny to his then four-year-old daughter. It was an arrangement that benefited both of them since Lorraine had lost her job as a secretary in Butterfield when the business had closed down. Rissa called the woman Aunt Lorraine, who, in turn, considered the teen her niece.

"Thought I'd come by and check on you." Grady snagged a chilled bottle from the bucket. Smirking, he pointed to the loveseat with his beer. "Safe to sit?"

Mortification rolled through Jeremiah, and he ran a hand down his face, not meeting Grady's amused gaze. "Yes. And I thought we agreed to never speak of that again."

Needing a distraction, he peeked at his phone and nearly dropped it when he saw the screen. Dale had sent him a series of pictures. Each one was sexier than the last. Making sure Grady couldn't see them, Jeremiah tried to keep his eyes from bugging out and a moan from erupting from his mouth.

The first one was an image of his bare chest, with his hand resting on his lower belly, fingers buried in the coarse hair there, looking as if he was about to go lower. He wasn't wearing any pants, and the tips of his fingers were just brushing the band of his boxer briefs. The outline of his erection was clearly defined behind the snug material.

The next photo showed Dale's hand *inside* his boxers, gripping his long, hard length, his knuckles pressing against the navy blue material, showing how tightly he was holding himself. The head of his cock peeked out from under the waistband, deep purple and glistening with precum. Jeremiah's mouth watered in memory, and he swore he could taste the salty bitterness even now.

The third picture made Jeremiah's already half-hard cock plump up and stiffen fully. It showed a completely naked Dale with his fist wrapped around his dick, precum shiny on the tip, trailing down the side and over his hand. He appeared to be lying flat on his back in bed, working himself over, his knees splayed wide, balls hanging heavy between his legs.

"Jeremiah?" Grady's voice broke through his thoughts and the fantasies spinning around in his mind at the sight of the photos.

"What?" His voice croaked like he was going through puberty again. He cleared his throat and tried a second time. "Sorry, what'd you say?"

"I asked how things were going around here, but you seem awfully distracted. What's on your phone that has you so . . . I don't know . . . flustered? Is everything okay?"

"Nothing." His phone pinged again, this time with a video file. He inhaled sharply.

Oh God . . .

"Uh, s-sorry. Let me just . . . um . . . answer this . . . uh . . . text. Sorry, just . . . just some business I have to take care of."

> Stop! Grady is here! OMG Dale, I can't. You're killing me!

DALE

> I don't want to stop. It feels sooo good. Did you watch the video?

> I can't! Grady is literally sitting right beside me!

Crossing his legs at the knees, he did his best to hide his state of arousal. His jeans pinched uncomfortably, but the pain did nothing to dull the ache in his balls. Saliva pooled in his mouth, and he swallowed several times before he started drooling like a St. Bernard with a juicy bone.

After silencing the phone and its unexpected pornography, he glanced toward Grady but didn't meet his questioning gaze, instead focusing on the letters on the man's shirt. "Things are . . . um, good. Same as ever. Looks like we're going to have a good calving season. Profitable." Somehow, he managed to fall back on the familiar subjects of ranching and the cattle, the answers nearly automatic after a lifetime of similar conversations.

Grady's brow furrowed, but thankfully, he didn't question Jeremiah further about the texts. "That's great—hope this weather holds."

This time, instead of a ping, the phone vibrated in his hand.

DALE

Jay, I need you. My cock is so hard for you. I keep thinking about what it felt like to be inside your mouth. The sounds you made were so hot . . . so sexy.

Biting back a groan, he fought for composure. He had to stop looking at the screen every time a new message appeared, but it was like a train wreck—he couldn't *not* look. "Yeah, not too hot yet, huh? It's . . . uh . . . nice for a change." They could've been in the middle of a blizzard, and his answer probably would've been the same. He was too focused on the *sexts* Dale was sending him. Jeremiah had never experienced sexting, or even phone sex, before, but if this is what it was like, he wanted to do it often. Alone, of course, when he could take matters into his own hands—literally.

Two can play this game, he thought to himself.

Fingers flying over the screen, he answered Dale, half listening to Grady ramble on about a bar fight he and his deputies had broken up last night at the Spur and Bull.

> I keep thinking about it too. You tasted so fucking good. Your cock filled my mouth and throat just right. Makes me wonder where else you'd fill me just right.

DALE

> Oh fuck. Jay . . .

His phone didn't vibrate for a few minutes, and with disappointment, he thought that was the end of it. But when the device vibrated in his hand again, he nearly ejaculated in his pants as he fumbled the cell, catching it at the last second. Dale had sent him a picture of his cum-slicked stomach, his hand still holding his now softening dick, creamy-white jizz covering his fingers and knuckles.

> OMG! You didn't!

DALE

> Damn right I did. Don't come in your jeans this time ;) Get rid of Grady then go inside and watch the video I sent you. Send me one back. I want to see you come, baby. I want it so bad. But don't touch yourself until you're recording.

He didn't hesitate even one second, hitting the

button on the phone that would put it into sleep mode. "Hey, Grady, I'm sorry, but I have to call this guy . . ." he gestured to the darkened device, scrambling for a plausible explanation, "and . . . uh . . . sort out this mess about his . . . um . . . balls—bulls! They're . . . uh . . . supposed to be here for insemination in June, but now he's saying he can't get them here until July. I hate to cut your visit short, but this'll take a while. Rain check?"

"Sure, no problem." Grady stood, setting his now empty beer bottle on the porch rail. He paused a moment and stared at Jeremiah. "Sure you're okay?"

He nodded, unable to get to his feet without giving away the fact he had a raging hard-on. "I'm fine. Just . . . need to get this straightened out." Jeremiah suspected Grady saw right through him, that he knew something else was going on, but with his cock throbbing painfully, Jeremiah was too desperate to care right then.

"All right. I'll be seeing ya."

Jeremiah didn't even wait for Grady to drive off before he barreled into his house, slamming the door shut behind him and flying up the steps and down the hall to his bedroom. Tossing his phone on the bed, he stripped to his skin and flopped backward onto the king-sized mattress. He propped himself up on his pillows, not touching his aching dick yet, needing to see the video first.

Opening it up, he pressed play, holding the phone close enough not to miss a thing. Dale's face and upper chest appeared on the screen, his shoulder moving up and down, jerking in an unmistakable motion. The video shook a little, but not enough to be a hindrance. Dale's rough and rumbling voice filled the air. "Jay, fuck, it feels so good. I wish it was your hands on me. I love it when you touch me." The rhythmic sounds of flesh slapping flesh were loud in the otherwise still bedroom, competing only with Jeremiah's panting, moaning, and pounding heart. "I'm so hard it hurts, baby." The camera angled downward, showing Dale's hand wrapped around his thick cock. He'd applied lube, his skin slick and shiny with it.

Jeremiah watched, not moving, hardly getting enough oxygen to his lungs and brain, as Dale cupped his balls, tugging and rolling them in his palm. Jeremiah's own cock and balls ached, demanding the same attention, but he held off per Dale's earlier demand.

"Yeess . . . " Dale hissed as he gripped his length again, sliding his hand up and down, twisting his fist around the head with every upstroke. Jeremiah could see Dale's thighs tremble as the man jerked and moaned. Thrusting his hips upward, Dale fucked his fist hard and fast. He screamed when the violent climax hit him. The camera shook as cum splashed onto Dale's abdomen and chest while he babbled incoherently. After a few moments, the view shifted to show Dale's face again. He was sweating and gasping for air. The sexy, filthy bastard winked at the lens, and then the video ended.

Jeremiah was humping the air, his dick wet with his own precum, and he was sure if he touched himself, his orgasm would be brutal and fast. He quickly typed out a text and sent it.

> Holy hell! Fuck me that was so damn hot.

He grabbed a tube of lubricant from the bedside drawer and squirted some into his palm before rubbing his hands and fingers together, warming up the sticky liquid.

DALE

> Show me, Jay. Show me how hot you thought it was. Show me that gorgeous cock and how hard you are for me. Jack off for me.

Jeremiah groaned at the dirty words, swearing he heard Dale's voice whispering them in his ear. Commanding him.

After taking a moment to wipe the lube off one hand onto the comforter, he opened the video app and flipped the camera, pointing it down toward his lap. He hit record and wrapped his fist around his shaft. Grunts and moans flowed from his throat. His balls already tingled. It wasn't going to take long before he shot his load. He tried to talk like Dale had in his video, low and sensual, even though it felt weird when he was all alone. Hopefully, he sounded seductive instead of comical when the other man watched the video. "Dale, you're so sexy and hot. Goddammit, this feels fuckin' awesome. I wish it was your hand around my dick, getting me off."

He jerked himself in earnest, too impatient to draw it out, too needy and turned on. The sight of Dale working over his own dick was forever burned into his mind. He let his body take over—the sensations, the cravings, the *need*—and crude words flowed easier from his lips. "I want you here with me. I want you to bend me over and prep me with your tongue and fingers. Then I want your cock to split me open and fuck me into this big bed. Hard and fast the first time. Just to take the edge off. Don't pull out either—I want to feel your cum, so deep inside me. Oh, God! *Ahhhhhh*, shit!"

His orgasm ripped through him like a freight train. The force of it was nearly painful in its intensity. He allowed himself to make as much noise as he wanted, not tempering or holding back his reactions. Imagining Dale watching the video and jerking off again to it drove his orgasm higher and longer. He kept tugging on his cock and working every drop free until he was too sensitive to continue. Breathless, he made sure he angled the camera up his stomach and chest, showing Dale he'd come so hard that semen had reached his pecs. There were even some drops at the base of his throat.

With trembling hands, he ended the video, uploaded it to the message thread, and sent it to Dale before he could chicken out. He'd never done anything like that before and felt shy now that it was over. Dropping his phone onto the comforter beside himself, he reached over the side of the bed and snagged his T-shirt from the floor, using it to clean himself up.

Tossing the shirt in the direction of his hamper, he lay back and tried to catch his breath while he waited for Dale's response.

Chapter Fifteen

Slack-jawed, Dale stared at the video on his phone, hitting play again and watching it a third time. With his heart in his throat, he couldn't breathe, and even though he'd just come a few minutes ago, he was hard again. It took all of his willpower not to hop into his truck and race over to Jeremiah's house, pin him to the bed, and fuck him just like he'd begged for—bare and raw, hot and deep.

When the salacious video ended, he chewed his bottom lip and hit the button in the app for a face-to-face call. He didn't know if Jeremiah would answer but hoped he would.

A moment later, the man's flushed and sweaty face filled the screen, the sight making Dale groan out loud. "Oh, fuck, Cowboy, you are so damn sexy when you come."

Grinning shyly, Jeremiah shifted around on his

bed, getting comfortable. The dark green bedspread and pillowcase under his head contrasted gorgeously with his red hair, making his emerald eyes bright and mesmerizing. "I've never done anything like that before—I mean, the sexting and video."

"How was it?" Dale asked, satisfaction coursing through him at being Jeremiah's first at something as hot as that. If he had his way, there would be many more firsts for them in the near future. While he knew Jeremiah wasn't exactly naive—he'd told Dale about going to a gay club in Cheyenne to hook up with other men—Dale got the impression there were many things the cowboy hadn't experienced yet when it came to sex.

"Amazin'. Almost as good as if you were here. To be clear, though, that is not what I had in mind when I texted you earlier to say hello."

Laughing, Dale replied, "I bet not, but it was so worth it. That video . . . " He turned his phone, showing Jeremiah how hard he was again and that he was still naked, before bringing the camera lens back to his face. "I'll be jerking off to that video for months to come when you're not here in person. I love the filthy way you talked to me on it."

Sighing, Jeremiah closed his eyes and swallowed hard. "You're going to be the death of me, Marine."

"Maybe, but what a way to go, eh?"

There were several beats of silence before Jeremiah opened his eyes again. This time, instead of passion and desire or even amusement, there was wariness in them. "I wanted to ask you . . ." He blushed and glanced away. Dale had come to learn when his cowboy got like that, it was best just to give him a few moments to gather his thoughts and pick his words—he'd speak when he was ready. "What are we? What do, ugh . . . what do I call you?"

"What do you want to call me?" Words filled Dale's mind—*boyfriend, lover, best friend, partner.*

"I've never had a boyfriend before, but it feels a little too junior high for us. Aren't we too old for that?"

Grinning, Dale shook his head. "Not at all. Are you asking me to be your boyfriend, Cowboy? To go steady?"

Jeremiah paused for a moment, meeting Dale's eyes with a forthrightness that made his breath catch. "Yeah, that's exactly what I'm asking."

"Then consider yourself spoken for. I don't share."

With a growl, Jeremiah nodded. "Neither do I. While we're dating, there's no one else—for either of us."

"Just the way I like it." Winking, he pursed his lips and blew a kiss at the camera. "Did you eat dinner?"

Blinking at the subject change, it took Jeremiah a moment to respond. "Yeah, I did." He yawned, and then his gaze flickered up to the top of the phone and back down again. "I didn't realize how late it was. Between dinner, two beers, and coming so hard I thought my head would explode, I'm beat. Five o'clock comes early."

"That it does. Get some sleep. Can I text you tomorrow?" Dale forced himself not to push things and offer to run over and tuck Jeremiah into bed, preferably pressing himself tight against his back, skin to skin, their hearts beating in sync.

"Anytime. Maybe we can do dinner tomorrow night?" Jeremiah asked before his gaze dropped to his chest as his bottom lip disappeared into his mouth. His moments of shyness were so damn adorable.

"I'd love that. Night, Cowboy."

"Night, Dale."

The last thing Dale saw before the screen went black was Jeremiah's beautiful smile. Rolling over, he plugged his phone into its charger and set his alarm. Hope bloomed in his chest, hope for the future and the possibilities it held.

Three weeks later . . .

Dale took a drag from a bottle of his home-brewed beer as he stood at the island in Jeremiah's kitchen, as the other man put the finishing touches on the meat-lovers pizza he'd made from scratch for their dinner. Dale had ogled the man all evening, watching him knead the pizza dough, the muscles in his forearms and shoulders flexing and shifting surprisingly erotic.

Who knew cooking could be so much fun?

It was a Saturday evening, and the JP was quiet after the ranch hands had left a few hours ago for a big PBR rodeo in Cheyenne. Even Anthony had gone with them to see the professional bull-riding event, so Jeremiah and Dale had the ranch to themselves—a fact Dale knew his lover was relieved about.

While no one, other than Willow and Nathan, knew Jeremiah was gay and dating him, Dale was okay with Jeremiah's hesitancy and nervousness when others were around. He knew the man was trying and that the situation differed from what he'd experienced with Chris being in the closet. In that case, *no one* had known about them—they'd remained hidden behind closed doors or traveled far enough away that they wouldn't run into anyone they knew. With Jeremiah, there'd been small steps in the right direction, and hopefully, more would follow.

Dale and Jeremiah had joined Willow and Nathan for dinner or coffee and dessert several times over the past few weeks. During those occasions, Jeremiah had openly flirted with Dale and even held his hand and kissed him in front of the other couple, often making Willow squeal or swoon and sigh. Jeremiah felt safe with them, and Dale was willing to wait for him to take the next step in coming out. He had faith it was just a matter of time until Jeremiah was fully out—he could keep being patient, at least, for now.

A few evenings over the past several weeks, Dale had wandered over to Jeremiah's place for dinner or some beers on the porch—things that could easily be construed as acts of friendship—but he never stayed over or even too late. However, the other night, after dinner with Willow, Nathan, and baby Shannon, Dale and Jeremiah had returned to Dale's RV, where things had, understandably, gotten hot and heavy between them. They'd exchanged blowjobs and fallen asleep in each other's arms afterward. Jeremiah had kissed Dale awake the next morning at four-thirty to let him know he was walking back to his house. Since it'd been the first time they'd actually slept together, Dale appreciated that his cowboy hadn't just disappeared on him. Waking up in Jeremiah's arms was like a dream come true, and he was looking forward to the day it became a regular occurrence with them. He wanted it like he wanted his next breath.

They hadn't fucked each other yet—Jeremiah had confessed that, while he'd topped a few times, he'd never bottomed, a fact that blew Dale's mind. He wanted to be Jeremiah's first in the worst way but knew he had to be patient. Chris was the only man to ever be inside Dale, and he remembered how terrifying yet amazing that first encounter had been. When the time was right, and Jeremiah was ready, Dale would do everything in his power to take care of him and make it the greatest experience of the man's life. He fully antic-ipated being the bottom for as long as it took Jeremiah to be ready. And even if the man was never ready, Dale would be okay with that too. What they had was worth so much more than sex and worrying about whose dick went where.

It was a busy time of the year at both ranches, so many nights, the two men talked on the phone using the video chat feature on the texting app. Dale enjoyed getting to know Jeremiah better on a personal level. They'd discussed their childhoods, education, hobbies, trips they'd taken, likes and dislikes, and everything else that popped up in the easy conversations they shared. They'd laughed so much, his ribs had ached some nights.

A thought flashed in Dale's mind. Grinning, he waited until Jeremiah had slid the loaded pizza into the oven. "So . . . did you finish the wooden cock yet?"

Being a ginger, there was no way for Jeremiah to hide his embarrassment, a fact Dale loved. The other man sighed heavily as his neck, face, and ears burned bright. Dale chuckled. "Is that a yes or a no, Cowboy?"

Without a word, Jeremiah strode from the kitchen. Dale's eyes narrowed as he tracked his footsteps up the stairs and down the hall to his bedroom. A few moments later, he returned with his hand behind his back and his chin nearly touching his chest. A leering grin spread across Dale's face, and his cock stirred. He set his hands on the island and leaned on them, not taking his eyes off the beautiful flush on Jeremiah's face and neck. His mouth watered at the sight, and he wanted to lick the man from head to toe. "Show me."

Without looking at him, Jeremiah slowly brought his hand forward and held up his creation. Straightening, Dale rounded the island, stalked toward the other man, and took the phallus from him. "Damn, baby. This is gorgeous—and I don't mean that in a sexual way. Although, there is that."

Jeremiah had finished the carving, including thick veins and a flared and notched head. There was even a slit at the top. The wood had been sanded to smooth perfection, the grain rich, natural, and stunning. Several layers of clear sealant had been applied until it was slick and shiny. The cock was long and thick, and Dale's thumb and finger couldn't quite touch around the circumference. At the wider base was a pair of heavy balls, which could be used as a way to grip the sculpture or to stand it on its end. It truly was a work of art. It was lifelike and solid. He hefted it slightly, trying to imagine what it would feel like to use it to get himself off. Or better yet, have Jeremiah use it on him, or Dale could fuck Jeremiah with it while Jeremiah sucked him off. The possibilities had his own cock hardening and his mind racing.

Fuck.

"You're really talented, Jay. Willow mentioned you have a workshop here that you never invite anyone into. I'd love to see more of your work, but if that's crossing a line you don't want to yet, I understand. A lot of artists are quirky like that, and there's nothing wrong with it. I'd just love to see that part of you—maybe someday?"

"Maybe," Jeremiah responded with a shrug. "And you're right, my workshop is my sanctuary—it's where I can really be me."

Dale set the cock down on the counter, then hooked his fingers into the loops on Jeremiah's jeans, pulling him close. Dipping his head down, he brushed their lips together. "You can always be the real you around me—in fact, I prefer it. Now, tell me, can that thing be used for real?"

Biting his bottom lip, Jeremiah nodded—his blush that'd begun to fade, returning. "The sealant is safe. I . . . um . . . did research."

Dale chuckled as he raised his eyebrows a few times in succession, causing his cowboy to bark out a laugh and blush harder than before. He put his hands on Dale's chest and gave him a gentle shove. "Pervert. Before you blurt out any of those bright ideas swarming around in your head, let's eat. I'm starving, and the pizza's done."

After dinner and a make-out session that'd led to Jeremiah blowing Dale's brains out and coming in his own hand simultaneously, the two men cuddled on the couch in just their jeans and socks. The old John Wayne film *Big Jake* was on the widescreen TV above the fireplace and was the only source of light for them except for the one under the microwave in the kitchen.

Dale sat with his stocking feet propped up on the coffee table while Jeremiah was stretched out next to him with his head in Dale's lap. He loved the open floor plan of the house. The great room was huge, with exposed, dark-stained wooden beams in the vaulted ceiling. The entire fireplace wall was covered in river rocks and with a matching stone slab for the TV to rest on. The hearth and mantel conjured visions of Christmas decorations and matching red and white stockings, but he quickly shut that down. He was getting way ahead of himself there.

There was a half-bath off the hallway that led to Jeremiah's office. The country kitchen had both a breakfast nook with a two-chair bistro set and was attached to a formal dining room. Upstairs, there were three spare bedrooms and a full bath, in addition to Jeremiah's main bedroom and en suite bath. The man had worked closely with the builder and architect, completely renovating the place to get his dream house, and the results were stunning. Even the attractive but practical decor belied the fact it was a twenty-seven-hundred square foot bachelor pad. Each time he was there, Dale spotted more and more little details that showed Jeremiah's hand in the finished work of the house. Little carvings at the corners of the moldings above the doors, a figurine of a cowboy on a bucking bronc on the mantel, and even an oversized wooden bowl on the kitchen counter where Jeremiah kept fresh fruit.

Dale checked his watch. He didn't need to leave yet—Nathan had handled the evening chores so the foreman could have the night off—but he didn't want to be half naked on the couch with Jeremiah when the ranch hands got back. Ten to one odds, most of them would be three sheets to the wind, and at least one of them would knock on the back door, urging the boss to join them for a beer at the fire pit. One thing Dale had learned about Jeremiah was that he treated his employees like family—some of them had worked for him for over five years. In the ranching business, which often saw a fast turnover in hands, that was saying something.

As the movie credits began to roll, Dale ran his hand up and down Jeremiah's bare chest, enjoying the way the coarse, auburn hairs there tickled his palm. Goosebumps appeared on the cowboy's arms and shoulders, and he turned over so his face was pressed against Dale's groin. Dale could feel the heat of Jeremiah's breath through his jeans and moaned. With a mouth that was pure heaven, the man gave the best blowjobs Dale had ever had the pleasure of receiving. He refused to allow himself to think of where and with whom Jeremiah might've acquired such skills. Resolving himself to enjoy it, he spread his legs slightly, lifted his hips, and pressed his crotch harder against Jeremiah's face and mouth.

Neither of them heard a key unlock the front door, but when it burst open and then slammed shut, they both jumped to their feet, Jeremiah stumbling and nearly ending up on his delectable ass in the process. There was a loud thump in the foyer as if something heavy had been dropped.

"Jeremiah! You home?"

Dale's eyes narrowed at the unfamiliar female voice and the panicked look on Jeremiah's face as the man frantically searched for his shirt. He snatched Dale's black T-shirt up from the floor and tossed it to him as a petite woman in her mid-thirties strode into the room, flipped the light switch up, turning on the three lamps in the room, and stopped short. With her perfectly-coiffed auburn hair, stylish makeup, and the same startling emerald eyes as Jeremiah, this had to be his sister Jenna, the successful lawyer from Denver. Dressed in an elegant black pantsuit, high heels, and a red blouse, accented by diamond earrings and a gold necklace, she crossed her arms as her sharp gaze flickered back and forth between Jeremiah and Dale. She looked like a smaller, fancier version of Jeremiah. It was eerie.

"Huh. Well, this is unexpected and awkward, although it doesn't surprise me all that much. Sorry for the interruption," she said to Dale, giving him a small wave. "Hi, I'm Jeremiah's sister, Jenna. And you are?"

Dale pulled his shirt on before answering her. "Dale Harris. Nice to meet you, Jenna."

He stuck out his hand to her, which she shook, while Jeremiah stood there mute, his eyes still wide and his jaw nearly down to his knees. The blood had drained from his face, and he swayed on his feet, so Dale took a step closer to him in case the poor guy decided to faint.

"Nice to meet you too, Dale Harris. Why don't you two finish getting dressed or whatever?" she gestured toward Jeremiah, who still hadn't found his shirt and had his hands splayed across his chest and abs as if trying to hide every inch of his exposed skin. "In the meantime, I'm going to get a drink. I assume Daddy's liquor cabinet is unlocked and fully stocked as always?"

Jenna pivoted toward the hallway leading to the home office. Apparently, their father had always kept the beautiful wood and glass cabinet in there, and after the renovation, Jeremiah had returned it to its rightful place.

Clearly stunned that his sister wasn't freaking out about catching him half naked, cuddling on the couch with another man, Jeremiah's voice cracked when he stammered, "Um . . . s-stocked, yes. Unlocked . . . um, uh . . . no. With my . . . uh, goddaughter around, I thought it best to keep it . . . um, locked up. The key is —is right where it always is. Right there."

She glanced over her shoulder at them as Dale found Jeremiah's T-shirt under a throw pillow at the far end of the couch and handed it to him. "Your goddaughter? You only have one, right? Your new neighbors' daughter who was born last fall? Is she already an alcoholic, and you need to lock up the booze?"

Dale barked out a laugh while Jeremiah rolled his eyes and pulled on his shirt. Her teasing seemed to have eased the tension and astonishment a little, and he glared at her. "Same old brat. I just figured I'd get into the habit of locking it up for when she gets older. Now, go fetch three glasses and a bottle of whiskey. Then you can tell me what on God's green earth you're doing here."

"Oh, that's easy," she said with a nonchalant hand wave. "My career and life in Denver are over, and I'm moving back to the Rock."

Jeremiah's jaw nearly hit the floor again as she disappeared down the hall.

Well, okay then.

Dale closed the distance between him and Jeremiah and gently grabbed the man's chin to get his attention. "Listen, Jay, your sister obviously needs you. I'll head home." He kissed Jeremiah, not caring if Jenna saw them since it was evident she'd already figured out her brother was gay—something that seemed to have blown the man away. The siblings had a few things to discuss, and it was probably best that Dale wasn't around. He was sure they both had a lot of personal baggage to unpack, he was sure.

"Call me tomorrow." He phrased it as an order and not a request.

"O-okay," Jeremiah responded, but his focus returned to his sister as she wandered back into the great room with a full bottle of whiskey and three lowball glasses.

Jenna frowned at Dale as he pulled on his boots. "You're not leaving on my account, are you? Please feel free to stay. Obviously, I wasn't expected. No need for your evening with Jeremiah to be ruined because I'm insensitive and showed up unannounced."

He waved her off. "No worries, I've got things to take care of. He's all yours for the night. It was nice meetin' you. I'll probably see you again soon." He gave Jeremiah a quick peck on the lips. "Night, babe."

"N-night." Jeremiah stuttered, his eyes flittering back to Jenna. Smiling, Dale waved at them both and headed home.

Chapter Sixteen

Jeremiah wasn't sure what he was most stunned about—the fact his sister was actually there, that she wasn't surprised to find him in a compromising position with another man, or that she was moving home to the Rock.

She set the low-balls on the cocktail table and kicked off her heels before pouring three fingers of whiskey into two of the glasses. Picking up one, she downed her portion of the amber liquid like it was water and then filled the glass to the halfway point again.

Okay, well, they do call whiskey the water of life.

Running his hands through his hair, Jeremiah stared at her. "What the hell are you doing here, Jenna? And what the hell do you mean your career and life in Denver are over?"

She finished off the second glass almost as fast as

the first one, then shrugged. "As I said, I'm moving back to the Rock and figured I'd stay with my big brother until I find a place."

Before she could fill the lowball up for a third time, he took it and the bottle from her and set them on the table. He stepped closer and cupped her narrow shoulders. "What's going on, sweet pea? This isn't like you."

As soon as his old nickname for her cleared his lips, her calm, cool, and collected demeanor crumbled before his eyes. She burst out crying and threw herself into his arms. As he embraced her, Jeremiah didn't have a clue what'd happened, but he did know one thing—he had his sister's back no matter what.

Tonight, he'd let her cry. Tomorrow, he'd find out who he had to track down and kill.

The next morning, after a quick shower, Jeremiah sent Anthony a text message that he was taking a couple of hours off because his sister had arrived late last night unexpectedly. And wasn't that an understatement. After her crying bout, they'd talked more about Dale than anything else. Every time Jeremiah had tried to steer the conversation toward why she was now unemployed and moving back home, she changed the subject. Knowing his sister well, he'd let it go for the rest of the night with the full intention of forcing the topic this morning.

Jenna had worked hard to leave behind the small-town life Jeremiah loved so much. After graduating summa cum laude from the University of Colorado, she'd then enrolled in their law school and finished with top honors there as well. Upon graduation, she'd been hired by Waters, Byron & Cornell, a prestigious firm in the heart of Denver, and had quickly climbed the ranks with her intelligence and aggressive drive. Her goal had been to become a partner, and the last Jeremiah had heard, she'd been on a short list for junior partner. So, whatever had caused her to give it all up to return to the Rock had to be unexpected and significant, and he was determined to get it out of her over breakfast.

He'd just finished brewing a pot of coffee and cooking some bacon and was about to pour pancake batter onto a griddle when Jenna shuffled into the room, looking much different than she had the night before. Gone were the stylish clothes, hair, makeup, and jewelry. In their place were well-worn sweatpants, a U of C T-shirt that'd been washed so many times it was now faded and super soft, and a pair of fuzzy slippers. Her face had been scrubbed clean, and her thick, auburn locks were pulled up into a ponytail, making her look far younger than her thirty-six years.

She made a beeline for the coffee. "Ugh, please tell me that's fresh and you have hazelnut creamer."

"Of course, I have it. You're not the only one in this family who craves sweet caffeine."

"Yeah, well, the first thing I'm unpacking when my stuff gets here is my espresso maker."

He set the pitcher of batter down and turned toward Jenna, his brow furrowing. "You've already packed up your place? This is a done deal?"

"Mm-hmm." That was the only response she gave him while preparing her coffee.

He let her have a few moments of silence until after her first sip of what she often called "the nectar of the gods."

Keeping one eye on the griddle, he said, "All right. Enough of this. What the fuck happened, why did you lose your job, and why did you arrange to move back here without telling anyone? Wait a minute. Did you sell your condo?"

Taking a seat at the island, she shook her head and reached for a piece of bacon on the plate he'd set nearby. "Not yet, but it's on the market, and I'm hoping it'll go quickly. It should, since that area is in high demand right now. Perfect timing."

"Perfect timing for what? Damn it, Jenna—"

She held up a hand, cutting him off. "Hold your horses, big brother, and flip the pancakes. You know I hate burned ones."

Scowling, he grabbed the spatula and turned the golden circles over, glad to see he hadn't ruined them. "If you're gonna boss me around, I'll give it right back to you. Get the syrup and butter out, please."

Jenna snorted and climbed off the stool. "Well, since you said please . . ."

A few minutes later, they were sitting at the island, digging into their breakfast. Jeremiah used his fork to point at his sister. "All right, enough stalling, sweet pea. Tell me what the hell is going on."

Swallowing a mouthful of pancakes, she wiped her lips with a napkin, then reached for her coffee.

"Where to start?" she mumbled. Jeremiah didn't bother answering the rhetorical question and waited for her to continue. "About six months ago, I started dating this guy, Brett Carney. I think I mentioned him to you once or twice."

He nodded, trying to recall what Jenna had told him about the man. "You met him at some art gallery or something, right?"

"Uh-huh. The artist was the wife of one of the firm's bigger clients, so I went to her debut show to make an impression on the client and the partners. I figured I could make a few connections while I was there too. Stuff like that is done all the time when you're trying to climb the corporate ladder."

"Makes sense." He sipped his coffee, washing down the last of his breakfast.

"Exactly. Anyway, I was rubbing elbows and was introduced to Brett. He was good-looking, polished, intelligent, and charming—right up my alley. He called me the next day, and we started dating. He said he worked for an investment company—"

"He *said* he did? Does that mean he didn't?"

She sighed. "Oh, he works for them, just not in the way he led me to believe. You know that big case I've been working on with one of the partners for the past eight months?"

"Of course—it's a lawsuit, right? You said if your firm won, it would bring in huge recognition and business for Waiters, Myron, and Corndog, and possibly that promotion you wanted." Ever since she'd started with the company, Jeremiah had intentionally screwed up the owners' names, and as usual, Jenna rolled her eyes at him.

"Yeah, well, turns out Brett's position in the investment company was a cover for the fact he was hired to find out everything WBC had against the defendants in the case." Her nostrils flared, and there was a tightness around her eyes. "I'll give you one guess on how he decided to do just that."

"Oh, fuck, Jen. What'd he do?"

"I brought home my laptop with all my notes every night, so I could access everything on the firm's mainframe and do some more work. Apparently, when he'd stay over, Brett would wait until I fell asleep and then hack into my computer. He saw everything we had on the company we were going after. Every! Fucking! Thing! That bastard used me, and here I thought I'd finally found a great guy. Fucking asshole."

Jeremiah reached over and set a comforting hand on her arm. "How'd you find out?"

"One night, I woke up and went looking for him. He didn't hear me until it was too late, and I saw what he was doing. I threatened to bash his head in with my trusty baseball bat before I called the cops." Her eyes welled up. "After he . . . he fucking thanked me for the terrific sex because that'd apparently been a bonus of the job, and then he walked out."

She ignored Jeremiah's angry growl. "First thing in the morning, I reported what happened to Ron Schaffer, the attorney in charge of the case. Needless to say, he had a conniption. They had the IT guys go through my laptop and were able to trace everything Brett accessed, which was our entire case. It took all of ten minutes for the partners to vote to fire me, and I'm sure nine of those were spent cursing me out."

"Fuck. When did this all happen? Why didn't you call me?"

"Last Thursday. I didn't want to talk about it before now because I was bouncing back and forth between being in shock, wanting to commit homicide, and crying my eyes out over multiple pints of Häagen-Dazs. So, I spent the past week packing, arranging for movers, and getting a realtor."

He stood and pulled her to her feet and into his arms. "I'm so sorry, sis. Do you have an address for this asshole, so I can go kill him? We'll feed his body to Marty Olsen's pigs."

She snorted against his chest. "I wouldn't do that to the pigs—they'd probably get indigestion."

"It'd be worth it." After a final squeeze, he stepped back. "But why move back here? Don't get me wrong, I'd love to have you living in the Rock again, but there's got to be plenty of firms in Denver that would snatch you right up."

A miserable sigh escaped her. "Not after word gets out about how badly I screwed up. And trust me, it's probably the talk of every big firm down there right now. So, I decided to pack up and move back here. I've got enough in my savings to relax for a bit and figure out my next move. I'll let the hubbub die down and then start looking at New York, California, Chicago, and maybe Dallas. No matter what, I'll have to start from the bottom up again."

"What about starting your own practice here? I know it's not the metropolis you've grown accustomed to, but you still have friends here . . . and me. I miss you somethin' awful, Jenna."

Before she could answer him, there was a knock at the back door, and it swung open. "Hey, Jeremiah, I—"

Anthony stopped short when he noticed the boss wasn't alone. His eyes bulged a little as his gaze roamed Jenna's body from head to toe and back up again, and a smile spread across his face. Jeremiah wasn't surprised since his sister had garnered that kind of appreciative reaction from the opposite sex since high school. If he hadn't gotten used to it over the years and didn't know she could kick a guy's ass if need be, he might've had the urge to deck his foreman. That and he was one of the nicest guys Jeremiah had ever met, so he ignored the man's perusal.

As it was, it took a moment for Jeremiah to remember the two had never met before. Anthony had been working at the JP for about two-and-a-half years, and the only other time Jenna had been to the ranch for a visit had been when the foreman's uncle had been in his final stages of terminal cancer. Sadly, it'd advanced faster than the doctors had predicted. Jeremiah had given Anthony a month off to spend some time with his uncle and to help his aunt with the funeral and aftermath. The few other times Jeremiah had seen his sister over the past thirty months or so had either been in Denver or down in Arizona while visiting their parents. She'd missed the last few New Year's Eve parties at the ranch.

"Uh, Anthony, this is my sister. Jenna, this is my foreman, Anthony Garner."

The other man quickly removed his hat and stuck out his hand. "Pleasure to meet you. I've heard a lot about you from Jeremiah. He's awfully proud of you."

The smile that'd graced Jenna's face briefly while she shook Anthony's hand quickly disappeared with his last words. "Um, thank you. The same could be said for you—he thinks very highly of you." She glanced at Jeremiah. "Thanks for breakfast. I'm going to hop into the shower, and then I've got a lot of things I need to do today. We'll talk more later, and I'll even cook dinner tonight, okay?"

"Sure. Let me know if you need me for anything."

"I will." She gave Anthony a little wave, her usual vivaciousness missing from her countenance and attitude. "Bye. It was nice to meet you finally."

"Same here." The man didn't say another word as he watched Jenna leave the kitchen. When Jeremiah cleared his throat, Anthony shook his head. "Uh, sorry. She's even prettier than her pictures."

"You don't say." When he got no response, he raised an eyebrow. "Did you need something, or are we going to stand here and stare at each other all day while you fantasize about what my sister looks like naked?"

A blush accompanied the man's chagrined expression. "Sorry . . . uh . . . oh! Birdie threw a shoe, and Jackson's out of town for the week. Who do you want me to call?"

He ran a hand through his hair. Bye Bye Birdie was one of Jeremiah's favorite horses, and she was very particular about who she let shoe her. Jackson Coyne was a local farrier who had won her trust, and she wouldn't be happy he wasn't available. "Crap. A while back, he gave me the name of a woman who he recommended if he wasn't around. I have her card in my office and will give her a call. Why don't you check and see if any of the other horses need attention while I find out when she can come?"

"You got it." With a last not-so-subtle peek toward the hallway where Jenna had disappeared, Anthony slapped his hat on his head and left the way he'd come in.

Sighing, Jeremiah began to clean up from breakfast. It looked like it was going to be one of those days, and all he wanted to do was call Dale and ask the man to take him away from it all, if only for a few hours. Yup, he had it bad.

Chapter Seventeen

Two days later, Jeremiah hopped in his truck and drove to town. He had some errands to run, and Anthony had given him a list of stuff they needed from the feed and supply store. Given that he hadn't seen Dale since Jenna had shown up, Jeremiah was hoping for some privacy on the drive to call his boyfriend.

Boyfriend?

He still felt a little juvenile calling Dale that, but he didn't think they were at the partner stage yet. Though he was sure they would be if he'd just grow a pair and come out already. Willow had texted him earlier and said she'd overheard someone at the Pack and Sack talking about him and Dale. Apparently, there were whispered rumors and speculation about the two men spending a lot of time together alone, at both their homes, and disappearing for hours when they've gone out for drives with each other.

Unfortunately, there were only a few people that could've figured things out and started telling others— Willow and Nathan, their ranch hand, Shane Rivers, and Jeremiah's six employees. The JP was too far from town, and the Skyview Ranch was its closest neighbor, so no one else would've noticed or been able to track comings and goings easily enough to realize something was up. He'd trusted Willow and Nathan with his secret for a long time and knew they would never tell anyone without his permission or knowledge. And while he'd never told Anthony he was gay, even if the foreman had put two and two together, Jeremiah doubted he was the source of the rumors. That left six hands between the two ranches—three of which had worked at the JP for at least the past five years. Part of Jeremiah was in a twisted and convoluted knot about coming out, wanting to run and hide. Meanwhile, the other part of him wanted to rip the Band-Aid off, so he could finally be free to love who he wanted.

Deciding to finish his errands first, he'd call Dale on the way back to the ranch. It would motivate him to get in and out of Ducky's and not allow himself to get caught up in conversation.

The familiar drive passed quickly as sweet and sexy thoughts of Dale filled his head, and before he knew it, he pulled into the lot at Ducky's Feed and Supply. The sun had disappeared behind heavy gray clouds that were rolling in, and the wind had picked up, blowing up dust. A storm front that'd been forecast was earlier than expected. Hopefully, he could finish his errands and return home before it hit. They could definitely use the rain.

After double-checking he had his wallet, cell phone, keys, and shopping list, he climbed out of his truck, adjusted his hat, and strode inside.

He headed right for the desk where customers could place large orders and quickly requested an order for the fence posts and wire he needed, along with some lumber and other items. His workshop was getting a little low on materials, and like all ranches, fixin' fuckin' fence was a never-ending struggle.

"Will that be everythin' for you today, Jeremiah?" the owner, Dave "Ducky" Swann, asked.

He consulted the list one more time. "Yup, it looks like that should do it. When can it be delivered?"

"Day after tomorrow. We have another big order to fill first, and we'll have to wait for our next truck to come in before we can fill yours. Is that all right?"

"Sure, no problem."

Jeremiah handed over his credit card and waited while the man processed his payment. As he made a mental note to keep the receipt and add the total to that month's expenses in his accounting book, a voice from behind him jerked him out of his thoughts.

"Yeah, I hear Jeremiah likes to receive. Know what I mean, Carl?"

Nasty guffaws accompanied the not-so-vague slur. "Sure do. Urban here takes it up the ass—fucking queer."

Whipping around, Jeremiah glared at the men—Carl Skinner and Ken Larson, two of the biggest loudmouths and bullies around. They were about five or six years younger than Jeremiah, and like him, they'd lived in the Rock their entire lives. Anger and humiliation warred within him, making him hesitate in his response, which was the worst thing he could have done.

"Look at that! He can't even say nothin'!" Skinner cackled, his yellow teeth flecked with pieces of chewing tobacco and his unkempt beard speckled with brown stains from spitting the juice.

Shaking his head, Jeremiah snatched his credit card back from Ducky, who silently glared at the two assholes, and shoved past them toward the door. Their bawdy laughter followed him, and his face burned red-hot with shame. Why didn't he say anything? His feelings for Dale were deepening by the day, and he couldn't open his stupid mouth to defend his lover or himself? To defend what was developing between them?

"Hey! I wasn't done talking to you, Urban!"

Skinner and Larson had followed him out of the store, but it was the former who'd shouted at him. For some unknown reason, Jeremiah jerked to a halt. Why he was giving in to the bigoted asshole, he didn't know.

He whirled around and snapped, "What?"

"I said I wasn't done talkin' to you." Skinner took several steps toward him, his cocky grin making his face even uglier. "You a fucking *faggot*? Is what people been sayin' true? You love taking it up the ass and sucking cock?"

The insults sliced through him like a knife. Agony followed in their wake.

"No, I'm not fucking gay. Whoever told you that was lying, so just back the fuck off," Jeremiah snarled, wanting nothing more than to plant his fist in this bastard's face. But he couldn't. His gut tightened, and he immediately regretted his words, wishing a hole would open under his feet and swallow him. The first opportunity to tell the world he was falling in love with Dale Harris, and he'd balked. He should have said, "Yes, I'm a queer! I like dick—no, I LOVE dick! And I won't be cowed and made to feel like less because of it!"

But he said none of those things, even as his heart screamed them.

A slamming door caught his attention. Turning his head, he saw Dale glaring out at him from the driver's window of his truck before throwing it in gear. His tires squealed and smoked as he peeled out of the parking lot like the hounds of hell were on his bumper.

Thunder rumbled in the distance, adding to the foreboding Jeremiah felt. The sky was growing even darker while flashes of lightning streaked across the heavens as if the universe was pissed off at his behavior too.

Jeremiah didn't see Skinner's laughing face or hear the vile words the bastard continued to spew. The only thing that filled his mind and broke his heart was Dale's enraged and devastated face.

Racing to his truck, he didn't pause to think how it would look as he jumped in and tore out after Dale. His own shrieking tires added to the burned rubber smell hanging thick in the air. Jeremiah's heart beat a frantic tattoo in his chest, and bile seared the back of his throat. Without a doubt, the entire rumor mill would have confirmation he was gay within the next half hour, and he honestly didn't give a shit. The only thing he cared about was fixing the mess he'd created with a few careless words thrown out to save face in front of a couple of two-bit bullies.

He stomped his foot on the gas and roared after Dale. The drive flew by, passing in a blur, while his mind played a never-ending loop of regret and apologies in between self-flagellation. Strong gusts of wind shook the truck as the sky could no longer hold back the rain. At first, it was only a few drops slapping on the windshield, but then it quickly intensified. His wipers struggled to keep up with the downpour.

He turned onto Willow's drive, following the tire tracks Dale had left in the mud in his wake. The truck skipped to a stop in the loose gravel of the parking area next to the other man's pickup. In a panic, Jeremiah leaped from the vehicle, not bothering to turn it off or even close the door. He needed to get to Dale. To explain and beg forgiveness—whatever it took. He couldn't allow this to end them—not when he was falling in love for the first time in his life.

Rain pelted down in sheets hard enough to sting his face as he made a mad dash toward the barn. The lightning was closer now, stabbing through the humid air and illuminating the sky like a strobe lamp. The thunder was so loud that he could feel it vibrating the earth under his boots as he ran through puddles that had already formed. He was soaked to his skin in seconds but paid it no mind.

"Dale!" he shouted, sprinting through the open door of the barn, ignoring the warning barks of Johnny and June. Once they realized who he was, they would calm down.

The alpacas were huddled under covered shelters in their corral, while the goats and dogs were holed up in the barn, but there was no sign of Dale. Exiting again and rounding the corner of the building, he ran toward Dale's RV and then pounded his fist on the door, shaking the whole vehicle.

The door flew open, almost hitting him in the face. He faltered back several steps as Dale's furious face greeted him. "What?" Spittle shot from his mouth with the spat word.

"Dale, please. What you heard . . ." Jeremiah trailed off. The downpour battered his body as the weight of his feelings and what he needed to say to fix things crushed his shoulders. Fear like he'd never known cloyed at him, smothering him. At that moment, he wasn't afraid of what anyone said about him but that he could lose this man—this good, decent, beautiful man. That he may have lost him already.

He stammered, trying to get the words out, but they wouldn't come. A bolt of lightning streaked across the sky, and the crack that followed was near deafening. Jeremiah nearly jumped out of his skin as the air sizzled around them, but he kept his eyes on Dale. The storm raging overhead had nothing on what he saw in the other man's eyes.

"What *I heard*?" Dale shouted over the pounding rain and roaring thunder. "What? You mean, you denying us? Denying me? I was a fuckin' fool to ever get involved with a closet case! One redneck asshole confronts you, and you just let him walk all over you and everything we've been building! I've been patient and understanding, but that ends here, Jeremiah! I'm done being your dirty little secret!"

Dale's cheeks were flushed red with fury, sweat dotting his brow as his shirt and jeans darkened with the rain the wind was blowing through the door. His mouth was set in a grim line while anguish radiated out from his whiskey eyes.

Jeremiah's stomach clenched. He'd done that. He was the cause of Dale's pain, and the thought had his heart splintering.

He took a tentative step closer, water streaming off the brim of his hat. "Dale, I'm so sorry. He caught me off guard, and I-I didn't know what to say. No one . . . no one has ever called me a faggot before. I . . . God, it hurt. But I'd go back and take that hurt a hundred times over if it meant not doing this to you, to us." Hanging his head, he swallowed the burn of tears. "Dale, please."

"Jeremiah, no. I can't. I *can't*! My heart can't take this again!" His voice cracking and his eyes swimming with tears almost had Jeremiah falling to his knees. "I'm sorry you were spoken to that way, but it's part of being out. Yes, it sucks. Yes, it's humiliating. But I refuse to let anyone tell me who I have to love, and if it doesn't conform to their ideals and twisted morals, have them tell me I have to hide who I really am because it offends them. Fuck that. No one writes *my life, my happy ending,* but *me*!"

He hitched a thumb toward his own chest."Does shit like that happen? Yeah, absolutely, but I need to have confidence that when it does, you can handle it. It's not even so much that you denied being gay. I wouldn't want anyone to be forced to come out because some vulgar asshole announced it to the world like it was something disgusting and depraved. Your verbal reaction I can understand—you were caught off guard. But it was that you looked and sounded so *ashamed*! Ashamed of me! Ashamed of what we have together! Loving me is *not* wrong! I'm not something to be ashamed of! And neither are you!" He swallowed hard. "One day, I hope you can accept that, but I'm not waiting around anymore to find out."

The door slamming and then locking were the only sounds Jeremiah could hear before tears began to race down his cheeks, mingling with raindrops, and a sob lodged itself in his throat. Gasping, he turned away, dragging his feet back to his truck with his head down. He felt like he'd just been shot in the chest, his heart fracturing from the trauma. Only that would've been less painful.

Dale's right . . . I don't deserve him.

Gulping for air, fighting back screams of agony, Jeremiah climbed into his truck, his drenched clothes making it difficult. The rain hammering on the roof did little to drown out his thoughts of self-recrimination. He didn't look back at the RV. Dale had made things more than clear—Jeremiah had royally fucked up, and there was nothing left for him here.

Slamming the driver's door shut, he threw the truck into gear and drove back to his ranch in total silence, aside from his own choked sobs of pain and gasps of regret he tried to stifle. He parked in his usual spot before he knew it, realizing he'd made the short drive home totally on auto-pilot. As he trod toward the house, it was all he could do to keep himself at a walk and not run for his room like a teenage girl after her first breakup. The storm raging outside matched how he felt within—volatile and chaotic.

Anthony stood at the barn door, calling out and waving to get his attention, but Jeremiah ignored him. He had to get inside, needing privacy before he broke down for all to see. His soul screamed as pressure built in his chest, and if he didn't release some of it, he'd explode. Flinging the front door shut, he ran up the stairs, two at a time, leaving small, muddy puddles in his wake as he hurried to the sanctuary of his bedroom. Jenna was nowhere to be seen, a fact for which he was grateful.

He shut his bedroom door, locking it behind him. He stripped his wet things off—clothes, boots, and hat —and everything landed on the floor in a sopping pile. He ached, bone-deep—regret, embarrassment, unrelenting rage, all battling within him for release.

Entering the en suite bath, he avoided looking at himself in the mirror, turned on the shower, and stepped under the spray without letting the water warm up. The extra-large stall was easily big enough for two people, and he'd been fantasizing for weeks about having Dale in there with him. Now, that dream didn't seem like it would ever happen.

It's over . . .

Quaking under the cold spray, he fell to his knees, collapsing under the weight of his emotions. The valve he'd held tightly shut since he'd arrived back at the ranch, capping his sobs, let go. Screaming, he smacked his hands against the tile floor of the shower over and over until his palms were stinging and sore. Tears mixed with the water running down his face. Pulling at his hair, he bowed over his knees, putting his forehead to the floor and weeping his heart out. A piece of himself had been ripped out today, and the empty space left behind was a throbbing, bleeding wound. A Dale-sized chunk of his heart was gone.

Until then, he hadn't known he'd fallen in love with Dale. No longer in progress—it was a done deal and irreversible. It was a kind of soul-deep love they wrote songs and poetry about. The type that was etched in the stars and existed through time itself. And he'd fucked it up. Maybe beyond repair. He didn't know.

Curling into a ball, he stayed that way, sobs racking his body until his arms and legs shook uncontrollably under the water pelting him. The temperature had warmed up, but it couldn't penetrate his skin to his frozen soul. He stayed there until completely drained.

Finally climbing out of the shower, he didn't even bother drying off, shuffling, zombie-like, to his bed, where he buried himself under the comforter, face first, naked, shivering, and completely lost.

Chapter Eighteen

Jeremiah awakened the next morning with a pounding headache, and his eyes felt like he'd crossed a desert in the middle of a sandstorm without protection.

Crying yourself to sleep will do that to you, jackass.

Groaning, he rolled over and sat up on the edge of the bed. Feet flat on the floor, he set his elbows on his knees and his aching head in his hands. Based on the feel, his hair was sticking up all over the damn place, as if he'd put his finger in a live socket.

Going to bed with wet hair will do that to you, too, jackass.

His words of denial from yesterday slammed into him, a freight train of regret barreling down the tracks of his mind, derailing, and exploding in a fireball. He'd won the championship medal for fuck-ups of the decade.

"Crap." Clearing his dry, scratchy throat, he glanced at the clock. It was almost nine a.m., hours past when he was normally up, in the barn, and well into the workday. He didn't take sick days, ever—the only exception was when he'd had a stomach flu a few years ago and was afraid to pass it on to his employees. Well, that and the fact he hadn't been able to stay out of the bathroom and stop kissing the porcelain god. Those had been the worst two days of his life—until now.

He was honestly surprised Anthony hadn't shown up at his door yet, checking to make sure he was okay. Even Jenna was MIA.

Staggering to the bathroom, he caught sight of his naked self in the mirror and winced. There were dark, baggy circles under his bloodshot eyes, his hair was, as suspected, all over the place, and his already pale skin had a morbid gray tint to it. In effect, he looked like death warmed over. A whiff of the odor coming from his pits made him amend that, he looked and *smelled* like death warmed over. The cold shower last night hadn't included soap, just tears and heartache, and most of the water had merely struck his back before rolling to the tiled floor and down the drain.

Flipping on the shower to hot this time, he stepped in and washed quickly but didn't bother to shave the stubble from his face. His motivation only went so far today. After drying off, he brushed his teeth and dressed in an old pair of jeans and a ratty, black T-shirt he hadn't worn in ages—it fit his mood, though.

The smell of coffee hit him full in the face as he descended the stairs, but the sight that greeted him in the kitchen had him stopping in his tracks.

Jenna and Willow were seated at the breakfast table together, coffee mugs clutched in their hands. In near unison, they turned their heads and glared at him as if he'd kicked a dog in their presence. It creeped him out and made his balls shrivel. While they looked nothing alike, he got some serious *Shining*-twins vibes from them. Nothing good was about to happen.

While he should've been man enough to stand up for himself and Dale yesterday, he knew better than to argue with these two women. It was best if he followed orders and took whatever they were about to dole out. And he was certain they were about to lay into him.

"Jeremiah, sit." Willow pointed at the empty seat, and yup, that was her don't-fuck-with-me voice.

He sat, laced his fingers together, and then released them. Fiddled with a coffee spoon resting on a napkin. Glanced at both women and turned away.

"Stop fidgeting. Consider this your intervention," Jenna said, her tone just as stern as Willow's and brooking no argument from him.

Sighing, he leaned back in the chair, crossing his arms over his chest. "Can I at least have coffee first?"

"I guess," Willow snapped, but then she pushed her own mug toward him. "Here. Now, you're going to sit there like a ginger lump, keep your mouth shut, and listen. Got it?"

"Yes, ma'am," he replied in the only way he could think of that wouldn't result in the demons of hell raining down on him. He knew he wouldn't like whatever this was, but the alternative of what Willow and Jenna could put him through wasn't an option.

Raising the mug to his lips, he took a long drink, needing the caffeine before he had a pound of flesh stripped from him by the two women who meant the world to him.

"You, my favorite brother," Jenna started, and he snorted at the old joke—he was her *only* brother. Frowning, she raised her eyebrows, and he snapped his mouth closed. "*You* are an idiot."

"Thanks for that vote of confidence," he mumbled.

Willow patted his hand. "This comes from a place of love, honey, so deal with it."

He snorted again, not believing this was fuckin' happening right then. *An intervention? Seriously?*

"Well then, go right ahead—intervene, butt into my business, put your two cents in, or whatever." He waved his hand dismissively.

"You're gay," his sister announced with no fanfare as if he wasn't already aware of that fact. "And we love you. You being gay has zero bearing on how we feel about you." She glared at him and pointed at his face. "Also, fuck you very much for never trusting me enough to tell me. Not that I didn't know. Do you honestly think I didn't notice you stealing my

Cosmopolitan magazines and romance books years ago?"

Jeremiah flushed at the memory and stared at the table, unable to meet her eyes as humiliation rushed through him like a raging river. "I was afraid to tell anyone," he mumbled.

Reaching over, Jenna took his hand, and sympathy replaced the annoyance in her voice. "I know you were . . . and you still are. But you don't need to be. If you don't get a handle on it, you'll lose the best thing that's ever happened to you. I've never seen you like this before." She paused, then asked, "You love him, don't you?"

"I—" He caught himself, unsure if the first time he confessed his love for Dale should be to these two women and not the man himself.

"It's okay," Willow assured him. "We know you do. But the fact of the matter is, you don't have much time."

"What are you talking about?" Jeremiah's stomach clenched at the worry in her voice, the coffee turning sour.

She sighed heavily and glanced at Jenna before returning her gaze to him. "Dale came to me this morning. He told me what happened yesterday—not that I hadn't already heard about it. He gave his notice. He'll be leaving as soon as I can hire a replacement."

Jeremiah's heart stopped, and his lungs seized.

No. No. It can't be. He wouldn't . . .

Well, why wouldn't he, you asshole? You haven't given him a reason to stay, have you?

He stood so fast that his chair fell over with a crash, and he didn't have a single fuck to give. "I have . . . to . . . Dale," he stuttered, his heart racing as he hurried for the front door.

Quick footsteps followed him, and a small hand jerked him to a halt by his bicep. Willow moved between him and the door. "He's not there."

It's too late? Oh, God, no!

"Where is he then?" Jeremiah snarled like a cornered animal.

"He asked if Nathan and I could take care of the chores today so he could have time off. I don't know where he went."

Frantically searching his pockets, he felt for his cell phone and came up empty. Spinning around, he stopped dead in his tracks when he saw Jenna waving the device in the air. He snatched it from her without an apology and pulled up Dale's contact, hitting the button to call him. It rang once and went straight to voice mail. Hanging up, he called again and got the same response.

Fuck!

When the beep sounded in his ear, he flat-out begged, ignoring the fact Jenna and Willow were witnessing him falling apart. "Dale, please, call me. I need . . . we . . . I need to see you, baby. Please. I'm sorry. I'm so sorry." Thoughts of what he should say dried up, and he ended the call as his eyes stung. Shoving the phone into his back pocket, he sniffled, praying the impending tears wouldn't fall. After a few moments, he had his emotions under as much control as he could muster and lifted his gaze to Willow and Jenna.

His sister set a comforting hand on his arm. "We've got your back. He'll call—I know he will. Until then, you have work to do. I told Anthony you weren't feeling well and that you might be out later."

"Thanks . . . that goes for both of you." Tears burned his eyes again, but this time, they were from gratitude, not fear and regret. Willow and Jenna were right. The people that really mattered in his life loved him and just wanted him to be happy, no matter who that happiness was with or what it looked like. Their love and acceptance gave him the strength to finally go after what he wanted. *Whom* he wanted. And that was Dale Harris, the sexy retired Marine who'd manage to capture Jeremiah's heart. Now he just needed to track the stubborn man down so he could tell him that.

* * *

Dale listened to Jeremiah's voicemail for the third time in a row. It was almost noon, and he sat in his truck outside the Spur & Bull, the only decent bar in Antelope Rock, thinking about going in and getting loaded. He hadn't turned to booze to numb his emotions since the last time he'd gotten his heart broken. He knew the alcohol wouldn't help for long, but it would dull the pain for now.

Willow had knocked on his RV door early that morning. She'd seen his and Jeremiah's shouting match yesterday and had figured out the reason for it after hearing about the incident in town from the Rock's rumor mill. Thankfully, she'd waited. He'd invited her in and told her everything from his point of view, spilling his guts all over the tiny kitchen. He'd only managed to keep from bawling by the skin of his teeth. Jeremiah, as far as he was concerned, didn't deserve his tears right then. Maybe not ever.

There was a gaping hole in Dale's chest where his heart used to be. He mourned the loss of them, the loss of what could've been, and a blissful future he'd only glimpsed a fraction of. The possibility of forever had been spread out before them, and now . . . all he could see was an empty road and a solitary existence.

His cell phone vibrated in his hand. Glancing at the screen, he saw "Jay" and a picture of the two of them, their faces squished together with their hats askew and giant grins. He snarled, remembering the day they'd taken the selfie. Their happiness had been palatable, and if he thought about it too hard, he could still taste the peanut butter and strawberry jelly on Jeremiah's lips from the sandwiches they'd shared that day. Jeremiah had apologized for the simple lunch, explaining that he needed to go grocery shopping. Dale hadn't cared, though, as he'd licked the nutty flavor and sweet preserves from Jeremiah's mouth before following the line of his jaw, down his throat, then farther, showing his cowboy just how much he loved the taste of him.

His phone beeped with another voice message—this one he refused to listen to. Instead, he tossed the phone into the glove box, climbed out of the truck, and strode toward the bar. He hoped there was a dark corner he could hide in and drown his heartache. Hopefully, it was too early for any assholes to bother with him. A bar fight would be the cherry on top of the fucked up sundae his life was today.

After a long day of back-breaking work, Jeremiah had hoped he'd be exhausted enough to fall into bed and pass out. No such luck. Instead, he found himself all alone on his porch, sitting in his favorite chair with his bare feet propped up on the stump he used as an ottoman. He didn't even have the will or strength to whittle, which had always relaxed him.

How sad is that?

Dale still hadn't returned his calls or text messages, and Jeremiah was worried that he'd screwed up so badly that he'd lost all chance of the sexy Marine being a part of his future. The one man he ever considered coming out for, at the first chance he got to declare it in public, he'd shut down and denied who he really was. It shouldn't make a fucking difference to Jeremiah if Skinner, Larsen, or anyone else had a problem with him being gay. If he was in love and happy, truly happy, for the first time in his life, no one else's opinion mattered. He shouldn't be miserable until the day he died just because who he loved offended someone else. Let *them* be miserable, not him, and certainly not Dale.

"Mind if I join you?" Nathan's voice startled him from his morose thoughts as the man climbed the steps to the porch. He'd obviously walked over from Skyview. In his mid-thirties, Nathan still had the bearings of the Army soldier he'd been until last year. Having grown up in a small town, he'd settled into the Rock with little trouble, and Jeremiah was happy to call him a friend.

"Sure." Gesturing to the loveseat, he held up a beer in question.

His neighbor sat down and nodded. "I never say no to free beer."

Laughing, Jeremiah popped the top and handed it over. "That's usually my line. I'm assuming your wife sent you, huh?"

"Nope. I took it upon myself to come over." Nathan accepted the beer and took a long pull from it. "Willow can be . . . well, intense, as I'm sure you've figured out since meeting her. I wanted to see if you're okay. I won't pretend to know what you're feeling, but I *can* imagine how I would feel if Willow and I were apart—not good at all, my friend."

"I'm not okay, not even a little, but thanks for asking. Not good is one way to put it, yes." Jeremiah found himself opening up to Nathan, explaining his feelings more clearly than he'd done with Willow and Jenna. The other man had a calming presence and didn't push or pressure him. It felt a little bit like talking to himself.

He told Nathan about his fears growing up, how he'd seen other gay men ostracized and put down just for being who they were. His terror of letting his parents down and ruining his legacy. He explained his struggle between the desire deep within his soul to be loved for who he was and his need to be successful for the ranch and his employees. He had anxiety over losing vendors and clients just because he'd fallen in love with another man. He didn't want to walk down a street amid whispered rumors, fingers being pointed, derogatory names being yelled, perverted accusations being thrown, and possibly having his life threatened because he wasn't "normal" per some people's perception.

When his words ran out, and his throat felt hoarse, he realized his beer was empty and his heart felt a little lighter.

"Well. You're fucked, huh?" Nathan broke in, and Jeremiah felt his face flush.

"Apparently not in the way I want to be." He

laughed at his own self-deprecation, and even Nathan barked in wry amusement. After a moment, Jeremiah continued. "Dale would've been my first, you know? Well, my first in—in *that* way. I'd never . . . um . . . you know, before. Other ways, yes, but not . . . " He fought down the embarrassment of admitting that he was half a virgin at the ripe old age of forty-two, almost forty-three. He wasn't sure Nathan fully understood him, but he didn't have the guts to say, "I've never been on the receiving end of penetrative anal sex."

Thankfully, he didn't need to. His friend held up a hand, stopping any further attempts at an explanation. "I get it—don't need to go into more detail than that, thank you very much—but it's not over yet. Don't give up. I know you're no quitter."

Standing, Nathan set his empty beer bottle on the small side table and then clapped Jeremiah's shoulder. "I have to get home to my ladies, but I want you to know you're a good man, Jeremiah Urban. Dale, or any other guy, would be lucky to have you. If the narrow-minded people in this town can't accept that, that's on them, not you. If they have anything to say about it, they can go through Willow and me first. And from what I hear, your sister will be standing right next to us. You've got people who care about you and have your back no matter what. Just remember that."

Swallowing thickly, Jeremiah nodded his thanks, unable to find the words to express how grateful he was for the couple's friendship.

After patting his shoulder again, his neighbor walked off the porch and across the field to the path leading back to his house and family.

Jeremiah sat there long after twilight descended, watching the stars flicker and twinkle all over the big Wyoming sky. A plan began to form in his mind as he stared into the heavens. Nathan was right—he was no quitter.

Chapter Nineteen

Jeremiah had found a new level of nerves as he stood outside Dale's RV. He'd already spoken to Willow and knew that Dale had finished with his morning chores. Yeah, he was ambushing the man and knew this had the potential to go horribly wrong. But Nathan's words came back to him.

You're no quitter.

Taking a deep breath and swallowing the urge to vomit on his boots, he knocked on Dale's door and waited. With his hat in his hands, he fiddled with the brim while repeating the words he needed to say in his head. He might've practiced them in the mirror earlier before walking over, but he wasn't going to admit to anything. He only had one shot at this, one chance to make things right with Dale, and he was determined not to blow it.

The door creaked slightly as it opened, and Jeremiah's heart beat faster, and his palms began to sweat. Then, the man he'd fallen for stood in front of and a few steps above him. Even scowling, he was beyond handsome. Jeremiah's breath hitched, and he swallowed hard. He wanted to reach out and touch Dale so badly, but he had to take this one step at a time.

"What do you want?" Dale demanded in a voice that was raspier than usual. It was then that Jeremiah noticed the man's bloodshot eyes and sallow skin. Dale looked like he'd been ridden hard and put away wet. Hope bloomed within Jeremiah—maybe he had more of a shot than he'd thought.

"H-hey," Jeremiah stammered before clearing his throat. "I almost didn't expect you to answer the door. But I'm so glad you did," he added in a rush before Dale could think to slam the door in his face. "I have a few things I need to say, and if you still want me gone after that, I'll go. I'm just asking that you please hear me out first."

Arching a brow, Dale didn't say anything, but after a moment, he nodded his agreement. Crossing his arms, he leaned against the door jamb, clearly not in the mood to invite Jeremiah inside.

Okay, we can do this right here. He's willing to listen, so get the fuck on with it!

"You were right—I'm letting my fear rule me. I have for a very long time, but I'm done. *Done* being afraid to let people see the real me. *Done* being ashamed of who I am and who I'm attracted to. *Done* being fucking alone while watching others be free to love whomever they want. I'm here to tell you that I'm going to come out. With you in my life or not, I'm going to do it. For me. Because I deserve to be happy. I'm so tired, Dale. So tired of hiding and pretending."

He took another deep breath. This next part would be even harder. He took a step closer, his gaze pinned on Dale's face. "I'm here to beg you to stay. Please, Dale, *please*. Don't leave the Rock. Don't leave Willow and Nathan. And please, baby," he swallowed past the lump in his throat, "don't leave *me*. We can work it out. I'll do whatever I have to, whatever you need me to do. Just . . . stay. Give me a chance to make this right.

"Having you in my life these past few months has made me the happiest I've ever been. I don't want to go back to the empty shell I was before. You make my life brighter and fuller. I've grown to really care about you, and it's not easy to say because it's never happened to me before, but I'm falling in love . . . I'm falling in love with *you*." His eyes welled up. "If you leave here, you'll take my heart with you when you go. If that's what you want, fine, you can have my heart—it's yours no matter where you are—but I sure hope that you'll consider staying here—with me."

Jeremiah had run out of words and felt as if he'd left a piece of his soul on the ground between them. Dale took a step backward, his eyes bulging and his jaw dropping. The man's reaction caused Jeremiah's stomach to bottom out, and he closed his eyes for a moment, trying to stem the flow of tears that threatened.

Have I just bared myself raw only to be rejected?

When he got his emotions under control as much as possible, he blinked and then focused on Dale's face. What he saw there had a sob lodging in his throat. Dale was smiling, his eyes bright—glimmering even—and his cheeks glowing. After a moment, though, he shook his head, schooling his features, and stepped down from the RV so they were on the same level. "Jay, baby, I'm not sure where to start. I don't know where you got the impression I'm leaving, but I have no intention of doing so. Antelope Rock is my home now, no matter what happens between us."

Jeremiah heaved a sigh of relief. "Thank fuck."

"Did you mean it?" Dale tucked his hands into the back pockets of his jeans and met Jeremiah's gaze head-on—no hesitation, no fear, just taking the bull by the horns, so to speak.

"I meant every word." Reaching forward cautiously, Jeremiah cupped Dale's scruffy jawline. "You've been stealing my heart, bit by bit, for a while now."

Dale grinned and chuckled. "Not that. I knew that, and the feeling is definitely mutual. What I meant was, are you really ready to come out?"

Straightening his spine, he gave the man a curt nod. "Yes. Today, in fact. With or without you. I'll stroll right through town waving a rainbow flag if I have to, but honestly, I'm hungry. Can I take you to lunch?"

Again, there was no hesitation, just acceptance and what seemed like joy in Dale's expression. "Absolutely, Cowboy. Is the Rock Diner okay? I have a hankering for a burger."

When Jeremiah agreed, Dale spun around, stepped up, leaned into the RV, and grabbed his hat, keys, wallet, and phone from the counter. Putting his hat on and adjusting it, he stepped down into Jeremiah's space, brushing his chest up against Jeremiah's, not giving him an inch. Tilting his head, Dale kissed him softly but didn't allow Jeremiah to deepen it into something more. Something he craved far more than a damn burger. He wanted to bask in this feeling inside him, to touch and grasp and taste every inch of Dale's body. He wanted his sighs of pleasure and his screams of ecstasy. He needed his laughter and joy, his sorrow and pain. Jeremiah needed all that Dale was, even while, in return, he gave himself over to the safekeeping of Dale's capable hands.

With a final peck on the lips, Dale put a few inches between their bodies. "That's all you get until after lunch, baby. If I do more than that right now, I'll drag you inside and take everything you have to give, and then I'll take some more."

Jeremiah gulped. "What's wrong with doing that?" His cock ached and throbbed in his jeans at the erotic images Dale's words conjured up.

"Nothing, but let's save that for later. I want you free, baby, really *free* to be with me, completely and in every way."

"O-okay."

Dale reached out and took his hand, and at that moment, Jeremiah fell the rest of the way. He wouldn't be alone. Dale was going to be there, by his side, while Jeremiah did the scariest thing he'd ever faced in his life. Having his lover's support meant the world and eased the fear of telling his neighbors and friends who he really was.

* * *

Dale drove them into town, trying to keep the combined anxiety and elation coursing through him to himself. This was a milestone in Jeremiah's life, and it could go one of two ways—they'd be able to love each other, out in the open, in this Podunk town, or they'd be scorned to the point Jeremiah would never forgive Dale for forcing his hand. But, damn it, they were both in their early forties—too old to be playing cat-and-mouse games, hiding who they were and who they loved. If the entire town, sans Willow and Nathan and some of the ranch hands, turned their backs on them, Dale honestly wouldn't give two shits. They weren't the people who made him happy —only one man had Dale's heart soaring and the ability to bring him to his knees—Jeremiah Peter

Urban, the sexiest cowboy Dale had ever laid eyes on.

Glancing over, he saw Jeremiah biting his lip and running his palms up and down his thighs. Reaching over, Dale grabbed the closest hand and squeezed. "I'm going to be right by your side every second. I won't leave you. If it gets to be too much or people are too awful, we'll leave."

Jeremiah's chin trembled, but then he swallowed, straightened his shoulders, and threaded his fingers with Dale's. "Thank you. I-I can do this. I know I can. Willow, Jenna, and Nathan all gave me something of a talking to. They said no one would care, not the people who really count. They said that the people who matter most in my life already know, or have suspected, and love me, no matter who I choose to love."

"Yes, they do." Dale brought Jeremiah's hand to his mouth and kissed the knuckles, earning him a genuine smile from the man.

A few minutes later, they arrived at the half-full and familiar Rock Diner lot. Dale recognized some of the trucks parked there and knew Jeremiah would likely know who they all belonged to and who they would face when they walked into the place.

He found a spot in the back corner of the lot and pulled in before killing the engine. "Ready, baby?"

Jeremiah glanced around, then let out a slow breath and nodded. "Y-yeah. Although, I could really use a kiss first—you know, for luck."

Grinning, unable to resist even if he wanted to, Dale leaned forward and pressed their lips together. As always, the taste and feel of his cowboy's mouth under his made Dale's cock twitch and his blood heat. He could kiss Jeremiah all day and never tire of it. Sliding his tongue along Jeremiah's, Dale swallowed the other man's moan. Giving and taking, advancing and retreating, they made out for a minute or two until they were both half hard and breathing heavily.

Pulling back an inch, Dale said, "There, that should give you plenty of luck—not that you need it." After smacking a loud final kiss onto Jeremiah's smiling mouth, he added, "Come on, I'm starved. Let's eat lunch so we can get to dessert."

Laughing and following Dale's lead, Jeremiah climbed out of the truck. Stopping at the rear bumper, Dale held out his hand to Jeremiah and waited. If they walked into the diner hand in hand, there would be no mistaking them as just two friends having lunch. Their declaration would be loud and clear—they were a couple.

With only a slight tremor, Jeremiah took his boyfriend's hand.

Chapter Twenty

Jeremiah's palm was sweating against Dale's, and he hoped like hell the other man didn't mind too much because there was no way he was letting go now.

You're no quitter.

He repeated the mantra in his mind, over and over, as Dale opened the diner's door and led them inside. The place was about three-quarters full with the lunch crowd. Heads turned toward the door, as was usual, but instead of immediately returning to their meals, the gazes of the patrons and staff, men and women he'd known all his life, lingered. All chatter ceased, and the only sounds reaching Jeremiah's ears were the clatter from the kitchen, someone's baby giggling, and the pounding of his own heart. Everyone's eyes were pinned on the couple's clasped hands, and Jeremiah raised his chin and squared his shoulders. He wouldn't be cowed or ashamed, and he almost dared anyone to tell him otherwise. He and Dale were doing nothing wrong, nor would Jeremiah be made to feel like he was less because of who he really was—never again.

"Where do you want to sit, babe?" Dale asked, glancing around at the few empty booths and tables.

"By the window." Jeremiah pointed to a booth at the front of the restaurant, and Dale led them over to it, never once letting go of his hand. When Dale sat down and slid in, Jeremiah moved to sit across from him, but the other man shook his head, tugging Jeremiah into the booth beside him. He'd no sooner sat when Dale urged him closer, so they were pressed against each other from shoulders to hips to knees, and before Jeremiah could blink, the Marine's arm was around his shoulders.

Jeremiah met Dale's gaze and saw the question in his eyes. *Is this too much?* Nope, not even close.

"This is nice," he said quietly, meant for Dale's ears alone. The back of his neck and his cheeks burned from the stares directed their way, but there was no turning back now—not even if he wanted to. He had a brief thought about grabbing Dale's face and kissing him to really give the lookie-loos something to gawk at, but he didn't think he was ready for that yet.

Dale's grin was so bright that Jeremiah swore it illuminated the room more than the sun streaming through the windows. "It sure is."

A throat clearing drew their attention. Crystal Fox,

the diner's owner, greeted them both with a smile. She hadn't brought over any menus since everyone who lived in Antelope Rock knew it by heart. "Hi, guys. What can I get for you?"

There was no disbelief, revulsion, or hostility on her face—just friendliness and kindness, as always. Swallowing his surprise and relief, Jeremiah managed to stammer out an order for a bacon cheeseburger, fries, and a Coke. When he was done, Dale ordered the same.

"I would've gotten the onion rings, but I won't subject you to my onion breath," Dale said with a wink after Crystal left them to give their order to the kitchen staff.

Even though he was still jittery, Jeremiah appreciated the other man's levity. "I'll have to remember to return the favor sometime."

"I'll be sure to remind you, Cowboy."

George "Georgie" McDaniel appeared and carefully set two glasses of ice-cold Coke on their table, seemingly not surprised or fazed to see them acting as a couple. "Hi, Jeremiah. Hi, Dale. Ms. Crystal said these are for you."

The twenty-one-year-old man was a fixture in the Rock, working part-time at the diner as a busboy and also bagging groceries at the Pack & Sack. He had Down syndrome, but it never slowed him. A hard worker, he also had a heart of gold—his tender heart and sweet nature always drew smiles from the customers. He could easily recall names of people he'd met, and even if you only went into the diner or grocery store occasionally, he'd still remember yours after hearing it only once. He lived with his aunt, a schoolteacher, ever since his mother passed away three years ago from cancer. Most of the townspeople kept a watchful eye on him, helping out when his disability might be an issue or someone was being cruel to him, which only happened occasionally.

"Thanks, Georgie," the two men said in unison before he hustled away to clean off a table that'd been recently vacated.

Conversations around them resumed, although there was more whispering than the usual chitchat this time. Jeremiah fought the urge to scan the room to see the reactions on everyone's faces. He was certain there was a combination of shock, disgust, and even a little understanding and acceptance. But those last two were probably in the minority and would be for a while until the town got used to the idea of a gay couple in their midst.

Taking a deep breath and letting it out slowly, Jeremiah relaxed a little into Dale's side, giving himself a moment to relish the freedom he felt. He was in a restaurant, on a date, with a man, and the world hadn't come to a grinding halt, the sky hadn't fallen, and God hadn't struck him down. Maybe everything was going to be okay.

Meeting Dale's amber-colored eyes, Jeremiah

allowed himself to do something he'd never thought would be possible in public—he smiled at his boyfriend. Hope and joy filled him, and the heavy weight that'd been on his shoulders for the past few days suddenly lifted. At that moment, he felt lighter than he had in his entire adult life. In fact, it was as if he was soaring high above a blissful sea of clouds.

That is until a snide voice broke into his happiness. "What the hell is this? You a fucking queer now, Urban? A goddamn pussy?"

Jeremiah stiffened, then glared up at the man he'd known since elementary school standing beside their booth. Dale had also tensed and then started to move his arm. Shaking his head no, Jeremiah silently told his man to keep his arm where it was. Where it belonged. He knew he'd gotten his point across when the limb settled back down on his shoulders.

Anger rose within him at the years of self-doubt and self-hate that'd dictated his entire existence. But he was done with all that. Never again would he back down because he feared the reactions from intolerant and sanctimonious homophobes.

He glanced toward a nearby table where a couple he knew sat with their six-year-old daughter. "Joe, you might want to cover MaryBeth's ears."

His mouth gaping, Joe Parsons slowly reached over and did as suggested. Jeremiah scowled at the asshole in front of him again. Thirty years or so of denial and fear morphed into courage and irritation with a touch of sarcasm. He pulled up his proverbial britches and let loose. "Yeah, I am, Schneider. And if you've got a problem with that, well, that's too fucking bad."

His gaze flitted around the restaurant as he held his chin high and raised his voice. "I'll say it again for those in the back who didn't hear me the first time. News flash, for any of you that care, although it's beyond me why you'd give a good goddamn who I love, this is nothing new—I'm gay. I like dick."

There were a few audible gasps and snorts that he ignored. "Always have, and always will. And this is Dale Harris, my *boyfriend,* and I'm looking forward to the makeup sex we're going to have as soon as we get home later. If you can't accept that, I don't give a flying fuck. We're here to stay. Get over it."

Frank Schneider sneered at him. "Really? No shame, huh? You're a fucking pervert."

That was exactly why Jeremiah had let their semi-friendship drift further apart as they'd gotten older. The man was a bigoted Asshole with a capital A. Feeling at a slight disadvantage with the man staring down at them, Jeremiah got to his feet, and Dale slid out of the booth behind him in silent support. Jeremiah appreciated it, along with the fact his lover was letting him take control of the situation. "Am I now? That's rich coming from you, Frank, since I know all about what you keep in your sock drawer. Yet, you don't see me judging you for your taste in porn."

Raising an eyebrow, Jeremiah held Schneider's gaze, letting the man remember when they'd been in their early twenties and had gotten drunk together with two other guys, and he'd shown everyone the stack of Japanese snuff porn he kept hidden. It had all been fake, Jeremiah had assumed, but if the asswipe could be comfortable getting off to simulated rapes and murder, then Jeremiah sure as fuck had nothing to be ashamed of, either.

"Fuck you," Schneider snapped, his already pug-like face growing even uglier with hate.

"Nah, that's my job," Dale said with a wink. Jeremiah almost burst out laughing as Schneider's face turned purple. "Or sometimes, his too. We switch—keeps things interesting if you know what I mean."

The couple did no such thing, having not had penetrative sex yet, but this fuckwit didn't know that. Schneider was about to spit out a retort when the diner's front door opened and Grady and another deputy wandered in, presumably to have lunch. Jeremiah's cousin stopped in his tracks and eyed the three men in a standoff. "Afternoon, Jeremiah. Dale. Problem?"

It wasn't a surprise Grady hadn't greeted Schneider since the asshole hated the sheriff after being busted three times for DUIs and losing his driver's license. The bully stepped back and wiped his hand across his mouth, probably because he didn't want to be slapped with a disturbing the peace or harassment charge and thrown into the county jail for an overnight stay. It wouldn't be the first time.

Mumbling, "fucking fudge packers," Schneider stormed off, slamming the door to the diner behind him on his way out.

Less than a second later, Grady's radio squawked as the dispatcher reported an accident with injuries on the other side of town. Lunch would have to wait for him and his deputy as they rushed out the door. Jeremiah had no doubt Grady would call him later to find out what the hell he'd missed at the diner, whether he got the story through the town's gossip mill or not.

"Listen up!" Crystal stood at the swinging door to the kitchen, her hands on her hips as she scrutinized the faces of her patrons. The petite, fifty-year-old woman's expression was stern and unyielding. She tilted her head toward Dale and Jeremiah. "These two men are paying customers, and they're welcome here anytime they wish. Just like all of you are. I pass judgment on nobody since the last time I checked, I hadn't qualified for sainthood yet. If any of you have a problem with that, there's the door. If not, shut up, keep your eyes to yourself, and eat your meals. I won't have any derogatory talk, harassment, or finger-pointing in my diner!"

Kam Fox, one of Crystal's two adult sons, stood behind his mom's shoulder, his white apron stained with grease and a meat cleaver in his large fist. A good foot taller—just like his twin brother Ged—he towered over her. For a small woman, she'd produced two giant-assed offspring. Kam was the main cook at the diner, and Ged was one of Jeremiah's ranch hands. Both were good men who had done their mother proud.

A high-pitched, childlike voice rang throughout the diner. "Everyone deserves love! Ms. Crystal says so." Georgie nodded decisively and thrust out his chest, almost daring anyone to disagree with him.

"You heard him," Kam added, placing a paw-sized hand on his mother's shoulder.

Not a single other person in the place spoke up for or against what'd already been said. One and all returned their attention to their own lunches and companions, and calm fell over the large room again.

"Thanks, Crystal, Kam, Georgie." Jeremiah dipped his chin to each in turn, deeply touched by their show of support.

Crystal smiled back. "No problem, sugar. Sit back down—your meals will be right out."

Spinning around, she patted her son's chest as she walked by him into the kitchen. With a final lingering glance at Jeremiah and Dale, which Jeremiah couldn't decipher, Kam followed his mother.

"Well, that went better than you probably expected," Dale murmured enough so only Jeremiah could hear him after they retook their seats.

"Better than I could've ever imagined," he admitted.

"Other than that guy who only missed getting

decked thanks to your cousin's impeccable timing." Dale took off Jeremiah's hat and ran his fingers through the man's hair. "Though next time, baby, you should tell him that gay men aren't pussies—it takes a real man to take a dick up the ass."

Tipping his head back, Jeremiah roared with laughter. "That remains to be seen, Marine."

Winking, he sipped his Coke and relaxed back into Dale's loose hold.

I could so get used to this.

The thought startled him. He suddenly realized he really *could* get used to it now. There were no more walls, no more secrets, no more fear. He was out. It was a done deal, and there was no looking back. Nearly giddy, he felt light-headed and was thankful he was sitting down.

"Hello, boys." Mrs. Barbara Bradley, the elderly mother of Antelope Rock's mayor, Joe Bradley, had stopped at their table and smiled at them. She'd been Butterfield's head librarian for longer than Jeremiah had been alive and had only recently retired. While the Rock had always been her home, the town was too small for its own public library.

"Afternoon, Mrs. Bradley," Jeremiah responded while Dale said, "Good afternoon, ma'am."

The octogenarian held her hand up to the side of her mouth as if ready to relate a secret. "I just wanted to say good on you both. You make a very handsome couple. Mr. Harris, I hope you know you've got a wonderful man here, and if you do him wrong, then I have a great-nephew I can introduce him to." She pointed at Dale and narrowed her eyes at him. "Food for thought—keep it in mind."

Dale wasn't the only one clearly trying to hide an amused grin. Beside him, Jeremiah used a hand to cover his own mouth as Dale nodded at the woman. "Yes, ma'am. I will. And I agree with you—Jeremiah's a good man—and I promise to do right by him."

"You do that. Now, have a nice lunch, boys, and tell your folks I said hello, Jeremiah." With a little wave and a wink, she headed for the door.

Jeremiah faced Dale with an expression and feeling of disbelief and then elation. His coming out really was going to be okay. While there would always be jackasses like Schneider, Skinner, and Larson, there would also be kind and accepting people like Jenna, Willow, Nathan, Mrs. Bradley, Crystal, Kam, and even Georgie. At that moment, he vowed the latter would be of more importance to him from then on.

For now, though, he did something he'd always dreamed of doing, something that'd been unthinkable before he'd fallen for Dale—he kissed his boyfriend. On the mouth. In public. And it felt amazing.

Chapter Twenty-One

Jeremiah was waiting for his nerves to tumble around in his gut like a washing machine, but all he felt was joy. Elation. Freedom. And desire.

I'm out! I did it, finally!

Sure, he fully expected more blow-back and whispered slurs, but the weight he'd carried on his shoulders his entire adult life had been lifted. He felt so light that he was certain he could rise into the air and drift away at any moment. Keeping him anchored, though, was Dale, his hand gripping Jeremiah's tightly as he drove them back to the JP.

He couldn't wait until they were alone and behind closed doors—not the figurative one he'd just escaped through. He wanted to make love to Dale.

With Dale.

Under him.

Over him.

Around him.

And in any position they could contort their bodies into that connected them in the most primal way.

Neither were young men anymore, capable of several bouts of sex throughout the night, but he would bet his favorite belt buckle that they both had at least two rounds in them. The anticipation alone would ensure that.

"What are you thinking about so hard over there?" Dale asked, squeezing Jeremiah's hand as he steered the truck onto JP's long drive.

"Your dick in my ass."

The truck jerked and swerved while Dale cursed before getting the vehicle under control again. He glared at Jeremiah. "Thank fuck we weren't still on the main road! Jesus Christ, babe."

Jeremiah howled, clutching his stomach as amused tears filled his eyes. "Oh, man, you're strung pretty tight, huh?"

"Fuck yeah," Dale barked, then stomped his foot on the accelerator, hurrying them down the dirt road at a rate that threatened the truck's suspension. They fishtailed to a stop next to Jeremiah's truck, sending a cloud of dust billowing up around both vehicles. "Get in the damn house and strip to your skin. Wait for me on the bed."

"Bossy much?" Jeremiah arched a brow.

Dale scowled at him, his stubbled jawline so tight it could cut diamonds. "Oh, Cowboy, you have *no idea.*"

"Shouldn't our first time be a little more romantic?" He knew he was poking the bear, but it was so much fun.

The man growled before answering, "We'll do romantic lovemaking on round two. This one, this first time, I need you bare, raw, and dirty. But don't worry, I know this is a first for you. Don't let my overbearing attitude and greediness scare you." He cupped Jeremiah's cheek, brushing a thumb along his lower lip and staring deep into his eyes. "I'd never hurt you—you know that, right?"

Breathing heavily while his rigid dick begged to be released from the confines of his jeans, Jeremiah tentatively drew Dale's thumb into his mouth before running his tongue along the calloused pad. Imagining it was Dale's cock he was worshiping, he hollowed his cheeks and sucked—hard. Dale's pupils dilated, and a gasp left his lips. Pulling his finger from the wet and eager mouth, Dale grasped Jeremiah's chin. His voice was raspy yet demanding. "Answer me, babe—do you trust me?"

At that moment, Jeremiah fell a little more in love with the man. "Yes, I trust you. One hundred percent." His face burned with his next words—a confession that Dale needed to know. "I've never bottomed before, but I've played with . . . with toys and such."

His mind briefly flashed to the wooden dildo he'd

carved, which he hadn't used yet. "I'm not a *total* stranger on what to do or what to expect. And I've topped before."

"God, the thought of you using a dildo on yourself . . . crap, I can't think about that, otherwise we'll never make it inside before I take you. But that's good—I mean, that you know what to expect. However, I'll still be careful with you—as much as I can, anyway. We'll get to a point when I won't have to be gentle. That's when I'll be balls deep in that sweet ass of yours and you relax around me. I'll be able to slide into your tight little hole as far as I want." He leaned forward and brushed his lips across Jeremiah's in the sweetest of caresses. "And at that moment, I'm going to make you *mine.*"

When Dale retreated and pointed to the passenger door, Jeremiah gulped but didn't say another word. He leaped out of the truck and ran inside as fast as he could manage with his cock hard enough to pound nails. Thank God Jenna had told him earlier she was spending the afternoon and evening shopping and having dinner with a few friends in Butterfield.

He reached his bedroom before his anxiety started to rear its ugly head. Trying to quell his fears about potential inadequacy, he toed off his boots, kicking them carelessly into the corner next to the dresser, and then made quick work of his clothes. He was so turned on, he knew it wouldn't take long for him to come. Hopefully, Dale wouldn't be disappointed. Over the past few weeks, Jeremiah had learned what an amazing lover Dale was—his talented hands and mouth had wrung Jeremiah dry on multiple occasions. But this time, it would be different. This was sex on an unparalleled level. He was giving himself to the other man, not just his body but his soul.

Stepping over to the bedside table, he pulled open the drawer, found his half-full bottle of lube, and tossed it onto the mattress. He looked at the strip of condoms resting in the drawer but left them there. They wouldn't need them anymore—both their test results had come back negative the other day. Thank God because he couldn't bear the thought of anything separating them. Not even a thin barrier of latex.

Dale had told him to get on the bed, but he hadn't said how. An image flashed in his mind, but he wasn't sure if he was brave enough to go through with it. He imagined himself kneeling on the bed, propped up on one hand while the other worked between his legs, stretching and loosening his dark hole. He'd be positioned with his ass facing the door, so the first thing Dale saw when he came into the room was Jeremiah with two . . . no, he thought, better make it three, fingers in his own ass, prepping himself.

Moaning at the fantasy, he realized he was fisting his cock, slowly stroking himself as his mind went wild.

When the door opened, he froze, facing in the opposite direction. The door clicked shut, and Dale's booted footsteps came closer before stopping directly behind Jeremiah. He shivered, feeling the other man's body heat blanketing the bare skin of his back. He wanted every hot, silky inch of Dale's flesh pressed against his own.

"You're not on the bed, Jay. Was my order not clear?"

Glancing over his shoulder, he replied, "Um, I . . . uh, kinda got distracted."

Hands clutched his hips, pulling until his back was tight against Dale's still-clothed chest, his ass against a denim-covered hard-on. There was something unbelievably erotic about being naked while his lover was fully dressed. Jeremiah arched his spine, reaching back and wrapping his arms around Dale's neck. Rubbing his ass against his man's crotch drew a moan from deep inside both of them. Jeremiah felt needy, as if his skin was too tight and would split open at any moment. Dropping his gaze, he saw his cock was an angry red as pearly fluid leaked steadily from the tip.

"What did you get distracted by?" Dale whispered against his ear before licking and biting the lobe softly. His hands roamed Jeremiah's chest and abdomen, seemingly everywhere at once. Jeremiah shivered again, curling back deeper into Dale's hold.

"I-I . . . He cleared his suddenly dry throat. "I was picturing myself kneeling on the bed, ass up, fingering myself open for you." All his normal shyness and embarrassment seemed to have fled. He felt bold, true, and whole in a way he'd never imagined he could.

"Oh fuck, Jay!" Dale's hips bucked forward.

"Would you like me to do that for you?"

"Hell, yeah, but not today." Dale spun him around, grabbed his head with both hands, and took his mouth in a ferocious kiss. Jeremiah brought his arms up around Dale's waist, then snaked his hands down to grip the Marine's delectable ass cheeks.

After a few moments of feasting on each other, Jeremiah tore his mouth free from Dale's. "You have too many clothes on."

He jerked Dale's shirt free from his pants, tugging and pulling until it came up and over the man's head and flew across the room.

"Yeess," Jeremiah hissed, running his hands all over Dale's chest, loving the feel of the soft strands tickling his palms. "I love how hairy you are." He flexed his fingers into Dale's pecs, squeezing the firm muscle and flicking his thumbs over his nipples, eliciting a groan from the man.

"I love that you love it."

Jeremiah bent his head, licking from Dale's neck to his collarbone before biting down hard enough to leave a mark. Working his way back up the man's throat, he kissed and sucked, tasting the salt of sweat and the elusive essence that was all Dale. The sexy Marine was so damn delicious.

Scraping his nails down the other man's back, Jeremiah used only his fingertips to explore every ridge and valley of the fine physique that haunted his dreams.

Every inch of Dale was sculpted to perfection. Artists of yore would've vied for the man to pose for them so they could immortalize him on canvas or in marble.

Roaming his hands back up Dale's chest to his shoulders, Jeremiah stopped with one hand on either side of his lover's neck. He pulled away enough to let their gazes meet. The deep brown of Dale's eyes was nearly gone, swallowed by his dilated pupils. He looked as high as a fucking kite, floating above the clouds. Warmth spread throughout Jeremiah's body, and euphoria filled his mind, knowing he had such a strong effect on this amazing man. *His* man.

"I want to taste every inch of you. Can I do that? Do you want me on my knees?"

Molten lava flared in Dale's eyes. "I'll never say no to my dick in that luscious mouth of yours." He undid his belt buckle and jeans before shoving them and his boxers down toward his feet, where they rested scrunched on top of the boots he still wore.

Without hesitation, Jeremiah dropped to his knees, excitement and need thrumming in his veins. Bracing both hands on Dale's hips, he leaned forward, tucking his face into the juncture between Dale's thigh and crotch and inhaling deeply. He could get drunk on the man's scent. Musk and soap, tinged with sweat—it should be gross, but it was the most incredible ambrosia Jeremiah's nose had ever experienced.

Running his tongue down along the crease of Dale's groin, he felt the coarse hair tickle his mouth and chin. He moaned in delight. Dale was so masculine in every way that it demolished Jeremiah's self-control. What he felt for this man went deeper than his bones. Every cell in his body rejoiced over being with Dale in such an intimate way.

Skimming his palms up and down Dale's thighs, Jeremiah took his time, enjoying the feel of heavy muscles twitching under his hands. The effect he was having on his lover was heady. Dale's cock stood hard and thick, jutting out from a dark thatch of hair, his balls hanging heavily underneath. Lifting one hand, Jeremiah wrapped his fingers around the base of the shaft, jacking it a few times. Precum leaked from the tip, a shiny drop at a time. Swiping it with this thumb, Jeremiah tilted his chin up, meeting Dale's eyes before he stuck his thumb in his mouth and sucked the salty-sweet fluid off.

"Delicious," he whispered before bending his head and taking Dale's perfect cock into his mouth. Moaning around the length, he paused a moment, loving the weight of Dale's hardness against his tongue. Blinking up at his lover, he suckled and laved like he was savoring a popsicle on the hottest day of the year.

A grunt was forced from Dale's lips. "Baby . . . shit!" With a whimper, he buried his hands into Jeremiah's hair, urging him closer and pushing his cock deeper into Jeremiah's mouth. "Please. Jay, you're killing me here."

Humming softly, Jeremiah relaxed his jaw and

sank slowly, taking as much of Dale into his throat as he could. He gagged briefly before breathing through it and forcing himself to take that final inch until his nose was pressed into the wiry hair of Dale's groin. He swallowed, working his throat muscles around the head of Dale's cock.

"Ugh!" Dale cried out, pulling back then thrusting forward, gentle but deep. So deep. "That's it. Fuck. You're perfect."

Up and down, Jeremiah worked Dale over. He gripped the man's length with one hand, matching the rhythm of his mouth, while his other hand cradled Dale's balls. He rolled them gently with his fingers, gripping them and pulling them down just a little. Not enough to bring Dale to his knees but to add a taste of erotic pain. Dale's breath stuttered, and he moaned, long and loud. "Yes. I love that."

Jeremiah's own dick throbbed. The need to get off was excruciating in its intensity, but he didn't touch himself. He didn't want to take his hands off Dale to meet his needs. Pulling off the man's cock, Jeremiah put two fingers into his mouth, getting them as wet as possible. He met and held Dale's gaze as he placed the soaked digits behind Dale's balls, brushing against the tender skin until he found his ultimate target.

Pausing at the puckered entrance, Jeremiah waited for permission to continue. Dale nodded and widened his stance, giving Jeremiah easier access. After rubbing his fingers a few times over and around Dale's hole, he swallowed the man's cock in one smooth gulp while, at the same moment, pressing a finger deep inside him. Dale's back arched, and he shouted, thrusting forward into Jeremiah's mouth and then back onto the finger impaling him. Muttered curses and pleas for more filled the air. Pulling his finger free, Jeremiah spit on two of them before returning to the dark depths of Dale's body with both. Stretching the tight walls and gaining ground with each thrust, Jeremiah searched for and found the man's prostate, lavishing it with attention.

Dale gripped Jeremiah's head harder as he fucked his mouth and came with a feral roar. Jeremiah swallowed quickly, determined not to miss a drop of the thick cum being pumped down his throat.

When the stream ran dry, Dale pulled himself free of Jeremiah's mouth and hand, stumbling backward until he sat heavily on the bed. "Fuck!"

Panting and sweating, he closed his eyes and flopped back onto the mattress, his arms splayed and his feet on the floor with his jeans and boxers still wrapped around his lower legs.

Jeremiah wasted no time, scooting forward and ridding Dale of his boots and the last of his clothes. Grinning and feeling a bit smug, he asked, "Liked that, did you?"

Clearly, it was a rhetorical question, but he still wanted an answer. It wasn't every day he could reduce a man to a babbling, incoherent mess.

"I . . . loved it and . . . as soon as my lungs, muscles, and brain . . . . are working at full power again . . . I'm going to return the favor. Promise."

Chuckling, Jeremiah got to his feet, climbed onto the bed, and straddled Dale, who was clearly in a state of euphoria. He rubbed his ass against the slightly sticky, half-hard cock under him. Dale's hands came up, palming Jeremiah's ass cheeks, spreading them apart, and caressing the cleft between them.

"C'mere," Dale ordered softly, urging Jeremiah upward until he had a knee on either side of Dale's shoulders and his groin hovered over the man's chin. When Dale parted his lips and stuck out his tongue, Jeremiah didn't miss a beat, gripping the base of his cock and slowly feeding it into the welcoming mouth. Warm, tight, and wet pleasure exploded and surrounded him.

"God, yes." Leaning down, he held himself up with his palms and fucked Dale's face. Everything with this man was different, better, sharper. Blowjobs were more powerful, kisses more intoxicating, and touches so hot they nearly burned his skin. Jeremiah was already addicted to all of it and craving more as every second passed, never wanting to stop.

A finger ran down the crack of his ass. Dale's teasing, advancing, and retreating drove Jeremiah out of his mind.

"Please, Dale, *please!*" He didn't care that he was begging shamelessly. He felt hollow and was desperate with the need to be filled. Jeremiah heard a *snick* of the cap of the lube opening—he had no idea how or when Dale had grabbed it—and then cool wetness dribbled down the cleft of his ass, making him shiver and arch his back. Dale's fingers were there a second later, spreading the liquid around his hole. One finger breached him, just a bit, before pulling out and stroking back and forth over his rim.

"Babe, please." He relaxed as much as he could, knowing it would be easier for both of them. A gasp was forced past his lips when Dale sucked hard and, at the same time, sank his finger in all the way. "Ah . . . shit!"

The pressure felt amazing. There was a searing burn, but it passed quickly, morphing into sheer plea-sure. Dale plunged his finger in and out of Jeremiah's body a few times, but then the burn was back, sharper, as he added a second finger. Jeremiah instinctively clenched.

Releasing Jeremiah's cock, Dale used his free hand to caress Jeremiah's ass cheek. As their gazes met, Dale murmured, "Easy, baby. Let me in again. You can take it."

Taking deep breaths, Jeremiah slackened his body and pushed back against the intrusion. Just when he thought there was no way it would happen, both fingers popped past the tight ring of muscle, sliding in all the way easier than expected.

"Yes, that's it." Dale nuzzled Jeremiah's balls as he

worked in and out of Jeremiah's hole, pressing on his prostate and sending a near-electric shock of pleasure arcing through him. Dale stared up at him in awe. "Fuck, you're so sexy. I love this. I could finger you all day. You're so hot. I can't wait to feel you wrapped around my cock. You're going to strangle me, and I'm going to enjoy every minute of it."

"D-Dale—" Beyond that, Jeremiah was at a loss for words as his lover pressed a third digit inside him. "Ugh." Pain flared, but only for a moment. Then, all he knew was indescribable and unending ecstasy. If Dale's fingers felt this incredible, how would Jeremiah survive having the man's thick cock inside him? He'd surely die from the thrill of it, but what a way to go!

"Do you think you're ready?" Dale rested his head on the pillow and gazed up at Jeremiah.

He slammed his eyes shut, trying to reel in the urge to explode. Through gritted teeth, he responded, "If I get any more ready, I'm going to blow all over your face."

He didn't know how he'd held on as long as he had. His orgasm was right there, so close he could almost taste it.

"Then let me up, baby." Dale pulled his fingers free, making Jeremiah moan, and smacked his ass, which earned him a grunt and glare.

Jeremiah lifted his leg and moved to Dale's side, eager to be filled again by the man's recovered erection. "How do you want me?"

"Hands and knees. That'll be the easiest way to start—for you, anyway. I don't know if I can handle watching my cock sink inside you. It's good you got me off already. Otherwise, I might come the second I'm balls deep."

His cock jerked at Dale's words. His body was slick with sweat, and while his nerves about taking a man inside him lingered, it was a distant worry. He *wanted*, and he *needed*. Not much else registered in his mind right then.

"Hang on. Come here." Dale knelt before him, closing the distance between them until they were chest to chest. Cupping his jaw, Dale drew him in for a kiss, and Jeremiah went happily. He'd never tire of kissing this man. Dale's tongue plundered Jeremiah's mouth, pulling him against his own hard body and rubbing their weeping cocks together. Jeremiah thrust helplessly against his Marine. He moaned into Dale's mouth, sucking his tongue and biting at his lips, driving them both higher.

Reaching down, Dale fisted his hand around both their cocks, stroking them together. The man was incredibly hard again, as if he hadn't come mere minutes ago.

Jeremiah mewled against Dale's lips. "Fuck, that feels amazin'. I could come just like this."

As if spurred on by his declaration, the pumps came faster, with their combined precum serving as lube.

"So, come. Come all over us, baby. We have all day and all night. And all the days after." Kissing his neck, Dale encouraged him as he licked up to his ear, which he bit—hard. "Come for me, Jay. I want to see it. I *need* it. Then I'll make you fucking come again when I'm buried balls deep inside you."

Dale's dirty words, coupled with the heat of the erection clenched hard against his own, had Jeremiah reaching for his climax. But it was the sounds of their combined pleasure that sent him over the edge. He grunted, wet heat bathing his abdomen as he shot cum over Dale's fist and both their cocks. Shuddering, he let Dale stroke him through the orgasm that seemed never-ending.

Finally spent, he nearly collapsed onto the mattress, but Dale grasped his hips and supported his weight. Heaving for oxygen, Jeremiah rested his forehead on Dale's shoulder. His cum had painted Dale's sculpted chest, abs, and still erect cock, and he nearly came again at the sight.

"Fuck that was hot." Dale grasped his own shaft, using Jeremiah's cum as lube as he jacked himself.

The mesmerizing action held Jeremiah's attention, and he groaned. "You're going to be the death of me. Sex has never been like this for me. Ever."

"Good. Get used to it because if I have anything to say about it, you won't be having sex with anyone else. Ever. Again." Dale growled, jerked Jeremiah closer, and smashed their mouths together. He kept the kiss brief, though, pulling free quickly before Jeremiah could take it any further. "Hands and knees, Cowboy. I want you. Right. Fuckin'. Now."

Jeremiah didn't hesitate to comply. Why Dale's orders turned him on so much, he didn't know, but he wasn't going to question it—not when there were much better things to do. Spinning around, he braced himself on his palms and spread his legs. Lowering his head, he tilted his pelvis and offered himself up to his lover in the most primal of ways.

"Fuck, yes." Dale glided his hands up Jeremiah's back and then down again to his ass, where he squeezed and massaged the muscular flesh. "I love your ass. I swear to God, Jay, you're the sexiest thing I've ever seen. I want to bury my face right here." Dale split him open, then used his thumbs to stroke his cleft and circle his entrance. "I want to eat you until you beg me to stop, and then I want to eat you some more."

"Oh, God." Unable to form any sort of meaningful response beyond those two words, Jeremiah folded his forearms and rested his head on them.

"You'd like that, wouldn't you?" Dale asked before the *snick* of the lube being opened again resounded, and liquid was squirted directly onto Jeremiah's hole. Nimble fingers spread it around, pushing some inside before retreating and teasing his rim.

"Y-yes." Forcing himself to stay still, he bit down on his forearm, letting the pain save him from shooting his load again before Dale ever got inside him. Even though he'd fantasized about it often, he'd never received a rim-job or given one, for that matter. It was too intimate of an act for a one-night stand, which was the same reason he'd never bottomed before, even though he'd been almost desperate to know what it felt like. He'd never trusted someone enough to give up that part of himself—until now.

"We'll save that for another time, baby. I can't wait to be inside you anymore. I've wanted to fuck you since the moment I saw you. Did you know that?"

"No," he responded with a hoarse croak, not really sure what the question had been. He was too far gone to care as Dale sank three fingers into him again, scissoring them apart, stretching him. Shockingly, Jeremiah's cock was hard again and leaking all over the bedspread. He couldn't remember the last time he'd recovered that fast. "Oh, fuck! Dale, please—I'm ready."

"You're ready when I say. I told you, baby, I won't hurt you." Dale smacked one of Jeremiah's ass cheeks, eliciting a muttered curse. "At least not in a bad way. Oh, you'll be sore tomorrow, but it'll be the good kind of sore. Every time you sit down or take a step, you'll remember that I was here. That you belong to me now."

"Oh, God, yes!"

The fingers were pulled free, and Jeremiah felt the head of Dale's cock press against his entrance. He instinctively tensed but then remembered to relax as a hand ran up his back, soothing him.

"That's it. Nice and easy. Take a deep breath and let it out."

As soon as Jeremiah exhaled, Dale pushed forward, popping the tip of his cock past the tight muscle, holding still with just the head inside, allowing him to adjust. Jeremiah winced at the fierce burn, feeling like he was being split apart. The Marine was well-endowed—thick and long—and Jeremiah had known taking him would be a challenge the first time. Hell, maybe every time.

"Just breathe, baby." Dale leaned forward to kiss along Jeremiah's shoulders, easing the tension there. "The pain will pass. Push back when you're ready to take more."

Jeremiah's cock had softened upon Dale's entry, but as he relaxed further and started to press back onto the cock lancing him, he began to harden again. He was so *full*, the stretch was just this side of painful, but it was morphing into pleasure, mingling together into a sweet, addictive fire as Dale pressed deeper into him.

"Oh fuck. Dale. That's . . ." Pushing back and spreading his legs a little more, Jeremiah slowly welcomed Dale, inch by inch, until he finally bottomed out. As the multiple sensations assailed him, Jeremiah didn't know which way was up. All he knew, at that moment, was Dale—the thick girth deep inside him, groans in his ears, and the feel of his lover's sweat dripping onto his own back.

"Yeah?" Dale panted, holding Jeremiah's hips and digging his fingers in. There was no doubt they would leave bruises for tomorrow. The thought of Dale's mark of possession on his skin turned Jeremiah on, and his balls grew heavy. "You okay, baby?"

"So good. Please, Dale, move. Please."

And he did. Pulling out halfway, he held himself there for a few seconds before thrusting forward, punching a sharp *ah* from Jeremiah's lips. Again and again, Dale fucked in and out of him, sliding out further each time until just the head of his dick was inside Jeremiah, who clenched his hole, trying to draw Dale back inside.

"Oh, fuck, do that again," Dale ordered as he plunged forward—hard. Skin slapped against skin. Their balls bounced off each other. With each clench and release, Dale gasped in response. Jeremiah propelled his hips backward, meeting each of Dale's forward thrusts. His body was looser, accepting the intrusion easily now—craving it.

They were both coated with sweat and trembling under a tidal wave of emotions. Dale shifted his hips slightly on his next thrust and hit Jeremiah's prostate, sending sparks of intense pleasure shooting through him. Jeremiah face-planted into the mattress to muffle his scream of ecstasy.

"There it is. I knew you'd be able to take me, baby.

It's like you were made for me and only me. Fuck, it's so hot watching my cock disappear inside you."

As Dale pummeled his sweet spot, Jeremiah wailed, "Just like that! Dale, oh, God, don't stop!" He bucked in time to Dale's advances, chasing his orgasm that loomed just beyond his reach. He could feel it building in his balls and ass, the pressure so intense, he instinctively knew his orgasm would wreck him in the best of ways.

Suddenly, Dale pulled out, leaving Jeremiah empty and gasping in confusion, but both were short-lived. Dale wrestled him over onto his back, shoved his legs up and apart, and plunged back into his ass in one hard stroke. Jeremiah grunted, the air knocked from his lungs under the force of Dale's tumultuous lovemaking.

The Marine snarled as a potent fire raged in his eyes. "I want to see your face when you come. I want to watch as I fuck every drop of cum out of you."

Jeremiah grabbed his own cock and jerked himself as Dale pressed his legs further back, almost folding him in half. Dale smacked Jeremiah's hand away. "No. That dick is mine, and you're going to come hands-free. You've done it twice now, and I get to watch this time."

"F-fuck!" Jeremiah grabbed Dale's shoulders, holding on as the man railed him, fucking him hard and deep. Over and over, pegging his prostate with every pass. Jeremiah lifted his hips, meeting him, moving with him, against him, forcing himself up and down on Dale's cock desperately. Dale possessed him in every way. He was stretched around his cock, pressed into the bed, loving every single second.

"Remember what I said? I said there'd be a moment when I make you mine. That's now, Jay. You're *mine*." Dale leaned down and growled in his ear before nipping at his lobe.

"Yes, I'm yours. Always. Yours. Oh, my God." Jeremiah knew he was babbling as tears seeped from the corners of his eyes, but he couldn't help it. He was bombarded by a multitude of sensations from all sides, aware of only his lover and what he was doing to his body and soul.

"Now, Jay. Come for me." Dale lifted one of Jeremiah's legs up and onto his shoulder and increased the pace, the change in angle allowing him to go deeper than before. The pressure built higher with every slap of Dale's hips against his own, sending Jeremiah a little closer to the edge of bliss. His cock bounced between them, untouched, smearing precum all over both their stomachs, combining with their sweat.

"Dale . . ." Jeremiah gasped as his orgasm rushed forward and slammed into him. His back bowed, and he screamed. Cum exploded from him, thick and hot, coating his stomach and chest, but he didn't stop slamming his hips up to meet Dale's continued assault.

"Jay . . . fuck . . . ugh!" Dale thrust again, once, twice, and then froze, holding himself as deep as he could inside Jeremiah as he came. The hot rush of his cum seared Jeremiah's sensitive tissue, and at that moment, he knew without a doubt he was owned. There would never be anyone else for him again, only his beautiful lover.

As Dale's orgasm eased and the rigidity of his muscles began to fade, his seed spilled out of Jeremiah's ass and onto the sheets below. They were both covered in sweat, cum, and lube, but Jeremiah didn't care. He lowered his leg off Dale's shoulder until he could wrap both legs around the man's slender hips. Burying his hands into Dale's dark hair, Jeremiah pulled him down until they were attached from mouth to groin. He kissed Dale, gently exploring the man's mouth, sucking on his lips and tongue, not ready to lose the miraculous connection they'd just forged.

"Baby . . ." Dale murmured against his lips. His cock softened and slid free from the dark confines of Jeremiah's body. Jeremiah mourned the loss, even as he winced at the sting and soreness that were left behind.

"That was . . ." Words failed him.

"Yeah. It was." Dale peppered Jeremiah's cheeks, eyelids, and forehead with the gentlest of kisses before propping himself up on his forearms. He brushed Jeremiah's hair off his face where it had fallen, sticky with sweat.

Staring at the other man's handsome face, Jeremiah finally found the words he'd wanted to say. He could no sooner hold them back than he could stop the sun from rising. "I love you."

Surprise and then tenderness filled Dale's eyes. "I love you too." Grinning, Dale kissed Jeremiah again, this time on the mouth, before rolling over onto his side. "Come here."

Wrapping an arm around Jeremiah's waist, Dale tucked him against his chest. It was almost too hot to cuddle like that, both of them still sticky with sweat and cum that were beginning to dry, but Jeremiah didn't care. A shower would happen just as soon as he was sure his legs would hold him, but for now, he was right where he wanted to be.

With his face pressed into the slope of Dale's neck, Jeremiah felt the need to clarify his earlier declaration. "I didn't say it because of the mind-blowing orgasms either, although those were definitely appreciated. But I really do love you, Dale. More than I ever thought it would be possible for me to love someone."

"Jay," Dale began, lifting Jeremiah's chin with a finger. "I know it's not just the sex. This thing between us, this connection? It's rare. Most people don't get to feel something as real as this. Now that I have it? With you? I'm never letting it go. You're mine, and I'm yours. Nothing can change that now."

Smiling with his whole heart, Jeremiah kissed his Marine, his lover, his best friend, his partner, and, maybe one day, his husband.

Chapter Twenty-Two

They eventually made it to the shower, where the bench came in handy for when Jeremiah made Dale sit and pull his legs back, so he could kneel and eat him out until he came. With the sounds Dale was making driving him crazy, Jeremiah jerked off and came all over the shower floor. It seemed rim-jobs were one of Dale's favorite things, and Jeremiah discovered a new-found appreciation for it himself if nothing more than to hear his man babble and plead. Jeremiah couldn't wait to top him, to take him apart slowly and show Dale that he wasn't the only one capable of forcing a hands-free anal orgasm.

They washed one another, worshiping each other's slick and soapy bodies as they reveled in their newly declared love. They laughed like fools, drunk on their feelings, joy bubbling up inside them both, unable to be contained. Jeremiah had never been so happy, never thought he could have this with someone. He wouldn't let it go, let Dale go, or allow anyone to bring them down.

When they were finally clean, Jeremiah grabbed a towel from the rack outside the shower and dried Dale off, enjoying his freedom to touch the other man so intimately. "How about I get us something to drink, and then we can take a nap before dinner? You wore me out, Marine."

"I'd love nothing more than to curl up with you, baby." Dale rested his head on Jeremiah's shoulder, softly kissing him and licking stray water droplets off as Jeremiah used the now-damp towel on himself. "But this has been the longest lunch break ever, so how about I go get the animals taken care of, and I'll come back for that dinner?"

"Okay. I should probably check on Anthony and the guys anyway. They're used to me being around most of the day after lunch."

Both men wrapped towels around their waists and went in search of their clothes. Everything they'd worn earlier was scattered in disarray throughout the bedroom. Bending forward to untangle his boxers from his jeans, Jeremiah winced and hissed at the pain in his ass.

"Sore?" Dale asked from behind him before gripping Jeremiah's waist and pulling him back against his muscular chest.

"Yeah, but in a good way." Glancing over his shoulder, he smiled at Dale, his lover who was no longer a secret. "It was worth the wait. I'm glad my first time was with you."

"Me too, Cowboy, me too." Dale spun him around, cradled his face with big, warm hands, and took his lips in a blistering kiss. Jeremiah melted in the man's arms and was disappointed when the kiss ended all too soon. Dale gently pressed his lips to Jeremiah's forehead. "Let me cook for you tonight?"

"I never say no to blowjobs, cold beers, or home-cooked meals." Grinning, Jeremiah moved away and dropped his towel, loving how Dale's eyes immediately drank him in. Stepping into his boxers and pulling them up, he made a show of adjusting his cock and balls.

"Such a fuckin' tease."

Jeremiah winked. "You love it."

"I do, I really fuckin' do. But if I give in every time, we'll never get out of this bedroom, and if that happens, I'm pretty sure I'll get fired, no matter how much Willow likes me." Dale dressed quickly. "I'll see you tonight. Six, okay?"

"Six is perfect. Your place?"

"Fuck no! You have a nice grill and a giant deck."

Laughing, Jeremiah couldn't resist and gathered Dale into his embrace. "Okay, I see it now. You're just with me because of my big . . . deck."

Snorting, Dale gave him a loud smacking kiss on the cheek. "Yup!" He popped the "p" at the end. "I love your big, beautiful, hard . . . deck." He grabbed Jeremiah's hips and thrust his pelvis forward several times.

"So mature, Marine. So very mature."

"Hey, you started it!" Dale let Jeremiah go and swatted him on the ass.

"Okay, okay, so I did." With joy and contentment coursing through him, he searched the floor and found his shirt and jeans. "Get going before I never let you leave."

"That wouldn't be such a bad thing, Cowboy. It might be worth getting fired." Winking and tipping his hat, Dale strode out of the bedroom, whistling as he descended the steps and went out the front door.

Smiling from ear to ear, Jeremiah shook his head and finished getting dressed. He'd just had wild monkey sex in the middle of the afternoon with the man he loved and honestly didn't care if anyone else knew about it. In fact, he wanted to shout it from the rooftop. Hmm. Maybe not. The last time he'd climbed up on the roof, he'd been a teenager and had broken his arm. He'd have to find another way to celebrate, preferably when Dale returned for dinner and Jeremiah got him naked again.

* * *

"Hey, Ethan! Gimme a hand for a bit!" Anthony shouted from where he stood in front of the horse barn.

Ethan Rivers waved in acknowledgment at the JP's foreman before turning off the hose he used to rinse the filthy ATV he'd ridden earlier to check out a fence line. The ground had been muddy from an overnight storm, and the little boy in him hadn't been able to resist plowing through a few of the larger puddles. Yeah, despite being twenty-eight years old, he was still a kid at heart—something that seemed to annoy his fiancée, Lacey Morrison, more and more as their wedding date approached, and it was still fifteen months away.

His friends had all told him he was crazy to propose after dating her for less than a year, but for him, it'd been the next logical step. Now, he was thinking that logic might've been skewed. Don't get him wrong—Lacey was a great girl—beautiful, intelligent, and fun—but lately, she seemed more excited about the wedding than about spending the rest of their lives together. And that had Ethan wondering if he'd made the biggest mistake of his life when he'd gotten down on one knee with the ring he'd spent months saving for.

At the side of Jeremiah's house, an engine roared to life, catching Ethan's attention as he strode toward the barn where Anthony was waiting for him. Dale Harris's truck did a U-turn before driving away. Since yesterday, when the gossip about Dale and Jeremiah "making a scene" at the Rock Diner had spread like wildfire, it now made perfect sense why the foreman from the neighboring ranch had been at the JP so much lately. Like everyone else, Ethan had been shocked to learn both men were gay and secretly dating. While he'd heard rumors about Dale screwing both men and women—whoever caught his eye, really—Jeremiah Urban's coming out had blown everyone's minds. Well, at least most of the people Ethan knew. Some of the Rock residents he'd spoken to said they'd suspected the man swung that way since they'd never seen him date any women. But then again, Jeremiah hadn't seemed to date anyone of any gender for the nine years Ethan had worked for him.

He didn't care one way or another who his boss dated—it wasn't his business or anyone else's—but what bugged the hell out of Ethan was the dream he'd had last night after finding out Jeremiah was gay. As a young, red-blooded man in his prime, Ethan was used to having erotic dreams, some raunchier than others. However, last night's had freaked him out a bit. The person who'd invaded his unconsciousness hadn't been his hot fiancée or even some sexy movie starlet he would never have a chance in hell with. Instead, Ethan had experienced a wet dream with someone else completely in mind—Kam Fox, fraternal twin brother of Ethan's coworker, Ged.

What the hell had that been all about?

Seriously, they were both straight, as far as Ethan knew, so it defied his logic why he'd had one of the sexiest dreams he could ever remember, and it'd involved another guy.

While Ethan had become good friends with Ged, he didn't run into Kam often enough to be more than just acquaintances. Waking up to cum covered sheets with thoughts of hard muscles and rough stubble abrading his skin had been downright bizarre.

Shaking off the unwanted memories of last night's titillating fantasy and the stirring in his groin, he approached Anthony. "What's up?"

"I need someone to hold the new gate for Cricket's stall while I install it." The mare was one of the dozen horses on the JP. Two nights ago, a garter snake had entered the equine barn and the horse's stall. Cricket had freaked and kicked the gate a few times, breaking one of the hinges and the lock. Thankfully, she hadn't injured herself, but she had managed to kill the non-venomous snake, which they'd found stomped to death in a corner the next morning, with the horse not happy it was still within her view.

Last night, Cricket had been placed in another unoccupied stall and had made her displeasure about that known by trying to nip Ged when he'd hung up her feed bucket. The fussy horse did not like any upsets to her routine.

"Sure."

Following Anthony into the barn, Ethan paused for a moment to let his eyes adjust to the darker surroundings. The overnight squall that'd raged had been followed by a pristine, cloudless sky that morning, brightening their part of the world again. He loved how everything smelled after a storm, fresh and new, like the world had been washed clean, albeit temporarily.

Anthony opened his mouth to say something, but both men froze when they heard a loud male voice spewing malice. "—fucking fudge packers. Should've known the asshole was queer. If I see him looking at me twice, I'll kick his fucking ass before shoving a branding iron up it."

"You and me both. Last thing I need is people thinking I'm a faggot because I work for him."

Ethan should've known there would be some negative reactions among the ranch hands to the news the boss was gay—and these two would've been on the top of his list if he'd made one. The first voice belonged to Simon Benson, and the second to Ferris Baxter.

Before Ethan could react, Anthony stalked toward the far end of the barn where the two men were supposed to be cleaning out the stalls. Instead, they were sitting on bales of hay, doing nothing. Well, actually, Benson was sniffling, wiping his nose, and quickly shoving something into his pocket upon hearing them approach. Yeah, he was doing something all right, and it sure as fuck wasn't work. Despite the man's attempt to brush away the evidence of the cocaine he'd been snorting, there was still some white powder under one nostril.

Both men scrambled to their feet as Anthony reached for the nearest one, who happened to be

Baxter, grabbing him by the shirt and shoving him roughly against the door jamb.

"What the fuck?" barked Benson.

"That's my question!" the foreman roared, getting into the coked-up man's face. "What the fuck? Instead of working, you're sitting on your goddamn asses, slamming the man who signs your paycheck over something that's not any of your fucking business!"

Before Benson could stop him, Anthony thrust his hand into the pocket of the man's jeans, pulling out the small vial of white powder.

"And what the hell is this shit?" he snarled, holding it up in front of Benson's red, sweating face.

"Fuck you, man! Give it back!"

Standing several inches taller than Benson, the foreman could hold the vial out of his reach. Benson made a grab for it and missed before changing tactics and taking a swing at Anthony, who easily dodged the wildly thrown punch and returned one of his own. He connected with Benson's jaw, sending him back onto his ass, as dust and hay flew up around him.

Wide-eyed, Baxter took a hesitant step toward Anthony, but Ethan moved, blocking his path. "Don't even fucking think about it."

As expected, the other man held up his palms and retreated. He'd always been a follower, not a leader, and when confronted, he usually backed down. Most of the time, he wasn't a bad guy, but unfortunately, he'd chosen to pal around with Benson and his thug cohorts. While Benson had only worked at the JP for six months, Baxter had been there for over a year.

Anthony threw the vial to the ground and crushed it with his foot with a snap, grinding the heel of his boot down, making doubly sure the drug was unusable as Benson screeched, "Nooo!"

Fire flared in his eyes, and his face flushed as he got to his feet, stumbling in the process. Spittle shot from his mouth as he jabbed a finger in Anthony's direction. "Damn it! Do you know how much that shit costs, you son of a bitch?"

"I don't give a flyin' fuck!" The muscles in Anthony's neck corded as his nostrils flared. "You're both lazy and, worse, drugged up! Add in your homophobic bullshit attitudes, and you're both fired!"

The blood drained from Baxter's face, but he remained silent as Benson continued to rant. "Fuck you, Garner! You can't fire us—you don't own this place!"

"No, I don't. But Jeremiah gave me full permission to fire anyone if I need to, and trust me, after I tell him why I canned your asses, he'll agree with me. Now, pack your shit and get the fuck off the ranch!"

Damn. Ethan had never seen Anthony that pissed before, but from the looks of things, Benson and Baxter would have to be the stupidest people on earth right then not to obey the man's command. The foreman was taller, broader, and undoubtedly stronger than both of them put together. After a moment's hesitation, they seemed to realize that.

Benson grabbed his hat from the dirt, where it'd landed when Anthony had decked him, and smacked it against his thigh, sending a brown cloud flying, before slamming it onto his head. While it appeared he wouldn't go toe-to-toe with the foreman, Benson still had some bluster in him. "Screw you, Garner! Screw you! You and that faggot can go to fucking hell! You *all* can go to fucking hell!"

Anthony's voice dropped dangerously low. "If you're not off the property in the next ten minutes, I'll break your legs, and you'll be hauled out of here on a stretcher. Get. Now!"

Clearly knowing he was fighting a losing battle, Benson stomped away, cursing and spitting, with Baxter close on his heels. The latter at least had regret in his eyes as he followed his buddy out of the barn and toward the bunkhouse.

Ethan shook his head at the two men's retreating backs. "Un-fucking-believable."

Keeping an eye on his former employees and making sure they kept moving toward the bunkhouse, Anthony replied, "But not unexpected. I'll talk to the other hands later. I won't tolerate that shit, and Jeremiah shouldn't have to deal with it, either. In the meantime, get the shotguns. I wouldn't put it past Benson to fuck up the place before leaving. I'll watch from here until you get back."

* * *

Anthony was still steaming mad when Jeremiah came out of his house about forty-five minutes after those two shitheads had left the property. He hated that he had to tell his boss he'd just fired two of the JP's employees a couple of weeks before they planned to cull the cattle. The process of weeding out the inferior animals because of infertility, low productivity, poor genetics, or advanced age usually resulted in removing about fifteen percent of the cows and bulls to increase the quality and profitability of the herd.

He also dreaded telling the newly outed man *why* he'd fired the two bigots.

Jeremiah's smile fell when he spotted Anthony. "What's with the face? Who pissed in your cornflakes?"

He crossed his arms and tried to relax his scowl. "I fired Baxter and Benson a little while ago and escorted them off the property."

The boss stopped short, his eyes widening. After a moment, he let out a heavy breath and nodded. "Okay. What happened?"

"Between the cocaine I found Benson snorting, the punch he threw at me, and the homophobic slurs they were slinging in your direction, it took me all of two seconds to can them."

"Shit." Jeremiah ran a hand down his face and then glanced around, taking a few moments to digest the information. Finally, he eyed his foreman and asked, "You okay?"

"Yeah, I'm fine." Before the other man could say anything more, Anthony held up his hand. "Jeremiah, look. It's nobody's business but yours who you date. I'm not one to judge. The only place labels belong is on bottles. In fact, one of my nephews is gay—just came out last year—he's nineteen, though the family suspected he was struggling with his sexuality for a few years before that. Anyway, we—*I* couldn't be prouder of him. He's got the guts to live his life on his terms, and that's what I want for you too—everyone deserves that. I've already talked to the rest of the hands, and you have some staunch supporters here. None of them seem to have a problem with you and Dale being together—if they do, they're keeping it to themselves. They all volunteered to step up and cover the extra work until we can replace those two assholes."

Jeremiah's gaze dropped to the ground, and he swiped at his eyes a few times before lifting his chin again. "Thank you for that, Anthony. You have no idea how much I appreciate your support—everyone's support. I'll get an ad in the paper and put out some feelers. Hopefully, we can fill those slots before we start culling. If we can't, I'm sure Willow and Nathan will let us borrow Dale and Shane for a few half days. Anything else I need to know about?"

Anthony's gaze shifted over the other man's shoulder, where a gunmetal gray BMW convertible pulled in next to the house. He shouldn't stare, waiting for Jeremiah's gorgeous sister to climb out of the $85,000 vehicle, but he couldn't help himself. His breath hitched when she appeared. Jenna wore her auburn hair up in some complicated twist that had him wishing he could remove the clip holding up her silky tresses to run his fingers through them. Mess her up a little and shatter her careful control. He didn't know much about women's clothes, but in her pretty yellow sundress, she looked like she'd just walked off the cover of a magazine. At least she'd completed the outfit with a pair of new, brown Lucchese boots—she was on a cattle ranch, after all—but the damn things had to have cost a pretty penny. The woman obviously had expensive tastes. Too expensive for him.

Damn, he was a glutton for punishment. The woman was so far out of his league and had more or less told him so last night when he'd come across her walking around the grounds of her childhood home. With her fancy car, designer clothes, gold and diamond jewelry, and highfalutin law degree, she'd never be interested in a man who smelled like cattle every day and had barely graduated from high school. Even knowing she deserved a man in a three-piece suit on her arm, it didn't stop him from wanting her anyway.

Even though she'd grown up on the ranch, Jenna no longer seemed to fit there. She'd moved up in the world, and Anthony didn't belong on her level. Oh, at first, she'd been polite about turning him down when he'd asked her to go out with him on Saturday for dinner or drinks, saying thank you and that she wasn't interested in dating anyone right then. But he'd been able to read between the lines easily.

Then he'd let long-subdued feelings out of the locked box where he kept them in the back of his mind. The ones that stemmed from being the poor kid from the wrong side of the tracks, who'd gotten bullied through all twelve years of school back in Holden, Montana. His former hometown was basically the same size as Antelope Rock, but Anthony had never felt comfortable there. In the Rock, he had friends and people he'd started to consider family. As a kid, he'd longed for kin he could feel close to instead of being raised by grandparents who'd never shown any open affection toward him or each other. To them, Anthony had been an obligation thrust upon them after their nineteen-year-old daughter had overdosed on meth three years after giving birth to him. When he'd struck out on his own at the age of eighteen, his grandparents had probably been happy to be done with him. The two of them were long gone now, and he hadn't even been able to convince himself to go back to Holden for either funeral.

Watching Jenna as she wyaved at them over her shoulder before going into the house, he'd bet a hundred bucks the greeting had been for Jeremiah alone. Anthony couldn't help but think that he'd been dead on with his impression of her last night. After she'd turned him down, he'd paused a little, then told her they could go out as friends or neighbors getting to know one another, and she'd snapped at him. "Do you spend so much time with dumb cattle that you can't hear a no when a woman says one?"

Her snide remark had gotten his hackles up, and his temper had gotten the best of him. He'd snarled back, "Why, yes, Princess, even dumb hicks like myself can understand a no. Excuse the hell out of me for trying to be friendly."

Jeremiah glanced over his shoulder and then back to his foreman with a little smirk. "Problem, Anthony?"

He tore his gaze from the back porch door Jenna had disappeared through and shook his head. Nope, not gonna go there. The last thing he needed to do was pine for a stuck-up bitch who happened to be the boss's little sister, no matter how much she revved his engine. "Nope, no problem, and there isn't anything else you need to know about—at least, not that I can think of right now." He gestured toward the horse barn. "I've . . . uh . . . got work to do."

"Uh-huh."

The knowing bastard was all but laughing at him as Anthony spun on his heels and strode toward the barn. Maybe he'd get lucky, and Cricket would kick him in the head and knock some sense into him. Lord knew he needed it.

Chapter Twenty-Three

Dale turned off Jeremiah's grill and brought the platter loaded with baked potatoes, bell peppers, corn on the cob, and steaks inside to find the handsome cowboy had just finished setting plates, silverware, pilsner glasses, and condiments on the over-sized dining room table. He'd also lit two candlesticks and put them on either side of a vase filled with the flowers Dale had given him when he arrived earlier. Jeremiah had blushed at the sweet gesture, but Dale knew the man had appreciated it. After all, he'd told Jeremiah he would romance him, especially since the cowboy had never experienced someone doing that to him before. With the intimate atmosphere of the dining room, it seemed Jeremiah planned to do some romancing of his own.

Dale glanced at the table, looking for the best place

to set down the food platter. Usually, they ate at the island or bistro set in the kitchen, on the back porch, or in the living room while watching TV. Until now, he hadn't gotten a good look at the matching table and chairs that could comfortably seat eight people. Deep and wide, the dining table was more than large enough for the two of them, and it didn't take much to envision the surface filled with all manner of dishes for holiday dinners.

"That smells amazing, babe," Jeremiah said as he poured them each a glass of the homemade beer Dale had brought over. They both had a bottle of it earlier, and Jeremiah had proclaimed it was the best batch yet. Dale made a mental note to order the ingredients to brew more of it. Maybe Jeremiah would like to make it with him. They could make a date of it. He'd ask him later.

"Thanks. I hope it tastes good too. You sure Jenna doesn't want to join us?" As far as he knew, she was upstairs in the spare bedroom she'd moved into for the foreseeable future.

Jeremiah shook his head. "I asked twice, and she said no both times." He sighed. "She's got a lot going on in that head of hers right now, so I'll give her the space she asks for."

"Okay, just checkin'." Before he put the platter down, Dale noticed the center of the table was inlaid with the JP brand. The intricate design was breathtaking. A light pine color contrasted beautifully with the darker stain covering the rest of the surface. The craftsmanship that'd gone into the piece was really impressive. "This table is gorgeous. Where'd you get it made?"

Jeremiah blushed and ducked his head before mumbling, "I, uh . . . I made it."

"*You* made this?" Dale gaped at him before depositing the food near the two place settings and then running his fingers delicately over the inlay. "Jay, this is gorgeous. I knew you'd made Shannon's cradle and . . . *ahem* . . . a few whittling projects." He winked, loving how Jeremiah's face colored an even deeper shade of red at the veiled mention of the sex toy he'd made. "But I didn't know you crafted things this large. I'm dating a freaking artist! A very talented one at that."

"Stop!" Jeremiah laughed, burying his face in his hands. "It's just something I did after my parents moved away while I was waiting on the renovations on the house to be finished. This room needed a big table, and I couldn't find one I liked in the stores, so," he shrugged, "I made one in my workshop. The chairs too. And two leaves go in here and there." He pointed to two thin lines that ran the table's width on either side of the center design. "With those in, it can seat twelve people."

Taking the chair at the head of the table, he sat and grabbed his beer, downing half of it in one go. His face was still crimson as his gaze flittered around the room. Damn, the man was so cute when he was being all shy and self-conscious.

Dale pulled a chair away from the table, examining it closely and noticing how the colors matched the rest of the set perfectly. Above the spindles, the back of each chair had a design of interlocking horseshoes burned into the wood. As he sat, he almost felt guilty for putting his full weight on one because they were so beautiful—true works of art.

"Do you think you could show me your work-shop?" He reached over, taking Jeremiah's hand in his own. "Please? You're more talented than I realized, and I want to know every part of you."

Blushing, Jeremiah squeezed his fingers. "Yes, I'll show you. After dinner, though, because I'm starving."

"I can't wait."

"Don't expect too much. It's mostly a large work shed covered in sawdust and filled with half-finished projects."

"No doubt it's as amazing as you are." Dale winked, then began filling both their plates with the hot food. When he finished, his gaze went to the inlaid design again. "I just can't get over this table."

"I could get you over the table," Jeremiah replied cheekily, cutting into his steak and popping a bite into his mouth.

"You . . . Jay." Dale snorted out a laugh, delighted

that Jeremiah was joking about bending him over the table. Pointing at the sexy cowboy with his steak knife, Dale couldn't stop the silly grin that spread across his face. "You first."

He loved this playful side of Jeremiah, and he resolved to do what he could to bring it out more often. Jeremiah hadn't let the events of the day get him down. Two of his hands had been fired after getting laid out in the barn over homophobic slurs, yet here he was, smiling, laughing, and making jokes. Warmth settled into Dale's belly that had nothing to do with the beer and good food and everything to do with the joy this man brought into his life. The love and peace he'd filled Dale's days with. Eyeing Jeremiah, he knew right then he never wanted to be without his cowboy again.

Fifteen minutes later, Jeremiah leaned his chair back on two legs, groaning as he patted his stomach. "Holy shit, Dale. You keep cooking like that, and you'll have to roll me around. I'll be the size of a house."

"Never. I'll make sure you get plenty of exercise." Standing, he pushed their plates aside and reached out his hand for Jeremiah to take. "Come on, Cowboy, show me this famous workshop of yours, and then I'll help you clean up. The walk will help us settle our stomachs too."

"All right. But I'm nervous as hell. Jenna and my parents are the only ones who've ever been in it. Not even Willow has been inside."

That announcement startled him—none of Jeremiah's friends or extended family had *ever* been inside his private sanctuary. Wow. Dale thought about commenting on how he'd been inside Jeremiah's *body* that afternoon and how could the workshop be more intimate than that but decided not to. This was obviously something very important and personal to Jeremiah, and he didn't want the man to think he wasn't honored to see the place. "There's nothing to be nervous about. I'm not going to be judging you. I just want to experience what you do—I want to see it through your eyes. After this, you never have to let me in there again if you don't want to."

Since it'd been pointed out to him before, Dale knew which building the workshop was in and led Jeremiah there, holding his hand all the way. He loved how Jeremiah didn't look around, wondering who might be watching them. He was embracing being out with a grace and open-armed freedom that made Dale's heart swell with pride. His man was doing so well.

They'd eaten later than usual, and twilight would arrive soon. Behind them, in the western sky, hues of oranges, pinks, and purples swirled together as the gilded sun prepared to dip below the horizon. The shadows cast by the two men stretched out in front of them as several bats flapped their wings overhead. Around them, dozens of crickets warmed up for their evening symphony.

"Here we are—as if it's not obvious enough." Jeremiah shrugged before unlocking the door with a key from his pocket. The building was a smaller barn set apart from the others on the large property. Even from the outside, it was apparent this structure was used for something other than animals and their associated needs. The sweet, woodsy smell of sawdust greeted them as Jeremiah pushed open one of the giant double doors, just wide enough for them to walk through.

Once inside, he took a few steps to the right and flipped a switch, flooding the interior space with light from several rows of overhead lamps. There were long racks holding lumber against one wall, while in the center of the room, a workbench stretched nearly the length of the barn. The other long wall had saws, routers, and a lathe pushed up against it. Thanks to the sawdust, the place was dirty, yes, but Jeremiah kept it well organized and brightly lit. Shelves full of various stains and cans of who knew what took up the back wall. Tools were neatly organized on pegboards. Everything seemed to have a place.

The workbench held what appeared to be a half-finished rocking chair at the far end, some sort of shelf in the middle, and at the end closest to the door, there rested a large wooden barrel, like one used to age whiskey. Intrigued, Dale pointed to it. "What's this?"

Jeremiah shrugged again, rubbing his hand against the back of his neck and shuffling his feet on the sawdust-strewn floor. "Just, uh, something I bought. I, um, thought I could take it apart and make you a rack to store your beer."

"Jay. . ." Staring at the barrel, Dale was speechless. Never had he thought Jeremiah would devote what little free time he had to make something for him.

"I know, it's dumb . . ."

Whirling around, he quickly closed the distance between them and cupped Jeremiah's face in his hands, stopping any further protests with a deep kiss. "Stop it. It's not stupid. It's the nicest, most thoughtful thing anyone has ever done for me. And we weren't even really *together* together until today, so you did this before we'd committed to each other. That makes it mean even more." Resting his forehead on Jeremiah's, he blinked and took a deep breath to force back the tide of his emotions. "Thank you," he whispered.

Jeremiah pulled away just enough so their eyes could meet. "For what? I didn't even start on it yet."

"Shut up, Cowboy. I love you. That's what's important here, right now, at this moment. And you love me. I knew it—I could feel it—but now I can see it too. I don't know what I did to deserve you, but whatever it was, I'm grateful for it. Now kiss me, dammit."

"Oh, Dale. I love you too." Jeremiah's eyes watered with a mixture of emotion as he followed Dale's command and kissed him deeply, thoroughly, and oh-so passionately.

* * *

Later that night, Jeremiah's phone vibrated and slid across his nightstand, loud enough to wake him. He snatched the thing before it could disturb Dale snoring softly next to him. Blinking a few times, he tried to read the numbers on his bedside clock and groaned when they finally came into focus, telling him it was only a little after one a.m. He had to be up in four hours, and whoever was calling him better have a good fucking reason, or there'd be hell to pay. He swiped the screen to answer the call without bothering to check the caller ID.

"Lo?" he mumbled, keeping his voice low and running a hand over his face.

"Jeremiah? It's Grady—sorry to wake you, but it looks like your fence next to the main road was cut— we've got your cattle all over the place."

"Fuck me." He groaned again, deeper and longer. "Give me a few to get dressed and haul Anthony and the hands out of bed. We'll be right there."

Disconnecting the call, he rolled over and nudged Dale to wake him. There was nothing more he wanted to do than cuddle up to the man again and fall back to sleep, but ranch work was never done, even at one in the morning.

"W-wat?" Dale muttered, still mostly asleep.

"Grady called—there's fencing down, and cattle are in the road. I've gotta go, but I'll be back as soon as I can." After kissing Dale's bare shoulder, Jeremiah swung his legs over the side of the bed while swiping the screen on his phone. He opened his contacts, preparing to wake his foreman up.

"'lright." Dale climbed from the bed, stumbling a little. "I'll come help."

"Baby, no, go back to sleep. We got this," Jeremiah protested, waiting as the phone rang and rang. Anthony was a notoriously heavy sleeper, and he fully expected to need to call several times before the man finally heard the ringing. Maybe it would be faster just to go pound on the door of his cabin.

"Shut up."

Dale was apparently a grumpy brute when he was woken up in the middle of the night. Chuckling at the adorable, bear-like growling noises his lover was emitting, Jeremiah gave up on calling Anthony and stood to get dressed.

"Shutting up. If you want to haul your ass out of my big, warm, comfy bed to help me chase cattle, fine. Who am I to stop you?"

Dale glared at him before raising an eyebrow while pulling on his pants—sans boxers. Damn the man. "Who, indeed? Let's go, Cowboy. Get a move on. I want to get back into that big, warm, comfy bed with you as soon as possible."

"Yes, please."

Less than ten minutes later, after waking the hands and banging on Anthony's door until it opened, they pulled their ATVs out onto the road, turning left toward the flashing red and blue lights of Grady's vehicle. Jeremiah slowed down, carefully scanning the fence as he did. It was easy to find the break, not only from the few dozen cows milling around the hole but by the two fence posts that had been torn from the ground, as well as the wire being cut. This was no accidental break—someone had deliberately done it. If a driver had lost control of their vehicle and hit the fence, the posts would've been knocked farther into the pasture and not where they were, lying on the shoulder of the road.

Anger tightened his jaw as Jeremiah stopped his quad and climbed off to survey the damage, pulling a flashlight from a pack of supplies that was always strapped to the back of the ATV.

Anthony stopped his four-wheeler next to Jeremiah's, followed closely by Dale.

"This looks shitty," Anthony said unnecessarily, earning him a glower from both Jeremiah and Dale.

"No? Really?" Jeremiah was rarely sarcastic, but when people fucked with his livelihood and that of his workers, he had a right to be pissed off and salty.

"Sorry, boss." The foreman gestured to where the ranch hands, Ethan, Austin, and Ged, were pulling up in the latter's truck, the bed loaded with two of the new posts that'd been delivered less than twenty-four hours ago, a large spool of fencing wire, and tools. "Me and the boys will get started on rounding up the cows. We'll do a count in the morning and make sure we got them all."

"Let me talk to Grady, and then I'll give you a hand."

Dragging his attention from where his flashlight beam shone on the damaged fence, Jeremiah met Dale's gaze, finding fury that matched his own flaring in the man's eyes. After a moment, Dale squeezed Jeremiah's upper arm. "It'll be okay, babe. I'll go give them a hand."

Nodding in response, he strode toward where his cousin's vehicle blocked the road, its flashing blue and red lights creating a disco effect in the middle of the night. Grady had just finished setting up flares farther up the road where there was a moderate curve. The last thing they needed was for someone to come flying around the blind spot and start plowing through the men and the herd.

"Grady, what the fuck?" He clicked the button of his Maglite on and off several times as rage burned through him.

The sheriff tossed some extra flares into the back of his SUV. "Looks like someone cut the wire and dragged the posts out. At first, I thought maybe someone drove off the road or something, but it's obvious this was deliberate. Also, I, uh, found this." Grady held out a transparent evidence bag containing a piece of paper, his face stony and more than a little pissed off. "I didn't want to show this to you, but I think it's best if you know so you and Dale can be on guard."

Jeremiah's gut tightened with dread as he reached

for the item. Turning his flashlight back on, he held the light to read the chicken-scratched message written in black ink on the paper.

This is what fags like you deserve! Get out of our town before we cut you next!

His hand tightened into a fist. When Grady grabbed his wrist, Jeremiah realized he was close to destroying evidence. Relaxing his fingers, he gave the note back to the man and then ran his hands through his hair. "This is. . . fuck." He hung his head, doing his best to wrangle his emotions so he could communicate without screaming or punching something.

"Any idea who might've done this?"

He shrugged as he glanced around at the cows milling about, seemingly unperturbed that their prison break had been thwarted. "A few. Anthony fired Ferris and Simon this afternoon after they were talking smack about Dale and me. Could've been them. I also had a run-in with Carl Skinner and Ken Larson at Ducky's and another with Frank Schneider over at the diner. And I'm sure there are more homophobes in the Rock who haven't had a chance to confront me yet. That list will probably grow over the next few days."

If Grady was shocked that Jeremiah had basically just confirmed he was gay, the man didn't show it. He'd undoubtedly heard it from the rumor mill by now, but here was the proof. "Well, let me handle this, but stay on guard. I'd start carrying that pistol of yours, too, if I were you—Dale, as well, if he has one."

He clapped Jeremiah on the shoulder. "We're going to find who did this, and we'll file as many charges as possible against them. I wish the state legislators would get off their asses and pass the damn hate crime laws. Forty-seven out of fifty states have them, and we're not one of them. You'd think after that college student was tortured and killed twenty-plus years ago, it would've been a no-brainer, but apparently, it's not a requirement for lawmakers to have brains. I'm telling you this, though, cousin, I'm not letting these assholes get away with bullshit like this. I promise. Not in my fucking town."

Jeremiah nodded his gratitude before searching for Dale and spotting him, shooing a cow back through the hole in the fence. He'd do anything to protect the love of his life—anything.

"We'll be careful, but I'm not hiding. Not anymore. Never again."

A small smile appeared on his cousin's face. "I'd never ask you to. I love seeing you this way—been a long time coming. I'd never ask either one of you to give up the happiness you've obviously found. These fuckers," he held up the evidence bag, "they're the ones who are wrong, not you two."

"Thanks, Grady." He gestured toward where his employees and Dale were rounding up the cattle. "I better go help them so we can all catch a little more sleep before the workday really starts."

"I'll give you a hand."

"By the way, what the hell are *you* doing working in the middle of the night? Doesn't the top spot come with perks?"

Grady laughed wryly as he pushed on a cow's flank to urge her toward the opening to the pasture. "Yeah, it does. But there was a structure fire earlier over in Butterfield. A few of the volunteer firemen were injured when a wall collapsed. Nothing serious, though, but the chief suspected it was arson, so I let Rissa know I had to head over there with the fire inspector. This job definitely got a little easier since she became old enough to stay home by herself. I was just cruising through the area on my way home and came across this mess."

"Well, I'm glad you did. There could've been a couple of hundred cows out here if it was a few hours from now before someone else passed by." While the road that ran past the JP and Skyview ranches saw a lot of use during the day, in the middle of the night, it wasn't a busy thoroughfare.

As they worked, Jeremiah debated how he would tell Dale about the note. He couldn't keep it from him —there was no question of that. They were both being threatened, and he'd never forgive himself if something ever happened to his Marine. He just hoped and prayed this test wouldn't be too much for their new relationship, that they'd survive it, and the stress wouldn't fracture what they'd begun to build.

* * *

Jeremiah took a deep breath and raised his hand to knock on Willow's front door. Things were beyond good with Dale, the threat from last night notwithstanding, and he felt the time was finally right to have a conversation with his sister and Willow about manipulating him. While he knew their intentions were good, he was a grown-ass man and didn't need them interfering in his love life now that he actually had one.

Knock. Knock.

While waiting for the door to open, he tried to keep his temper on a tight leash, which was a little difficult after the unexpected escapades in the middle of the night. He didn't want to yell at them, but the longer he stood there, the more irritated he became at their meddling.

With both Jenna's SUV and Willow's pickup truck parked by the side of the house, he knew they were both there, but there was a possibility they were on the back porch and didn't hear him. He knocked again, just short of pounding on the door. If he didn't get an answer, he'd walk around to the back of the house to search for them.

This time, however, Willow's voice rang out almost immediately. "Come in!"

A small snort escaped him as he remembered when she'd first moved to the Rock and had been appalled most residents didn't keep their doors locked during the day—something that apparently wasn't the case back in Philadelphia. Such was life in a small Wyoming town. However, after last night's threat, you could be damn sure Jeremiah would be locking his doors whether he was home or not for the foreseeable future.

Turning the knob, he pushed the door open, entered, then closed it again before striding down the hallway to the kitchen after noticing the living room was empty.

"Jeremiah? Since when do you knock? What's up?" Willow was sitting at the table and turned back to continue feeding Shannon, who was in her highchair and wearing more of the mashed-up sweet potatoes than was probably in her stomach. The baby drew a smile from him, as his goddaughter always managed to do. Her presence would keep what he had to say on the more civil side, at least.

When he didn't answer her, Willow glanced back over her shoulder and took in his stiff posture and sour expression, her own face falling. "What's wrong?"

"Where's my sister?" he asked, only wanting to have this conversation once.

"Um. She's, uh, in the bathroom."

Jenna had mentioned that morning that she was coming over to hang out with Willow and Shannon for the afternoon while Nathan ran some errands. Jeremiah had waited until he saw Nathan's truck leave before heading over. He doubted the man would appreciate him confronting his wife this way, but he felt it needed to be done—for him and the sake of their friendship.

"Jeremiah, is everything okay?"

"No, it's not, but I want to talk to you and Jenna together."

Willow's eyes narrowed, and the corners of her mouth pulled downward. "You're scaring me." She picked up a wet washcloth and cleaned off Shannon's face before lifting her from the highchair and setting her down to play.

From down the hall, he heard a door open, and moments later, his sister joined them in the kitchen. When she spotted him and noticed the tension in the room, she glanced at Willow before settling her gaze on him. "Jeremiah, what are you doing here? Something wrong?"

"Sit down. Both of you." He pointed to the kitchen table, waited until they sat down, then took a seat himself. "I have something to say, and you're both going to listen. Understand?"

Willow twisted her fingers together, anxiety distorting her pretty face. "Okay, but is Nathan okay? You're really scaring me."

He shook his head. "Sorry, I didn't mean to frighten you. Nathan is fine. This is about you two and the lie you told me. You said Dale was quittin' and movin' away. He wasn't—in fact, according to him, as pissed as he was at me, the thought never crossed his mind. While I appreciate you were both trying to help me, the way you went about it was underhanded and unacceptable. I'm a grown man—older than both of you—and you treated me like a child who's easily manipulated into doing your bidding."

"Oh, Jeremiah," Jenna began, but he held up his hand, halting her words.

"Yes, things worked out between Dale and me. We're together now and committed to one another. I'm happier than I've ever been. In part, I suppose I do have you two to thank for that, but I'm telling you this, if you ever pull that sh—crap on me again, we're going to have a serious problem." He'd stopped himself from swearing just in time. He was really trying to clean up his language in front of Shannon, and there was no reason not to start getting into the habit early.

Willow reached a hand across the table to him, but he ignored it as she pleaded, "Jeremiah, please forgive us. We're so sorry, but we just wanted you to be happy and couldn't think of anything else to help get you and Dale back together. In Jenna's defense, it was my idea. Please, don't be mad at her."

He huffed out a breath. "I'm not mad—I'm hurt and disappointed."

"Oh, God, that's so much worse." Jenna dropped her forehead into her open hands and groaned. "Mom's been using that line on us since we were little, and dammit, it always works." She gave him a wry look. "I'm sorry, big brother. You have to know what we did came from a place of love, I swear. We didn't want you to lose the best thing that's ever happened to you."

He nodded. "I know that, sis. But can you imagine how I felt? I thought the man I was falling in love with was so pissed and disgusted with me that he was going to *move away*. Forever. It very nearly broke me. To think I'd finally found someone that made me feel brave enough to come out, who was worth all the fear and uncertainty, then to think he was going to leave." Shaking his head, he swallowed, trying to force down his emotions.

"Fuck, Jeremiah, I'm so sorry," Willow cried as fat tears ran down her cheeks.

This time, when she reached for him, he took her hand in his and squeezed it gently. "I forgive you, sweetheart. You're my best friend. I'll always forgive you." He made eye contact with Jenna. "And you're my favorite sister, so the same goes."

"I'm your only sister." She stood, stepped behind him, and wrapped her arms around his neck before kissing the top of his head. "I'm sorry too, big bro. I really am. It just broke my heart to see you so sad. All I've ever wanted was for you to have the happiness you deserve."

Patting her hands, he let a moment of silence fall over the room before clearing his throat. "Okay, enough of this. I got everything off my chest and accepted your apologies. It's done. Now," he glanced over his shoulder, "I want to know what's going on with you and my foreman, Jenna."

His sister's face turned a deep scarlet, and she let go of him and snapped, "Nothing. Nothing is fucking going on between me and that . . . that . . . that heathen."

Frowning, she huffed and flopped back onto her chair, ignoring Jeremiah's and Willow's amused and curious expressions. Recalling the conversation with Jenna about her moving back to the Rock, he decided to drop the subject. Whatever was going on between her and Anthony was none of his business, just as he'd pointed out to the two women moments ago that they needed to stay out of his own relationship issues.

Instead, he pointed to the glass jar on the counter across the room. "Now, that's two dollars in the swear jar, one from each of you—yes, I was keeping track." He grinned as they grumbled and dug cash out of their pockets. At this rate, Shannon's college fund would be fat and happy by the time she graduated from high school.

A few minutes later, after helping himself to a cup of coffee, Jeremiah sat back down and prepared for the next conversation he needed to have with the two women. Since Jenna was currently staying with him, and Willow was his best friend and immediate neighbor, Nathan and they all needed to be aware of the threat against him and Dale. Taking a deep breath, he blew it out slowly. "All right. There's something else I need to talk to you both about. You might want to get your money back out because I have a feeling you'll be adding more to the swear jar before I'm done."

Chapter Twenty-Four

Dale pulled his truck to a stop outside Ducky's, put it in Park, and quickly reviewed his list before getting out and striding toward the doors. Muttering under his breath not to forget to swing by the post office and pick up a package for Willow, he forced his mind to focus on what he was doing. He was anxious to finish the errands quickly, so he could finish his workday early and spend the late afternoon and evening with Jay. Despite the incident with the cattle and hate-filled note, last night had been amazing.

After they left Jeremiah's workshop, they'd gone back to the house and watched a movie before retiring to the bedroom. Making love to Jeremiah—and making love is exactly what it'd been—had made Dale feel complete. A piece of himself that he hadn't even realized was missing had clicked into place. Now, he didn't want to be apart from Jeremiah, even for one night. It was way too soon to live together, but he was desperately hoping for some more sleepovers—hopefully almost every night.

"Look, it's that fucking faggot." The snarled slur drew his attention, freezing his blood and sending a shot of adrenaline surging through him. Grady's warning came back to him, that someone might want to hurt him and Jeremiah, and his advice that they arm themselves.

In Wyoming, any legal resident of the United States, twenty-one years old or older, who could lawfully possess a firearm was allowed to carry a concealed handgun without a permit. The state also had a "stand your ground" law, which meant if a person feared they were in danger of imminent death or serious bodily injury, they could employ deadly force against the person threatening them. Unfortunately, Dale had left his pistol at home, convinced he didn't need it while working at the ranch and forgetting to grab it before he headed into town.

The source of the derogatory comment was that bastard, Schneider, who was leaning against the wall next to the entrance to Ducky's, smoking a cigarette. Benson and Skinner flanked him. It seemed like a few of the homophobic assholes in the Rock had found each other.

Great, it's a party!

Dale kept his mouth shut, resolving to get inside

the store and not engage. Just like bullies in a school-yard, the best thing was to ignore them as much as possible. Their weapons were just words. Hateful, disgusting words, but all the same, he could be the bigger man and walk away. No matter how much he wanted to beat all three of them to a pulp and show them exactly how hard this queer could hit.

Schneider stepped forward directly into Dale's path. "Boy, I was talking to you."

"Get out of my way." Dale kept his eyes trained on Schneider, even though his military training made him hyper-aware of what else was happening around him. The other two assholes pushed off the wall and circled Dale, boxing him in. The hair on the back of his neck rose—this was quickly becoming dangerous. He was surrounded and outnumbered. *Shit.*

He shoved his list into his pocket, settling his weight evenly on the balls of his feet and readying himself for the fight that was sure to come. His gut was in knots at the expectation of violence. He could feel the tension crackling in the air around him. His mind calmed, and he relaxed into a defensive stance. His time in the Marines had conditioned him for situations like this. Three-on-one wasn't a fair fight, and he was sure he was about to get his ass kicked, but he'd be taking at least one of them down with him. Maybe two if he was quick enough.

"I don't think so. You need to get it through your thick skull you're not wanted. This town doesn't need perverts like you in it." Schneider poked him in the chest as he spoke.

"Don't fucking touch me. This is your one chance. Walk away. Now." He fought to put as much authority into his voice as possible.

"Oh, look at that, boys! This fairy has some bite to him," Benson taunted. "We don't got to do shit, faggot."

Schneider flicked his lit cigarette at Dale's face. While Dale was able to dodge the butt, it was just enough distraction for him to get caught off guard. Someone, probably Skinner, shoved him in the back, and Dale's foot shot out in response, connecting a kick to the guy's gut. An *oomph* followed it, even as Dale stumbled off-balance. He recovered quickly, knowing that every second counted.

He raised his fists, protecting his face, and shouted, "Come on then, you fuckers!"

A red haze of rage fell across his line of sight as his fists shot out, connecting both jabs and punches. He blocked as many of the strikes aimed at him as possible but took just as much damage as he dished out. The assholes fought dirty. Dale knew he had to stay on his feet as long as possible, hoping someone saw the fight and called 9-1-1. If they got him to the ground, it would be all over. They'd kick him to death.

After taking a sucker punch to the jaw, he spit a mouthful of blood into Skinner's face, following it with a perfect jab to his nose which gave way with a rewarding *crunch*. The redneck staggered back, squealing and holding both hands to his nose as he bled all over himself and the sidewalk.

With no time to reap any satisfaction, Dale turned his attention back to Schneider. Pivoting his weight to his back leg, he kicked the man in the ribs, his shin making solid contact. With a pain-filled yelp, Schneider twisted away, grabbing his side protectively while glaring daggers at Dale, who was holding his own better than expected. If they'd rushed him all at once, it would've been over by now.

While Schneider paused a moment to catch his breath, Benson took his friend's place, swinging with strength but little finesse, although still managing to tuck his meaty fist into Dale's side. Grunting in pain, he whirled around, striking out as he moved. His powerful haymaker punch connected with Benson's jaw with a sickening *crack,* and the man crumbled to the sidewalk, out cold. Sirens wailed in the distance, but they couldn't get there fast enough for Dale. Spitting blood, he turned back to Schneider, who shouted something unintelligible and threw an orange-sized rock at Dale's head. He tried to duck, but it still glanced off his skull, just above his ear, making him see stars. He stumbled, and Schneider rushed forward.

Something metallic reflected the midday sun, sparkling as Schneider swung his fist, and Dale, stunned by the rock, couldn't move fast enough to avoid the blow. His stomach burned white-hot before he realized the bastard had pulled a knife and he'd just been sliced open. The pain and dizziness in his head overwhelmed everything else, but his abs felt scorched and wet. He ignored it for a moment.

Rage surged through him, and he advanced on Schneider, determined to end this once and for all. A wave of weakness crashed over him, making his legs shake and bringing him up short. *Fuck.*

His injuries had to be worse than he thought. He struggled to stay on his feet, buying some more time for the deputies to get there.

Off to Dale's right side, Skinner had managed to get back up and held onto a post on the feed store's front porch for support. His eyes widened at Schneider still brandishing the knife. "What the fuck? Are you crazy? Don't kill him!"

Yeah, what he fucking said.

"Watch me!" Schneider responded before pressing forward again, clear, murderous intent in his eyes. The knife was tight in his fist, gleaming and ready to gut Dale.

Dale's surroundings began to spin and blur. Despite his best efforts to remain standing, his legs gave out, and he fell to his knees. Glancing down, he gasped in horror at the sight of his own blood. His formally white shirt was stained a deep ruby, and his jeans were quickly becoming saturated as well, the wash of blood soaking the fabric down to his knees.

"Fuck . . ." Everything grew hazier as white and

black spots danced at the edges of his vision. He blinked rapidly, trying to clear it, but it was useless.

"Sheriff! Drop the knife! Hands in the air!" The voice shouting sounded familiar, but Dale couldn't place where he'd heard it before—it seemed so far away and almost garbled. Other sounds were muffled like he was underwater.

Trying to stem the blood flow, he clutched his stomach as he swayed on his knees, suddenly so dizzy he couldn't hold his head up. His last sight before he pitched forward was his hat tumbling from his head and falling onto the bloody sidewalk.

"Jay . . ." he whispered before his world went black.

* * *

"Any word?" Grady stopped in front of Jeremiah and held out one of two coffees he'd probably gotten out of a hospital vending machine. The ER's waiting area bustled with midday activity, but Jeremiah ignored everyone, his gaze remaining pinned on the door leading to the treatment rooms.

Taking the proffered drink, Jeremiah shook his head as Grady sat in the chair beside him. "Not since the paramedic who brought him in came and told me Dale woke up after they started an IV and gave him some fluids. He said it looked worse than it really was after they were able to clean up some more of the blood and get a good look at the wound. Apparently, the doctor said it would need a lot of stitches but wouldn't require actual surgery. I asked, but I can't go back and sit with him until they finish stitching him up. Something about reducing the risk of infection or some bullshit like that."

It'd been about an hour since the ambulance had screamed into the hospital's parking lot with Jeremiah's pickup truck hot on its ass. By the time he found a parking spot, they'd already whisked Dale inside. The only thing Jeremiah had been able to do was go to the registration desk and give a woman there Dale's information—which, surprisingly, was everything but the man's insurance carrier. He hadn't realized how much he'd learned about Dale over the last few months. Somehow, he'd managed to tell the woman what she needed to know without yelling or breaking down and bawling his eyes out.

Then, the torturous waiting game had begun.

Not long after, Jenna and Willow had rushed in and succeeded in calming Jeremiah down from a panic attack that'd been slowly closing in on him with each second that passed. His skin had felt clammy from a cold sweat as his hands trembled. Apparently, Grady had called them to come stay with Jeremiah so he wouldn't be alone. Nathan had remained home with Shannon but demanded updates every half hour.

While Jeremiah had appreciated his sister's and best friend's support, he'd gotten tired of their attempts to comfort him in between unbearable silence or random stilted conversation. He finally told them to take a break in the cafeteria for a bit and bring him back something to eat—not that he could stomach anything right then. Instead of sipping the coffee Grady had given him, he set the cup on a small table beside his chair. Just the thought of eating or drinking anything made him nauseous. All he could see in his mind was the copious amount of blood that'd stained Dale's clothes and his bruised and ashen face as they loaded his unconscious body into the ambulance.

"Dale's strong. He'll be good as new in no time. I have his hat in my truck, by the way."

"Thanks." He glared at Grady. "What the fuck happened? All I know is there was a fight, and it was three against one."

His cousin filled him in on what witnesses had told the responding deputies. As Jeremiah listened, his outrage grew as his stomach roiled violently. When he finished the recap, Grady lifted his Stetson and ran his hand through his hair. "Anyway, all three are under arrest for aggravated assault and battery. Schneider will also be facing charges for possession of a deadly weapon with intent to harm and attempted murder. When he pulled out the knife, the witnesses heard him threaten to kill Dale. He's still on probation from his last DUI, so he won't be granted bail. I doubt any of them will see the light of day for quite some time."

"I hope karma takes a huge bite out of his ass before someone shivs him in jail." It was the first time in Jeremiah's life he'd wished death upon someone, and he hated the feeling, but that fucking asshole could've killed Dale. Jeremiah didn't think he'd ever forget the terror he'd felt when Ducky called him to tell him Dale had been ambushed.

He dropped his head into his hands. "I should've never come out. Dale's hurt because of me, and it could've been so much worse. I can't help but think he'd be better off without me."

Grady grasped Jeremiah's shoulder and squeezed hard, commanding his attention. "Don't say that. Don't even think it. You hear me? There will always be people who hate others because of who they love, what color their skin is, what god they pray to, what side of the tracks they grew up on, who they voted for, and what uniform they wear. You think I haven't had my share of harassment and threats because of this badge?" He pointed to the gold star on the left side of his pressed, white button-down shirt. "It's nobody's right to demand you conform to their ideals. Dale makes you happy—more so than I've ever seen you, Jer. Why should you be alone and miserable just to please others? Don't let those pieces of shit make you give up the best thing that's ever happened to you. It's one of the reasons why your folks and mine don't talk anymore and why I barely talk to my parents. I—"

Jeremiah's eyes narrowed as he stared at Grady. "What're you talking about?"

He knew his mother and her sister had a big fight

about something when he was in his mid-teens. It'd put a huge rift between them, but even after all those years, Jeremiah's parents still wouldn't tell him what it'd been all about. Apparently, his cousin knew more about it than he did.

Grady cocked his head to the side. "You really don't know what they fought about back then, do you?" When Jeremiah shook his head, the other man continued. "Well, shit. Looks like I get to be the one to fill you in. The fight was over you."

"Me? What the fuck?"

"Yup. It was during a summer barbecue at the JP when I was twenty-two or twenty-three. My parents suspected you were gay and told your folks something along the lines of 'make sure he gets straight again,' otherwise, you'd be going to hell. They even told them to send you to one of those conversion camps so you wouldn't turn your cousins gay too—as if that's how things work."

Unable to formulate a verbal response, Jeremiah's eyes were huge as he gaped at Grady. He had no idea anyone had guessed he was gay back then. Hell, he'd still been figuring it out himself around that time.

"Your mother had a freaking conniption and told my mother off, saying she didn't care if you were gay, straight, bisexual, or screwing aliens. As long as you weren't messin' around with farm animals, there wasn't a damn thing wrong with you. And, yes, those were her exact words—I can still hear her sayin' them too.

Anyway, she kicked my folks out of the house, and to my knowledge, the only time they ever said another word to each other was at Grandpa Jack's funeral, and they were barely civil then. Of course, that didn't stop my brother and sister and me from visiting y'all whenever we could. It didn't matter to us."

He'd always known Aunt Anna and Uncle Henry were frequent churchgoers, but he never suspected it went beyond that to the point they were religious fanatics and intolerant bigots. Then again, it'd been forever since he last saw them, and come to think about it, they hadn't exactly been friendly toward him at his grandfather's funeral. He'd thought that'd just been a carryover from their fight with his parents, not knowing he'd been the cause of it. "Holy shit. How do you know all this?"

"I was *there*, but I don't think any of them realized it—they were all too busy yelling at each other in the kitchen. You, Jenna, and the other kids were all scattered around the ranch, practicing your ropin' or something—I forget. The rest of the adults were outside too. What I *do* remember is I had to go to the bathroom and heard the whole thing through the back porch door. It was pretty bad—I was surprised there wasn't any bloodshed. My folks were livid—they were halfway home before they realized they'd left me at your house. I'd caught a lift with them to the barbecue because my car was in the shop, and they completely forgot."

He snorted since he could actually picture that in

his mind. It wouldn't have been the first time they'd forgotten their son somewhere. Jeremiah remembered hearing about one time his aunt had left Grady at a Walmart when his cousin had been around eight or nine and checking out the toy department.

"It was the first time I'd realized how bigoted my parents were, so it wasn't really a shock when they forbade me to marry Leah because she was Jewish."

The hits just kept coming. Jeremiah rubbed his jaw, his late-day scruff abrading his fingers. "Are you kidding me? Is that why you two eloped to Vegas?"

"Yup. Leah's parents were gone, and mine refused to come to the wedding, so we did our own thing. It didn't matter to my folks that she didn't practice her religion and that any kids we had would be raised Protestant. As it is, they barely have a relationship with Rissa, and I doubt they'd even have that if she wasn't baptized.

"The point is, Jeremiah, when I met Leah, I knew almost immediately she was the love of my life. There was no way I would let anyone dictate to me who I could or couldn't love—not even my parents. So why are you letting some two-bit redneck assholes dictate who you spend your life with?"

Why indeed?

"Jeremiah Urban?"

A woman dressed in blue scrubs stood at the door to the patient area, glancing around the waiting room, and Jeremiah jumped to his feet.

"That's me!"

She smiled at him. "Mr. Harris is all stitched up and asking for you."

Relief coursed through him as he practically ran across the room with Grady on his heels. Jeremiah's cousin put a hand on his arm. "Hey, I'm glad he's going to be okay. You go on in and reassure yourself, but I'll need to talk to him in a few minutes with one of my detectives who's on the way. I'm just going to make a few phone calls first. All right?"

He nodded. "Yeah, sure. Thanks."

The nurse held open the door for Jeremiah and then pointed to the far end of the treatment area. "He's in that room down there in the first bed, resting comfortably with the pain medications we gave him."

"Thank God." He moved to stride down the open area between closed-curtain cubicles but then stopped and glanced back. "And thank you too."

"My pleasure."

Jeremiah entered the room the nurse had indicated and peeked around a curtain to see if he was in the right place. He swallowed a gasp at the sight of Dale lying still and pale on the gurney, a white blanket on top of him and tucked around his shoulders. His eyes were closed, and there was a small cut and a knot high above his right ear. An angry purple bruise had formed on his jaw, and his bottom lip was split. An IV line ran from one arm to a pole, and leads snaked out from under the blanket to a heart monitor that beeped in a steady, comforting rhythm.

After sliding the curtain shut behind him, Jeremiah pulled a lone chair closer to the bed and sat. He removed his hat, setting it gently on the bed beside Dale's leg, and then reached out and carefully took Dale's hand, being mindful of the IV catheter and his split, bloody, and bruised knuckles. His man hadn't gone down without a helluva fight.

"Oh, baby . . ." Jeremiah whispered, not wanting to disturb Dale's rest but unable to hold in his grief, worry, and rage anymore. Jeremiah had waited over forty years for the man who would steal his heart, and in the blink of an eye, he'd almost lost him. He wished Grady would give him five minutes alone with each of those bastards so he could rip them apart.

When he'd gotten the call from Ducky, alerting him to the fight, Jeremiah had been out of his mind with fear. He raced into town just in time to see a bloodied Dale on a stretcher, his shirt cut open, being loaded into the ambulance. Meanwhile, Grady and several of his deputies had the three other men in cuffs. A large crowd had gathered, and there'd been a pool of blood on the cement walkway near the entrance to the feed store. Jeremiah swore his heart had stopped right then. He hadn't had time to get out of his truck before the ambulance had taken off with its lights flashing and siren blaring, so he followed it straight to the hospital, breaking a few traffic laws along the way. Not that he cared. Nothing else had mattered then except getting to the man he'd fallen in love with and finding out how badly he'd been hurt.

"Jay. . ." Dale struggled to speak, his eyelids fluttering open as the heart monitor beeped faster.

"*Shh*, baby. Relax. Everything is okay." Jeremiah kissed the tips of Dale's fingers, then used his free hand to stroke the man's forehead gently.

"I'm so glad you're here." With his eyes unfocused, Dale's voice had a soft and dreamy quality that Jeremiah assumed was coming from the painkillers.

"Of course, I'm here. I was so worried about you."

Dale gave him a big, dopey grin. "I got my ass kicked, didn't I?"

Jeremiah huffed, then chuckled. "From what Grady told me, you held your own until the knife came out."

"Yeah, fuckin' cheater." Dale pulled his hand free from Jeremiah's grip, then reached up and cupped his jaw. Jeremiah closed his eyes and leaned into the touch, relief a living, breathing entity inside him. Dale's thumb caressed his cheek. "God damn, Cowboy, you're so damn pretty. Those freckles drive me crazy."

A snort escaped him before a grin spread across his face. "You're high."

"Probably. It feels awesome—I'm floatin'. You know what else is awesome?" Dale wiggled around, pushing the blanket down to his waist, exposing his bare torso. They hadn't put one of those useless gowns on him, so a dark bruise that'd formed over Dale's right rib cage was visible. Lower than that, a large, clean, white dressing covered what Jeremiah assumed was the stitched-up knife wound.

"It's so damn hot in here," Dale complained. "Fuck. Wait, that's not awesome. That's not what I meant." That dopey smile was back. "You, Jeremiah Peter . . . um, Peter . . . Peter-Pumpkin-Eater . . . uh, Urban—that's it! Sorry, babe. Anyway, you're awesome. You're an awesome person. You're awesome in the sack. You're an awesome boyfriend. Just . . . wow. You blow my mind, baby. Everything about you is . . ."

He trailed off, his eyes glassy and staring at the ceiling as he limply rotated his hand in the air. "Fuck, what's the word I'm looking for?"

Jeremiah's whole body shook as he tried not to burst out laughing and disturb any other patients. "Awesome?" he supplied with a giggle.

His gaze dropped to the large bandage again, and all the mirth from a moment ago drained from him. Swallowing thickly, he met Dale's stoned gaze, giving up the fight against his tears and letting a few run down his face.

"Aw. Don't cry, Jay." Dale crooked his finger at Jeremiah. "C'mere. Gimme some sugar, Cowboy."

Leaning forward, he kissed Dale, trying to be careful, but his lover wasn't having it. The man grabbed him by the ears and jerked him forward, smashing their mouths together.

Mumph.

Dale let him go as quickly as he'd grabbed him. He suddenly looked sober. "I thought of you, you know? When I fell, Jay, and I thought I was gonna bleed to death on that sidewalk, my last thought was of you and how much I love you."

"Oh, Dale, I love you too." He leaned forward, resting his forehead on Dale's shoulder. "I almost lost you today. The thought of never seeing you again . . . God, I wanted to die with you."

"I'm here, baby, I'm here, and I'm not going anywhere." Dale ran his fingers through Jeremiah's hair, petting and soothing him. Then, the drugs kicked in again. "Nothing can take me away from you, not even death. I'd haunt the hell out of you. Spy on you in the shower and shit."

Laughing past his tears, Jeremiah kissed the bare skin of Dale's shoulder, breathing his scent deep into his lungs and holding it there. He wanted Dale to be a part of him, and in turn, he needed to be a part of Dale. "I'd rather have you alive and well, and you can watch me in the shower any time you want, as long as you get in there with me."

"It's a deal, Jay." Dale's heavy eyelids closed as the painkillers dragged him toward sleep once more. "Fuck me—these drugs are . . ."

"Don't say it."
"Awesome."

Chapter Twenty-Five

It'd been six days since the events at Ducky's, and Dale was recovering well. The ER doctor had wanted to err on the side of caution and admitted his patient overnight, so they could monitor him and give him IV antibiotics. After they'd transferred him upstairs and settled him into a room, Dale had slept off and on all night while Jeremiah dozed in a chair that he'd pulled up next to the bed. By 10:00 a.m. the next morning, Dale had gotten the all-clear to be released.

Now, most of his pain was gone, but he was still stiff and had to be cautious not to tear out his thirty-six stitches. So, no lifting much of anything and lots of rest.

Before leaving the hospital, Jeremiah had insisted Dale stay with him at the JP for the duration of his recovery, at least until the stitches came out. Since

Willow and Nathan agreed, Dale had reluctantly complied. He'd said the only reason he wasn't happy about it was because he felt like an invalid when he was so used to doing things independently. The only person who hadn't treated him with kid gloves was Jenna, and damn if he didn't keep telling her he loved her for it.

Over the past few days, Jeremiah quickly learned that Dale was the worst patient in the history of patients. One would think a Marine wouldn't be such a baby about being couch-bound, but if the guy was awake, he was complaining.

However, Jeremiah would gladly listen to every whiny word if it meant his man was here with him. It'd been a close call. If that asshole had stabbed instead of slashed, there was a good chance Dale wouldn't be alive to drive Jeremiah crazy.

"Babe, come on. Put down Tal Bauer's book, and let's get you cleaned up. My folks will be here soon." Jeremiah leaned over the back of the couch, peering down at a pouting Dale. John and Patricia Urban had decided last week to come for a visit after finding out that Jenna had moved back home. After hearing about Jeremiah's coming out and his boyfriend ending up in the hospital because of it, they'd still insisted on coming to support both their children and Dale, who they apparently couldn't wait to meet. All those years that Jeremiah had thought he'd done a great job of hiding who he really was hadn't been necessary—at least not in his immediate family's eyes. His father and then his mother had gotten on the phone with him and told him how proud they were of him and that they loved him no matter what his sexual orientation was. Jeremiah had ended the call with relieved tears rolling down his cheeks before bawling like a baby on Dale's shoulder while making sure he didn't hurt him.

Dropping his Kindle onto his lap, Dale glared up at him, but that intense glower only made Jeremiah's grin grow wider. He was too cute, with his midnight hair sticking up all over and a week's worth of scruff on his cheeks. "You're saying I stink?"

"Yes, I am, Marine. Come on—a shower will make you feel better."

"Actually, Jay, the only thing that's going to make me feel better, besides sex, is getting out of the house. I hate this sitting around bullshit." He gestured to the e-reader. "And speaking of which, you do realize that the closest thing to sex I've had all week is in Bauer's books—which are freaking hot, by the way. Ethan and Jack are killin' me here, and what the fuck? Siberia? Again!"

"I'm very aware, you big baby. And I know they're hot—I'm the one who told you to read them. And yes, everything seems to go down in Siberia, huh? You think it's bad now, wait until you get to Sasha and Sergei's books. Don't worry, I won't judge you for crying—I'm sure Tal has that effect on all his readers." The author wrote some amazing gay romance/suspense books, and Jeremiah had read every one of them so far. He thought getting Dale into one of the series was a good way for him to pass the time while lying on the couch, and apparently, he'd been right.

Circling to the front of the couch, Jeremiah reached down and grasped both Dale's hands. "Up you go. Swing your feet over and stand up slowly." Dale had lost quite a bit of blood and still got dizzy when he stood up too fast. Another reason why he was forced to stay in bed or on the sofa for at least another few days. Most of the bruises started to fade, and his split knuckles were scabbed and healing.

"Ugh . . ." Dale groaned but did as he'd been instructed. "I know I've been a pain in the ass. I'm just not used to being taken care of or needing to be, for that matter. I feel helpless, and I fuckin' hate it."

"You haven't been a pain in the ass. Besides, it's your turn to bottom anyway."

Dale's eyebrows shot up, and his mouth fell open. "Did you just make a sex joke?"

"Yup." Jeremiah ducked under Dale's armpit and gently grabbed his waist before slowly walking him to the downstairs bath. He was beyond grateful he'd had it installed during the remodel since it meant that Dale only had to do the stairs twice a day. While Dale recovered from the attack's physical trauma, Jeremiah was recovering from the *emotional* trauma. The thought of

Dale going back to live on the Skyview Ranch after the stitches came out was something Jeremiah tried to avoid. Dale belonged in Jeremiah's bed, and if he had anything to say about it, the only thing Dale's RV would be used for is if they went on vacation.

"Out and proud, making sex jokes, and introducing me to your parents—you've come a long way since I caught you ogling me at the rodeo, Cowboy."

Jeremiah blushed but, for once, didn't look down at his feet. Instead, he met Dale's eyes and found them watery with tears. When one droplet slid free, Jeremiah reached up and brushed it away with his thumb. He shifted to stand in front of Dale, facing him while still supporting him. "It's your fault, you know. You loving me gave me the courage to embrace who I am finally."

He sank his hand into Dale's hair and brought him forward for a deep kiss. "Your love set me free."

"Oh, Jay," Dale whispered against his mouth before kissing him back and tangling their tongues together.

Jeremiah felt Dale harden against his stomach, making him groan and thrust gently. It took everything inside him to end the kiss. Unfortunately, they didn't have time to get carried away—his parents would be there soon, and Jenna was out running some errands, and who knew when she'd be back. "Let's get you cleaned up, babe."

"I love you."

Jeremiah cradled Dale's whiskered face between his palms reverently, joyfully. "I love you too. So much."

"Hurry up and get me naked. Even if we can't do much about it, I need to feel your skin against mine."

Dale took Jeremiah's hand, and together, they slowly made their way to the bathroom. As he carefully undressed Dale, then himself, Jeremiah's heart was full, nearly bursting with love for this man. He was sure he must be dreaming.

There's no way this is my life now, is there?

If it was a dream, he hoped he never woke up.

* * *

Jeremiah and Dale sat on the porch swing together, content in their silence. Dale had been tired after the shower, but Jeremiah convinced his reluctant patient that some fresh air would do them both some good. Jeremiah had taken off every day since Dale came home from the hospital, only doing the bare minimum of administrative tasks and leaving the outside ranch work to Anthony and the hands. However, he'd promised to return to his normal routine tomorrow.

Dale was doing well enough to be alone for most of the afternoon, and after all, Jeremiah was only a text away, and Jenna was around when needed. A moving van filled with her stuff finally arrived three days ago, and she'd had the company take it straight to a storage unit in Butterfield. She'd met them there to grab a few boxes and things she wanted at the house, but most of her possessions were now safely stored away. Jeremiah had no idea how long his sister planned to stay with him. He had no qualms about it, though, as long as she ignored the sounds coming from his bedroom after Dale got the all-clear for physical activity. If she had a problem with it, well, she could invest in some noise-canceling headphones and a sleep playlist.

"I gotta say, you were right. It's nice to feel the sun on my face." Dale's head was tipped back, and his eyes were closed as he basked in the sunshine. His jaw and upper lip were now devoid of scruff, thanks to Jeremiah, who was happy to see some color returning to his man's cheeks.

"Just remember that—I'm always right."

Cracking open one eye, Dale did his best to glare but failed miserably. The goofy smile he sported ruined the effect.

The sound of an approaching vehicle drew their gazes, and Jeremiah was surprised to see Grady's department SUV coming down the drive.

"Wonder what he wants," Dale said.

Hopefully, Grady's visit was just a casual one. He came out to the JP to record Dale's official statement the day he'd been released from the hospital. The case was headed for the grand jury next week. Between the witnesses and Skinner agreeing to testify against

Schneider and Benson, who were behind the cattle getting loose, the DA was positive he'd secure an indictment. Dale's testimony wouldn't be needed until the actual trial, but that was months away.

"Not sure." Jeremiah stopped the rocking motion of the swing with a booted foot on the carved footrest. They waited as Grady exited his SUV and climbed onto the porch.

"Hey, guys." Tipping his hat, Grady joined them, leaning against the railing. "I'm mighty glad to see you up and about, Dale. You scared about ten years off my life—ten years I can't afford to lose, by the way."

"Trust me, Sheriff, I feel the same." Dale reached out and took Jeremiah's hand, squeezing it tightly.

"Not that I mind the visit, but what brings you out here today, cousin? You look like you've got something on your mind."

Grady crossed his arms. "Well, I have a bit of a favor to ask of you. Remember Troy Downing?"

Jeremiah's blood turned to ice at the mention of the name. While he wasn't from the Rock, the murderer had been from Cheyenne, and the events surrounding his trial and conviction had been on the tongues of everyone in the state for months about six years ago. The bastard should be burning in hell after what he'd done.

Dale cocked his head at the tension coursing through Jeremiah and broke into his thoughts. "Babe? What is it?"

"Yeah. What about the son of a bitch?" Jeremiah asked Grady, with a shake of his head, ignoring Dale's question.

"I guess you haven't been watching the news all week—the conviction was overturned, and he was released."

"You're shitting me!" Jeremiah exclaimed. "How the fuck did that happen? Don't tell me he got out on a technicality or some bullshit like that."

"No technicalities—he's actually innocent of all the charges. You probably don't know, but Troy is Beth Loach's cousin on her mother's side. She asked me for a favor, which is why I'm here. But first, let me explain since Dale here looks like he'll burst if he doesn't get some answers soon. Don't try to deny it—you're just as nosy as everyone else in the Rock, Jeremiah and Jenna included. I think there's something in the water."

Grady took off his hat and slicked back his hair before settling the brown Stetson back onto his head. "Quick recap—Troy was convicted of the triple murder of his wife and two young children about six years ago. The evidence led right to him, all of it circumstantial, yes, but the DA had him dead to rights. His kids were drowned in the bathtub, and his wife was strangled with a lamp cord."

Dale nodded. "This sounds vaguely familiar. I think the trial ended about a month or two before I moved to Redworth. He was sentenced to death, right?"

"Yup. The jury convicted him in under two hours —it took less than that to vote for the death penalty. He's spent the last five years on death row up in the state pen while his lawyers tried everything they could to at least get the death sentence overturned. Then, two weeks ago, new evidence came to light. Turns out, the wife had a secret lover. The guy recently was killed in a shootout with police over an unrelated drug bust at his home. When the police processed his house, they found . . . God, this is so fucked up. They found a snuff film of the murder of Troy's wife and kids. It didn't take the police long to identify Troy's family in the video." Grady paused, taking a deep breath. "In the video, he recorded himself explaining how he killed them and framed Troy for the crimes. He kept the damn video as a trophy, the sick bastard. Hell is too good for him."

Gaping, Jeremiah blinked several times before he found his voice again. "Motherfucker. Unbelievable." He took a sip of his iced tea, letting the shocking news settle in his brain for a moment. "I had no idea he was Beth's cousin. How the hell did she keep that quiet?"

"He begged her to—wouldn't let her attend the trial either, even though she knew in her heart he was innocent. He didn't want the stigma of his alleged crimes to affect her career here. You know damn well people would've demanded she be fired just because she was related to a man who'd been convicted of killing his wife and kids.

"Now, I'm telling you all this in confidence. It'll get out eventually, but for now, Beth would like him to be able to settle in town without the gossip mill chewing on him, at least for a little while. As soon as that happens, I'm sure the press will descend on the Rock like dogs chasing a bone, trying to get an interview with him. In the meantime, his lawyers are trying to convince him to sue the state. He's not sure what he'll do—still needs time to comprehend he's a free man and not about to face a literal firing squad."

Due to a shortage of the drugs required for lethal injection, Wyoming was considering offering a firing squad to carry out death penalties.

"No problem—we won't say anything," Jeremiah said, answering for both of them. "Obviously, I know how to keep a secret."

Grady snorted in response. "Yeah, I can see that."

"Holy shit—what happens now?" Dale asked the question Jeremiah hadn't voiced yet.

"Well, that's what I stopped by for—as I said, I need a favor."

Jeremiah narrowed his eyes, not sure what his cousin was getting at. "What's the favor?"

"Troy needs a job and a place to lay low for a while. Prison messed him up, as you can imagine. It'll take him some time to adjust to being on the outside. Unfortunately, Wyoming isn't a compensation state—he'll have to sue if he wants to get any money for the wrongful conviction, and that can take years, and the payout isn't guaranteed. He spent a good part of his life working on ranches, so he knows what he's doing. Beth says he refuses to stay with her long-term. I wasn't sure if you replaced Baxter and Benson yet. Can you help him out?"

Jeremiah glanced at Dale, raising his eyebrows.

"What are you looking at me for? This is your ranch, not mine," the other man protested. "My input stops at the Skyview's fence line."

"Yeah, well, since you're gonna be living here, you get a say in who else does as well."

The corners of Dale's mouth ticked upward as he stared at Jeremiah. "Oh really? I'm living here now?"

"Aren't you?" Jeremiah smirked, then brought his lover's hand to his mouth and gently kissed the still-bruised knuckles.

Dale opened and closed his mouth a few times, clearly too stunned to respond immediately. "Ugh, well, yeah, I guess I am."

Grady chuckled. "He's got you there, Dale."

"Yeah, well, we're gonna have to work on your romancin', Jay. You know, wine and dine me a little before asking me—no, *telling* me I'm movin' in."

"Congrats, you two." The sheriff pushed off the railing, straightening to his full height. "Troy will be coming to the Rock either way, but if he has a place to stay and a job lined up for when he gets here, it would be good for his state of mind."

Jeremiah shrugged his shoulders. "If Dale is okay

with it, I am too." When Dale nodded, Jeremiah continued. "Sounds like the man got dealt a raw deal—we'd be happy to help him get back on his feet. And you're correct, I do need some more hands. It would have to be on a trial basis, though. Say, ninety days?"

"Understood, and thanks, guys. I'll let Beth know. He should be here by the end of the week, so I'll bring him over to introduce you. His lawyers have him holed up in a hotel in Cheyenne until the press dies down a bit and they can get him out of there without anyone being the wiser."

"Sounds good." As Grady started for the porch steps, Jeremiah added, "Hey, don't forget—dinner here tomorrow night with my folks. They can't wait to see Rissa."

"We'll be here."

* * *

After Grady left, Dale stared at Jeremiah while scratching his temple. "Um, tell me something. Did I just agree to move in with you? How the hell did that happen?"

"Simple. You love me, I love you, and we'd rather be together than apart, right? I have all this space, and it's not like you've got a long commute or anything." Jeremiah lifted Dale's hand and, this time, kissed his palm. "Seriously, though, if this week has shown me anything, it's that I want you here all the time. I love having you in my home and bed. I'd love for you to stay, but if you're not ready." Jeremiah heaved an overly dramatic sigh. "I'll try to be patient until you are. Just don't make me wait too long . . . you know, there are other fish in the sea."

"Oh really? Last time I checked, Cowboy, we ain't near no sea." He grinned. "Jeez, when you decide to do something, you just go balls-deep committed, don't you?"

Chuckling, Jeremiah bumped his shoulder against Dale's. "I guess so. Why wait, though? It's not as if either of us are getting any younger."

"You don't have to sell me on this, Jay—I'm right there with you. Being here with you this week . . ." Dale swallowed thickly. "Yeah, I'm more than happy to move in."

Leaning over, he kissed the love of his life, losing himself in the feel of Jeremiah's mouth against his own, his taste, and the electric zing that always hit him whenever they touched. Dale could spend hours just making out with him and never tire of it. The abrasion of Jeremiah's scruffy cheeks against his own and the small gasps and sighs that always escaped his lover would never get old.

The unexpected sound of a car door shutting had them reluctantly breaking the kiss and straightening. Dale didn't recognize the man striding toward them and highly doubted it was Jeremiah's father since he was alone and bore no family resemblance. There was a small blue car parked next to Jeremiah's truck. It was one of those new all-electric cars with a nearly silent motor, which explained why they hadn't heard him pull up. Also, they'd been so wrapped up in each other that the rest of the world had fallen away, as it always did when Jay kissed him.

The man cleared his throat sharply, frowning in blatant disapproval. "I'm not surprised by such a shameful display from this . . . godless man . . . but I'm disappointed in you, Jeremiah Urban. Your parents raised you better than this."

Thrown for a loop, Dale gaped at the self-righteous man standing at the foot of the porch steps, his arms clasped behind his back as he scowled at them. In his midsixties or so, he was slender and a few inches shy of six feet. His pinched face appeared ruddy from years of sun exposure, and his dishwater gray hair was slicked to the side in a tragic comb-over that did nothing to conceal his baldness, instead drawing more attention to it.

"And who the fuck are you to say anything about it?" Dale snapped, anger surging within him at the judgmental prick dropping by unannounced with his holier-than-thou attitude.

"My name is Pastor Preston Whitehouse—I'm the head of the church Jeremiah's parents used to attend before their fall from grace," the man replied, as snidely as possible, as if his name alone explained what he was doing there. He wore black trousers and an ivory, short-sleeved, button-down shirt, but it was the Tony Lama cream-colored pirarucu boots, which had to have cost around $500, that caught Dale's attention. Between them and the expensive electric car, the man lived high on the hog for a small-town pastor. "Jeremiah used to attend as well, and I can see the results of him turning his back on the good Lord."

Dale growled at the asshole. "Great. Just what I needed this week—a self-proclaimed prophet who thinks his shit don't stink." He didn't regret cursing in front of the guy because, with that attitude, the *good pastor* didn't deserve even a drop of Dale's respect. "If you're here to preach to me about—"

"Dale—" Jeremiah interrupted, but Dale raised his hand, cutting him off. The last thing he wanted to do was cause trouble for Jeremiah and his family—even with a sanctimonious jackass like this guy. They'd lived in the Rock for decades and knew everyone far better than he did. So, for now, Dale would try to hold his tongue.

The pastor took the sudden silence between the other two men as permission to get on his high horse. "I'm here because I wish to ascertain if the rumors I heard were true. I was very concerned for the sake of Jeremiah's soul. I see now that I'm too late. You have corrupted the boy with your evil ways."

Boy? Dale would gladly tell the man that what Jeremiah had in his pants was nothing close to "boy" size.

He glanced over at Jeremiah and was pleased to note his face was beet red, with rage reflecting in his eyes. Dale looked on with awe as his cowboy stood, squaring his shoulders and straightening his back. Jeremiah had just opened his mouth, no doubt to tell the pastor exactly what he thought of his visit and preaching, but the arrival of a silver sedan stopped him. All three watched in interest as a man and woman exited the car and strode toward the porch. Dale got a glimpse of what his lover would look like in twenty-five years as the man who was undoubtedly Jeremiah's father ascended the steps, his wife on his arm. Tall and still fit, though a little soft around the middle—probably since he wasn't putting in long hours on the ranch anymore—he was still a striking man. His red hair had faded to white and strawberry blond for the most part.

From the way Jeremiah's father glared at the pastor like the God-fearing man was something he'd found on the bottom of his boot, this was going to be good. Dale grinned excitedly and settled in for the show.

"Mr. Whitehouse, your presence here assures me we've arrived just in time." John Urban stopped two feet away from the other man. His wife, Patricia, stepped over to Jeremiah, kissing his cheek, before giving Dale a friendly wave when he tried to stand, insisting he remained seated.

Meanwhile, Whitehouse seemed oblivious to the evident tension in the group as he plastered on a relieved smile. "John! Patricia! Bless you—I'm so happy to see you two. Maybe you can help me talk some sense into these boys. Living in perverted sin. It's shameful, I tell you."

"The only thing I see that's shameful, Whitehouse, is you." John's voice was so frigid that Dale was surprised they couldn't see his breath floating through the air. The man was clearly not happy to see the pastor standing on JP property.

Whitehouse frowned. "John, I don't understand. You support this?" He pointed back and forth between Dale and Jeremiah. "This affront to the good Lord? Engaging in sodomy and living together as two men were never meant to?"

Patricia broke in, placing a hand on her enraged husband's chest when he moved to advance on the pastor. "John, your blood pressure." She faced White-house and scowled, and at that moment, Dale knew he would never want to piss the older woman off. She would rain fury down on anyone who crossed her family. "I wouldn't send my teenage son away to a conversion camp when you and my sister practically ordered me to, and I'm certainly not going to condemn him now. It's not your place to tell my son who he can and can't love, and it's also not your place to tell me I have to do that, either. I love my son and support him, no matter what, and if God has a problem with that, then he can tell me himself on my Judgment Day." She moved to the side, giving the man a clear passage to the steps. "Leave. Now. You weren't welcome then, and you damn well aren't welcome here now."

"Mom? Dad?" Jeremiah seemed stunned, his head ping-ponging between his parents and the pastor as if watching a table tennis match.

"Hush, Jeremiah—let us handle this," Patricia gently corrected him, showing that no matter how old her offspring was, she was still the protective mother she'd been all his life.

"Yes, ma'am," Jeremiah replied, but he reached for Dale's hand, gripping it tightly.

Whitehouse's lips curled back in disgust as he pulled a white handkerchief from his pocket to wipe his brow. "You don't seem to understand any better now than you did then. These two men are sin incarnate. Leviticus 18:22 says, 'Do not practice homosexuality, having sex with another man as with a woman. It is a detestable sin.' "

Patricia put her hands on her hips and leaned forward. "'Let he who is without sin cast the first stone,' John 8:7. Are you without sin, *Pastor*? And before you answer that, let me remind you I know all about your youthful . . . indiscretions." She raised an eyebrow at the man, seeming to look down her nose at him even though she was the shorter of the two. Whitehouse's face turned to granite, his jaw clenched in pious fury, but the outraged woman before him didn't let him get a word in. "Love is *never* a sin, and I'll not argue with you any further. Not now, not ever again." She pointed toward the steps. "Now, you've been asked to leave—I suggest you do so before I have to call my nephew. And you know just how Grady feels about you, don't you?"

Without another word, Whitehouse stormed off, getting into his eco-friendly car and slamming the door shut. As the man drove off, Patricia smiled and brushed her hands together as if getting rid of some dirt. "Now that the local hypocrite's been taken care of, Jeremiah, sweetheart, introduce me to your young man." Dale barely kept a burst of laughter from escaping at being called a "young man." Holding out both hands, Patricia reached over and grasped Dale's hand between her own while still talking to her son. "I've heard so much about him from your sister as well. I have to agree with Jenna—he's quite handsome—though the words your sister used were a little less polite."

Jeremiah chuckled. "Yes, he is. Dale, this is Patricia and John Urban, my parents. Ma, Dad, this is Dale— he's . . . um . . ." Jeremiah trailed off, his nerves clearly coming to the surface and getting the better of him.

Dale winked at Jeremiah, loving the blush that painted the man's face, before holding out his free hand for John to shake since Patricia still wasn't letting him stand. "Ma'am, sir, it's a pleasure to meet you finally. I'm Dale Harris."

"Jeremiah, where are your manners?"

"Sorry, Ma, I think I lost them back there when you and Dad told off the pastor." Jeremiah gestured to the two empty chairs on the porch. "Why don't you two have a seat, or would you rather go inside?"

"Let's go in—I could use a cold drink while we sit and chat," Patricia said.

John clapped Jeremiah's shoulder. "Come on, son, let's do as your mother says. That's her mama-bear tone, and you know as well as I do it's best not to argue with her when she wants to *sit* and *chat*."

"Oh, hush. You make me sound like an ogre."

Her husband kissed her cheek. "Prettiest darn ogre I've ever met."

Shaking his head at his parent's antics, Jeremiah helped Dale to his feet, and they followed the couple into the house. Patricia led the way as if she owned the place. Dale had to remind himself she used to—this had been her home for most of her life, and she still treated it as such.

"Where's Jenna?"

Jeremiah replied, "She ran to Butterfield to get a couple of things she forgot in the storage unit, and then she was going to stop at the Pack & Sack for a few things for dinner. She should be back soon."

Moments later, they were seated around Jeremiah's large dining room table, glasses of sweet tea in front of each of them. Despite the older couple's smiles and relaxed demeanor, the tension felt thick and awkward as Jeremiah stared at his parents. Dale wasn't sure if he should say something to break the ice. Even with Jeremiah's conversation with them on the phone the other night, it was the first time he was ever introducing a male lover to his folks. That alone was enough to make Dale feel anxious for him too.

Patricia sipped her drink, then set the glass to the side. "So, I want to get this right out there. Jeremiah, sweetheart, I love you. Your father loves you. We always have and always will. As we said on the phone, we don't care who you date, only that you're happy. Does Dale make you happy?"

Jeremiah beamed at him, and the love and adoration Dale saw on his cowboy's face would've brought him to his knees had he been standing. Jeremiah nodded, his gaze never leaving Dale's. "Yes, Ma, he does—happier than I ever thought I could be. I love him, and he loves me. I never imagined I would ever be so lucky to find someone this wonderful."

"I'm so glad." Tears sparkled in her eyes as she reached across the table, clasping Jeremiah's hand with her right and Dale's with her left. "Love each other, even when it seems too hard and scares the crap out of you, and you'll be just fine."

"Your mother's right, Jeremiah," John added. "If you're happy and cared for in return, we couldn't be more pleased. Don't let anyone tell you different."

Jeremiah freed his hand from his mother's grip and covered his face with both palms as sobs tore free from his chest. Dale didn't hesitate and, ignoring the pain in his stomach, wrapped his arms around Jeremiah's shoulders, holding him close.

"Oh, honey . . ." Patricia started crying in earnest as well, and Dale felt his own emotions rise. Even John swiped at his eyes a few times.

A thump sounded to the right of Dale, and everyone's gaze swung toward the noise. Jenna had dropped a tote bag and now stood there with her hands on her hips, scowling at all the tears she saw. "All right. What did I miss, and whose ass are we kicking now?"

Chapter Twenty-Six

One week later. . .

Dale winced slightly as he pulled his shirt off. He could finally get around without too much discomfort, thanks partly to Jeremiah's hovering and careful nursing. Patricia had also insisted on doing her part to look after him as he healed until she and John had returned to Arizona two days ago. Dale had gotten to know Jeremiah's parents well over their visit, and more than once, they'd told him to consider himself part of their family. He'd been more than happy to accept. With his own parents gone for at least fifteen years and no siblings, being mothered and included in family conversations and decisions felt foreign, but he could easily get used to it with the Urbans. He felt like he belonged in a way that he wasn't sure he ever had before, even in his own family.

Yesterday, Dale had convinced Jeremiah to let him ride along on one of the ranch's ATVs and be his official gate opener while they'd checked the fence line. There'd been one stipulation, though. Dale had only been allowed to ride on the back of his cowboy's four-wheeler, which he really hadn't minded since that meant his groin had been nestled against the man's fine ass for the duration.

After a long day in the fresh air, he'd slept like the dead and woke this morning feeling almost like his old self. He'd waited until Jeremiah had left the house to start the workday before driving himself over to Skyview and checking on the alpacas. Nathan, Willow, and Shane had everything well in hand.

He'd hung around, catching up on some paperwork and supply orders. It was boring, but he had to do something to feel useful. It was rare for him to take any time off from his job, and he itched to be back in the thick of things.

He'd eaten lunch with Willow and Shannon, enjoying the time with them, before leaving for a follow-up appointment with his doctor. Fortunately, he could see the man at the clinic in town and not have to travel to Butterfield. He'd walked out of the office, free of stitches and cleared for increased activity. While he still wasn't allowed to lift much of anything for another week or so, he'd been encouraged to move around as much as he could tolerate.

His brain immediately flashed to Jeremiah and the

memory of them in bed together. They'd only made love that one time before all this shit had gone down, and Dale was more than anxious for a repeat. The trouble would be convincing his boyfriend he was well enough for . . . *extra-sexy-curricular* activities.

He glanced at the clock again, grinning at himself before dropping his pants and striding naked into the bathroom. If Jeremiah followed the same routine as he'd done all week, he'd walk into the bedroom just as Dale got out of the shower.

Quickly cleaning himself, he paid extra attention to his dick, balls, and hole. If there was even a smidgen of a chance that Jay would do a repeat of that fantastic rim-job he'd given Dale last time, he wanted to be prepared.

As he turned off the shower, he heard the bedroom door open and then shut again. Grinning, he did a half-assed job drying himself off before wrapping the towel low around his hips. Glancing down at himself, he shrugged and changed his mind. He dropped the towel.

"Babe?" Jeremiah called out.

Dale replied by opening the bathroom door. He stood in the doorway, gripping the jamb above his head while his other hand stroked his cock slowly.

"Dale?" Jeremiah asked, his face flushing pink and his breath coming faster as he trailed his gaze from Dale's head to his toes and back up, stopping where his hand was working himself to full hardness.

"Yes, Jay?"

Jeremiah swallowed thickly, his throat bobbing. "Wh-what are you doing?" he rasped.

"Well, what I'm doing is hoping *you* could do *me*." Smirking, Dale stalked into the bedroom, advancing on his lover. "After all, you did say it was my turn to bottom next, right?"

"Um, yes, I-I did say that, did-didn't I?" Jeremiah stuttered, his eyes glued to Dale's now hard and leaking cock. "But, uh, are you sure you're, you know, up for that?"

"Oh, I'm definitely *up* for that." Winking, he reached down, tugging on his balls, making himself groan. "I need you, baby. It's been two weeks since we've had sex."

"I'm not fucking you." Clearly distracted, Jeremiah fumbled to unbutton his shirt before cursing and ripping both it and his undershirt up and over his head. Dale licked his lips, wanting nothing more than to taste all the peaches and cream skin Jeremiah was revealing.

"Huh? Why not?"

"Because I don't think I can be gentle, and you're not healed enough for that. But there are other things we can do." Jeremiah unbuckled his belt, unfastened his jeans, and tugged them down his legs before kicking them aside, leaving himself standing in just his skintight, black boxer briefs that cupped and outlined every solid inch of his impressive erection.

"Yeah? What's that?" Dale managed to force the

words from his throat—Jeremiah literally took his breath away—although his words were croaked like when he'd gone through puberty a lifetime ago.

"Get on the bed, Marine, and you'll see as soon as I'm done taking a quick shower to wash this stink off."

While his cowboy took one of the fastest showers ever, Dale did as ordered and waited impatiently in the middle of what was now *their* bed. He loved the bossy side of Jeremiah that emerged when they were behind closed doors and he forgot his worries, focusing only on them and the pleasure they brought one another. His voice even sounded different, deeper and more commanding whenever he took control.

Appearing in the bathroom doorway, Jeremiah briskly ran a towel over his body, then tossed it on the floor behind him. Dale didn't think he could get any harder than he already was, but when Jeremiah opened the top dresser drawer and pulled out a bottle of lube and the wooden dildo he'd carved, Dale's cock proved him wrong.

Pinning Dale with an intense stare, Jeremiah swaggered toward him, smirking. He stopped at the foot of the bed and leaned into Dale's personal space without touching him. Dale practically whimpered when Jeremiah said, "I'm going to fuck you with this." He held up the dildo and wagged it. "That way, I won't risk hurting you. After I make you come all over yourself, maybe I'll let you suck me off."

"Oh fuck." Dale moaned, then fell back onto the

bed, planting his feet and spreading his legs in a blatant invitation. Eager and excited.

With his still dripping hair clinging to his head, Jeremiah climbed onto the bed and knelt between Dale's legs, setting both the toy and lube aside. "First, give me that mouth."

Leaning over Dale, he carefully kept his weight off him and took his mouth in a blistering kiss. Jeremiah must've brushed his teeth, too, because he tasted minty-fresh. Their tongues dueled as each man stole the other's breath. Dale gripped Jeremiah's head, tugging on his wet hair and kissing him back desperately. Groaning at the deliciousness of his sexy cowboy, Dale tried to urge the other man's body down onto his, but Jeremiah wasn't having it.

Pulling his face back, Jeremiah shook his head. "No. I won't hurt you."

"But—"

"No buts . . . well, at least not the verbal kind." The corners of his mouth ticked upward as he slid his hand down Dale's side to his hip, then dipped it between his ass and the bed, gripping a cheek. "Now, this kind of butt is fair game tonight."

"Jay . . ."

"Yes, baby?" Jeremiah tapped his finger gently against Dale's hole, drawing a hungry growl of need from him.

"Hurry up and get that damn toy inside me before I do it myself."

Chuckling, Jeremiah sat back on his heels, hooking Dale's legs over his arms so the backs of his knees rested against Jeremiah's elbows. Jeremiah gripped the backs of his thighs and pushed his legs up. "Comfortable? Nothing hurts?"

"All good. Don't stop."

"Bossy much? Topping from the bottom? Someone seems to have forgotten who's in charge tonight. Let me remind you—it's not you. Now, hold them there."

Dale complied eagerly, unashamed to admit he was desperate—not just for the sex, but for the carnal connection with Jeremiah. He felt vulnerable in that position, exposed, the air brushing against his most intimate parts. He moaned, loving it.

"Needy, huh?" Jeremiah teased as he opened the lube and poured some on his fingers. Circling his slippery digits over Dale's hole, Jeremiah smirked down at him before sliding his index finger into him.

"Argh," Dale groaned, unable to hold it inside. He pushed back, trying to draw Jeremiah's finger deeper.

"You like being topped, don't you?" Jeremiah asked, pulling his finger free and adding a second. The burn intensified, but Dale welcomed it. It passed quickly, changing into the delicious fullness and stretch he'd been craving.

"By you? Hell, yes." Dale grunted as Jeremiah shoved his fingers deeper, harder, and faster, scissoring them apart and stretching him. His cock ached, and he was so rigid it hurt. "Please, Jay . . ."

"Mmm. I love how you beg so sweetly."

It seemed the cowboy had found a different level of confidence over the last few months, and it was so fucking hot. Pulling his fingers free from Dale's body, Jeremiah used his already sticky hand to lube up the dildo, winking at Dale as he prepared it. Dale nearly came at the sight alone, the anticipation nearly killing him.

"Ready?" Jeremiah asked as he placed the tip of the toy against Dale's hole.

He answered by relaxing and bearing down, trying to draw the dildo inside himself. Jeremiah stared into his eyes as he pushed forward, breaching that first tight ring of muscle.

"Oh, God!" Dale cried out—it was so hard and stiff, he wasn't sure if it would work. But as he began to loosen up, and it sank deeper, he moaned, long and loud. "Oh, fuck, yes."

"Holy shit, that's so hot." Jeremiah withdrew the wooden cock slightly before sliding it in farther. "Can you take it all?"

"Fuck me, Jay, goddammit, yes, I can take it all." He tried to shove his pelvis down to impale himself farther, but Jeremiah's hand on his hip halted his movements.

"You'll take what I give you—at my pace. Stay still."

Jeremiah's words and his commanding tone nearly

undid Dale, but he was determined not to come before the whole thing was in his ass.

"Fuck, Jay . . ." He threw his head back, his legs trembling as the toy was pushed deeper inside him before finally stopping. The wide base rested against his ass cheeks, and he realized the entire length was pressed inside him.

Staring at Dale's ass, Jeremiah palmed his own erection. "So sexy, baby. I could blow just from the sight alone. One day soon, it'll be my cock I'll be watching disappear into that perfect ass."

The cowboy had found his dirty-talking ability, and Dale was loving every second.

"Baby, please," he whined, knowing he was flagrantly begging but too far gone to care. He was stretched and so full that he needed Jeremiah to move the dildo. Panting, he canted his hips and hissed when the dildo shifted and brushed his prostate.

"Shh, I've got you."

There were no words after that. Jeremiah wrapped his free hand around Dale's cock as he fucked him. Easy and slow at first, but as Dale lost his mind, babbling and pleading, the other man worked the wooden dick in and out, increasing the speed and intensity. Dale's balls tingled, and his cock throbbed painfully as his orgasm built. Jeremiah adjusted the angle of the toy slightly the next time he thrust it in, hitting Dale's prostate directly, causing him to howl as cum shot from his dick. He bucked and cried out, coming for what felt like a lifetime.

As his orgasm began to wane, he gasped for air. His heart hammered in his chest. "Holy shit, baby."

Jeremiah wordlessly tugged on the end of the phallus, and Dale got the hint, relaxing so it could be eased from his body. He winced slightly—it had been quite a while since he'd bottomed. He'd be feeling that tomorrow for sure.

Jeremiah tossed the toy off the side of the bed with a *thunk* before straddling Dale's hips, though he was careful not to put too much pressure on his belly. Dale's hands came up, clutching Jeremiah's thighs. His cock was red, the head nearly purple and shiny with precum.

"My turn," Jay growled before reaching down and swiping some jizz off Dale's belly and using it as lube on his own cock.

"Oh fuck, that's hot." Dale moved his hands to Jeremiah's ass, cupping the cheeks, squeezing rhythmically, and spreading them.

"Love your hands on me," Jeremiah said with a moan, his hand flying on his cock, jerking up and down, the slick sounds obscene and almost enough to make Dale hard again.

He teased his fingers down Jeremiah's crack, brushing against his hole but not pushing in. "I love touching you."

"Oh, fuck, yes." Jeremiah panted as sweat dotted

his brow and bare chest. He was gorgeous as he took his pleasure.

"That's it, baby, come on me." His words seemed to send the cowboy over the edge, and he grunted, throwing his head back as he came, decorating Dale's chest with his release.

When Dale urged him down, Jeremiah gave up resisting and laid on top of him, smearing their cum between them, sticking them together in a glorious mess.

"I love you so fuckin' much," Jeremiah whispered against Dale's neck, kissing him softly and licking the sweat off his skin, making him shiver in response. "I'll move in a second, as soon as I can feel my legs."

"I love you, too, Cowboy. Forever." Dale wrapped his arms tighter around his man, ignoring the twinges of pain the action caused. He'd endure much worse if it meant keeping Jeremiah plastered to him. He never wanted to let him go or leave this bed, resolving at that moment he was going to make sure it really was forever. Smiling softly, he kissed Jeremiah's bare shoulder, his heart fluttering with his resolution.

Epilogue

Dale wiped his palms on his pants again, unable to settle his nerves. The past fifteen months had been a roller coaster for him. Moving to Antelope Rock and settling into the new job, meeting and falling for the love of his life, getting stabbed, recovering from that, moving in with Jeremiah —there'd been a lot of changes for them both. Thankfully, most of them had been positive.

Dozens of party-goers now gathered for the annual New Year's bash Jeremiah threw in one of his barns. Fewer people had chosen to attend this year than previously, though, a fact that hadn't escaped Jeremiah's notice. He attributed the drop in guests to his coming out, but he was fine with it, saying he'd rather the people who had a problem with him being gay not come to his home anyway. He wanted to ring in the new year surrounded by family and true friends, unwilling to compromise who he was anymore. Dale wholeheartedly agreed and supported him.

"Nervous?" Nathan asked, joining him where he stood outside the barn. Even with the frigid winter temperatures, he was sweating bullets.

"I might puke. Does that answer your question?" It wasn't a lie.

Chuckling, Nathan clasped him on the shoulder. "I remember the feeling well. When I proposed to Willow, I was shaking like a leaf. Turned out pretty good for me, and it'll be the same for you. I know it."

"You think?" he asked his boss and the man he now considered a close friend.

"Absolutely, dude. Jeremiah loves you beyond reason. Everyone can see it whenever he looks at you. Plain as day. He's not only going to say yes, but I'd bet money he cries too."

Dale's mind flashed back to a few nights ago, when he'd had Jeremiah under him so desperate and on edge that tears had streaked from his eyes, running down his flushed cheeks as he'd shuddered with need. He was so pretty when he cried, which was a fucked up thing to think, but it was what it was. Happy tears anyway— Dale would sooner cut off his own arm than hurt his cowboy for real.

"Dale?" Nathan prompted. "Ready?"

"Yeah. Yeah, I am. I told him forever, and I meant it."

"Come on, I'm freezing my ass off. Let's do this thing."

They made their way back inside, where the party was rockin'. Jeremiah, Dale, John, Anthony, and the ranch hands had spent the week between Christmas and New Year's clearing out the place. For the rest of the year, this particular barn was used mainly for equipment. Whatever they hadn't been able to temporarily fit up in the loft or in the other barns and sheds on the property was under large tarps behind the building. The inside had been cleaned and swept before the rented tables and chairs arrived. Flanking the small stage, where a country band was performing, there were two eight-foot Christmas trees, fully decorated with ornaments, red bows, and white lights. Illuminated garland was draped everywhere, and strategically placed snowmen, Santas, and reindeer decorations completed the festive theme. Coupled with the scent of pine hanging heavy in the air, it was a Christmas wonderland come to life. Apparently, the hoe-down was a tradition John and Patricia Urban had started the year before Jeremiah had been born, and it'd taken place annually without fail ever since.

Dale weaved his way through the tables and chairs around the dance floor's perimeter, where half the guests were doing the latest line dance. Nathan joined his wife at the end of one of the rows, and like last year, they were out of step from everyone else. Both of them had two left feet when it came to dancing and didn't care at all, spending more time laughing at each other than actually dancing. It was part of the fun.

Spotting the man who would hopefully be his father-in-law very soon, Dale stepped over to him. A grin spread across John's face. "You look terrified, son."

"Well, that's good because I *am* terrified. What if he says no?"

"From how Jeremiah looks at you, that's not gonna happen. My son loves you as much as you love him, and Patricia and I can't wait to welcome you into the family officially."

Dale wished he was as confident as everyone else that Jeremiah would accept his proposal. The only people that knew it was coming were Patricia, John, Jenna, Willow, and Nathan, and that was because they would all play very important roles tonight. It hadn't taken Dale long to know he wanted to propose—in fact, it'd been on his mind since he'd moved into Jeremiah's house and bed permanently. The problem had been finding the right time—a special way to pop the question. Once this great idea had come to mind, he'd gotten busy asking the five people closest to them to help him out. Of course, they were all thrilled to take part. How Willow had kept it quiet this long, he'd never know.

John checked his watch. "Getting close to midnight. You ready?"

He chuckled wryly. "I hope so. Otherwise, Willow will kick my ass if I don't go through with it after all the planning."

The older man slapped his shoulder. "You'll do just fine. Let's get this done before my wife bursts and gives it away. I can't remember the last time Pat was so excited."

In a preplanned move, John strode to the stage, where the lead singer gestured for him to step up and take the mic as the band finished a song. Meanwhile, Dale found Jeremiah talking to Anthony and joined them, putting his arm around his lover's waist. The spicy aroma of Jeremiah's cologne, combined with his own unique scent, hit Dale's nose, making his mouth water. To be near his cowboy was to want him, and hopefully, after tonight, he'd have him for the rest of his life.

Jeremiah looked as handsome as ever in his best black jeans, a white button-down western shirt with a silver and black leather bolero tie Dale had convinced him to wear. Black boots and a Stetson completed the yummy package. Dale was dressed similarly, but his shirt was cobalt blue—Jeremiah had given it to him for Christmas.

John tapped the microphone twice. "Can I have everyone's attention?" He waited momentarily for the din to die as the guests turned toward him. "As I say every year, thank y'all for coming and helping us usher in the new year. This is the forty-fourth anniversary of this annual tradition, and it recently occurred to me that I've had the privilege of starting the countdown every year. I think the time is long overdue for me to pass that honor onto my son, Jeremiah, don't you? After all, the JP is his now."

A round of applause and whistles filled the barn. Beneath Dale's arm, Jeremiah froze before glancing around, clearly needing a moment for his brain to catch up with what was going on. Dale gave him an encouraging squeeze. "Go on. Git up there, Cowboy."

Jeremiah side-eyed him, and Dale gave him a gentle shove toward the stage. The man finally seemed to get his head on straight, then approached where his father held the microphone to him. Dale moved closer, waiting for the right moment. His heart beat like a drum in his chest, and his stomach rolled.

This is it.

Taking the mic, Jeremiah put his hand on his father's shoulder. "Uh, thanks, Dad. You know I don't mind you doing the countdown." John shook his head, and Jeremiah shrugged. "Okay, then. Thank you. It's an honor to step up, but I doubt I'll ever be able to fill your shoes. Give my dad a hand, everyone. And my mom. Because of them, this party is one of the fondest memories of my youth and something I look forward to every year." After the clapping rose and fell again, Jeremiah checked his watch and frowned. "Um, it's a little early, though. We still have about fifteen minutes to go."

That was Dale's cue. Stepping out of the crowd, he stopped in front of the stage and pulled a small box from his pocket before getting down on one knee. At first, Jeremiah didn't see him because he was facing John, but then his father nodded in Dale's direction, and the cowboy turned.

A hush fell across the barn as Jeremiah stilled, and his jaw dropped. He blinked a few times, then came dangerously close to dropping the microphone. Thankfully, John stepped in, took it from him, and handed it down to Dale.

As sweat broke out on his brow and his heart rate surged, he held the microphone up in front of his mouth. "Jay, the first time I met you, I thought you were trouble." There were a few chuckles from the crowd. "The second time I met you, I *knew* you were trouble. The third time we met, I knew you were the man who could break my heart. But then the next time we saw each other, I knew you were the man I would lose my heart to."

Jeremiah's eyes filled up, and Dale swallowed hard, determined to get everything he felt for this man out in the open for everyone to hear without breaking down himself. "I knew you were the one who would own my heart and soul for the rest of my life if we just gave it a chance. I fought it like an idiot, but it was a losing battle.

"Sometimes, I thought I'd pushed you too hard and screwed up for good. But you were fighting too—your fears, your demons, and even me. You battled your way into my heart, and now it belongs to you and only you. I've told you countless times that I love you, and it's forever. Now, I want to make an honest man out of you."

He grinned, then took a shuddering breath. Using the hand holding the mic, he opened the box and revealed a matching pair of wedding bands he'd spent hours searching for. They were black zirconium inlaid with koa, a Hawaiian wood. He'd known they were the perfect choice the minute he spotted them. "Jay, will you do me the honor of marrying me? Right here. Right now."

With tears rolling down his face, Jeremiah nodded and stepped toward him, evidently forgetting he was on the elevated stage. When he stumbled forward, Dale jumped up, catching and steadying him. As his head bobbed up and down, Jeremiah clutched Dale's face. "Yes, yes, yes! Yes, I'll marry you! Of course!"

He threw his arms around Dale's neck and kissed him thoroughly as the party guests cheered, clapped, and whistled. Suddenly, Jeremiah drew back and stared at him. "Wait a minute? Did you say right here and now? Like *now* now? How?"

"Well, technically, it won't be legal—we'll have to go fill out the paperwork for the marriage license and do it again, but in the meantime, your dad took one of those online courses yesterday, and he can perform the ceremony."

Still stunned, Jeremiah glanced around the barn, his gaze taking everything and everyone in as he wiped the tears from his eyes. "Oh, my God. I-I can't believe you planned all this."

Willow and Nathan stepped forward. She held a small bouquet of wildflowers. "We've been asked to be your matron of honor and best man. If that's all right with you."

Jeremiah hugged his best friend. "Of course, it's all right with me, Willow-girl. If it weren't for you and those damn alpacas, Dale and I never would've met."

Nathan held up four white and blue boutonnieres, handing one each to Dale, Jeremiah, and John before pinning one onto his own chest. Willow's friend Maddie was an amateur photographer, and Dale had asked her to bring her equipment without confessing his secret, but he suspected she'd figured it out before-hand. Willow had been in charge of making sure the other woman was ready to capture the proposal. Now, Maddie clicked away, getting a ton of pictures of the happy couple and their family and friends. Dale couldn't wait to see the memories captured and lined up on the mantel in their living room. He never thought he'd be here—he'd hoped for it, of course—and now that it was happening, he was happier than he ever thought possible.

Jenna appeared at Jeremiah's side holding a basket of white rose petals and baby Shannon, who wore a festive navy blue and white dress. About six weeks after Dale had been attacked, Jenna rented a townhouse in Butterfield and opened a small law practice a few blocks away. It looked like she would stay in Wyoming for now, but they knew she still wanted to work for a big city firm. Dale hoped things worked out for the best for her.

As Shannon reached into the basket and threw some petals into the air, laughing in delight, Jenna smiled at her brother. "Your goddaughter and I are your official flower girls."

"Thank you." Jeremiah kissed the baby on the cheek, then turned to face Dale again. The man's forest green eyes sparkled, his cheeks were flushed with happiness, and his smile practically reached both ears. "All right, Marine, let's do this. I'm yours—forever."

At the stroke of midnight, Dale kissed his new husband. "I love you, Jay."

* * *

EXTENDED EPILOGUE AVAILABLE!

J.B. and Samantha hope you've enjoyed *Wistful in*

Wyoming. If you'd like to read a special, eight-chapter extended epilogue to Dale and Jeremiah's story, sign up for our newsletters, and you'll get it for free!

Click on the following URL (or enter it into your browser) to claim your free digital copy today!

dl.bookfunnel.com/10abmjy9aj

Other Books by J.B. Havens

Zombie Instinct Series

Molly: The Beginning

Molly: Immersion

Molly: Reemergence

Steel Corps Series

Core of Steel

Hardened by Steel

Forged by Steel

Bound by Steel

Solid Steel

Steel Corps/Trident Security Crossovers with Samantha A. Cole

No Way in Hell

Anthologies and Short Stories

Beyond the Night: An Anthology

Ashes & Madness, A Molly Everett Short Story

High Tech/Low Life: An Easytown Novels Anthology

About J.B. Havens

J.B. Havens lives in rural Pennsylvania and is a wife and mother of three, a boy and twin girls. She has a love for a good cheesesteak and anything that involves coffee or chocolate. When she's not caring for her family, she is busy researching and writing her next novel.

Find JB on her website where you can find character bios and even a short story or two. She loves to hear from readers, so reach out and tell her what you think!

Connect with J.B.

Facebook
Haven's Haven Facebook Group
Twitter

Other Books by Samantha Cole

*******Denotes titles/series that are only available on select digital sites. Paperbacks and audiobooks are available on most book sites.

THE TRIDENT SECURITY SERIES

Leather & Lace

His Angel

Waiting For Him

Not Negotiable: A Novella

Topping The Alpha

Watching From the Shadows

Whiskey Tribute: A Novella

Tickle His Fancy

No Way in Hell: A Steel Corp/Trident Security Crossover (co-authored with J.B. Havens)

Absolving His Sins

Option Number Three: A Novella

Salvaging His Soul

Trident Security Field Manual

Torn In Half: A Novella

Burning For Him

*****HEELS, RHYMES, & NURSERY CRIMES SERIES**
(WITH 13 OTHER AUTHORS)

Jack Be Nimble: A Trident Security-Related Short Story

*****THE DEIMOS SERIES**

Handling Haven: Special Forces: Operation Alpha

Cheating the Devil: Special Forces: Operation Alpha

THE TRIDENT SECURITY OMEGA TEAM SERIES

Mountain of Evil

A Dead Man's Pulse

Forty Days & One Knight

THE DOMS OF THE COVENANT SERIES

Double Down & Dirty

Entertaining Distraction

Knot a Chance

THE BLACKHAWK SECURITY SERIES

Tuff Enough

Blood Bound

MASTER KEY SERIES

Master Key Resort

Master Cordell

HAZARD FALLS SERIES

Don't Fight It

Don't Shoot the Messenger

THE MALONE BROTHERS SERIES

Her Secret

Her Sleuth

LARGO RIDGE SERIES

Cold Feet

*****ANTELOPE ROCK SERIES**

(CO-AUTHORED WITH J.B. HAVENS)

Wannabe in Wyoming

Wistful in Wyoming

AWARD-WINNING STANDALONE BOOKS

Where the Broken Bloom

Scattered Moments in Time: A Collection of Short Stories & More

*****THE BID ON LOVE SERIES**

(WITH 7 OTHER AUTHORS!)

Going, Going, Gone: Book 2

*****THE COLLECTIVE: SEASON TWO**

(WITH 7 OTHER AUTHORS!)

About Samantha Cole

USA Today Bestselling Author and Award-Winning Author Samantha Cole is a retired policewoman and former paramedic. Using her life experiences and training, she strives to find the perfect mix of suspense and romance for her readers to enjoy.

Awards:

Wannabe in Wyoming (co-authored by J.B. Havens) won the bronze medal in the 2021 Readers' Favorite Awards in the General Romance category.

Scattered Moments in Time, won the gold medal in the 2020 Readers' Favorite Awards in the Fiction Anthology category.

The Road to Solace (formerly *The Friar*), won the silver medal in the 2017 Readers' Favorite Awards in the Contemporary Romance category.

Samantha has over thirty-five books published throughout several different series as well as a few standalone novels. A full list can be found on her website.

Sexy Six-Pack's Sirens Group on Facebook
Website: www.samanthacoleauthor.com
Newsletter: www.samanthacoleauthor.-com/newsletter-signup

facebook.com/SamanthaColeAuthor

instagram.com/samanthacoleauthor

bookbub.com/profile/samantha-a-cole

goodreads.com/SamanthaCole

amazon.com/Samantha-A-Cole/e/B00X53K3X8